By Katherine Lampe

The Caitlin Ross Series

The Unquiet Grave
She Moved through the Fair
A Maid in Bedlam
The Parting Glass
The Cruel Mother
Demon Lover

The Fits o' the Season

Other

Dragons of the Mind: Seven Fairy Tales

The Unquiet Grave
A Caitlin Ross Adventure

Cover art by Matt Davis, www.rockandhillstudio.com

All songs traditional except "Caitlin's Spell Song" copyright © 2007 Too Big Cat (ASCAP), lyrics and music by Katherine E. Lampe

ISBN: 978-1-514-68375-0

The Unquiet Grave

A Caitlin Ross Adventure

Katherine Lampe

"My lips they are as clay, my love,
My breath is earthy strong,
And should you kiss my clay-cold lips,
Your time will not be long."
The Unquiet Grave, Traditional

For Michael
Who told me how to get into the cellar

Chapter One

Stepping through the pub's shiny new oak and etched glass doors sent a jolt down my spine exactly like running headlong into a brick wall. Then my brain kicked in and began listing all the ways the barrier I had encountered did not resemble a wall at all. I could see right through it, past the scattering of tables and booths to the antique mahogany bar at the other end of the room. I checked my head and face. No blood, no lumps. I hadn't been knocked unconscious, as far as I could tell. And a wall would have prevented the rest of my band, Red Branch, from entering as well as me. But when I looked up I could see them making their way to the stage in the back room behind the bar. Their voices, raised in eager discussion of our upcoming gig, wafted back to me like a tune played slightly off-tempo.

Then one of them paused and looked over his shoulder. I saw his face move from puzzlement, as he realized I no longer followed, to concern, as he saw me leaning against the front doors in a daze.

"Caitlin!" He dropped his gig bag and the case holding his bodhrán, the Irish frame drum, and hurried to my side. "Are you all right?"

Not a wall, then. I straightened and shook off the shock of impact, marshaling my senses in my best attempt to determine what had happened. My mind quested towards the point of impact with the caution of a bomb squad approaching a suspicious package. Almost at once I felt it again. Violent nausea leapt from the pit of my stomach all the way up my throat; I gagged and swallowed it back. My nostrils twitched. I couldn't smell anything. All the same, I received the distinct impression of the sick-sweet stink of something old and rotten. The kind of smell that gets right under your clothes and into your skin, a clinging stench no amount of bathing will eliminate. It had no touch, and yet my skin crawled. I felt an almost uncontrollable urge to flinch away, or to curl up into a ball so as to present as little surface area as possible.

At the touch on my elbow I did flinch, jerking my flute case up in self-defense. I started to cry out, but in the next moment my vision cleared and I found myself looking into the twilight blue eyes of my husband and bandmate, Timber MacDuff.

"Watch it, aye?" He grabbed my wrist before the flute case could smash into his nose. His mouth opened, whether to deliver a rebuke or caution I'll never know because just then he got a good look at my face and I saw the words drain right out of him.

"Caitlin, love! What is it?"

Timber gathered me into his arms and for a minute I rested against his chest, smelling the comforting smell of him: sawdust, woodsmoke, sage and sweetgrass, with the faintest hint of the fine whisky we all drank—in moderation, of course—before a gig. It blanketed the thick un-smell and his arms held at bay the horrible un-touch, giving me a much-needed space to pull myself together.

I took one deep breath and another. My stomach still heaved, but I felt stronger. With an effort, I detached myself from my husband's torso and stood on my own two feet.

"Tim…." My voice came out in a squeak. I grimaced and tried again. "Timber, there's something there." I cocked my head towards the interior of the pub.

He regarded me for a long moment, irritation warring with resignation on his face. At last, resignation won and he shrugged, running a callused hand through his unruly, dark curls.

"Aye. Well, we knew that, didn't we."

I sighed and nodded.

With a shake of his head that said more than words, Timber reached for my gig bag. I relinquished it without comment. It helped, a little, to pass the black Gatemouth with its weight of whistles, microphones and various other musicians' paraphernalia to someone bigger and stronger than I.

"Come on, then. We'd best be seeing about the set up before those dafties bollux it up." He started back towards the stage, paused, and glanced back at me. "You'll be all right?"

I nodded again. I wouldn't like it, forcing myself through the wall of sensation that stood between me and my work, but it wouldn't take me by surprise again.

I took a step and felt the strangeness close around me. I could almost hear its voice—or did I hear more than one? It tickled my inner ear like a putrid feather from something the cat left under the bed and then forgot,

"Help…Please…Help…Please…Please…"

I closed my eyes and kept going. I knew I should never have taken this gig.

Timber and I located Frank Delacourt and Lisa Bristol, Red Branch's other two members, drinking beer in a booth at the pub's rear, to one side of the stage where we would soon be playing. I endured a few minutes of the guitarist and fiddler's

raptures over the recently remodeled Emerald Isle's facelift, and their grandiose schemes for using our gig as a stepping stone to bigger and better things. Then I lost patience with the whole business and went in search of the pub's new owner, leaving Timber to make sure all the instruments got tuned and the stage got set up.

I found Mr. Casey behind the curved bar, serving bottled Killian's to a couple of early arrivals while a rugby match played without sound on the television screen over his head. We hadn't met in person before; he'd left the remodel to his contractor while he finished up odds and ends of business in New York. We'd dealt with all the contractual details over the phone and by fax.

I knew from our conversations that he had been a banker before taking early retirement, but he looked less like a banker than a football player: big and wide, especially through the torso. The white button-down shirt he wore strained over muscles better developed than I would have expected for a man of his former station and age, which I took to be about fifty-five. His legs, or what I could see of them behind the bar, were somewhat slimmer but just as muscular, encased in brand new Wranglers. Altogether, he posed a somewhat threatening figure and I would have felt ill at ease if not for his pleasant, round face, now sporting a welcoming smile under wide blue eyes and a shock of black hair in the late stages of going grey.

"Mr. Casey?" I stretched out my hand. "I'm Caitlin Ross. Of Red Branch."

The small, neatly manicured hand he extended over the bar seemed out of place on his beefy arm, but it latched onto mine with a knuckle-popping grip. "Call me Casey. Everyone does." The accents of Midtown and the Bronx warred in his voice. "Do you have everything you need?"

I nodded. "We'll be starting in about twenty minutes, just as soon as we get everything set up."

A sudden burst of over-amplified acoustic guitar from the back room made both of us flinch, the more so when a discordant squeal of out-of-tune fiddle joined in. I made out the first few bars of our opening number before Timber bellowed at Frank to turn it down and the sound abruptly cut to a less deafening level.

"You've done wonders with this place." I ran my hand across the smooth mahogany surface of the bar. Late evening sunlight streamed through the front windows and danced across the array of glasses and bottles behind Casey's back, and I remembered how dismal and shabby the interior had been when Timber and I had visited the place in one of its previous incarnations. I wished the care put into the setting would soften the odd, dark atmosphere, which I could still feel swirling around me. Perhaps given time it would.

"It's always been a dream of mine to have a place like this. My grandfather used to take me to his favorite New York haunts when I was small. The strength of the Irish community, refusing to be swallowed by the big city, affected me more than anything has, before or since." He wiped an invisible speck from the bar, his eyes misting over. "After school, I spent every vacation in Ireland, looking for the best aspects of all the best pubs. I think I've managed to incorporate many of them here."

He looked up, his eyes narrow and serious, all traces of mist gone. I thought I would not like to see such an expression on a person with the power to grant or deny me a loan.

"But I must be frank with you, Ms. Ross. I've heard quite a bit of music in pubs, and Red Branch isn't up to the standard I'm used to. The CD you sent me has a certain spark, but overall it lacked cohesion. I only hired your group because I'm trying to fit in here and that means hiring local people whenever possible."

I had wondered. Casey struck me as wealthy enough to bring in the Chieftains if he wanted, and he hadn't needed to tell me he desired only the best for his bar. Still, his words hit me like a slap in the face. I might question the quality of my band every day; I still didn't like hearing a complete stranger criticize it.

"The music industry has changed, Mr. Casey. Once upon a time, a band played out a great deal, hoping to land a recording contract. Now you have to have a recording almost before you can get a gig, so you make one as soon as possible and hope the venue can see the potential behind the flaws." I shrugged. "Besides, it's an old CD. I'm afraid it doesn't quite reflect our current abilities." True enough. We played better live than our CD suggested. I hoped it would be enough to satisfy Casey. He'd paid in advance for the gig, though, so it wouldn't much matter if he threw us out in disgust halfway through the first set.

"I'm surprised you haven't made a new one, then."

"Money is always an issue for independent musicians. Studio time doesn't come cheap, even here. Couple it with reproduction, artwork and all the rest of it…. That adds up to a lot of gigs."

He gave me a calculating look, the blue eyes I had thought so merry flat and cold. I saw it for the merest instant, then it vanished and he smiled again. "Well, if you do well here tonight, perhaps we could come to some kind of agreement."

"Perhaps." Maybe I should have been pleased, but the vagaries of his mood put me off and I found I didn't like him very much. How could you like someone who first insulted you and then offered you money? "Listen, I'd better get back to the rest of the group. I'm pleased to have met you," I lied.

"Think about what I said," he called after me.

Think about it? I couldn't help thinking about it. I only hoped the whole conversation wouldn't ruin my ability to perform.

"Jerk," I muttered under my breath as I grabbed my flute and climbed onto the stage for the minimal sound check the circumstances demanded.

I'd never played to such a crowd as packed the Emerald Isle by the time we started. Hordes of red-faced merrymakers called greetings from table to overflowing table; more milled around the bar or lined the walls. Children from toddlers to teenagers ran about underfoot, tripping up the waitresses and making general nuisances of themselves. The din about deafened me.

Behind the bar, Casey dispensed pint after pint, his face wreathed in a jovial landlord's smile. I wondered if he'd be so pleased if he knew how little the success of his opening night meant in the long run. Lots of local families held reunions around the Fourth of July, which had just passed, and anyplace serving food and drink benefited from the influx of out-of-towners. Five years in Gordarosa had also taught me that any business could expect record crowds for the first month or two, until the new wore off. Then people decided they couldn't afford the high prices, or they didn't like the food, or the entertainment didn't appeal to them and they began to drift away. If luck held, a core crowd kept coming back. Usually those people had been going to the same restaurant or bar in the same location for years and didn't care what name hung over the door or who owned the premises. This particular location had a reputation for attracting hard-drinking, violent types. That didn't say much for Casey's continuing in the light-hearted, family pub vein in which he had started.

The gig went about as well as I had expected it would, which meant Lisa's fiddle line faded in and out, Frank from time to from to time changed his guitar rhythm to something completely different from the way we had rehearsed it, and for long stretches I felt as if I were keeping the whole thing going through the force of my flute and my will. At least Timber's bodhrán gave us a solid backbeat, and when he sang, the house stilled, spellbound. Lisa's songs also went over pretty well—better than mine, as usual. I had a fondness for the kind of long, sentimental ballads that sent everyone in the house to the bar for another round. I could never tell whether my delivery brought up such intense emotions that the audience needed to drown their sorrows, or whether my musical choices simply bored them to tears. I suspected the latter.

To my surprise, Casey seemed pleased with us. During our first break he came around to the band table with a pitcher of draught Guinness. I made a big show of sorting through my whistles while he chatted up the others. He mentioned the possibility of steady work, maybe as a session band, maybe as something more. I watched carefully for the hardness I had glimpsed in him before, but didn't see it. The rest of the band loved him. I thought I was losing my mind.

Inspired by our patron's attention, or by the Guinness, or by both, Red Branch charged into our second set with unusual energy. The audience responded by clapping, stamping their feet, and swilling beer at an alarming rate. I thrilled to the rare experience of Red Branch functioning as single unit, sheer joy in the music washing away all my worries about the band's quality and our future together. However, I became alarmed when one pickled customer, who had been doing a Riverdance imitation in the aisle, tripped and ended up under a table. Taking this as a sign that we needed to back off and give our fans time to recover, I decided to skip ahead in the playlist and caught the rest of the band's attention with a wave of my flute.

"'Kilnamartyra Exile,'" I mouthed.

Timber set down his bodhrán at once and left the stage looking relieved; sweat poured down his ruddy face as he staggered toward the bar. Lisa started to protest my choice, then shrugged and followed him. Behind me, Frank struck up the opening of the old emigration ballad I had named. I stepped up to my mic and began to sing,

"I am a lonely exile, who left my own dear nation

To seek a situation in the land beyond the foam,
I have traveled cross the ocean,
Midst hardship and through danger,
And for years I've been a stranger
To my own dear native home...."

As always when I sang, my eyes roved out over the audience, seeking a particular individual to whom to direct my words. That's when I noticed the old man.

He might have been the exile of my song, so lost and alone he seemed. Hovering between the two tables directly in front of the stage, he stared up at me with such an expression of sad longing on his face that I faltered going into the second verse. Lisa, who had taken a seat with a co-worker from the middle school, broke off her conversation long enough to glare at me. Frank, bless him, vamped an extra measure while I found the words; sometimes he really did come through.

I had never seen the old man before. This struck me as unusual; after five years in Gordarosa I knew pretty much everybody in town, at least by sight. I wondered if he might be someone's father or grandfather up for the Fourth, maybe out of the nursing home for a weekend; he had that unkempt look about him. He wore a battered derby over grey hair that stuck up in two tufts over his ears. Aside from its expression his face held little of interest. Bushy white eyebrows sprouted in profusion over eyes that might have been blue, and a bulbous nose sat slightly off-center between jowls covered with wiry sideburns. His mouth gaped open a little as if in astonishment at the sounds coming in at his protruding ears.

"I've hunted for prosperity, and still it has eluded me,
And bleak misfortune followed me wherever I did roam..."

Prosperity certainly did seem to have eluded the poor fellow. His clothes sat ill on him, rumpled and dusty as if he'd pulled them out of a dumpster. Something else bothered me about them as well. I frowned down from the stage, trying to pinpoint the trouble without losing the thread of the song.

Suit coat with sleeves frayed at the cuffs. Trousers trying hard to keep a crease and failing. Suspenders, some kind of white shirt, scuffed boots. You could have seen any of it on a workingman in a bar for the past hundred years. Then it hit me. His clothes were so ordinary I hadn't seen it at first. I hadn't realized the cut of his suit was a hundred years old.

Then he took off his hat, and I saw something else I hadn't seen before. Some blunt object had bashed in the left side of his head and I could see bits of brain and gore spattered in the wiry grey hair. I closed my eyes and told myself to keep singing; I had reached the middle of the third verse and would be finished soon. I looked again; the old man still stood there. He reached into his shirt pocket for a handkerchief to blot the blood streaming over his ear. The left side of his mouth sagged alarmingly as he flashed what I took to be a smile of apology for his mangled appearance. A piece of skull dropped from his head onto his shoulder.

Into the fourth verse now and can I please just get through this song so I can run to the ladies' and sick up? I barely noticed that the house had grown still as a church. No customer coughed; no child cried. Not even Timber had ever held an audience's attention as I held this one's. Every eye was glued to me and every one held same rapt expression that had called the old man to my notice. The attention would have pleased me, once. Now I cared for nothing but the song, because only my intense need to finish the song kept me from passing out.

Finally I came to the end:

"And when my days are over and Death has come and taken me…"

I choked on the mention of death, but kept going.

"It's fondly I'll remember thee, Dear Land that I adore."

I tagged the song with the requisite "that's it," and the house erupted into more applause than any song of mine had ever earned. The old man put his hat back on and gave three slow, soundless claps. His eyes met mine and his mouth moved. I could just make out the word it formed:

"Please... Please..."

He stared at me a long minute. Then he turned and walked, through the tables, through the applauding people sitting at the tables and straight through what I knew to be a blank wall.

CHApTER TWO

I did not sleep well that night. I often did not sleep well after a gig, but lay tossing, going over the performance and wondering how it could have been improved. That night, however, our performance was the farthest thing from my mind.

The scene started replaying in my head as soon as I turned out the light. Over and over I watched the old man's head disintegrate as his rotten lips mouthed their silent plea. Over and over he walked through the tables, through the wall: an unremarkable character transformed into something monstrous. Did he have any connection to the sensations that nearly had knocked me off my feet upon first entering the bar? Probably. His appearance had made my skin crawl in the same way, had instilled me with the same nausea. Did he have any connection to the bar's name as a bad luck spot? Perhaps. A hundred-year-old ghost could account for a lot of bad luck.

I might have asked myself why he had appeared to me, but I already knew.

I rolled over and watched the minutes flash past on my nightstand clock. Three forty. Three forty-five. Three… My eyes closed and I drifted into a familiar dream. I walked up a windswept hill in the dark. Overhead, the stars fought a full moon. A door in the hill opened and a man came out, a man with flaming hair and eyes the color of the stormy sea. He took my hand.

"Ah, that's the Old Blood speaking," my grandmother Llewellyn had said when I told her of the dream once, long ago. "It's Brenda Maddox you see. She slept on a Fairy hill, and the Bright Ones took her, and no one in mortal lands saw her for a year and a day. Then she came back, big with child, and no one could name the father. They married her off to a neighbor boy, and they came across the sea. But the Old Blood comes out in her daughters from time to time." Here, she poked me in the nose and cackled.

She died soon after, and no one else in my family wanted to hear about the Old Blood.

The dream changed. Five years old, I sat on the floor of the room I shared with my sisters, making balls of light. Seven balls, all the colors of the rainbow, danced around my head and I laughed with the pleasure of it.

My sisters came in, fifteen and seventeen. At first, absorbed in chatting about some boy or other, they didn't notice me. Then they did, and their faces grew mean with fear.

"Stop it," said Una, the elder.

"You're not allowed," the younger, Mairghread, chimed in.

I let the balls vanish. "Is it true you're going to marry David?" I asked Una.

Her face went dead white and her hand pressed her belly in a gesture I didn't understand. She took a step forward, as if she meant to shake me, then stopped. "Where did you hear that? You little spy!"

"He's no good for you," I went on in a toneless voice. "He'll break your heart."

Una ran out of the room, screaming for our mother. Mother came in. She didn't fear me. She grabbed me by the shoulders and slapped me across the face, so hard my head snapped back. I didn't understand what I had done wrong, and no one bothered to explain.

My mother and sisters left the room. I crawled into bed, drew the shadows about me, and huddled there for a long time.

Disturbed, I roused a little and looked at the clock again. Three fifty-five.

My family didn't manage to beat the magic out of me, for all they tried. I practiced in secret, and my skill grew. As soon as I could, I left home and looked for the others like me I knew must be out there. But although I learned ritual and divination, and many other things besides, I found few who could match me—a true witch. Finally, I settled in Boulder, Colorado, and made an attempt to blend in with the New Age community there. I kept a shop and read cards, and guarded my real nature from all but a few. Until Timber came to draw me out of my shell, I lived a quiet, almost Mundane life.

I shifted in my half-sleep, knowing what was coming, not wanting to face it but helpless to stop it. My mind, freed from the control I kept over it by daylight, raced on toward the inevitable.

Timber persuaded me to use my skill in service to others. For a short time, we worked together, blessing houses, healing, laying ghosts.

Laying ghosts. My unconscious brain caught at the concept and I flinched, not knowing why.

Then we stumbled into a situation where our combined powers were not enough. And like a fool, I went in search of more. I didn't get it. Instead, I got a warning of what would befall me if I continued in my course.

I saw a shining figure, a road leading into fire. And then I saw walls. Long, beige walls narrowing to a point in the distance. I walked between them on shuffling feet, and the walls closed me in.

I sat bolt upright, completely awake, stifling the scream rising in my throat. Shuddering, I glanced at my nightstand. Only a few minutes had passed, but it felt like a lifetime.

After that vision in Boulder, I'd run. Swearing I'd never use magic again, I'd left everything—shop, clients, even Timber—and fled to tiny Gordarosa on the Western Slope. Five years had gone by since then, and in all that time I'd never willingly used my powers. Sometimes they took me unawares. From time to time I experienced flashes of vision, or the force of magic flowing through me. But always, I had been able to fight it back. Until tonight. Until the energy in the Emerald Isle sent me reeling and a ghost appeared.

Slowly, my breathing steadied. As silently as I could, I extricated myself from the blankets and the cats hemming me in on all sides and got up. Timber made a little murmur of protest, but soon enough edged into the warm spot I had left and sank back into sleep. In the dark, I pulled on an old sweatshirt and sweatpants. Still silent, I left the bedroom and padded downstairs, feeling the hardwood risers slick and cool under my bare feet, flinching when the boards creaked. It would have been a soft sound by day; in the stillness of the night it seemed as loud as a shout.

In the living room I turned the stand-lamp on low. Its dim glow illuminated familiar and comfortable things: the big, squashy sofa upholstered in soft green plush where I spent hours reading, the tweed armchair that was the first piece of furniture Timber and I had bought together, the coffee table Timber had built from odds and ends of oak left over from a construction site, strewn with tool and gardening catalogues. In one corner an antique étagère that had belonged to my grandmother held china animal figurines I had collected since childhood, presided over by a large Bast on the top shelf. Another wall displayed a series of monotypes of Irish standing stones by a local artist. Floor to ceiling bookshelves took up most of the remaining wall space, crammed with everything from history and religious subjects to sheet music and the odd romance novel. I spent a lot of time in this room and more than any other in the house it spoke of safety and of home. But tonight I didn't know if its reassurance would be enough.

Sighing, I made my way to the kitchen to make a cup of tea. When the kettle boiled, I snatched it from the burner before the whistle could waft upstairs and disturb my sleeping husband. My hands shook as I filled the mug Timber had given me for Yule, but I managed not to slop boiling water all over myself.

Back in the living room, I sat cross-legged on the couch and shut my eyes. I sipped my tea and tried my best not to think of anything at all. It wasn't easy. In my head, the old man's head dissolved and his mouth moved, over and over. I felt like throwing up.

After a time, I heard the bedroom door open. Timber appeared at the top of the stairs, blinking sleep from his face as he adjusted his ratty brown sweatpants around his hips.

"Could ye no sleep, then?" Thirty years in America had not managed to erase the Scots burr from his voice; when he hadn't slept, as now, or when strong emotion moved him, it became even more pronounced.

I shook my head. He came down and sat beside me on the couch. He stroked my hair, his face flickering through a wide range of expressions as he tried to decide what to say.

"Is it the band again?" he asked at last. "I know it gets to ye. The bickering. The lack of professionalism. Frank and Lisa having such high-flown ambitions when they dinna show any willingness of doing the real work of making good music. I dinna ken, love. If it weren't for them, I'd be happy playing in the kitchen, with maybe a wedding now and again…"

"No, no, it isn't the band," I said in a rush. "Not tonight. Tonight they were pretty mild. And the gig went well. You heard Casey. He's thinking of hiring us as house band."

"Aye, I heard him." Timber looked far from pleased. "But I'm not so sure a steady gig at the Emerald Isle would be a good idea. That place has an evil reputation, and well-earned. We both have cause to know it."

I remembered. Timber and I had visited the bar only once before Sean Casey took it over. That had been before our marriage, soon after we had moved to Gordarosa. Both of us had drunk far more than usual and ended the evening by having the most vicious argument of our life together. I hadn't run into any psychic wall, though, and I wondered why.

"Ye didna want to take the gig in the first place, I seem to recall," Timber went on.

"No," I admitted. There were too many stories about the place, and what I heard scared me. Patrons got violent. Owners went bankrupt, or just gave up and left. One had simply disappeared. There had even been a murder, shortly before Timber and I came to town. "But it was too good a thing to pass up. As Frank and Lisa pointed out. Repeatedly."

The corners of Timber's mouth tightened. "Ye shouldna let them push ye around the way ye do."

I shrugged. I didn't want to talk about Frank and Lisa. I didn't know if I wanted to talk at all.

"Is it what happened?" he asked in a cautious voice, knowing he was approaching dangerous territory.

"What happened?" I echoed.

"When ye went in. Whatever it was, ye looked sick to death."

"I'd really like another cup of tea," I said, not meeting his eyes. "Would you put the kettle on?"

"Caitlin. Tell me."

I didn't want to. I knew how he'd react. However, keeping secrets from my husband was the next thing to impossible. He'd have the story out of me sooner or later; better let it be sooner.

Taking a couple of deep breaths, I related everything I had sensed and seen from the time I entered the bar, from the wall of overpowering sensation to the vision of the old man. I didn't even leave out the words that had come to me, though I didn't advance any theories as to what they might mean.

"I'll make that tea now," he said when I had finished. "Or shall I start the coffee?" The summer sky had grown lighter as I talked; morning birdsong drifted through the open living room window and hummers zoomed around the feeder hung outside.

"Tea, please." I managed a smile. "I'm still hoping to get some sleep."

He disappeared into the kitchen. At the sound of him filling the kettle, three cats emerged from the bedroom and pelted downstairs squalling to be fed and let out; I heard the rattle of dry food hitting various dishes and the back door opening and closing several times.

To my surprise, Timber's return roused me from a doze. Feeling the couch sink under his weight I shook myself awake and accepted the steaming mug he offered me with an appreciative sniff. Celestial Seasonings' Tension Tamer for both of us. Smart man.

"Poor old bugger." Timber shook his head sadly and took a thoughtful sip from his mug. "Trapped in that place for a hundred years."

I sighed, wishing for once that I'd married a man who would tell me that ghosts didn't exist and that the whole incident could be explained as a hallucination brought on by repressing my frustration at the band. Timber, however, knew better. When we'd met, he'd been a half-trained shaman trying to locate a missing master. Suspecting the disappearance was no Mundane matter and not trusting his own abilities, he'd gone looking for help. He'd literally pulled my name out of the psychic listings in the Boulder Yellow Pages. Eventually, one thing led to another. Yes, Timber knew all about me. Almost.

"It explains a lot, of course," he went on. "The fights, the failures…even the death. An angry spirit can stir up all kinds of bad feeling."

"He didn't seem angry to me," I felt moved to say. "Only sad. Upset."

Timber waved away my distinction. "All the same. Now that we know what we're up against, we can do something about it."

I gazed into my tea mug, not wanting to meet his eyes.

"What?" His normally gentle voice touched the edge of impatience. He had to know what was coming. We'd argued about it before, the one sore spot in an otherwise harmonious marriage.

"You know I won't get involved," I said at last.

He flushed from his beard to the roots of his disheveled dark hair. Frustration poured off of him and his throat convulsed as he swallowed back a harsh response. When he spoke he had mastered the urge to snarl at me, but I still felt his struggle to keep his emotions in check as if it were my own.

"Because you decided to keep out of anything…" He searched for an inoffensive word. "…Unusual. Aye, well. Ye canna just cut out half your soul and expect to live a full life."

The old argument made me feel as if I had swallowed half a dozen razor blades. My eyes filled with tears at the pain of it.

"You knew what you were getting when you married me," I said softly.

"Aye. I did." I knew he was remembering that we almost hadn't married at all, and wondered if he regretted that we had.

"No regrets," he said, as if he were the psychic. "You're the only woman I will ever want, magic or no. But I miss the woman you were."

I tossed the tears away with the back of my hand, before they could overflow. I missed that woman, too. Sometimes I missed her so much.

"I'm sorry," I told him. "But I won't get involved in this. You can look into it if you want, but you'll have to do it by yourself."

"Won't you even help on the Mundane end?" he wheedled. "If I'm to send the poor old fellow to his rest and free the bar of his influence, I'll need all the information I can get. My guides might give me some, but they do like a person to exhaust all avenues before troubling them. If this ghost has been around as long as we think, someone must know his story. The library might have records, or the Historical Society. It would save me a lot of trouble if you'd look into it for me. Besides, you're so good at that sort of thing."

I shot him a wary glance. His face displayed only innocence, without a hint of the cunning mind behind his wide blue eyes. By itself, his request seemed reasonable enough. Still, acceding to it might be the first step on the road to perdition. Once I started looking into the ghost's story, I doubted I could refrain long from bringing my other powers to bear on the case. I suspected Timber thought the same.

"I'll think about it," I said in tones that meant, "Not a chance in Hell."

He nodded, apparently satisfied. I wondered what other heinous tricks he planned, to get me to change my mind. Whatever they were, he'd probably spring them on me at the worst possible moment. I resolved to stay on guard.

I yawned; the hour and the stress had taken their toll. Confiding in my husband had helped, despite our little disagreement, and I thought I might finally be able to sleep. Timber opened his arms to me and I was only too glad to settle back against his warm chest. I was dozing when I felt his lips move against my hair.

"I thought I'd start by looking into the remodel."

"Oh? Why?" I asked sleepily, then came fully awake with a silent curse. So much for staying on guard.

He chuckled at my reaction. "Well, if the history of the bar is anything to go by, that ghost has been haunting the place for a hundred years. But you, powerful psychic that you are, never saw him before last night."

"Timber, I've only set foot in that place once before." I chose to ignore his pointed reference to my abilities. "Maybe he was busy."

"Aye. And maybe he had no reason to show himself, then. Maybe he does now."

"What are you getting at?" I asked, curious in spite of myself.

"Perhaps something about the remodel upset him. Ghosts don't like change, aye? But Casey's made some pretty big changes, getting the Emerald Isle ready for business."

I thought about that. "True, as far as it goes. But Timber, that place has been remodeled about a gazillion times. There have been three owners in the last five years. You'd think if the ghost were going to be upset at a change in décor, he would have shown it before now."

"Perhaps he did and we just didn't know enough to see it. There was that murder, after all. Or it might be this remodel was different."

"Like the excavations disturbed his grave or something?"

"I'm not sure they did any excavating. But aye, something like that."

I closed my eyes, casting my mind back to the ghost's appearance before the stage and further, to the moment I had entered the bar. Something in Timber's theory struck me as not quite right. One might expect a ghost to show anger at the violation of his grave or the disruption of his routine. But this ghost had not struck me as angry. For a minute I quested after the true feeling. Sadness, yes. And something else. Something like….

Then I realized what I was doing and sat up in a rush. I fixed my husband with a stern glare.

"I'm not helping you," I told him. "I'm not getting involved."

"Of course not," he replied in much the same tones as a mother whose toddler has just announced she'll never eat spinach again. "Come on back, love. You're tired. Things will look different after a rest."

"In your dreams," I said and turned my back on the treacherous comfort he offered. At least, that's what I intended to happen. Instead, I found myself wrapped once more in his arms, the rise and fall of his chest rocking me steadily towards sleep.

"You can't live with half a soul," I heard him say, and I wanted to slap him for bringing that up again when I was so relaxed.

But I was already gone.

Chapter Three

I had half expected my sleep to be broken and full of nightmares. Instead, I remained in a state of blissful unconsciousness until well into the afternoon, when a cat jumped from the back of the couch directly onto my bladder and jarred me awake.

I was drinking my second cup of coffee when the drumming started upstairs and the scents of cedar and sweetgrass wafted down. Timber had commenced his investigations, then. Trying not to let the steady, pulsing rhythm carry me away, I wondered if Timber were right about my living with half a soul. Probably. Souls were a shaman's business, after all.

It would be so easy to succumb to the pull of my powers. Reaching out last night had taken less thought than breathing. And it had felt so good. Maybe it wouldn't hurt if just this once...

Then I thought of the shining figure on the hill, the fire, the shuffling feet and the walls closing in, and shook my head. No. I couldn't risk it. The consequences of returning to a magical life would be too severe.

I had never told Timber why I had stopped using my powers. Maybe I should. Maybe it would help him understand.

As I thought of my husband, the drumming ceased. I heard a door open, then close. Timber trudged down the stairs, looking weary. When he saw me, his face did not light up. But he sat on the couch beside me and took my hand. His clothes smelled faintly of incense and sweat.

"I'm not getting anything," he told me. "Caitlin, I need you."

I hated to disappoint him. I did it anyway.

"No," I said.

"For feck's sake, Caitlin! This is the first time in five years I've asked ye for anything!"

"No," I repeated.

For a moment I thought he would shake me, and I half wished he would. Then he threw my hand into my lap and stalked back upstairs without another word. After a while, the drumming started up again.

Timber didn't speak to me for the rest of the day.

Monday, I rose an hour earlier than I was accustomed to do, which is to say before Timber left for his job as foreman on the site of a new custom home construction project on one of the mesas outside town. I hesitated over going downstairs and seeing him off. I didn't want to hear any more about how much he needed my abilities. Even more, I didn't want to find he was still upset with me. But when I finally screwed up my courage and ventured downstairs, I found he had gotten over his fit of pique. He flashed me a wide smile and swept me off my feet for a kiss that denied we had ever had any difference of opinion at all.

When he released me, I stumbled to the coffeemaker and poured myself a cup. I stared into it balefully while leaning on the counter. Even without ghosts, mornings were not my best time.

Timber glanced at the clock on the stove. I already knew that if he was still home it couldn't be too much after seven; I didn't want to know the details.

"You're up early." He finished putting his breakfast things in the dishwasher and started it running.

"It does happen." Taking a swallow of coffee, I leaned on the kitchen counter to watch him put his lunch together. At one time I had made a point of getting up when he did to make his lunch and breakfast, but after a couple of weeks suffering my morning temper he'd informed me he'd rather do it himself.

"Any special plans?"

I tried not to read too much into his question, though his voice held an insinuating note I didn't much like.

"No." The back door stood open; I wandered over to it and stuck my head out. "Maybe pull some more weeds before it gets too hot." In the arid western summer, that meant before ten a.m.; with my tendency to sleep late, more often than not the weeding didn't get done until evening, if at all.

"I may be late. We're on the roof today."

"Remember your water. And your hat!"

"They're in the truck already." Lunchbox in hand, he gathered me in his arms and planted another hearty kiss on my lips. His embrace felt so good I wished I could stay there all day. I sighed. No such luck.

"Don't work too hard."

Reluctantly he released me. "Ye ken I won't."

He looked as though he wanted to say more. I tensed, waiting for it, but he only deposited a chaste peck on my forehead and disappeared through the door. A minute later I heard the truck start up, followed by the crunch of gravel as Timber rolled off down the drive.

I carried a second cup of coffee into the office, where I spent a half an hour perusing the latest internet headlines while waiting for the caffeine to jump-start my brain. At one point I caught myself about to Google "ghosts" and dropped the mouse as if it had burned me. What was I thinking? That it wouldn't hurt? That I'd just run off a couple pages of information for Timber's use? Sure, and then I'd read them, and then I'd look for more, and before I knew it I'd be poking around at the Emerald Isle, inviting contact from any supernatural entity that happened to be in the vicinity. I knew better than to start. But,

"I need you," Timber had said. How could I refuse to meet that need?

"Balls," I said to anything that might be listening.

I shut down my internet browser and left the office.

I had been working in the garden for perhaps an hour and was just settling down to deadhead the roses when I heard the distinctive crunch of a vehicle coming up the gravel drive. I couldn't see the car. The perennial bed ran from the south side of the house to the east; the drive came in at the northwest corner of our property and continued around the north side of the house to Timber's shed in the back. I wasn't expecting any visitors. From the way the shadows fell across the garden it was still early—ten o'clock at the latest. Anyone who knew me knew better than to drop by before noon. For a minute I considered the possibility that Timber had come back after some tool he had forgotten. For another minute I thought about reaching towards the person with my mind, just to see if it happened to be anyone I knew. I turned away from that notion with a brutal twist of my brain. Timber would find me or he wouldn't. Anyone else, I didn't care to see. I kept working.

The vehicle stopped. I heard a door open and shut; it didn't sound like a truck. Not Timber, then. Footsteps went clickety-click up the path leading from the drive to our front door. The clickety-click warned me the visitor was not someone I knew—probably not even a local. Footwear in Gordarosa ran to boots, sneakers and rafting sandals; these sounded like high heels. No one around here wore heels except to go to church or court. I decided to pretend I wasn't home.

The doorbell chimed faintly from inside. After a minute it chimed again. I continued clipping, waiting for the retreating clickety-click to signal that my caller had given up. It didn't come. Instead, I heard the creak of our screen door being opened, followed by a determined rapping on the solid oak entry door.

"Hello?" A woman's voice called in the interval between raps. "Is anyone home?"

This visitor was not going give up easily. I could keep hiding in hopes she would go away, but she just might opt to camp out on the front porch until someone appeared. Deciding I'd better go see what she wanted, I thrust my pruning shears and my trowel into my weed collecting bucket, brushed myself off and headed around to the front of the house.

"May I help you?" I asked as soon as I rounded the edge of the house. I kept my voice cool. I am not fond of unexpected visitors, even when I know who they are.

The woman whirled to face me and I allowed myself a smug smile as a glimpse of her clothes confirmed my suspicions: definitely not a local. She wore a smart business suit, a tailored black jacket and matching short skirt, with a hint of white silk peeping from beneath the jacket's collar. Pearl grey hose encased long, shapely legs and expensive black sling-backs had made the distinctive clickety-click on my front walk.

"Ms. Ross?" She took a hesitant step towards me. The uncertainty of the movement seemed foreign to her, and I received a momentary impression of something fierce crouching behind a harmless façade.

Her beauty literally stopped my breath. The black suit hugged a figure curved in all the right places. The exposed skin of her throat glowed milky white and her lips arched in a perfect red bow. Shining black hair cut in a swing bob style framed a flawless, heart-shaped face. All in all, she put me in mind of Snow White—or the evil queen, I couldn't tell which. A look in her eyes might have helped, but they were obscured by chic designer shades revealing the merest hint of delicate, arched brow.

"I'm Caitlin Ross." I would admit that much, but no more. In my experience, only religious proselytizers and process servers in Gordarosa dressed as this woman did. I didn't think I had done anything to merit a visit from one of the latter, but then, the former didn't as a rule call you by name.

She came down the steps towards me, holding out a hand tipped with long, burgundy nails. My own grubby fingers and dirty jeans wreaked fleeting havoc on my self-esteem, but I managed to take it with confidence. We stood on my turf, after all.

Her grip was neither too harsh nor too weak; her palm felt cool and not in the least damp against mine. Impressed, I sized her up again. At second inspection, she did not present as corporate a figure as I had first thought. Rings circled every finger of both hands, thumbs included. A few held semi-precious stones; most were engraved silver. Two silver chains showed at her throat, and when she brushed her hair back I saw at least six piercings in each ear.

"I'm Breda Ni Fhearraigh." She pronounced the Gaelic without stumbling, but I could tell it had taken practice to learn. She wasn't a native speaker. In fact, her accent sounded frankly American without any overtones to hint at where she came from. I guessed she had Gaelicized her name in an attempt to reclaim some lost cultural heritage. In English it would have been "O'Farrell." "Forgive me for turning up unannounced, but I had to see you."

"Did you, then?" I wondered why, but I refused to show any curiosity.

She flashed a smile meant to be apologetic. "I know I should have called. I did stop at the coffee shop downtown to use the phone book. They asked who I was looking for and when I told them, they gave me directions here. So I decided to chance finding you at home."

And trust to rural hospitality, I thought, wishing the days when uninvited intruders were as likely to be met with a shotgun as with a welcome had not vanished so long ago. I wondered which one of the Sunshine Bakery crowd had been so helpful. Not that it mattered. Tiny Gordarosa respected no one's privacy; what people didn't know about you they happily made up.

"I got your name from a mutual acquaintance in Boulder," Breda Ni Fhearraigh went on. "Susan Connor? When I told her I was coming here she remembered you had moved out this way and said I should look you up."

I remembered Susan Connor, a skeletal executive's wife with delusions of arcane wisdom and a taste for questionable spiritual authorities, who had frequented my magic shop downtown.

"And why should she say such a thing?"

"Well…." She had the grace to look uncomfortable, and I could tell she was about to ask for something. She didn't prove me wrong. "I need a reading."

My stomach lurched and I froze for the count of three. I had to admit I was tempted. I enjoyed reading Tarot. Besides, interpreting the cards didn't take any special ability, just a quick mind and a head for symbols. It needn't go any farther.

Sure, and an alcoholic could stop at one drink.

"I don't do that anymore."

"Why not? She said you were the best."

As I couldn't recall ever having read for Susan Connor, I took this with a grain of salt. "It's none of your business why not. I think you should leave now."

"Please." She laid her expensive manicure on my elbow. "I need help. My fiancé came out here for a job last spring and I haven't heard from him since. I'm really worried."

I thought it wouldn't be the first time a man had come west to start a new life free of old attachments. I said, "You need a psychometrist then, not a cartomancer. Tarot can't tell you about other people, only about yourself."

"I know that," Breda snapped. "Do you think I haven't tried anything else? In Boulder?"

I suppressed a wry smile. In Boulder, clairvoyants came a dime a dozen, most of them worth about that much.

"I heard more than I can stomach about becoming a being of white light, but nothing useful," she continued with a grimace that made me like her better. "I thought maybe someone closer to the place Jake went…."

"You know, it seems a little odd to me, trying to locate your boyfriend with a psychic. If it's so important, why not hire a private detective or something? There are some out here. I think."

She shook her head, making her bobbed hair swing about her face in an appealing way. "It's not like that."

"Like what?"

"Like what you're thinking." She smiled impishly.

"Oh, so now you're the psychic?"

"Come on, it's obvious, isn't it? A guy wants to break off his engagement so he disappears. Maybe there's another woman he likes better." Breda shrugged. "But Jake wasn't like that. We told each other everything. If he'd had doubts, he would have said."

"And you would have been perfectly fine with that."

"I'm not saying there wouldn't have been sparks. But I would have understood. Eventually." Another impish smile. "Anyway, Jake wouldn't have been so frightened by the prospect of an argument that he'd disappear to avoid it. If he had been, we would never have gotten engaged."

She was a fireball, right enough. I tried to peg her sign and had just decided upon Aries when it occurred to me that thinking about astrology might lead to other things the way smoking marijuana supposedly led to heroin addiction. Damn, this was hard!

"That doesn't explain why you prefer to use…alternative methods to locate him."

"Jake was…mixed up in some stuff."

From the tone in her voice she didn't mean gangs or drugs or contraband firearms. "Occult stuff."

She nodded. "He was always talking about mystic secrets and lost knowledge. How there were powers out there no one remembered or understood, and if he could just find the right key he could use it to unlock the universe. He could get a little manic about it, but I thought it was kind of cute."

Oh, brother. I thought Jake sounded like a nut she was better rid of.

"Before he came out here, he was really excited. He thought he was on to something. He wouldn't tell me what, only that he wanted to test his theory someplace out of the way. I think…I think maybe it didn't work out."

She paused. I rubbed the bridge of my nose between my eyes, where I suspected I had a headache starting.

"Let me see if I'm hearing you right. Your boyfriend's one of those saps who get taken in by all that Golden Dawn Ceremonial Magic shit."

I made my voice harsh on purpose; I'd seen quite a few of the type and had no patience with the narcissism and just plain foolishness they got up to. I also hoped Ms. Ni Fhearraigh would get a clue and leave before our conversation went any farther.

"He thinks he's discovered the Greater Key to Solomon or something that's going to give him power. So he comes to Gordarosa to test it out, in case something goes wrong, because if some demon gets loose and eats a bunch of hicks no one will care. But you think maybe the demon ate him instead."

"That's about right." Her face turned chalky and her voice might have come from a stone.

"And you want a psychic to find out what happened because if you took this story to the Mundanes they'd laugh you off the face of the planet." I sighed. "Look, Miss Ni Fhearraigh, most of that ritual magic stuff is crap. You're about as likely to call up the Universal Mind with a spell from some book as you are to reach the White House by dialing random numbers into a phone." Of course, it did happen. I shrugged. "Even if you got through, the Universal Mind would probably hang up before you got out two words. It's not like a genie granting wishes from a bottle."

"What about demons?"

"What about them?"

"Do you believe in them?"

I knew should end the conversation. Right now. I couldn't.

"Depends on what you mean. Sure, I believe there are a lot of entities out there, many of which we don't entirely understand. But as far as the Judeo-Christian cosmology and all the subsequent ritual pseudo sciences built on it, I'd have to say no."

She tried a different tack. "You don't think someone could raise a demon?"

"If the so-called demon had some reason to want to participate in that kind of thing, sure. Most of the ones who do don't have any real power. They're just playing games. You can't even be sure they're demons. Muck around long enough with a Ouija board and you're certain to contact something that says it's the Lord of Hell. Is it? Provided there is a Hell at all, why would its Lord bother with the sort of people who muck about with Ouija boards? You'd think he'd employ a legion of minor imps for that kind of work. Any CEO on this plane would."

Before last night, I hadn't even talked about supernatural matters for five years. Now here I was, discussing demonology with a total stranger. It felt good, more than good. Timber was right; I'd been functioning on half a soul.

Breda's lips thinned in thought. "Playing games. But a person could be caught in a demon's game."

"Happens all the time. Those entities feed off a person's fears and hopes and what-have-you. They suck you in. But they only can work with what's inside you. If you're strong, you figure that out."

"And if you're not?"

I didn't answer. The unfortunate truth was that a lot of people who got heavily involved in occult subjects were not strong and, in fact, were all too ready to let others have power over them. Guru or demon, it didn't matter.

"You seem to know a lot about it."

"In my time I've known a lot of people who mucked about with Ouija boards." As a teenager, I done it myself. That had been a bad time. "Automatic writing, too. I wouldn't recommend it."

She proffered her hand. "Well, you've given me a lot to think about."

"I'm sorry I couldn't help you." Strangely enough, I meant it. I had a sense about people, if not always the wisdom to use it, and I liked Breda Ni Fhearraigh. I wished she would go far away, taking her problem with her, but at the same time I regretted I wouldn't have an excuse to see her again. "Listen, I'd bet your man found out his great key was useless nonsense and went off somewhere to get over his embarrassment. He'll turn up."

"I hope so." She turned back to her car, then stopped. "It's just that he never turned up for his job, either. He didn't even call them. It's not like him, it really isn't."

"What job?" Except in fruit picking season it was unusual for a person to come to Gordarosa looking for work, still stranger to line up a job and then never show up.

A raven flew up from the neighbor's hayfield and passed overhead, croaking three times. I shivered. I already knew Breda's answer.

"He's an architect. He was supposed to be supervising a bar remodel, a place called the Emerald Isle."

I looked at her for a long moment, seeing not her lovely face, but the porcelain mask worn by an Oracle. Fighting oracles never did anyone any good, as any number of stories pointed out. Fate always caught you up in the end.

I walked to the front door and held it open.

"I think you'd better come in."

Chapter Four

"We met in college. NYU," Breda told me as we waited for the kettle to boil. "I'd never known anyone like him before. Even then he was into the magic thing. He had this theory about architecture, how you could plan a building around special dimensions and such, so it drew the power of the universe right in."

"Not a new theory."

"I suppose not, but I didn't know it then. He went on about it like some people go on about the latest movie. He was always buying weird books and stuff from places like The Devil's Advocate—that's an occult shop in Chelsea."

I nodded. I knew of it, though in my own short time in Manhattan I'd never visited it. I considered Smith's, the Midtown shop specializing in rare, out of print books and scholarly works on everything from Auras to Zoroaster, as well as the latest New Age writers, more up my alley.

"And he'd get so excited when he found something to support his theory. Once he found a whole book about the mysteries behind the designs of the pyramids and he crowed for days."

I thought he couldn't have been looking very hard, if he'd only found one book on the subject. Even I knew there were tomes and tomes on mystic architecture, and I had never felt any great desire to study the subject.

"Where did he come from?"

"New Orleans. From the wrong side of the tracks. He…didn't talk about his past much."

Breda had removed her sunglasses on entering the house, which was rather dim—I preferred natural light—and her eyes, a startling pale blue that made a sharp contrast with her dark hair, gleamed earnestly.

"He made me feel so special. Sharing that kind of thing with me, you know?" she said, and I knew she didn't mean Jake's southern birth. "Like a whole new world opening up in front of me, one I'd imagined must be there but never dreamed was real. I majored in business," she added, as if it explained everything.

"Business?" I would have pegged her for something much different. Something in the arts, maybe.

"My family wanted it."

"What did you want?"

"Do you know, I never thought about it." She smiled an apology. "I just always knew what they wanted for me and so I did it."

Well, I knew how that went, too.

The kettle whistled then, and I got up to tend to it. "What will you have?"

"Oh, anything."

"Black or herbal?"

She thought for a minute. "Do you have any green tea?"

"Sure."

In the kitchen I dumped lukewarm water out of the two small teapots I'd been warming. To one I added several tea-spoons of loose green tea; to my own, a handful of chamomile flowers from my herb bed. I filled both pots with boiling water and placed them on a tray along with the tea strainer.

Back in the dining room, Breda hadn't moved. She perched pensively on the edge of her chair, staring straight ahead. I shooed my black Angora, McGuyver, off the table—readings always attracted him—replaced him with the tray and went to the china cabinet in the corner for a couple of the Royal Dalton cups I'd inherited from my grandmother Ross.

"You'll want to let that steep a bit." I set a cup and Breda's teapot near her elbow and carried my own to the other end of the table. "Do you need anything else? Honey? Sugar?"

She shook her head and I sat down. The speed with which all the little phrases and rituals to set a client at ease came back amazed me. People who came for Tarot readings fell into two categories: those who believed and those who didn't. I'd seen my fair share of each. Non-believers came as a lark, or out of curiosity, or because they hoped to prove you a fraud. Believers came for confirmation, for options, for someone to tell them that, despite all odds, everything would be all right. Non-believers and believers shared one thing in common, however. Everyone who sat down at the cartomancer's table was afraid. It didn't matter whether they were about to have their first reading or their hundred-and-first. They all had one thing that, whether they knew it or not, they hoped and prayed the cards wouldn't reveal. Unfortunately for them, what they feared usually turned out to be the thing they most needed to hear. Fortunately for me, I knew how to deal with it. Most of the time.

I poured myself a cup of tea, not a little nervous, myself. Not because I hadn't touched the cards in so many years: that didn't trouble me. Wondering where this reading would lead me put my heart in my throat, though. Sure, Tarot reading didn't require my special gifts. But the cards had a way of calling them up, whether I meant to use them or not. And a raven had croaked three times flying over my house and Timber said he needed me. I knew that Timber, at least, wouldn't be satisfied with half measures.

I swallowed.

"Ready?" My voice rang too cheerful by half. I hoped Breda wouldn't notice.

Breda nodded and I passed her three purple velvet pouches identical but for small variations in size.

"The first thing I want you to do is choose one of these decks. You can take the cards out and look at them, handle them, anything you want."

She considered no more than a minute before handing one of the pouches back to me. "That one."

"You don't want to look at the cards?"

"No. That's the one."

"Okay." I set aside the pouches she hadn't chosen and spilled the preferred deck into my hand. I knew before looking at it which deck Breda had selected, and that alone told me a great deal. The images it contained were dark, powerful, daunting. This consultation did not involve a trivial matter. Breda would have choices to make, and some of the choices might change her life. Little stuff like that.

I began to shuffle the cards without looking at them, feeling my mind fall into the beginnings of a mild trance state. A sense of serenity washed over me; all my own doubts and fears vanished in the certainty of my skill and the sure knowledge that whatever happened here would be right and good.

"Have you ever had a reading before?" I heard my own voice as if from a distance; it was lower-pitched and more rhythmic than usual.

"Yes. Several times."

"This is a different deck than the ones you may be used to. Some of the images are quite unusual."

"Does it matter? Which deck I chose, I mean?"

I smiled to myself. Some things were better kept secret. "Each deck has its own peculiar energy; each is suited to different situations. I find the client generally chooses the deck that has the most to tell her."

There was a silence punctuated by the sound of shuffling cards.

"How did you learn to do this?" Breda asked.

"My sister had a deck. The 1 JJ Swiss, I believe, though I don't remember very well. I was only nine or ten, but it fascinated me. I kept asking my parents for one. They finally caved in and gave me a deck for my twelfth birthday." More than twenty years later, I still couldn't understand how it had happened. They'd usually been so keen to deny my abilities, so ready to discourage my interest in the occult. Maybe Fate had intervened. "It was a department store Rider Waite knock-off—the Rider Waite is the deck you see most. It had nice colors, but left out a lot of the symbols. It came with a little faux parchment booklet of meanings, which I promptly lost. I used to lay the cards out and tell myself stories about them. It wasn't until much later that people began to teach that as the best way of going about it. It's all about what you see, really."

"The symbols don't mean anything?"

"Of course they do, but I like to look at it from a more Gestalt perspective. What they mean to me, and to the client, is more relevant than any arbitrary learned association. Anyway, I've been messing about with cards ever since. Done some book reading along the way, but it hasn't changed my methods much. Here." I slapped the cards together and passed them across the table. "Do you know what you're going to ask? Remember, it's better if it's something about you."

"I thought I'd ask how I should go about finding Jake."

"Good enough. Now, sit up as straight as you can in your chair so that you're still comfortable. Both feet flat on the ground." I checked her posture. "Good. Take a few deep breaths and let them out."

I did the same and went on, keeping my voice low and rhythmical. The voice kept on talking, leading Breda through a standard meditation designed to bring her thoughts into focus. My Reader's mind watched her relax. Good.

"Now, remember your question?" I asked after we had finished the meditation and I had instructed Breda to open her eyes. "I want you to take the cards and shuffle them—shuffle them any way you like—and as you shuffle, imagine your question going down into the cards. Shuffle until you feel done; it can be as long or as short a time as you want."

She shuffled. Tarot cards are quite a bit bigger than playing cards and many people have difficulty wrapping their hands around them; some just stir them around on the table. But Breda, with a look of intense concentration on her face, managed the standard method.

"Cut the deck in three with your left hand," I said when she had done.

She did so and I gathered up the three stacks of cards this process created in reverse order, also in my left hand. I had always done it that way, even before learning that the left hand was controlled by the right side of the brain and was, therefore, less subject to rational control and more subject to psychic influence. Or so the books said. To me, it just felt right.

I laid the deck down in front of me and sat there for a minute, feeling the cards under my fingers as I sent a silent prayer to whatever powers might be listening to guide me. Finally, I removed the card from the very bottom of the deck and set it aside, face down, on the table.

"Okay. I'm going to lay the cards out one by one. I'll tell you a little about each as it comes up and then more as the reading progresses and patterns emerge. This first card is your Apparent Self. That is, the obvious ways you present yourself to the world and the ways you've been working in the material plane."

I turned over the first card. It showed a man on a running horse. In his raised right hand he carried a spear poised as if he were about to fling it at something out of sight.

"You're strong and determined, used to getting your own way." Breda gave a nervous titter and I smiled. "You have a great force of will and tend to rely on it to the exclusion of all else. By that I mean, when you're presented with an obstacle you want to muscle your way on through along the most obvious path, rather than look for options or side routes that might not be apparent right away. You tend to act and speak without thinking or worrying about the consequences, because you believe you'll be able to deal with those later. This makes you somewhat reckless. You aren't devious and have a hard time believing people around you might not be playing straight with you. So, in looking for Jake, you're taking a straight route—it seems simple to you, a matter of hunting him down. You think if you're determined enough you're bound to succeed."

I glanced up from the card. Breda's eyes had become very wide.

"All that from one card?"

I could have told her I hardly needed the card to tell me what she had displayed so clearly by doing nothing more than turning up at my house. The Spear Knight had merely confirmed what I already knew.

"This is your Deep Self," I said, turning over the second card and laying it to the left of the first. "You might call it the things going on with you that aren't immediately apparent, or a message from your subconscious. Often what's going on in the Deep Self is at odds with the Apparent Self."

"Why's that?"

I thought a minute. "The Apparent Self, a lot of the time, is made up of learned patterns of behavior. You know, the way you are without thinking about it. Obviously, everyone learns those patterns for a reason and they're usually enough to go on with. But sometimes you find yourself in a situation where the pattern doesn't work. The Deep Self gives you information you need to break the pattern and move on. But change is hard work. The pattern doesn't want to be broken."

The second card showed an old, stone archway with a single spear standing before it, barring the way. Overhead, clouds boiled in a grey and threatening sky. The card was reversed, that is, when I laid it in place the image appeared upside-down.

"Seven of Spears." I named the card for her. "You're protecting something. Trouble is, it's not the thing that needs protecting. And it's not what you think it is. You can't even see it, because all your considerable will is focused outward, to ward off attack, and you can't see what's going on behind your back. You're facing the wrong direction."

"Protecting something…Jake?" Breda frowned. "And he's not what I think?"

"You said it, I didn't." Again, I thought it didn't take a psychic to know that. "Taken with the first card, I'd say you're pretty much banging your head against a wall and pretending the wall isn't harder than your skull. You need to turn around and go through the door."

She took a thoughtful sip from her cup. "But what's the door?"

"Well, maybe the third card will tell us." I laid it out above the other two, so that the three cards formed a triangle. "This is your head: what you think about the situation. The spread I'm using mirrors the parts of the body; we have the center and the head, and we'll get to the hands and feet. Also, the right side and the left side correspond to the material and non-material planes. Oops, no door here. Or too many, take your pick."

Breda leaned over the table to see. The third card, another reversed one, depicted a castle at the far side of a lake. The water reflected the castle's lit windows, but in place of the rest of the stone fortress, the lake gave back a wavering image of a green hill. The castle door was shut. A dark hole led into the hillside under the water. In the foreground, a single cup stood on the lakeshore.

"Seven of Cups. Tarot has four suits, just like regular playing cards." Since she'd had readings before Breda most likely knew this, but a bit of review never hurt anyone. "In most decks the suits are Swords, Wands, Cups and Pentacles, which correspond to the modern Spades, Clubs, Hearts and Diamonds. In this deck they've replaced Wands with Spears and Pentacles with

Stones. Each suit is associated with a magical element—Air, Fire, Water and Earth—and also with a quality. Swords represent Intellect; Spears or Wands stand for Will; Cups are emotion and Stones or Pentacles are physicality."

"That's the minor arcana, right?" Breda twisted a lip at me. I smiled back.

"Am I sermonizing too much? Sorry. Sometimes it helps to give people a context, though." And talking about the deck's structure kept me grounded in the here and now, less open to my other senses. "You're right; the suit cards are known as the minor arcana, the lesser secrets."

"What about the greater secrets?"

"I'll tell you about them if any turn up." I hoped none would. As a rule, the more minor arcana showed up in a reading, the less the reading's cosmic significance; the more Major Arcana, the greater. The disparity between the offensive and defensive elements of the first two cards already showed me Breda had some weighty personal work ahead of her. I didn't want any Major Arcana indicating something more.

I tapped the card in front of me, drawing our attention back to the reading.

"You think you know where you're going, but you don't. You see something solid and real, but your eyes deceive you. You'll notice there's no bridge to that castle, no obvious path; to get there you're going to have to swim. Remember Cups and water both mean emotion. You're relying too much on your will—the Spears we've seen—and not enough on your intuition. To solve your problem, to find Jake, you're going to have to learn to forget what you think you know and go at things in less obvious ways. But that's going to take you places you don't expect, and you need to be on your guard."

I glanced at Breda again, but she didn't seem to have anything to say, so I went on, laying the fourth card at the lower left side of the spread, angled with its top edge perpendicular to the bottom left corners of the two central cards.

"Left foot," I said. "That's the spiritual grounding, the non-material basis of your situation: where all this is coming from, ultimately."

I had turned another dark card. To the left it pictured a barricade made of sharpened stakes; three of the stakes had severed heads impaled on them. A narrow stream flowed at the base of the barricade from the center of the card to its bottom. A sword floated downstream, pointing towards the bottom of the card. In the distance, a single tree stood on a hill and over the tree a waning moon hung in an overcast sky.

"Ugh!" Breda shuddered. "At least that one's not reversed."

"Well, it is, actually. In this spread, the center is the reference, so this card is reversed to center." I pondered a minute. However dark the card I always tried to interpret it in as positive a way as possible; I liked to leave clients with a sense of hope, rather than utter terror. On the other hand, the nine of Swords didn't give me much to work with.

"You're afraid," I said at last. "And with good reason. There's bad stuff happening, stuff so bad you've constructed this great wall around it, all full of nasty things to warn you away if you get too close. You know what it is."

"Don't you?" For the first time Breda sounded a bit waspish. "You're the Oracle."

That kind of comment didn't bother me anymore. Frightened people often took out their discomfort on readers. I shrugged it off. "It's an Oracle's business to speak in riddles and a Seeker's business to solve them. Your journey, not mine."

She settled back into her chair with a grimace.

"You know what it is and you know what to do," I continued. "Problem is, you're not using your knowledge. In fact, you've thrown it away. You're like a green soldier on a battlefield who throws away his weapon when the fighting starts because all he can think about is getting away from there before he shits himself. You need to pick your weapon up and turn around."

The phrase caught at me: Turn Around. It wasn't the first time that had come up.

"Right hand." I reached for the next card. "That's tools available to you on the material plane. This-world help."

I laid it in place at the upper right corner of the spread, in a line with the card I had just finished with. When I saw the image on it, my stomach fell into my feet like a hunk of lead.

"Oh, shit," I whispered. Breda sat up with a start, staring wildly from card to card, straining to see what I had seen.

"What is it? That doesn't look so bad."

It wasn't, not for her. For her it was great.

A serene-looking woman dressed in white with a blue cloak embroidered in elaborate patterns about her shoulders sat enthroned in a marsh, under the twining branches of leafless trees. An open book lay in her lap; in her hand she held a sword. Behind her, a flight of cranes filled the evening sky.

The deck Bread had chosen called this card The Lady of the Lake. Most others called it The High Priestess. I knew any number of ways to interpret her appearance. In the depths of my soul, I knew the proper interpretation of her showing up in this reading, and it was not the one I would have chosen.

I'd hoped not to turn up any Major Arcana. Now I had, and the implications scared me silly. I didn't give two pins for cosmic influences in Breda's life. Until that moment, however, I hadn't given up wishing I could escape the cosmic influences in my own.

Words from a book I scarce remembered rose unbidden into my head. *A woman of power who walks in the Otherworld. One who inspires the seeker to face the hard truth.*

She was me. And her appearance informed me in no uncertain terms that I couldn't hold myself aloof from the goings-on at the Emerald Isle any longer. And as if a ghost hadn't been bad enough, now I had a forsaken fiancée and a missing magical architect to cope with. I felt like sobbing and throwing the remaining cards through the window.

Outside, a raven chuckled as if to tell me that's what I got for fighting my inmost nature.

Right away, I made up my mind not to tell Breda the whole truth. No rule said I had to. I might be bound to help her, but I wasn't fool enough to believe I had no say in what form my help took.

"You have access to a great deal of knowledge that will help you," I said, choosing my words carefully. "Knowledge about hidden things, esoterica. Listen to the wisdom of those around you, and trust your own intuition."

I turned the next card in a great hurry.

"Wait, that's it?" Breda sounded astonished, as well she might after the detailed information she'd heard so far. "That's all?"

I shrugged. "Sometimes you don't get much."

She frowned and I wondered whether she believed me.

"Maybe I can tell you more when we see the rest of the cards," I went on before she could ask any more questions. "Only two to go. This one is your left hand: non-material tools, maybe a spirit guide."

I turned the next card with a shaking hand and laid it in the upper left corner of the spread. It showed the doorway to a shrine. Within stood a cloth-covered altar lit by two candles; above the altar, a Celtic-looking cross. An overturned cup blocked the doorway; wine ran over the floor into the foreground. The eight of Cups, reversed.

"You're within reach of a force of spirit that will make you very powerful. Problem is, there's emotional baggage keeping you from reaching it. Stop letting the emotional baggage get in your way and take your power. Let's turn the last card and see what it says." I was rushing to get through the reading now; The Lady of the Lake had upset me quite a lot and I wanted to get rid of Breda so I could lie down.

The last card, in the bottom right corner, showed a tower being struck by lightning. Another Major Arcana called, appropriately enough, the Tower. So, cosmic forces were moving in Breda Ni Fhearraigh's life as well as in mine. The thought didn't reassure me.

"Right foot. Material grounding. Some would say, the outcome. Well, your world is falling apart." I delivered this news in the perky tones of a kindergarten teacher instructing her charges in the niceties of dental hygiene. Breda looked murderous. I half expected her to slap me.

"You're in this situation because your world is falling apart, and your world falling apart is the resolution to the situation. Basically, this card means out with the old and in with the new, in a big way. You can't become the person you're meant to be until you turn loose the person you are. See the spiral light coming out of the tower? That's the power you release by allowing change to happen."

"This isn't telling me how to find Jake!" Breda complained.

"Isn't it?" I sighed, relenting a little. I had a responsibility to give her all the information I could, no matter how much I wanted her to go away and leave me alone. "There's a lot here about deception, looking in the wrong places, focusing on the wrong things, ignoring the right ones. You're playing the game the way you think it should go, not the way your gut instinct tells you to play. You're running all over trying to get other people to tell you what to do, but you know what you should do. You want some psychic to tell you, 'Look in the third door from the left in your grandmother's attic, he's there, waiting for you!' But if that's all there was to it, you would have hired a P.I. You've taken on a quest, but you're forgetting that a quest isn't about finding an object. It's about finding yourself."

"That's bullshit," Breda spluttered, her blue eyes flashing ice. I'd hit a nerve. "You're no better than those quacks in Boulder, all talking about ascension to a higher plane and beings of crystal and whatnot."

"Doesn't do any good to curse the Oracle," I replied evenly. I hated this part of any reading. People liked to talk about finding themselves and embracing their personal power, but no one liked to be told they had to do it.

"You can give up the quest. In fact, I'd advise you to. Forget Jake. Go back to Boulder, or New York, if you prefer. That's the easy way out. Because if you keep looking, you're going to have to change. And the longer you resist it, the more it's going to be thrust on you and believe me, you won't like it." So much for being positive.

She glared at me. "What's that?"

I followed her gaze to the card I had set aside in the beginning. "That? That's the bias card. It represents the issue least relevant to the reading."

"What is it?"

I turned it over. When I saw the image, I couldn't help myself; I laughed.

"What?" She grabbed at the card, glanced at it and back at me. "What?"

A man and a woman faced each other in a forest glade, their eyes full of longing. A magnificent white stage loomed between them. The Matthews called this card The White Hart, but traditional decks called it The Lovers.

"It's not about Jake. It's not about you and Jake. It's about your life and what you do with it."

She didn't like that, not one little bit. I hadn't thought she would.

I could have told her a lot more. I could have told her the work ahead of her consisted more of getting rid of the material attachments blinding her than of pursuing some kind of spiritual destiny. I could have told her will and wit and even her intuition weren't going to be a heck of a lot of help if she didn't start dealing with the reality of the here and now. I could have told her there would be answers if she would only start asking the right questions. But I didn't tell her any of that. She was gathering up her sunglasses and bag, obviously through. And I knew that, whatever help the future had in store for her, from me or anyone else, everyone setting out on this kind of quest sets off alone.

"Here." She thrust something into my hand. "Thank you for your time. I'll see myself out."

Her sling backs went clickety-click down the hall. The front door opened and closed, and pretty soon I heard her car start up and go crunching down the drive.

I opened my hand, revealing a crisp, new hundred-dollar bill.

Shaking my head, I began gathering up the cards from Breda's reading and shoving them at random back into the body of the deck. I saved The Lady of the Lake for last. Her wise eyes seemed to wink as she gazed up from the card, smiling her Mona Lisa smile.

I knew I hadn't seen the last of Breda Ni Fhearraigh.

Chapter Five

After Breda left, I lay on the couch, swallowing over-the-counter medications and moaning pitifully, wishing Timber would sense my distress from across town and come home to take care of me. I would have felt better, had I been able to believe I was truly ill. However, I knew my headache and upset stomach were nothing more than a psychosomatic reaction to seeing my own destiny spelled out in Breda's reading and as such should be easily conquered by accepting my fate with fortitude and keeping a stiff upper lip. But my lip insisted on wobbling and fortitude remained stubbornly out of reach, and I made myself feel even worse than I had to by berating myself for being a coward and a whiner, and calling myself a lot of other nasty names.

I'd never been much good at either sustained self-pity or sustained self-abuse, however. In time, my native good sense kicked in—or maybe it was just that the medicines I had gulped down had finally taken effect—and I sat up to take stock.

Item one: I'd nearly drowned in a tide of psychic goo at a bar with a bad reputation. Shortly thereafter, I'd seen a ghost. Item two: A complete stranger had shown up on my doorstep, seeking a line on a person who had disappeared while employed at that same bar. And this stranger had convinced me to read her cards, when I hadn't done any such thing in years. Item three: The Lady of the Lake had appeared in Breda's reading, indicating I was doomed to become involved in the whole sorry mess. All this had happened within a few days, after five years during which my life had contained so little supernatural activity that I had come to regard Gordarosa as a psychic dead zone. Clearly, something big was going on.

I remembered the old adage: to make the gods laugh, tell them your plans for your life. I didn't know if I should blame the gods or some other entity for my current situation, but I thought whoever was responsible must be rolling.

Still, I knew a thing or two about dealing with otherworldly beings. People tend to swallow whole anything they suspect has a supernatural source because they forget that gods, spirits, fairies and so forth have a much different world view than your average mortal and don't always have mortal interests at heart. I was not about to forget that little detail. I also knew that though gods et al can cajole, threaten, blast flocks and fields and otherwise make life pretty unpleasant for mortals who don't fall in with their plans, they can't actually force a person to do anything. We may jump when the gods say "frog," but we still get to choose how fast and how high.

When Timber got home at a little after five, I informed him we would be dining out. I'd spent the rest of the afternoon deciding what to do next and hadn't concocted anything in the way of food; I also hoped telling Timber of my change of heart in a public setting might limit his response to a single "I told you so."

We ended up ten miles down the highway in Murtaw, at the Maroon Bells, an adobe diner-cum-bar named for a mountain range a hundred miles away. Despite the Tex-Mex menu, the food was bland, but the soothing décor more than made up for the flavorless dishes with lots of little booths set in dark hollows between vigas festooned with tropical vines. Best of all, most of the patrons were older ranchers and their families, so the likelihood of being interrupted by someone we knew was much smaller than it would have been at one of Gordarosa's trendier spots.

Timber had already perceived the change in me, but held his peace until the waiter presented us with the obligatory chips and salsa. Then he jumped right in.

"You have a look on your face. What's up?"

I dipped a chip, crunched it and swallowed.

"I've changed my mind."

"Aye? About what?" The glint in his eye belied the necessity of the question.

"About getting involved in the Emerald Isle business. I'll help."

"Oh? And to what do you owe this about face?"

I shrugged; I had decided to keep Breda and her reading to myself a little while longer.

"I still won't use my gifts. But I can do research. Maybe between the two of us we can figure out what's going on."

To his credit, he didn't ask me what happened afterwards. We both knew Timber was more than capable of laying a ghost without my help. As for Breda's missing fiancé, I'd cross that bridge when I came to it.

"So, did you find out who did the remodel?"

"Aye. Chap named Brett Cable."

I compared the name with the Rolodex in my brain and drew a blank. "Do we know him?"

"I've never worked with him. Word is he's decent enough—less of a hard-ass than some and better organized than most."

"And? Did the ghost cause any problems?"

Timber took a swallow from his bottle of Beck's dark. "Nothing caused any problems. The whole project came in on time and under budget. Six months, start to finish."

"That's weird. Especially for a place with the reputation that bar has." I selected another chip. "No fights between the framers and the drywallers? No arguments about pay? No bloody accidents involving runaway circular saws?"

"No, no and no." He dumped the remaining crumbs from the chip bowl into his hand and tossed them into his mouth. "Did you expect something of the sort?"

"It wouldn't have surprised me." I sipped my margarita and made a face; it tasted vaguely like Chloraseptic.

"Dave the plumber did tell me they were expecting some Outside guy on site—an architect, I think—but he never showed. He sent blueprints, though."

I remembered Jake's obsession with magical architecture. "Anything weird about those?"

"No hidden chambers or secret passages, if that's what you're thinking. Or so Dave said. He doesn't have the keenest mind, ken, but I think he would have noticed."

The waiter appeared with our food and we fell silent while he fussed over us. We declined more chips and salsa. Timber ordered a second beer. After what seemed like an hour, the waiter admonished us to be wary of our very hot plates and left to bother another table.

"So it seems the remodel didn't irritate our man with the bashed head." I poked at my taco salad without enthusiasm.

"You said yourself that he didn't seem irritated. Just sad." Timber spoke through a mouthful of burrito.

"True. But it bothers me. With the reputation that place has, an angry ghost would make sense. A sad ghost doesn't. And what hit me when we first walked in wasn't sadness…." My words trailed off as I groped for the feeling. Unable to put a name to it, I shrugged. "Whatever is was, I can't imagine it inducing violence and mayhem."

"There was no violence and mayhem Saturday night. Unless you count some of the dancing." Timber's second beer arrived; he grabbed it and shooed the waiter away before he could start fussing over us again.

I remembered the jigging drunk who had ended up kissing the floor and grimaced. "Ouch. Michael Flatley has a lot to answer for. But that's what I mean."

My husband nodded wisely. "Aye. A pissed off ghost wouldn't take well to people holding a *ceilidh* on his grave. He'd put a stop to it somehow."

"You'd think." I shoved my plate away.

"You were the only one to see him, weren't you?"

"As far as I know. No one else screamed and ran for the exit, anyway. I may be the only one who's ever seen him. You'd think if he showed up a lot we'd have heard about it by now."

My husband nodded and looked smug.

"What?"

"I don't think the ghost appeared because something disturbed him. I think he appeared because he finally had access to someone capable of seeing him."

I swallowed back a momentary recurrence of the afternoon's nausea. Timber patted my arm.

"You're right, love. That ghost isn't pissed. That ghost wants something. From you."

I should have known. I would have known as soon as the apparition showed up, if I hadn't been in such a hurry to deny it had anything whatsoever to do with me. When Joe Blow from Hoboken sees a ghost, it could be a random manifestation. When a powerful psychic sees a ghost, chances are the ghost has an agenda.

"Damn and double damn." I cursed as I trudged down the highway Tuesday afternoon, on the way to the Historical Museum, where I hoped to get some idea of the spirit's identity and what he wanted. Ideally, he'd require me to do something Mundane, like find his bones and give them a decent burial. I could do that. I could probably even manage to solve his hundred-year-old murder—always supposing, of course, that he had been murdered, which I thought likely; the bashed-in head didn't point to death by natural causes. If the ghost wanted his killer brought to justice, however, all bets were off. Unless the perpetrator was ancient beyond reckoning, he'd be dead by this time, too. In my reading on occult subjects, I'd come across several spells for forcing dead souls to atone for their crimes in life; I had no intention of trying any of them. The justice of whatever powers ruled beyond the grave would have to suffice. I hoped the ghost at the Emerald Isle would understand that.

At the end of my brisk, mile long walk in the blazing sun, I discovered the Historical Museum was closed. The sign on the door gave the hours as Mondays, Wednesdays and Fridays from noon to five, with Saturdays by appointment.

"What now?" I muttered, leaning against the clapboard wall.

"Library," I answered myself. The local section might have an old newspaper or something that hadn't found its way to the Historical Society archives. If not, any information at all on the subject could give me a place to begin. I turned around and started back the way I had come.

Two miles later, I received some good news and some bad news. Although the local library didn't have the old newspaper I had hoped for, the catalog did list quite a few books on ghosts and hauntings not written by authors named Koontz and King. That was the good news. Unfortunately, the head librarian kept them all under lock and key—along with any volume mentioning Witchcraft, Astrology, Numerology, Palmistry, Shamanism, Scientology or Dream Interpretation and the collected works of Bruno Betelheim and Carl Jung, all of which she considered the "Dark Arts"—apparently to keep them from leaping off the shelves and infecting innocent children with wrong ideas. Mavis had left on two weeks' holiday only the day before and none of the other librarians had access to the "restricted section."

"That's what I get for choosing to live in a small town," I muttered as I stalked across the street to the post office. I was well aware that, on a metaphysical level, making a decision is akin to wearing a t-shirt with "Mess with the Idiot!" written on it in big flashing letters; the gods love to test a person's resolve, which is why so few people keep their resolutions.

I could get the information another way. A simple shift in consciousness—the merest blink of the Inner Eye—would put me in contact with a whole host of spirits who liked nothing better than to gossip about mortals. One of them was sure to know everything about the ghost from his name to his shoe size. And psychic research would be much less sweaty than all this walking around.

"I won't do it. I won't!" I informed my post office box, garnering me a suspicious glance from a passing old lady.

I didn't even have any good mail.

Now in my experience, the best way to deal with powers that seem intent on messing with you is just to go on about your business, pretending you haven't noticed. Sooner or later whatever is testing you—or, if you like, whatever has it in for you—will realize you're serious and leave you alone. Sometimes they'll even decide to help you. One problem with this tactic is, unseen powers almost always have a great deal more stamina than mere mortals; in other words, a person usually gets tired of the obstacles a lot sooner than the powers get tired of inventing them. The other problem is, it's often hard to determine what's meant to be a help and what's just more bullshit.

That was my question when I ran into Sean Casey.

After picking up my mail and disposing of half of it in the convenient trash can the post office staff kept by the front door expressly for such a purpose, I headed back down Main Street towards First. This, I should point out, is not the route I usually took back home. I could get there that way, but as Main Street ran into the highway five blocks from town and First dead-ended in a lumberyard after about the same distance, taking that route meant walking several miles, most of it in the wrong direction. On the other hand, Third Street ran straight east towards the mountains for a little over three-quarters of a mile before spilling right into my driveway. That Tuesday, however, I needed very much to prove to myself that I could make a dent in the ghost problem without recourse to my unusual abilities. As neither the Historical Museum nor the library had given me much help, I decided to go have a peep at the Emerald Isle.

One glance through the window told me the place was packed with what looked like Gordarosa's entire population. Midweek, at a full hour after the usual lunch rush, I thought this strange, even for a new place, and I wondered if Casey had taken out ads in the Aspen and Glenwood papers, trying to attract the summer tourist trade. If so, it had worked. As the door opened to admit yet another party I caught the clink of cutlery, the low roar of conversation and a snatch of something Irish—Patrick Street, I thought—playing on the house sound system. All in all, it seemed very merry times were to be had within. I wondered how the ghost felt about it. I wondered how long it could last.

Well, that was pointless, I thought, and rounded the corner onto First. Then I heard myself being hailed.

"Caitlin Ross! Just the person I wanted to see!"

I turned to see Casey waving at me from the doorway, looking flushed and jolly and rather as if he'd been indulging in his own wares. He wore a pristine white polo shirt with "The Emerald Isle—Gordarosa, CO" embroidered in Kelly Green uncial script on the breast around a shamrock; Casey had a bar towel bearing the same logo thrust into his belt. I could imagine both shirt and towel pinned up behind the bar alongside hefty price tags.

"Mr. Casey." I inclined my head a fraction. "What can I do for you?"

He showed his teeth. I think he meant the expression for a smile, but it put me in mind of something reptilian from a Michael Crichton novel.

"I've been wanting to talk to you about having Red Branch as our house band here. Do you have a minute?"

I had to think about it. I wasn't in business mode, but I could make the transition without too much trouble. I didn't relish the thought of going into the bar without some kind of moral support, but I'd have to check it out again sooner or later, and Casey's invitation gave me a good excuse to get it over with. Besides, I didn't have any good reason to turn him down. I could have made up another appointment, but I was sure he'd see right through me. I'm a terrible liar.

"Okay." For some reason I felt like adding that my friends would know where to look for me if I didn't come home by suppertime. I restrained myself.

He held the door open for me. As I crossed the threshold I braced myself, anticipating the psychic miasma that had hit me before, but the only shock I experienced was the normal shiver that comes from entering an air-conditioned room after walking down a hot, dusty street. Curious. Of course, the place had been virtually empty the last time I'd entered it; perhaps the presence of so many living souls had some sort of damping effect. Had I still felt the strangeness, the first night, even after the joint started its proverbial jumping? I couldn't remember. Until the ghost showed up, I'd been focused on doing my job.

"Let's go into my office; it's quieter there." Casey steered me past the slightly off-center hostess station, towards a graceful, arcing staircase leading up to a gallery where a few isolated tables looked out over the main room. The wall to the left featured a big mirror panel with the Emerald Isle logo done in gold paint. The far end of the gallery featured a discreet service station that I knew from my own restaurant experience would house a hot plate for the coffee pot, a sink and ice maker, extra cups and water glasses, and a bus tub. At the very top of the stair was a heavy oak four-panel door with an ornate brass knob. This Casey unlocked with an equally ornate key and gestured me inside.

If the rest of the Emerald Isle was elegant, the room beyond the oak door was positively luxurious. Though merely ten feet from the door to the opposite wall, it stretched forty in length, the entire width of the building. A forest green Berber carpet covered the floor; Victorian pressed tin panels painted white made up the ceiling. Above the waist-level cherry paneling the walls were plastered in a soothing shade of mint, and the light spilling in from two arched windows looking out over First Street gave the whole room a gold tinge, like sun through leaves.

The furnishings, though sparse, were the best quality. A rank of cherry file cabinets stood at attention along the long wall opposite the door, each drawer carefully labeled in black italics upon a creamy card bracketed in brass. A set of three barrister-style bookcases, also in cherry, covered the far wall: a tall one on either side of another arched window that gave a rather unfortunate view of the roof of the Western Realty office next door, and a smaller one beneath it. Books packed all the shelves, all of them hard cover editions, some of which looked quite old. Casey's desk, a seven-foot Gothic monstrosity in carved walnut, stretched diagonally across the corner between the filing cabinets and the bookshelves. Before it stood two wing chairs upholstered to match the carpet. Aside from this, the room was empty.

I find a degree of emptiness in a place more agreeable than overcrowding; I like to feel I can move around without running into occasional tables and knocking over knickknacks. This time, though, the emptiness gave me a shiver; the asymmetry disturbed me. The stretch from the door to the desk seemed as infinitely long, yet as dismally abbreviated, as the walk from the cell to the gallows.

"Do take a seat, Ms. Ross." Casey closed the door behind him. On this side, it had been paneled and plastered to match the surrounding walls, so that when it shut the office seemed to have no entrance or exit save for the windows. Even the doorknob had been camouflaged; it blended into the paneling so well that I would not have been able to find it, had I not known it was there. I made sure I could locate it again after looking away before I perched uncomfortably on the edge of one wing chair.

"Now then." Casey clasped his hands on top of the vast desk before him and leaned forward with the mannerism of false intimacy so annoying in men of business. "I believe I mentioned downstairs the reason I wished to speak with you."

I nodded. "You did, and frankly, after your attitude the other night I'm surprised. You led me to believe that in your estimation Red Branch is not the caliber band you'd prefer to offer a situation at this establishment."

He sighed, his face the picture of weary regret. To me, the expression seemed studied.

"Ms. Ross, surely you don't hold that against me? It was a big night for me and, I have to admit, I was a little nervous. I wanted everything to be just so. If I took it out on you, I'm sorry." A self-deprecating smile did a little dance on his lips before he went on. "But I thought I made it clear even Saturday night that you had more than impressed me."

"And besides, there isn't anyone else." Not the wisest thing to say, perhaps, but I have never learned to play the games many people take for granted.

Casey grimaced, caught. "I stand by what I said. Your CD is ragged; I don't think you disagree with me there. As the CD was all I had to go on at the time, I think I can be forgiven for having qualms."

He had me there. Some days even I couldn't listen to our CD without wondering why in the world anyone who heard it would want to hire us.

"Still, what you lack in technique you more than make up for in energy, and that's what I'm looking for above anything else. Besides, you're bound to improve with time." He opened a desk drawer, took out a folder and handed me a sheaf of papers. "In light of that fact, I took the liberty of drawing up a contract. I'm prepared to be very generous, as you see."

He was. We charged five hundred dollars for a three-hour gig; what Casey's contract offered for three nights' work a week, Thursday through Saturday from nine to midnight, came to quite a bit more. In addition, after three months' satisfactory performance he would finance recording and duplication of a new CD, provided we gave him a producer's credit. Frank and Lisa would be thrilled. I should have been thrilled. Instead I felt as if I were looking at a ball and chain that was about to be welded to my ankle.

"Well? Do we have a deal?"

The rest of the contract was standard: the band provides this, the venue provides that. I had no good reason to hesitate, still less reason to turn it down. I knew if I did the others would have my head, in any case. Plus, being in Casey's employ would give me a perfect excuse to snoop around. Dammit.

"Just a couple things. We do play out in other venues, especially in the summer. In fact, we're already booked for a couple of festivals in the next month. I want it specified that we're free to take other employment, even if it means we can't be here on a night we're scheduled. We wouldn't demand payment for nights we couldn't be here, of course."

"I think that's fair. As long as you keep me posted." He made a note in the margin of his copy. "What else?"

"We have a standard clause in all our contracts. If we show up ready to play and the gig is canceled through no fault of our own, we still get paid." That clause was meant to protect us from flaky situations; we'd learned the hard way that we didn't want to work for anyone who objected to it. Driving two hundred miles to a rained-out festival and coming home empty-handed taught a lesson you didn't soon forget.

I didn't really expect Casey to make a fuss and he didn't. He simply made another marginal note. "Anything else?"

"I'll have to discuss it with the rest of the band, of course. But I'm pretty sure they'll agree."

"Good! I'll make those changes. Unless I hear otherwise I'll expect you Thursday. You can pop up and sign the contract then."

Thursday was two days away. I didn't usually accept gigs on such short notice, nor did I make it a practice to commit to anything without a contract signed well in advance, but I figured, what the Hell. The sooner I could poke around the Emerald Isle, the sooner the whole business would be over. At least, I hoped so.

That should have been the end of the encounter. But the powers that had put Casey in my path—or vice versa—still had a little something in reserve. As I rose from my wing chair, stuffing the contract into my stack of mail, my eyes wandered across the nearest cherry bookcase and fell on something they recognized. I experienced a momentary dizziness as my senses recalled another time in a place two thousand miles distant: a low-ceilinged room lit by modest fluorescents, the faint whiff of nag champa from a display of incense and Tibetan prayer beads, discreet harp music playing in the background. And books. On every side, tall shelves crammed with books, making narrow corridors like a maze leading into the dim recesses of subjects too esoteric to be discussed by anything but candlelight. Books on Eastern and Western mysticism, books on lost civilizations and UFOs, books on channeling and crystals and reincarnation and the magical use of healing herbs. Books on Spiritualism, on magic both Ceremonial and Earth-Centered, on Masons, Rosicrucians and other secret societies. And books on darker subjects still: Demons, black magic and Satanism, to name a few.

Smith's Books in Midtown Manhattan treated all these subjects as valid areas of scholarship, no more, no less. I tried to think of them in the same way. Despite that, it sent a frisson of fear down my spine to see a great many of those familiar volumes on the shelves in Casey's office.

Titles and authors spiraled through my brain. Israel Regardie. MacGregor Mathers. Eliphas Levi. Magicians, every one of them. The Secret Order of the O.T.O. and the Golden Dawn: hotbeds of spiritualism—and some said demon worship—at the turn of the last century. I looked for and found Aleister Crowley's *Liber Aleph* and *The Holy Books of Thelema*. I didn't look for books on Sacred Geometry, but found them anyway, right alongside a history of the Masonic Order and *The Lesser Key to Solomon*. All very old editions, maybe even firsts.

"Ms. Ross?" Casey's voice sounded as distant as the crash of waves on the Atlantean shore. "Are you all right?"

"Yes, I…." I couldn't tear my eyes away from those shelves. Was that the original *Necronomicon?* And the *Grammatica Daemonica?* And, "Excuse me, but is that *Great Light of the Ancient World?*"

"Ah. You noticed my collection. Yes, that's one of my prizes. Do you know it?"

"I've heard of it." Enough to know the copy before me belonged in a bank vault or a museum. A purported survey of mystical science from Ur of the Chaldeans to pre-Alexandrian Egypt, many occultists hailed it as the definitive guide to everything from building temples to raising demons. It had been out of print for more than a century and copies were rarer than the beards of women.

"You surprise me, Ms. Ross. I'd hardly expect such knowledge from a flute player in the boondocks." He smiled to take the sting out of his comment.

"I'd hardly expect such a collection from a banker turned pub owner," I replied, the wheels turning in my head. In my experience, no one amassed a substantial collection of anything without a strong personal interest in what it represented. So what did a library of rare occult books represent to Casey? And why had he brought them here, to a haunted bar?

"Even a banker needs a hobby. I might say, a banker especially needs a hobby. And rare books are a good investment."

Yes, but could that possibly be all? I threw caution to the wind.

"Why these?"

"The subject matter, you mean?" He shrugged. "You might say I fell into it. I used to frequent a certain bookstore on my lunch hour. They specialized in this kind of thing. The proprietor and I had a speaking acquaintance. He was rabid about rare and out of print books, always haring off to estate sales after this or that. I gather many of his customers were the same way. Occultists are always looking for that nugget of true knowledge, that original source they hope will shed light on what the ancients knew in less rational times." He covered a discreet cough with one hand. "Or so I'm given to understand."

He meant Smith's, of course. I'd already suspected as much, and his description of the owner confirmed it. But why did Casey frequent Smith's in the first place? Chance? Idle curiosity? Or something else?

"I was looking for a concrete investment already. Something I could see and touch and enjoy the way you can't enjoy stocks or bonds. Another friend suggested books. He collected them himself, eighteenth century poets, I believe. I hit on occult works in large part because of my association with Mr. Smith, but I must admit I was also drawn to the subject because it differed so from my everyday life. The idea of a conservative banker going home to a quiet evening of demonology amused me. It still does." He chuckled to prove his point. The sound chilled me to the bone.

"You've read all these? A lot of collectors don't, you know."

"I do, and I think that's a shame. Books are meant to be read." He spoke with some heat and I felt a fleeting sympathy for the man. Though it galled me to think Casey and I had anything in common, I shared his sentiment. I could never understand people who spent money on books and then left them to gather dust.

"Most of it's nonsense, of course," he went on, chuckling again. "Interesting nonsense, but nonsense all the same. Now if you'll excuse me, Ms. Ross, I really must get back downstairs. I know the staff can run everything perfectly well without me, but I like to think I'm indispensable."

Rising, he offered me his hand. I clasped it with my best business grip, noting his palm was damp. Interesting. When I tried to withdraw, his fingers tightened.

"It has been an enlightening meeting, Ms. Ross." The calculating look I had seen before flashed in his blue eyes again; I had to steel myself not to flinch or look away. It struck me suddenly that I had seen those eyes somewhere else in recent days, but I couldn't recall where. "I think we can have a long and profitable relationship. I look forward to signing that contract soon."

He released me then. I made my way unerringly to the hidden door and let myself out, more to prove I could than for any other reason. I had a feeling showing weakness in front of Sean Casey would not be a good idea.

Despite his claim that he needed to get back to the bar, Casey didn't follow me, a fact for which I was inordinately grateful. As the door clicked shut behind me, I imagined him in there, alone with his bizarre library. I had a brief, dizzying vision of him turning to the shelves behind the desk, opening the glass front of one case and removing an age-stained volume. Resolutely, I closed my inner eye before I could see which it was.

Chapter Six

"I hate Ceremonial Magicians," I told Timber that night, over a large glass of Laphroaig whisky. "They're so...smarmy."

The hall clock had just struck eleven forty-five, and I felt terrible for keeping him up when he had to be at work the next day. But the band met Tuesday nights and I hadn't wanted to go into the details of Casey's hobby before rehearsal. As soon as Frank and Lisa had left, still chatting excitedly about our great good fortune—as I had expected, Casey's offer had thrilled them no end—I'd let Timber have it, though. He'd heard me out with a stoic expression worthy of a Spartan warrior, then disappeared into the kitchen without a word. I'd expected tea and experienced a warm rush of gratitude when he returned with the whisky bottle instead.

"You dinna ken he's a Ceremonial Magician." Timber sipped, smiled and exhaled a breath redolent of peat. "He could be no more than a collector, like he said."

I cast my husband a dark look from under my brows and he drew away in mock alarm. "If you'd seen the collection, you wouldn't say so. Even if he started out innocently enough, it isn't possible to amass such a huge library of occult books without being affected. I bet he conjures spirits in the cellar every night."

"The Emerald Isle doesn't have a cellar."

"In his office, then. There's certainly space enough."

"You didn't see any paraphernalia, though, did you? No ritual swords in the corner? No antique censer prominently displayed? No…"

"No, I didn't see anything at all. But he could have all sorts of stuff locked up in his desk. It's huge."

Wrist stiff, I tossed back the last of my whisky. Timber raised the bottle, a question in his eyes. I thought about it, decided I'd better not and shook my head.

"Anyway, it would make sense. Messing around with Ceremonial Magic could easily disturb a ghost, even one that was resting peacefully."

"Which, if the location's bad reputation is anything to go by, this one wasn't. But if the magician knew what he was doing…."

"Most of them don't; that's the problem. They just don't think, Timber. At least, not in my experience." It cost me to qualify the statement, but I wanted to be fair. Somewhere out there, there might actually be a Ceremonial Magician who was not narcissistic, power hungry and rash. There might be one who was altruistic, cautious and thoughtful. I hadn't met him, though. "I'm not saying the sources aren't worthy…."

"Except for Crowley," Timber added on cue. He'd heard this rant before.

"In my humble opinion, Aleister Crowley doesn't constitute a source. He's a prime example of the idiocy that set gets up to. 'Do as thou wilt is the whole of the Law'—Please! I've never heard a viler piece of adolescent claptrap. His pimply fantasies have done a bigger disservice to western mysticism than anything else I can think of. And now he's lauded as a Magus by a bunch of developmentally arrested losers who spend all their time trying to conjure up succubi because they can never get dates with real women. It makes me vomit."

My husband poured another dram into his empty glass. "That's harsh."

"Oh, go ahead, give me another splash, too. I feel harsh," I sighed and flopped back onto the couch. "You know how I am about stupid people, and stupid magic people are even worse. They should know better. *Slàinte.*"

We clinked our glasses together. I tossed back the shot mine contained, thinking it had better be the last; I felt rather fuzzy in the head.

"So if the magician did know what he was doing," Timber began again, holding up his hand when I glared. "Let me finish. Say Casey does more with those books than collect them. And say there's more to his coming here than an innocent desire to open a pub like the ones in the old country. He's wealthy; he could have gone anywhere. Even if he had his heart set on the area, there are plenty of other businesses for sale. Why buy the one with the bad reputation? Why buy the one where nothing succeeds?"

I snorted. "I can think of a lot of reasons. Because he's so full of himself he thinks he can't fail, for one. Or because he doesn't give a cow pie for local superstition."

"You're being dim. If we're granting him magus status, we have to grant that he would care about local superstition. So why buy the place with the bad energy?"

"Well, maybe he didn't know." I hesitated, considering the idea. No, it didn't make any sense. Casey struck me as a careful man, one who always maintained control. He wouldn't make the kind of investment he had in the Emerald Isle without knowing everything about the place. When I realized this, the thoughts floating around in my muzzy brain snapped into a new pattern. "Or…he bought it *because* it had bad energy. Because it's haunted."

"Aye." Timber raised his glass in a toast. "He bought it because it's haunted. You and I both ken that repositories of psychic energy can give a real boost to magic work. Places where people have prayed for centuries. Battlefields. Even places where people have gathered in large numbers on a regular basis, like tourist attractions. And the Emerald Isle fits the bill on all counts."

"Crap," I swore. "So you think Casey is trying to harness the ghost's energy to…do whatever it is he's trying to do?"

"It's a valid assumption."

"No wonder the poor thing is asking for help. I wonder if freeing it will put a stop to Casey?"

"Entirely?" My husband shook his head. "I doubt it. Our Casey probably has more than one trick up his sleeve. Too bad we dinna ken more about sacred geometry; he may have designed the whole place to be a channel to the nether realms."

"He didn't design it," I said without thinking.

"Had someone design it, then. And killed him to keep him quiet, like those old tyrants used to do when they didn't want anyone to reveal their secrets. Didn't the architect disappear?"

I knew from his tone that he meant it as a joke, but my stomach still sank. The theory fit all too well with what Breda had told me. Timber still didn't know about Breda or the reading I had given her. Had he hit on the answer by chance?

"You're the one who hears the trade gossip. You tell me." Despite my best efforts to steady it, my voice shook.

"Are you all right? You look pale." He stretched out a big hand to caress my cheek, his face a mask of concern. "Caitlin, I was just kidding, aye? It was in bad taste. I'm sorry."

"It's nothing. I'm tired, is all."

"You dinna think…?"

"Of course not," I lied. I did think. That was the problem with Do As Thou Wilt being The Whole Of The Law. If you willed it, you could justify anything. Up to and including murder.

"Just take me to bed, Timber. Make me forget all this for a little while."

My wonderful husband received this request with an impish gleam in his eyes. "I think that can be arranged."

Much later, I remembered something else and poked him in the side.

"Timber. Timber!"

If he wasn't already asleep he wasn't far from it. Splayed across the bed, limbs ivory in the light of a half moon, his curls a dark wave across the pillow, he looked to me like Eros caught in the glow of Psyche's lamp. I hated to wake him.

"Eh?" He opened one eye. "What is it?"

"You never said in rehearsal. What do you think of that contract?"

"Gods, woman, couldn't it have waited until morning?" Smiling at my perversity, he raised himself on one elbow. "What do I think of the contract? I think, my darling dear, that whether or not Casey is planning to set himself up as the Magister Magnus of Gordarosa, anyone willing to pay as much money as he's willing to pay to engage a half-assed band like us, has something very deep to hide."

The next day being Wednesday, I finally made it to the Historical Museum.

It was a picture-perfect day for the mile-long walk along the road running along the back edge of town from my house to the highway. The temperature, cool for mid-July, hovered in the low eighties with just the slightest breath of humidity in the air. The sky was that piercing blue you only see in very dry climates, and though a smudge in the north over Black Bear Gulch hinted at afternoon thunderstorms, I'd lived in Gordarosa, on the edge of the Great Basin, long enough not to expect rain until I felt it on my skin. I would have enjoyed the walk immensely, had it not been for the questions troubling my mind.

Who was this ghost and what did he want from me?

Timber and I hadn't dealt with many ghosts. During our brief tenure as psychic interventionists in Boulder, several people had approached us to put down hauntings. Most of these had turned out to have more to do with the client's troubled psyche than with any restless spirit; a few had been genuine. Only rarely had I seen as clear a manifestation as I had at the Emerald Isle.

According to common wisdom, ghosts appeared for one of several reasons. Death might have come so suddenly that the recently departed person didn't understand he was dead and so couldn't move on to whatever afterlife awaited him. Or, the ghost might have left life with some task unfinished and couldn't rest until the business was resolved. Some ghosts feared the afterlife they had been brought up to believe in; others simply didn't feel like going. So they lingered, trying to wash that last load of dishes, or find their keys, or communicate with their loved ones. Or they just hung around in their favorite rooms, yearning after a world they could no longer touch, unable to move forward, afraid to move on. Most of them didn't cause problems—at least not intentionally. Violent hauntings involving flying objects and property damage usually turned out to be the work of poltergeists or other mischievous spirits. True ghosts might cause a sudden chill or an unexplained feeling of melancholy, rarely more. Even the strongest manifestations did little beyond appear at inconvenient moments and scare the heck out of people. But they didn't do any harm, and once the living understood this, they stopped freaking out. Quite a lot came to consider their ghosts as part of the family, and treat them with a kind of rueful respect, as one might an eccentric Great Uncle with the unfortunate habit of appearing at dinner without his trousers.

A meadowlark trilled from its perch on a phone line, calling me from my thoughts back into the glorious day. Along the road where I walked, clover, sweet pea and wild roses ran rampant in the ditches, filling each breath with the scent of warm honey.

The second cutting of the summer's hay lying in the fields waiting to be baled added its dry perfume to the mix, making me sneeze when the light breeze stirred it. Horses played in the pastures of the little farms along the way, their silky flanks bright in the noon sun.

The one truly troublesome ghost we'd encountered had been trying to protect the crumbling Victorian pile where he'd lived and died from new owners planning extensive renovations. At first I'd thought the Emerald Isle's ghost to be one of the territorial variety, as well. That would have accounted for the bar's nasty ambience, as well as the unfortunate events that kept happening there. The more I considered the matter, however, the less the explanation fit. As I'd told Timber, the ghost hadn't seemed angry, only sad. Nor had he produced any of the more theatrical manifestations of a haunting—flickering lights, moving furniture, spectral sounds and the like—meant to scare the living away. All he'd done was emote so strongly that he drove the bar's patrons to violence as a way of shedding the unpleasant energy.

Dealing with a territorial ghost held all the appeal of embarking on a course of court-ordered therapy with an inveterate wife-beater, so I was just as glad to put the possibility aside. That left me with two problems, however. First, what might induce the Emerald Isle ghost to move on and leave the living in peace? And second, what was Sean Casey up to and what, if anything, did it have to do with the apparition? The implications of finding a Ceremonial Magician parked on top of a restless spirit daunted me more than a little, so I had decided to focus on the first issue. If I could find out the old man's identity, I could, in theory, find out or deduce what he wanted. Once he got what he wanted, the ghost would depart—ideally, taking the Sean Casey problem with it.

The Historical Museum came into view as I crossed the bridge over the Gordarosa River, still high with runoff from an unusually good snowpack. Several years before, the Cottonwood County Historical Society had purchased the two clapboard buildings and moved them from their original locations down valley, where one had been a schoolhouse and the other the home of one of Gordarosa's first mayors. At the time the buildings had been in very bad repair, but the Society had done a good job refurbishing them and now the premises exuded a certain rural charm. Sagging porches had been shored up and broken windows replaced, and both the house and the school sported new white paint and bright green tin roofs. The grounds were a rainbow of regional wildflowers, artfully planted to give the impression of a natural mountain meadow. A discreet sign at the end of the gravel drive proclaimed: "Gordarosa Historical Museum Est. 2005."

Though Red Branch had played at a benefit to raise money to get the museum started, I had never been inside since the official opening, so I wasn't sure where to begin. The farmhouse sat closest to the drive and its door stood invitingly open—as good a place to start as any, I supposed.

I mounted the porch steps and went through the door to find myself in a farmhouse kitchen furnished in the style of the late eighteen hundreds. The room was empty.

"Hello? Is anyone here?"

My voice echoed eerily though the house.

The next room was a parlor of some sort, with stiff horsehair chairs arranged around the edges of a braided rug and a potbellied stove in one corner next to a full coalscuttle. A window framed by lace curtains the color of weak tea looked out onto the center's small parking lot; at its far edge one car lurked in the shade of a lone cottonwood tree. Someone was around, then.

The parlor door opened onto a hallway papered in a lurid Victorian pattern of pink cabbage roses and dark green vines on a paler green background. Fortunately, not much of the paper showed beneath the framed prints, photographs, and newspaper articles covering the walls. Flinching slightly under the stern gaze of a bearded gentleman identified as the Reverend James Thurston Overton (First Baptist), I opened the first door I came to and found myself in a cramped bedroom. The brass bedstead, which took up most of the available space, was piled high with quilts, the topmost in a wedding ring pattern. Several more quilts hung on a rack shoved between the bed and the wall, and at the foot of the rack an open trunk vomited forth a remarkable jumble of gloves, scarves, hosiery and other accessories. A dressing table shoved into one corner held not only a silver-backed brush and matching comb but also a number of jars and bottles whose faded labels identified them as various types of patent medicine.

"May I help you?"

I jumped at the voice close behind me. Turning, I saw a petite woman wearing the valley uniform of jeans, scuffed cowboy boots and slogan-bearing t-shirt—hers was black with "Gordarosa Historical Museum" in white, Old West style letters over the left breast. From the crow's feet around her eyes I thought her to be ten or more years older than my own thirty-six, but I could have been wrong. The dry climate of Western Colorado is hard on skin.

"I'm sorry, I didn't mean to startle you. I was dusting in the children's room," she held up a feather duster as evidence, "and I thought I heard someone, so I came to see if you needed anything. Most people just want to look around, but sometimes they have questions. I'm Missy Phillips."

She spoke in a very rapid, breathless fashion that, in addition to making her sound much younger than she appeared, gave me the strong urge to offer her a dose from the bottle of laudanum on the dressing table.

"Are you interested in old remedies?" she asked, following my gaze. "Most of those bottles came from the same guy, you can tell by the handwriting on the labels. He used to park his wagon under the old Gordarosa Bridge every summer and people would come from all over to buy his medicines. He claimed to have learned the recipes from the Utes and I guess they really worked. Of course, most people relied on homemade medicines and folk remedies. When I was a girl my grandmother still insisted that fried goose droppings were the best thing for burns, can you imagine! I think the laudanum bottle is from the first apothecary in town...."

"Actually, I came about something else entirely. The building downtown on the corner of First Street and Main..."

"The Connolly Building." She nodded wisely, making her dark curls bob around her elfin face. "What do you want to know?"

For no reason I could name I found myself reluctant to tell Missy Phillips I had come to the Historical Museum looking for ghost stories. "I wondered if you might have any articles about it. Or any old photographs or building plans?"

"Those would be in the schoolhouse. Follow me."

Brandishing her feather duster, she led me down the hall, out the door, and across a flagstone path bordered in miniature rosebushes. Three shallow steps took us to the schoolhouse door. Pausing briefly before entering, Missy pointed to a cast iron bell hanging in a bracket to the right.

"That's the original schoolhouse bell. We found it inside when we bought the building. Most of the other furnishings aren't original, but we tried to make it look as authentic as possible...."

It certainly did look exactly like a schoolhouse. Six old fashioned double desks stood on either side of a central aisle leading to a larger desk in the front of the room. On the wall behind this desk hung a blackboard upon which someone had written the proverb: "A wise man is strong, yea, a man of knowledge increaseth strength" in shaky script. The requisite stove and coalscuttle stood in one corner. It was rather dim, as the only light came from the windows: two in each of three walls. I wondered whether the students had been allowed lamps, or if they'd just had to strain their eyes and make the best of it.

"If you'll wait here, I'll get the folder. We keep the records in the lean-to."

I took a seat at one of the uncomfortable desks while Missy made her way to a door to the right of the blackboard. When she opened it, I caught a glimpse of stack upon tottering stack of cartons and boxes: the records, I supposed. I sighed and tried to get more comfortable. I might be here a while.

To my surprise, Missy returned after a very few minutes, a manila folder clutched in one hand. The folder was labeled "Connolly Building, 1898." It contained several yellowed photographs and a number of faded newspaper clippings. The very first one made me close my eyes and shudder.

It had come from the first page; under the masthead the date read November 16th, 1909. A bold, twelve point headline proclaimed "Connolly to Operate Tavern." The accompanying photograph showed a smiling, bewhiskered gentleman standing on the front steps of what I now knew as the Emerald Isle pub. His hair was darker and of course his head was in one piece, but I recognized him at once as my ghost.

The caption read: "Archie Connolly, son of the late James Connolly." Now I knew his name.

"He haunts that place, you know," said Missy from over my shoulder.

My eyes popped open. "I…I beg your pardon?"

She cocked her head to one side. "Well, it's not a very well-known story. The Chamber of Commerce takes a dim view of anything that might drive away tourists, you know. I'm not surprised you haven't heard it. Though haunted houses can be big attractions! I know of a place in Cripple Creek…."

"Archie Connolly?" I prompted.

She lowered her voice to a whisper; maybe she thought the Chamber had spies outside.

"Some people say he's the reason no business since Connolly's Tavern has done well in that building."

Without asking she came around the desk and crammed herself into the seat beside me.

"I remember my grandfather talking about Archie Connolly." Her hazel eyes misted over the way people's eyes do when they're looking backward through time.

"He knew him?"

"Oh, yes. Grandpa was a Bahr," she added, as if that explained everything. In Gordarosa, it did. The Bahrs had been instrumental in getting the mines going, in bringing the railroad to town, and in starting several churches. You didn't live long in Gordarosa without hearing about the Bahrs.

"The Connollys didn't actually build that place, you know. It had been there for a long time before they arrived. In fact, it's older than the town is. Mountain men used to trade furs there. But Archie's father—that was James—bought it at the turn of the century and put a lot of money into it. That's why they call it the Connolly building. James operated the place as a general store."

"I thought it had always been a tavern."

"Most people think so, but no. During the San Juan gold rush it was actually a brothel!"

"Not much between the two," I said, remembering a few period novels I'd read.

"Well, no. And according to Grandpa Bahr, people always did seem to…overindulge when they went there. Or so his grandfather told him."

"Overindulge?"

She giggled. "Oh, you know. Drink too much. Fight over cards. Fight over women. Start shooting if the place ran out of bourbon or if they didn't like the taste of the beer. It was the Wild West, after all."

"Interesting." I remembered Timber nearly getting into a fight over a game of pool, the one time we had visited the place. So the site's reputation pre-dated the ghost. I wondered what it meant.

"Anyway, everyone was relieved when James Connolly bought the place and turned it into a store. Then Archie inherited and went right back to running a tavern. Oh my, but people were upset! The Baptist Ladies' Society held a Temperance march on Main Street that went on for two days."

I was fascinated. "What happened?"

"No one smashed any windows, if that's what you mean." Missy giggled again. "One lady chained herself to the door for a few hours, but she had to go home to milk the cows. The rest milled about chanting slogans until the minister—that would have been Reverend Overton; his picture's in the other building—came down and quoted Saint Paul at them and made them leave. Everyone liked Archie, you see. He went to church regularly, donated to the mine widows' fund and all. And he kept a close eye on things, sent folks home when they'd had too much. So it pretty much blew over."

"And then?"

"Well, the state went dry in 1916—five years before the rest of the country, did you know that?" Telling the story, Missy's voice grew slower and more resonant; I thought I could hear Grandpa Bahr. "But Archie kept chugging right along, discreetly, of course. State inspectors didn't get out this way much and when they did, somehow they never found anything. Of course someone started a rumor that Archie had a secret room somewhere under the tavern, where he hid the goods."

"Was there such a room?"

She shrugged. "No one ever found it. And believe me, they looked, especially when Archie suddenly disappeared in 1922."

"Oh!" I jerked upright like a jack-in-the-box; Missy startled away.

"I'd heard an owner had vanished," I told her in explanation. "I didn't realize it happened so long ago."

"Ah." Reassured my reaction didn't herald the onset of a seizure, she continued her story. "Most people said Archie just got tired of the trouble and went off to start again somewhere.

It was one thing when only the state was dry, quite another when Prohibition hit the entire nation. People said it broke Archie's heart; that tavern was his life."

"And what did your grandfather say?"

"He was a young man then, not twenty-one. But he said Archie was no quitter. He would have done anything to keep the tavern running. So Grandpa Bahr figured he got involved with some shady folks—folks that could help when serving liquor became a federal offense. Except something went wrong and they killed him."

With a blow to the head, I thought.

"Nobody ever found any evidence he'd been murdered, and they never found his body, either. But afterwards the place went bad again. So now every time a business at the Connolly Building fails, the old-timers say that Archie's done it again."

"Have you ever seen him?"

Her eyes widened. "Archie's ghost? No. Actually, I've never set foot in the place, myself. Anyway, it's just a story. Part of local history, whether or not it's true."

I shuffled through the folder, feeling vaguely discouraged. I'd hoped for so much and I'd found—what? A local legend confirming that something haunted the Connolly Building? I already knew as much, had known it years before I'd seen anything. I guessed knowing the fellow's name might help; names were power and all that. But knowing his name didn't bring me any closer to knowing what he wanted.

I glanced at a photo of very young-looking men in World War I infantry uniforms posed stiffly in front of the bar, and another of a smiling Archie Connolly standing in a then-empty lot at the side of the building, beside a storm cellar door. Behind Archie I could just see the outline of a side entrance, the one his ghost had walked through Saturday night.

"If you're thinking that's the secret room, you're wrong," Missy informed me. "It really was a storm cellar: one room and no other doors. Anyway, it got filled in when they replaced the foundation in the fifties. And then the Taylors built Western Realty on that lot, so there's nothing there now."

I sighed. "And there's nothing else? No building plans or diagrams, anything like that?"

"There should be." Sounding perplexed, Missy took the folder from me and flipped through its contents. "That's odd. I could have sworn… That other man must have taken them. I did tell him not to."

I stiffened. "Other man?"

"Oh yes, didn't I mention it? He came in just before Christmas, asking the same questions you're asking. I remember, because I was putting up the holly. A nice young man, very handsome in a tall, dark way." She giggled.

"Not the new owner?" I asked, puzzled.

"No. I know Mr. Casey. This was definitely someone else."

And then it struck me. Jake. Breda hadn't described him, but I was willing to bet the handsome, dark man had been her missing fiancé.

I rose abruptly, nearly dumping Missy out of her seat in my haste to leave.

"Thank you. You've been very helpful."

"Uh…You're welcome. You found what you needed, then?"

Already halfway to the door, I didn't turn around.

"Yes. Yes I did."

Not what I expected. What I needed.

Jake had been here. Jake worked for Casey. Jake had taken something, maybe old building plans. That meant Casey had them, or at least had access to them. Did they contain information he needed? Or a secret he meant to hide?

I had no idea. But I was determined to find out.

Chapter Seven

In my dream that night I found myself sitting at one of the round bistro tables in the back room of the Emerald Isle. Although the room lay in darkness as complete as that of a tomb or a cave far underground, I knew my location from the stage, which shone with an eerie blue glow as if from a spotlight suspended somewhere in the ceiling. The blue glow reflected off a number of indistinct shapes, which resolved, as soon as I turned my attention in that direction, into Red Branch's sound system and equipment: microphone and instrument stands, speakers and amplifiers all arranged in neat rows, as if at any moment the band would appear and start playing. Looking around for the rest of the band, I felt a surge of irritation; they were nowhere in sight. Didn't they realize we had a gig? Now I would have to do it all by myself, pretending everything was the way it was supposed to be and hoping no one would notice.

I reached for my flute, which I usually kept with me, but it wasn't there. I had left it at home and I had no time to go back for it. I had sent Timber for it—of course, that's where he'd gone; he should be back any minute now—but where were Frank and Lisa? I couldn't hold an audience singing unaccompanied. They were probably in the bar. I'd have to go hunt them down.

"I gave my life to this place. Now look at it."

I glanced left to see Archie Connolly sitting across the table from me. In the way of dreams, I wasn't at all surprised to see him. His appearance didn't appall me as it had, either. He wore the same old-fashioned tweed suit and muslin shirt. His hat hid the damage to his head, but blood trickled down the left side of his face. He shook his head sorrowfully and made a clucking sound with his tongue.

"Damn shame, what they've done."

"What do you mean?"

"Can't you see it?" He raised an arm in a gesture that took in the whole of the room from floor to ceiling.

"I can't see anything. It's too dark." In fact, I could barely see across the table.

"Rotten, through and through."

"If it's so rotten, why don't you leave?"

"Can't leave." He sounded shocked at the very idea. "I gave it my blood. We're stuck with each other. It's an ill thing, this trying to get between us. Almost too late now, anyhow."

"Too late?"

Archie pulled a mammoth gold pocket watch from his waistcoat, consulted it and snapped it shut with a frown. "No, not much time left at all."

He lurched up out of his chair and pushed past me, headed for the side door. I found myself following close behind him, without any memory of leaving my own seat or conscious idea what I would do if I caught him.

At the doorway, he turned, raising one finger in a stern warning.

"You watch yourself, missy. I should never have got you involved. But you looked so pretty up there, singing that song. And a fellow needs help, he truly does. He can't always manage things all on his own. Especially where there's family involved."

The door closed behind him.

"Wait a minute…!"

I reached for the doorknob. My fingers met only plaster and paper, a blank wall. At the same moment, a hand closed on my elbow.

"That's not the way," said Lisa. She wore a slinky black dress that would have been appropriate on Morticia Addams and she had slicked her blonde hair back with some luminescent gel, making her head look hard and shiny, like an insect's. She turned me around and shoved me towards the stage.

"Over there."

I stumbled a pace or two, regained my balance and faced her.

"Aren't you coming?"

She pouted in a puzzled sort of way. "Why should I?"

I stood on the stage, alone. The house was utterly dark, not with the darkness that comes sometimes when the lights are shining in your eyes and you can't see past them, but with a thick, roiling blackness, as though the audience were populated by living shadows. I knew if I opened my mouth those shadows would surge down my throat and strangle me.

Somewhere in the middle distance a light flicked on, illuminating one round table. Casey leaned forward over the table and smiled.

"Sing for me," he said.

I must have checked to be sure I had my flute about five times before Timber and I left for what would be our first gig as house band at the Emerald Isle. Even then, believing that it was, in fact, in my gig bag, along with my whistles, playlists, microphone and various other odds and ends, was largely a matter of faith. Not being a person to whom faith came easily, this made me distinctly uncomfortable.

We arrived at the Emerald Isle at eight o'clock, to allow ourselves plenty of time to set up our equipment and run a brief sound check before beginning to play. To my surprise, Frank and Lisa's car was already parked in the alley by the loading dock. That had to be a first. Unless we all came together, they always arrived at the last possible minute. It shocked me even more to discover their amplifiers already on the stage and plugged in and their instruments ready and waiting on their stands. Passing Frank's guitar, I gave it an experimental strum. It was in tune.

"Will wonders never cease?" I muttered to myself. They seemed to be taking this gig seriously. I took it as a good omen.

I found Frank sitting in the booth we had occupied the last time we were all here, perusing The Mountain Market, a weekly advertising circular.

"Hey." I slid into the booth. "Anything good in there?"

He shrugged without looking up. "Lots of lost pets. Timber need help with the PA?"

"Yeah, I think he'd appreciate a hand." Sometimes I felt guilty for leaving the lugging and hauling aspects of band life up to others, but we'd agreed early on that my role as bandleader exempted me from physical labor. It meant Timber did most of the heavy work, but he claimed not to mind. "Where's Lisa?"

"Up front." He twitched his head in the direction of the bar, his dark face looking even darker than usual.

"You two fighting again?"

"This gig could be the start of something for us, Caitlin. Red Branch could go somewhere. But Lisa...as much as I love her, I know she's the weak link. She hardly practices, and when she does she plays the same mistakes over and over again. Then she gets discouraged and quits."

I gazed at my bandmate with honest amazement. I knew Lisa's issues with playing music very well; I just hadn't thought Frank understood them—or cared.

"I simply tried to suggest that she go about it another way, pay more attention. And she got all shirty with me. Like any criticism means I think she sucks. You know how she is."

I did know. I trod on eggs during every rehearsal. I put up with it because Frank and Lisa had been my friends before we started the band together and because I truly believed quiet support would go farther in the long run than bluster and threats. After a couple years, though, it was quite clear that Lisa didn't respond well to either.

"I know I'm not any great prize, myself." Most people would have accompanied this kind of declaration with a little self-deprecating smile, but Frank remained perfectly serious. "I never played this kind of music before Red Branch, not much anyway. I diddle around and waste time because I'm nervous. I get flustered and I forget things. You and Timber are the ones holding this band together. I know that. If we do make it big, it'll be because of you."

I clamped my mouth shut on the reassurances Frank's bald self-assessment had inspired. He'd done it again, deflected attention from his own shortcomings by praising me and Timber, instead of going one step farther and admitting he needed to change.

"If Red Branch makes it big," I said slowly and carefully, "it will be because of all of us, not just because of me and Timber."

"Caitlin, the two of you are the most talented people in this band. Shit, you're two of the most talented people I've ever known. Don't be afraid to admit it!"

"I'm not..." I began, but he had already gone to help Timber with the PA. He always had to have the last word.

I sat for a minute trying to regain my cool, knowing that if she and Frank had been fighting I would probably need it when I found Lisa.

I heard her before I saw her; for a small, cute person she had a remarkably strident voice, with a laugh like a donkey braying. She was sitting at the bar drinking a glass of stout and flirting with the bartender, an attractive young man who looked barely old enough to be serving alcoholic beverages. As always, she had dressed to show off her stunning figure, this time in a slinky black nothing near enough to the dress she'd been wearing in my dream to give me a shudder.

"…private parties mostly," I heard her say as I approached. "That is, when we can get time off from our tour schedule. We're really just doing this as a favor to Casey; he's such a dear. I don't know how long it will last; it's been such a busy summer. Last month we played with Altan at Telluride, and of course we're opening for Eileen Ivers at Four Corners…"

I rolled my eyes. We had, in fact, played in Telluride during the festival—in a bar at a session organized by some friends of ours. Altan had been one of the headline acts and we'd never come into contact with them. And Eileen Ivers was playing at Four Corners, but whether we would be there remained a matter of speculation. If we did get the gig at this late date, the festival committee would likely use us to fill an early morning slot far from the main stage.

The bartender gave me a slightly glazed look over Lisa's head; clearly her habitual name-dropping behavior meant nothing to him.

"Get you something?"

"Water, thanks. Actually, if you could get a pitcher and some glasses over to the stage area…."

"I'm on it." He hastened to make his escape. Lisa turned to me with her practiced frown.

"You finally made it." She made it sound as though I had waltzed in an hour late, rather than precisely on time. For all I knew, she and Frank had come early just so she could take that tone with me. It would be like her. Well, it wouldn't be a gig if I got through it without asking myself at least once why I considered Lisa my friend.

"Sound check in ten minutes," I said, refusing to be needled.

"So soon? We don't go on for an hour."

"Forty-five minutes. And I want to start on time, not still be fussing with levels when we're supposed to be playing."

"Fine. Geez, Caitlin, relax, why don't you. It's just a bar gig."

She gulped the last of her stout, slid off her barstool and flounced away towards the back room.

"And tell the guys I want to go over the Island Set while we have a chance," I called after her. "Your entrance is ragged."

Okay, so maybe I was a little needled. The jibe was probably lost on her anyway; she kept going as if she hadn't heard me.

So. The band was all present and accounted for; the equipment set up, or nearly so. Only one thing remained to do, and I felt more reluctant about it than any other aspect of the gig.

I had to sign the contract. I had to sign a contract drawn up by someone I strongly suspected of practicing Bad Magic in his spare time, who had stirred up enough vile energy that the resident ghost required me to put a stop to it, and who had some unknown and possibly malevolent reason for hiring my band in the first place.

I'd read the whole contract through several times and had been unable to find anything suspicious—no claims on my soul or those of my bandmates, no requirement I sign in blood, no weird mystical code I could see. But that didn't matter. Nor did it matter that I held a dim view of Ceremonial Magic and its effectiveness. Contracts have their own kind of magic. They're a kind of binding spell, represented in words and sealed by signatures, symbolic representations of the parties involved. By signing Casey's contract, I would be binding myself to someone I didn't much like and didn't much trust, with or without the magical complications. That kind of thing could backfire all too easily.

I wasted a minute or two wondering if there were any conceivable way I could get out of signing, and another minute or two trying to invent some clause that absolutely had to be included but I had somehow forgotten to mention at our initial meeting. Failing that, I spent a further minute reminding myself that contracts are essentially meant to protect the people who sign them. The protective nature would stand against any possibly negative effects…wouldn't it?

I sighed and headed up the stairs to Casey's office. I couldn't see any way around it; I had no choice but to sign and hope for the best.

There were voices in the gallery.

I blinked. All the tables were empty, as was the bus station at the end. Yet I still heard the voices, one male, one female, raised in anger. They got clearer as I approached Casey's office door—much clearer. I identified the man's voice as Casey's; well, that was a no-brainer. The woman's voice held a familiar note, though I couldn't quite place it.

The office door stood ajar, explaining why I could hear so well. My steps slowed. The polite thing to do would be to retreat downstairs until the storm blew over. I almost did. Maybe this argument, happening at this particular time, was a sign from the gods that I should not, in fact, sign the contract. If so it could be unlucky—not to mention disrespectful—not to take advantage of this opportunity for escape.

On the other hand, it could be that by putting me in a position to overhear, the Powers That Be were offering me a chance to learn exactly what Casey was up to. This interpretation of the situation suited my inherent nosiness much better. I edged up to the door.

"…trying to evade me!" said the woman's voice. "You know where he is!"

"Please keep your voice down!" Casey shouted. Then he went on in softer tones, "I don't think this is the time for this conversation. The bar rush will be starting any minute now. I don't want to air…"

"I can think of a good many things you might not want to air. I know what you get up to—both of you, though you're the one who put him up to it."

"I've told you, I don't want to discuss it."

"Fine. Then tell me what you've done with him and we won't have to."

"Done with…?" I heard Casey give a tired sigh. I could picture him running a manicured hand through his crisp black hair.

"He wouldn't have come here if it hadn't been for you. What are you planning? More demon raising? Did you think if you got someone else to help it would actually work this time?"

My hair stood on end. Demon raising? So I'd been right about the significance of Casey's library. No wonder old Archie took exception.

"I told you before. He volunteered to help me with the re-model. He sent the plans along, but he never showed up. I don't know where he is."

That was a lie. After learning what I had at the Historical Museum, I was sure of it. So was the woman.

"I don't believe you."

"That is abundantly clear," Casey snapped. Again, he gentled his tone. It seemed to me it took him some effort. "Honey, you're overwrought. I know how much this whole thing has upset you, but don't you think it's time to let it go? He obviously wasn't the person you thought. Accept that and move on."

A long silence followed.

"Maybe he wasn't the person I thought," she said at last. "But neither are you. I tried to pretend I didn't hear the things I heard or see the things I saw, but I can't pretend anymore."

Feet scuffed on carpet; I shrank against the wall. A shadow appeared in the office doorway.

"I'm not through with this!"

The door slammed and I found myself face to face with Breda Ni Fhearraigh. From what I'd heard, I wasn't surprised. I could have knocked her over with a feather, though.

"Ms. Ross!" she gasped. Lowering her voice, she hissed, "What are you doing here?"

"I could say I came up to sign a contract for my band, and it would be true," I replied in equally low tones. "It would also be true to say I was lurking in the hall, eavesdropping on a very interesting conversation. Which version of the truth would you prefer?"

"You didn't tell me you were in the band here."

"You didn't tell me you knew Casey. What's your connection with him, anyway? You seem pretty cozy."

She opened her mouth, thought the better of what she had been going to say and closed it again. Then she shrugged.

"Sean Casey is my father."

"Your father!" I blurted. My surprise lasted only a second. Of course. I'd thought her eyes looked familiar. They were his. But a piece of my half-remembered dream drifted into my head, making me shiver. What had the ghost said? "A fellow can't always manage on his own. Especially when family is involved."

I guessed I'd found the family in question. Damn precognition, anyway.

"Shh!" She laid a hand full of sparkly nails on my lips. "That office is pretty solid, but it's not soundproofed. Yes, he's my father."

"Why didn't you tell me before?" I dropped my voice back down to a whisper.

"I thought…." She looked around the empty gallery and pursed her lips. She wore plum lipstick today, to match the camisole and silk cardigan she wore with her black slacks and pumps. "Look, this isn't a good place to talk. Can we meet somewhere?"

"I'm playing until midnight. I won't be home until twelve-thirty at the earliest."

"Good. I'll meet you there."

"But…." I wondered when I was going to get the chance to explain things to Timber and how he would take it. Like a gentleman, I hoped.

"Later," she said firmly. "And Ms. Ross, let me give you some advice. Don't sign anything my father gives you. Not anything."

She pulled away from me and trotted down the stairs before I could say anything else. From the gallery I watched her stride across the bar and out the door.

"Caitlin!" bellowed my husband's voice from somewhere in the back room. "Come on, we need you!"

I glanced at Casey's office; no sound came from within. Was he waiting for me? If so, he'd just have to wait a little longer. Forever, if I had anything to say about it.

"Caitlin!"

I scampered down the stairs, fumbled my flute together and clambered onto the stage. Of a mercy, the whole band came in together when I gave the count for our usual warm-up number, a set of jigs we'd been playing so long I could have done it in my sleep. I didn't even falter when, halfway through, I glanced into the house and saw Archie Connolly's ghost, with Casey standing just behind him, looking vaguely blue and misty in the apparition's shadow.

The ghost gave his head a sad shake and walked through the wall. Casey smiled and moved his lips.

I could have sworn they were saying, "Sing for me."

Chapter Eight

That night's gig seemed to drag on forever.

Even at the time I knew it was one of the best performances Red Branch had ever given. The instrumental sets flowed like clean water, without any of the fumbling and faltering I had come to expect when we transitioned between tunes. The love songs moved people to tears; the martial ballads had them stomping their feet and clapping their hands until I thought someone would do himself an injury. I even caught Lisa smiling over the bridge of her fiddle once or twice, instead of wearing her habitual scowl. I should have been ecstatic. But all I could think about was getting the tedious business over with so I could hear what Breda had to say. In consequence, I went through the entire gig and all the subsequent rigmarole of signing CDs and chatting up fans—which seemed to take twice as long as usual—in a state bordering on exasperation. I think I actually growled at several people; anyway, they stopped approaching me and converged on Lisa and Frank, who lapped up the adoration with their usual studied charm and witty repartee. I wish now it hadn't been that way. I wish I had let myself enjoy the moment, but I guess it couldn't be helped. I guess you never do know until it's too late, when your career has reached its pinnacle.

One scary moment almost jolted me out of my fixation on what might be waiting for me at home. Just as Timber and I were finally leaving, Casey caught us at the door, wanting to know where the contract was and why I hadn't stepped into his office to sign it. Perhaps we could get the matter taken care of now?

I leaned hard on Timber's arm and cast him a meaningful, helpless look. My husband, bless him, understood what I wanted at once.

"I'm sorry, Mr. Casey, but my wife is quite tired."

"I really do need a signature..."

Timber is a big man under any circumstances, but in response to Casey's words he seemed to grow at least a foot. He has a useful talent that way. He looked down on the top of Casey's head, his blue eyes oozing disdain.

"Contrary to the glamorous myth of a musician's life, playing gigs is hard work, Mr. Casey. My wife has just done three hours of this work to your benefit, and she's tired." I poked my husband in the ribs; he was overplaying his role. His arm tightened around me, but he didn't let up. "None of us in the band would like her to conduct important business in anything less than her usual astute frame of mind, ken. Tomorrow will do as well as tonight, aye?"

Faced with an excessively broad, six foot four inch Scotsman who wore a twenty-inch dirk as part of his performance apparel, Casey had no choice but to agree.

"I do need it before the weekend is over," he said, by way of having the last word.

"I think we can manage that," Timber replied, foiling him. Then he swept me out through the door.

"What was that about?" he hissed at me as soon as we were alone in the truck.

"You'll see," was all the explanation I could manage.

He began to see as soon as we pulled up in our driveway, when a dark figure detached itself from the porch swing and strode purposefully down the walk to meet us. Breda, it seemed, had been waiting.

"What took you so long?" she demanded before I had slammed the truck door.

"Who's this, then?" Timber asked at the same time, coming around the hood to get between us.

"Timber, this is Breda Ni Fhearraigh, Mr. Casey's daughter. Breda, Timber MacDuff. My husband."

"Daughter?"

"Husband?"

They eyed each other like emissaries from two opposing camps, newly informed that they're required to lay aside hostilities and form an alliance. Timber's kilt and dirk made the sight all the weirder. Breda, contrary to what I had come to expect from her, was clad very simply in a dark sweatshirt, black jeans and black canvas high-tops. She'd even dispensed with most of her jewelry, and she looked like an operative for some secret branch of the government—or a skate punk; I couldn't decide which. I wondered briefly if I had stumbled into some bizarre urban fantasy novel. No, I decided. That would be too easy.

"Even Ceremonial Magicians can have families," I told my husband before adding, to Breda, "and I'm not the kind of Oracle that takes vows of perpetual virginity. Does this look like Delphi?"

"I hadn't thought…"

"Of course, I didn't mean…"

"No, neither of you did. Now, let's go in and get all this sorted out." I didn't know what "all this" was, exactly, nor did I have the least faith that the hour's conversation I felt up to would miraculously sort it out. But either the words, or my somewhat waspish tone, or a combination of the two, had the desired effect. The two of them followed me into the house. I could still sense them looking daggers at each other behind my back. But I could live with that.

While the kettle boiled and the tea brewed, I explained to Timber how I had met Breda. He raised an eyebrow when he heard I had agreed to do a reading for her, but didn't comment. When it came to the reading, I glossed over the details, only saying it had indicated there was more to Jake's disappearance than was immediately apparent, and that it probably had something to do with knowledge Breda had access to, but didn't fully understand. Hard as I found it to keep secrets from my husband, I respected client confidentiality. From the grateful look Breda shot me, I knew I had done the right thing. Besides, it would surely all come out when she told her side of the story.

Finding myself on a roll at that point, I went on to fill Breda in on the situation at the Emerald Isle, from its tarnished history, to the ghost, to my visit to the Historical Museum and what I had found there. When I mentioned my discovery of the ghost's name, Breda twitched.

"Connolly?"

"Yes." I narrowed my eyes. "Does that mean something to you?"

"And Jake stole documents for my father?"

"It looks that way to me, yes."

"You might have shared that little detail, love," Timber put in with a frown; I hadn't told him about Jake, either.

"Sorry. I had a lot on my mind. Anyway," I concluded, "Timber thinks your father bought a haunted bar because its very nature will add something to whatever magical process he's set in motion. And that's all we know."

I sat back on the couch. And waited.

We had gathered in the living room by then, and the first cups of tea had long since been drained. Timber and I had changed out of our stage clothes, he in the bedroom during a part of the story he already knew and I right there, barely pausing in my tale as I squirmed out of my bodice and kirtle and donned the sweats my husband tossed down to me. If my casual undressing in front of her caused Breda any consternation, she didn't show it. As for myself, well, once you've spent any part of your life on the performers' side of a stage it takes a lot more than showing skin to ruffle your feathers, so to speak.

The silence lengthened.

"I don't know where to begin," Breda said at last, gazing into her empty cup.

"I can think of a good place." I glanced at my husband, who responded by pouring more tea all round. "You told me Jake's interest in magic opened a whole new world to you. But your father is a Ceremonial Magician. From what I overheard on the balcony today, you knew it. So were you lying?" I hoped not, but not for the reasons one might think. Usually I could tell when people lied to me, but nothing Breda had said during the course of our first meeting had set off any alarms. I didn't like to think my early warning system might be rusty, especially not when I had Casey to deal with. That man, I thought, could lie to Lucifer himself, should the reputed Lord of Hell happen to show up at the bar.

"Not exactly," Breda admitted, and I heaved a sigh of relief. "You see, when I met Jake, I didn't know about my fa-ther's…um…hobby, I guess you would call it. My mother, Kitty O'Farrell, prided herself on being a practical woman. She had no patience with all the… 'mystic Celt idiocy,' is how she put it. She said it was no wonder the Irish had been persecuted throughout so much of history, if they insisted on holding onto such outmoded beliefs. Those as subscribed to them were sell-ing their people short in the name of a few moments' glory, she said. You should have heard her take on about the New Age movement! 'Self-hypnosis' was about the kindest thing she called it. My gran spoke the Gaelic, but mother wouldn't have it in the house; she said too many people associated the language with absurd notions of the little people and whatnot. She wouldn't let me study at the Irish Arts Center, or have any Irish friends unless she'd approved of them first."

Brenda's voice frayed on the jagged edges of old pain. I shoved a box of tissue in her direction, but she waved it aside.

"Mother insisted I study business. She wanted me to have a practical foundation for my life. There was no arguing with her. Not that I wanted to argue. I wanted her to be proud of me, so I just did what she wanted. But I always felt an emptiness in my life, something missing. That's why, after she passed away— it was breast cancer—I changed my name. I started going to the Irish Arts Center events, too. I was looking for something, and I thought if I did all the things she hadn't wanted me to do, I'd find it. But I didn't. I guess I'm too much like my mother in that respect. I don't like traditional music much." She threw an apologetic glance my way. "And I thought pining after the 'auld sod' was maudlin, and the political talk bored me to tears. So after a while I stopped going. But I still felt this incredible emptiness. Until I met Jake."

She smiled wanly. "From there, everything I told you is true."

I wondered if she hoped I would overlook her omission. As it happened, I caught it. "But you didn't tell me everything."

"No."

"Aye?" Timber growled. "And what, pray tell, did ye no see fit to share?"

Breda turned to face him. "Jake and my father hit it off right away. Actually, I wonder now if Jake only wanted to date me so he could meet my father. I gather Daddy has a reputation in arcane circles."

She grimaced ever so slightly, and I found myself admiring her. Not many people could share heart truths with virtual strangers at one o'clock on a Friday morning, and do it with no more than a grimace.

"I'd been seeing Jake a couple of months when I found out what my father did in his spare time. While my mother was alive Daddy kept very close. I can't imagine she wouldn't have known, but they probably had some kind of agreement about it—if he kept the magic under wraps she wouldn't make an issue of it, or something. After she died, though…. I don't know whether he got careless, or whether he figured he didn't need to keep the secret anymore, or whether he actually wanted me to find out. But he stopped locking the private study where he kept his collection. There was other stuff, too. Stuff I saw and then told myself I hadn't really seen. Stuff I overheard…."

Her voice trailed off and she gave her head a brisk shake. I ached for details, knowing she'd never give them.

"You may think it's funny, since Jake's interest in the occult excited me, but I didn't want my father to be involved in all that."

"No, it makes sense," I said. "We all have things in our lives we want to keep separate, and finding one's parents are involved tarnishes them. Tarnishes the parents, too. It would be like having your father turn up at a college party. Or like walking in while your parents are having sex."

To my surprise, Breda blushed. "Yes, it is like that. A shock to find out real grown-ups do those things. It makes you re-evaluate your whole way of looking at the world." She sighed. "So I tried to close my eyes to it. It got harder, though, when Jake started visiting my father when I wasn't around. I knew they were getting up to something. At first it was just a feeling. I'd come home after classes and find the two of them in the den…and although they never said anything out of the ordinary, never exchanged any overt looks, I just knew. It was like looking at two people and knowing they've recently been lovers. In fact, I even wondered if that could be the case and Jake and I had a huge fight about it before he convinced me otherwise. Then I wondered if I were losing my mind.

"As time went on—I haven't said, but this period of my life lasted a number of years—other things happened. It seemed the house smelled funny when Jake and my father spent time together. Several times I came home and found them locked in the study; I could hear chanting. I closed myself in my room until they came out, and tried to ignore it. After a while, it got to where they had no regard for me at all. If I walked in on a conversation, they just kept talking. Maybe they thought since I couldn't understand them it didn't matter…."

She paused again. Timber and I waited. I don't know what thoughts might be passing through my husband's head, but I was furious. Furious at Casey and Jake's casual messing about with forces they didn't understand in a way I considered both foolish and dangerous, yes. But mostly furious at Breda's denial. I wanted to ask her why she'd stayed in her father's house at all; she was obviously well enough off that she could have got a place of her own. More, I wanted to ask her why she'd stayed engaged to a guy involved in the stuff Jake was involved with. I didn't have problems with Ceremonial Magic, per se—well, okay, maybe I did—but Breda, for all her claims to being excited, was clearly uncomfortable with its place in Jake's life. I tried to keep my thoughts off my face, but I must not have done a very good job. She looked at me with a weak smile.

"It was such a small part of our relationship. Actually, it wasn't part of our relationship at all. It made him happy. How could I question that? I thought I just needed time to adjust. And…."

"Ye blamed your father." Timber finished for her.

"Well, I did. I still do. I don't think Jake would have gotten in so deep if my father hadn't led him on. And…."

"You didn't expect it would ever work." This time, I finished Breda's thought.

"You said yourself most magic doesn't."

I opened my mouth and shut it again. I hadn't said that, not exactly, but never mind.

"Besides, that's not what I was going to say," Breda continued. "I was going to say that I convinced myself they were only involved in some kind of boys' club, like the Elks or the Oddfellows—weirder, maybe, but essentially harmless. And it made me so uncomfortable because I was jealous of the time and energy Jake put into it when he should have been spending time with me. So I just kept trying to work on my attitude and see the thing in a more positive light."

"I see." I did see. No one likes being uncomfortable, and very few people have the strength of will to listen to what discomfort has to tell them, especially when that might mean confronting loved ones with their unacceptable behavior. I had seen people go through amazing intellectual contortions to avoid any kind of confrontation, telling themselves if they only showed more understanding the problem would vanish. I had been guilty of it, myself.

"So what brought them here?" Timber asked.

Breda took a swallow of tea. "From stuff I overheard I gathered Daddy was looking for something. Early last year, he found it."

"The bar."

"It must have been, yeah. He decided to take early retirement and come out here to fulfill his lifelong ambition of starting a pub. It may have been a lifelong dream, but I'd never heard him say any such thing before. He and Jake were thicker than ever, making plans. Then, last December, Jake told me he was coming out here. I never saw him again. I waited a few months, and in March I followed him as far as Boulder, where I had some friends. They put me in touch with…people. People who might help me trace him."

"That's true love, that is," Timber remarked. "Waiting three months to find out what's become of your intended. And then wasting another three before following him to his destination."

Breda colored, startling red patches standing out stark on her pale cheeks. "Well…things were strained between us. We had decided to separate for a while, to see if marriage was really the right idea. But I did…I do love him. It took me a while to realize it, but I do. And I got worried. I still wasn't really eager to throw myself behind whatever he was doing, but…"

Timber made a low noise in his throat, not mollified. I hushed him with a look.

"Why didn't you come here straight away if you knew where he was headed?" I asked.

"I didn't want to run into my father. He made it clear he didn't want me here."

"He didn't get here until just before the Grand Opening." But he had been in contact with Jake, of that I was sure.

"Well, I didn't know that, did I?" she said with some asperity. "Believe me, I didn't want to know any more about his plans than I had to, and he wasn't precisely sharing."

I thought of a spear planted in the ground before a crumbling doorway, keeping anyone from examining too closely the darkness within. In my mind, the spear metamorphosed into Breda. Her feet moved, turning her in a slow circle until she faced the doorway.

I blinked, and the vision shredded and vanished.

"And you have no idea what they were up to or what, exactly, they were looking for?" I said, coming back to the present.

She shook her head, looking sheepish. "No."

I thought about that, running my mind back over the conversation I had overheard on the balcony.

"Then what makes you think your father is attempting to raise a demon?"

Breda blanched. "I…did I say something like that?"

"You did." I nodded. "You asked him if he was planning more demon-raising, and if he thought getting someone else to help would make it work this time. I presume you were referring to his recruiting Jake."

"I don't know." She picked up her teacup, noticed her hands were shaking, and set it down again hastily.

"Think, Breda. You brought up demons when you first came to see me. You must have had a reason."

"I don't know," she repeated, and this time I was sure she lied. "Why would my father want to raise a demon?"

"You tell me. And stop playing around. You came to me for help and I can't give you any if you aren't completely honest with me."

"All right," she whispered. "I do think that's what they're up to. I know…I overheard…Daddy tried once before, back in New York. I think he did it just to say he had. Then Jake…"

"What about Jake?" I prompted when she didn't go on.

"Jake had…has problems." She sighed. "I told you he came from the wrong side of the tracks? Well, it hadn't always been that way. His family was well-off until he was about seven. Then a liquidator went after his father's company. They lost everything. It hit Jake hard. He never felt safe again. No amount of money, no amount of influence…Nothing was ever enough for him."

"I see." Power, influence, maybe even revenge. All very good reasons to want to bring a demon into the picture.

But Jake hadn't been seen in months. That left Casey, who had power and influence already. Would he really raise a demon, just to say he could?

"That's what worried me so much when Jake vanished," Breda continued. "That's why I started consulting psychics to find him. But then you said there aren't any demons and…"

"Whoa, wait a minute!" I interrupted. "I never said there aren't any demons. I said our definitions of the entities we call demons are flawed, because we presume we can understand and control them if we have the right ritual. I, myself, wouldn't want to take my chances with an otherworldly, essentially amoral entity to whom I hadn't been properly introduced, but some do."

Timber's eyes narrowed. "What are you thinking, love?"

I took a deep breath. All the events of the past few days had come into sudden, sharp focus, and they made a picture I didn't like at all.

"I'm thinking Sean Casey didn't just come here for a ghost. I'm thinking he came here to raise a demon. The one under the Emerald Isle."

Dead silence fell. I kept waiting for someone to break it by laughing. No one did, though, and as the silence stretched I gave up hope anyone would. Damn.

"That," Timber said slowly, "would explain a lot. A lot more than a mere ghost."

"I don't get it," said Breda.

I looked at Timber. Timber looked back and shook his head. I'd put the pieces together; it was up to me to explain.

"I told you that the Emerald Isle—or the Connolly Building, let's say—has a chequered past? The site has always had a reputation for violence. Well, let's suppose it's not just random bad luck causing that to be the case. Let's suppose it's the presence of a demon."

"Demons attract violence?" Breda frowned.

"Some entities *are* violence." Timber's face had gone dark. "Ye canna walk long in the Other World without understanding that."

"Well forgive me if I've never walked in the Other World at all," Breda snapped.

I spread my hands in a quelling motion and saw Timber bite back a retort. "It doesn't explain why the remodel wasn't troubled. In fact, since your father bought the place it's been unusually quiet. If we accept a demon, or some other violence-inducing entity, that doesn't make sense."

"It doesn't explain the ghost, either," Timber put in.

"I don't see what the ghost has to do with it."

"Archie Connolly is upset about something," I told Breda. "I think your father trying to raise a demon on his home turf would upset just about anybody."

We all thought for a few minutes. Then Breda asked,

"Why does the demon stick so close to the bar? Why doesn't it affect the whole town? For that matter, why doesn't it just leave altogether? Why should it hang around?"

Timber chuckled. "There goes your theory, love."

"That's a very good question," I said at the same time. No matter what Timber said, I couldn't seem to let the idea go. I didn't want there to be a demon, did I? Things would be so much simpler if there were only a ghost.

I just didn't believe in things being simple.

"I suppose it could have been bound there sometime in the past." I rubbed my forehead, thinking. "It's pretty unlikely, given the kind of people who usually try it and the way those spells usually turn out. But that might explain your father."

"How?"

"He might find the situation very convenient. He wouldn't have to raise a demon at all, just find a way to channel its power."

"Aye," Timber said, his voice rich with skepticism. "But how would he know where to look?"

I stared at him, stumped.

"Well…" Breda cleared her throat, looking uncomfortable. Timber and I both rounded on her.

"I dinna want to hear this, do I?" my husband said. In my heart I agreed with him. The demon's theoretical presence was complication enough. Somehow I knew what Breda was about to say would only make things worse.

"My great-grandfather—that would be my father's mother's father—didn't come from Ireland originally. He served in the Great War, and settled in Galway afterward. He didn't come back to America until after World War II. His wife died and he wanted to take his daughter away from the memories. That's when he emigrated to New York."

"Back to America? He came from here?" My mouth went dry. I'd been right; I didn't want to hear it.

"Yes. In fact, he came from *here*. From Gordarosa. And that's not all. You see, we had a lot of his old things in the attic. I found them when I was cleaning after my mother died. Some of them had his name on them. And it wasn't Casey. It was Connolly. Seamus Connolly. It never meant a thing to me until today."

I looked over at my husband. He had closed his eyes and leaned back on the couch as if relaxing, but his face had grown very tight around the mouth.

"Please tell me you don't mean what I think you mean."

"I can't, Caitlin; I'm sorry. I think…." She took a deep breath, just as I had done before sharing my idea about the demon. "I think Archie Connolly was my great, great uncle."

Chapter Nine

We went to bed soon after Breda's revelation. At three in the morning, we couldn't possibly have done otherwise. I had just about enough energy left to steer Breda to the spare bedroom, point out the bathroom door and locate an extra set of towels; I was absolutely unfit to discuss the possibility that she and the late Archie Connolly were related, or any of the implications thereof.

For a mercy, I slept without dreaming. When I came to, the clock read ten-thirty and Timber's side of the bed was empty. The smell of fresh coffee wafted up from the kitchen and I could hear running water in the bathroom down the hall, where someone was taking a shower. I pulled the sheets over my head and tried to go back to sleep, but it didn't do any good. My body still felt like a lead weight, but my mind was already turning the previous night's conversation over and over. If I didn't get up and talk to someone, I'd wear a hole in my brain.

I got dressed and went downstairs, where I found Breda and Timber drinking coffee at the kitchen table. Breda's hair hung in damp strands over her shoulders, leading me to the brilliant deduction that it had been she in the shower. She was completely absorbed in stroking the immaculate, white belly of our calico cat, Zathras, who lay in her lap, making biscuits in the air and gazing at her with adoring green eyes while purring like a low-flying aircraft. Across the table from Breda, Timber stared into space, his eyes vague and his jaw lax as an idiot's; he had a remarkable capacity to turn off any kind of brain activity when thought wasn't absolutely necessary.

"What are you doing here?" I asked my husband. "Didn't you have work today?"

"Providence intervened," he explained, rousing himself with an effort. "The electrical inspector can't come until this afternoon. We can't do anything else until the electric passes inspection. We have the day off."

Just as well. I shuddered to think of Timber working with power tools on three hours of sleep.

I poured myself a cup of coffee, pulled out one of our ladder-backed kitchen chairs and sat down. Disturbed by the sound of the chair screeching across the tile, Zathras fell out of Breda's lap and stalked away in a huff.

"So," I said. "Here we are. I don't suppose either of you has the slightest idea what happens next?"

They shook their heads in unison and I swallowed a moment's anger. Why did everyone always wait around for me to come up with the ideas?

"Very well, then. I think we should check out the rumor of a secret cellar," I went on. "Jake and Casey must have wanted something with those old building plans."

"You can't think it would be on there," Breda snorted. "Someone would have found it, if it even still exists. From what you said, people have been looking for it almost a century and no one ever has."

"I know. But it's the one place I can think of where Casey could indulge in his hobby without the whole neighborhood finding out, as well as being the perfect lair for a resident demon, trapped or otherwise. Timber, I want you to talk to Red."

"Red?" Breda asked, mystified.

"Red Foster, the town building inspector," Timber replied. "Do you want the blueprints, then? Dave the plumber did say…"

"That there was nothing weird about them, I know. And you were quick to point out that he's not the most reliable source. I want to see them for myself. All remodel blueprints have to be filed in the building inspector's office," I explained to Breda. "They keep them for a year, and they're a matter of public record."

"You expect the secret cellar to be marked with an X?"

"It's a long shot, but you never know. It's worth checking out. At least we'll be able to see crawl spaces and stuff. Chat Red up while you're at it," I told my husband. "He may know something."

"He knows a lot of things. Some of them even have to do with building." Timber chugged the last of his coffee and stood up. "I'd better be off, then. If I'm lucky, I'll be able to pry myself free before nightfall. You know how Red likes to talk."

He bent to kiss me on the cheek in parting. I laid a hand on his arm. "If you have time, see if you can locate Curtis, too. And don't forget we have a gig tonight!"

"I'm on it." Timber grabbed his hat and left through the back door. After a minute an engine roared and the truck crunched away down the drive.

"Who's Curtis?" Breda asked while the door was still swinging.

"Curtis Richards, the local cement guy. If the Emerald Isle needed any cement work, he'll have been the one to do it. It's another long shot, but…"

"Worth checking out," Breda finished for me. "And what are we doing?"

"We," I told her, downing the last of my coffee and wishing for more, "are going to verify a fact and look into a theory. And the sooner we do that, the sooner we'll know where to go from here."

Before we did anything, however, Breda insisted we stop at her hotel so she could change. She was staying at a turn of the century house downtown, just a block away from the Emerald Isle, which had been remodeled the year before into an upscale Bed and Breakfast. I still thought Gordarosa had little call for anything upscale, but they seemed to do all right, most of their trade being family reunions and out of town weddings. Breda had a lovely room on the third floor, with a private balcony over-looking the tree-lined street. The furnishings were ornate and Victorian from the antique walnut four-poster to the brass light fixtures, and I couldn't help but wonder how much Breda was worth. I wondered it again when we got in her car—I saw from the New York plates that it was no rental. I know nothing about cars, but I had read an article about this model a month or so back while waiting for a haircut. Though it resembled a flashy sports car, it was an environmentally sensitive custom job with a hybrid electric engine and a price tag close to what I had paid for my house. The interior reeked of leather, and affixed to the dash was a framed black and white headshot of a dark-haired man with gleaming white teeth—Jake, I presumed. He was very handsome. No wonder he'd caught Missy's attention.

"Where to?" Breda asked as she fastened her seat belt, newly-reclaimed earrings swinging.

"Up to the highway, then turn right."

At the Main Street crossing we had to wait almost ten minutes for a train coming down from Sunrise, loaded with coal. Breda was unusually quiet. I don't often feel the need to make noise, myself, but something about her silence unsettled me.

"Some of those trains are a mile long," I found myself say-ing as the last cars passed and the gates swung up. "Or it seems like, anyway."

Breda put the car in gear. "Do they bother you much? They're so noisy."

"Not really." I shook my head. "After a while you don't even hear them, unless some engineer leans particularly hard on the horn. We don't live too near a crossing, though. The worst thing is that there are so many crossings in town. Sometimes, if your timing's bad, you have to wait for the train three times just to get to the highway."

"That must be awful in emergencies." She turned onto the highway. "It sure is pretty here, though. Peaceful, too. I was getting tired of the bustle in the city."

I gazed out the window and tried not to roll my eyes. I'd heard the tone of her voice too often not to recognize in it the infatuation with rural landscape that causes city dwellers to move halfway across the country before thoroughly investigating living conditions in the quaint little towns where they plan to settle down.

"Income's the lowest in the state," I remarked. "If you can find a job."

"That's not really a problem for me."

I hadn't thought it was. Breda had "trust fund" written all over her. I had nothing particular against trust funds; still, I couldn't get over feeling antagonistic towards people with no visible means of support moving into an economically depressed area and driving up property values so high that the folks who worked for a living couldn't afford to stay there.

"Turn right here," I said. "Then take the first left."

Following my instructions, Breda pulled into the parking lot of the Historical Museum.

"What are we doing here?"

"Like I said, verifying facts. If Seamus Connolly was related to Archie Connolly," and of course it was too much to hope for that he wouldn't be, "they'll know it here."

I got out of the car, calling for Missy Phillips, who appeared from behind the farmhouse. At least, I assumed it was her—her arms were so loaded with wild sweet pea vines that I couldn't see her face, and she looked as though she were mating with some strange, fuchsia and green octopus.

"Well, hello again!" She dumped her load of wildflowers into a wheelbarrow parked by the flagstone path, allowing me to verify her identity. She wore the same t-shirt and jeans uniform as two days before, but she had made an unfortunate attempt to straighten her dark curls. Her hair resembled a badly used wire brush. "I thought some flowers would brighten up the place! Back for some more history? It gets to be addictive, doesn't it?"

"It certainly does." Breda gave me a skeptical look. Missy did not have much in common with the kind of expert source one usually saw on television. I decided to get even by introducing her. "Missy, this is Breda Ni Fhearraigh. She's visiting from out of town."

"Nee Yarra?" Missy tried uncertainly, missing the requisite gargle entirely. A pained expression flashed across Breda's face and I smiled to myself.

"Breda, Missy Philips, an authority on Gordarosa history." Missy preened; I'd hit the right tone with her. If I survived the Emerald Isle, maybe I'd go into politics. Not. "I had another question about Archie Connolly. Did your grandfather ever mention whether he had a brother?"

"Now that's a funny thing." Missy's eyes misted and she rubbed her chin in thought. "As a matter of fact, according to Grandpa, there was some talk about it at the time. You know, back then families tended to be large. But Archie was an only child."

"An only child?" I repeated eagerly, glancing at my companion. She looked disappointed. I wondered whether she'd feel the same if she knew what I did about demons and blood ties.

"An only child for many years," Missy continued, and my stomach lurched. "Then, when he turned twenty, his parents had another boy. The mother died of it—she was older, and dying in childbirth wasn't at all uncommon then no matter what the woman's age. Some men would have been overcome with grief and taken it out on the child, but James Connolly doted on his new son. He used to take him everywhere, all bundled up in a little coat. When he was working, he kept the baby in a cradle under the counter. They hired a woman to look after him, but she didn't have much to do."

"I wonder what Archie thought about that."

Missy leaned forward confidentially. "By all accounts he was none too pleased. He had been the sole son for twenty years, and he thought his brother terribly spoiled. When Big James passed on Archie tried to take his brother in hand, but I gather they never did get on too well."

"And the brother's name?"

"They called him James Junior, after his father. I don't believe Archie liked that much, either." From the way Missy spoke, you might have thought she'd been there.

"James!" Breda gulped. Her face had lightened when she heard about Archie's brother, but now it fell again. I reminded myself that she didn't know the Gaelic.

"Yes, but they said it in Irish, you know. Seamus. They called the boy Seamus Óg—James the Younger. And his father became Seamus Mór. Big James, I think that is."

"Yes, it is," I confirmed. "Do you know what happened to him?"

"Oh yes." Missy's face grew grave and her breathy voice dropped to a sorrowful murmur. "World War One happened to him. He had his eighteenth birthday two months after the United States entered the war, and he volunteered right away. He never came back. Killed at Verdun they said. Big James was already gone by then, or his heart would have broken. It even upset Archie. Everyone said he blamed himself for his brother's death."

That was interesting. I wondered what mysterious issue lay between the two brothers, that Seamus would allow Archie to think him dead and Archie would so readily accept the blame. It sounded like more than your garden variety sibling rivalry to me.

"Do you have a picture by any chance?"

Missy nodded. "Just the one I showed you the other day, but you can see it again if you like."

She disappeared into the schoolhouse and returned after a few minutes with the photo of the young men in uniform lined up outside Connolly's tavern.

"That's Seamus, in the front row."

For the first time I noticed that one of the faces had been circled. It was too small for any of the features to be evident, but Breda's face turned white.

"My grandmother Casey had a copy of this picture. In her album. She said it was the only photograph she had of her father."

"Your grandmother?" Missy's eyes lit up with an historian's avid interest. "You mean, Seamus Connolly didn't die at Verdun? Or…?" She raised her eyebrows and I knew what she was thinking. It didn't take long to father a child, and for a young soldier before a battle, well…

"No," Breda said. "He didn't die at Verdun."

"But that's wonderful! Why, you're not an outsider at all then! You must stop by some time and tell me all about it."

Breda said nothing more. She just kept staring at the photograph, and I realized she had not really believed in her relationship to Archie's ghost until that moment. It had been the hare-brained notion of a late-night bull session, almost a joke, not the kind of thing you expect to take with you into daylight and have it make any sense. The reality was just beginning to sink in.

I detached the picture from her damp fingers and handed it back to Missy. "Thanks so much. You've answered a lot of questions."

She nodded gleefully, mind still full of the chance to hear an unknown and unusual story. How unknown and how unusual it might turn out to be, she had no idea.

"One more thing…."

"Yes?"

"You know how that place—the Connolly Building—has always had such a bad reputation?"

"Yes; since the eighteen-sixties…"

"Tell me," I broke into her incipient lecture. It was another long shot, but I was in a winning mood. "Did the Connollys—Big James and Archie, I mean—did they ever have any trouble?"

"Well…." Her pixy face clouded. "You know, now that you mention it, I don't think they did. In fact, I'm sure of it. I remember Grandpa Bahr saying how it was always quiet there, during the Connollys' time. Why?"

Bingo! "Just a hunch. Thanks again."

I steered Breda back to the car. Time to go home. I needed some lunch, and Breda looked as though she needed a sedative; I hoped chamomile tea would be strong enough. If not, maybe whisky would do the trick. With the gig coming up that night, the prospect of fencing with Casey, and the extreme likelihood that I would have to explain my refusal to sign a lucrative contract to the belligerent half of the band, I felt I could use a drop myself.

Back at the house, Breda opted for iced tea, so I poured the last of it into a couple of quart-sized Ball jars and filled the stock pot to boil water for more. Counting out the fifteen tea bags required, I remembered all the chores I had neglected since becoming involved in the Emerald Isle matter, so once I got the tea steeping I started a load of laundry, washed the dishes and went out to turn on the well pump supplying water to the soaker hoses in the vegetable garden, which looked decidedly wilted. The spinach was a dead loss, so I yanked it up and tossed it onto the compost heap. Then I started to pull weeds, but the discovery of a zucchini the size of a baseball bat frightened me so much I had to retreat to the back porch.

"Jesus, what's that?" asked Breda, who had been watching me from the shade.

"I believe when they reach this size, the polite term is 'vegetable marrows.'" I laid my zucchini on the back porch table and pulled up my own chair.

We sat in silence for a minute or two, looking out over the garden. Then:

"That lady was really scary," Breda said.

"Who? Missy?" I chuckled. "Her hair isn't always so bad."

"That's not what I meant. It's the way she knew so much. She didn't even have to look it up. Do you think she knows as much about the whole town? Or is the Connolly family a special hobby of hers?"

"I think she could probably tell you something about everyone here. Everyone who's been here more than a couple of years, anyway. Small towns are the last bastion of Oral History, you know. They call it gossip. It's a most entertaining way to while away the long winter nights and the hot summer days."

"How terrible!" From her shocked expression, I could tell that Breda, like me, had come from a culture where being talked about was the last thing anyone wanted.

"Not really. Someone once defined gossip as the last sacred art. I believe it. Sometimes the things people want most to keep secret are just the things you need to know."

"But what if it's not true?"

"Strangely enough, that's not often the case. Sure, you sometimes get a wild speculation or an unfounded rumor. But most of them don't go far enough to do any real damage. And you know what they say; where there's smoke, there's fire."

"You don't really believe that, do you?"

I grinned. "To an extent, yeah, I do. People know what they see and know what they feel. It's when they let their biases get in the way of interpreting the facts that there can be problems. But face it, other people's lives are interesting. Who said, 'The proper study of man is man?' There's drama all around. Who needs television?"

Breda was quiet for a minute, digesting this. Then she asked,

"Why did you ask if the Connollys had trouble when they owned that place?"

"Checking out a theory." I shrugged. "You know how you asked last night why a demon would stay under the bar, given all the ups and downs? Well, maybe it didn't at first. Maybe it just visited from time to time. But we're assuming it is trapped there now and that's why Casey is interested." It seemed weird to call him by name, but I couldn't quite bring myself to refer to Casey as Breda's father. "I can't think of any natural circumstance capable of trapping demon. I mean, they travel through dimensions; what's a little rockfall? So, despite my inherent skepticism, I think it must have been bound at some point. Probably the Connollys did it, because that would make Casey's hearing about it from his grandfather all the more likely. How long did Seamus live, anyway?"

"He died before I was born. In nineteen seventy, I think."

"Which would make Casey…?"

"Twenty."

I nodded. "Plenty of time to milk the old man for information. Anyway, if the Connollys bound the demon, their respective businesses would enjoy a period of quiet. Missy confirmed that this was, in fact, the case."

"Why just bind it? Why not drive it out?"

"Don't know. Maybe they didn't know how, though you'd think a magician able to bind a demon wouldn't find getting rid of one any great problem." I shrugged. "Maybe binding it was easier. Or maybe they didn't want a demon loose in Gordarosa, with no guarantee it wouldn't come back. Take your pick."

Breda thought about this. I was impressed by the way she had accepted the idea of a demon. Not without question, but without too much trouble. Lots of people wouldn't have. But lots of people didn't have Sean Casey for a father.

"Then why did the situation get worse again after the Connollys' time? Wouldn't it still have been bound?"

"Well, as to that I can only speculate. We don't know what happened to Archie, you remember."

"He's dead," she said bluntly. "With his brains spilling out."

I swallowed. "Yeah, that we know. But how?"

"Is that relevant?"

"I don't know. It could be. Whether it is or not, the first thing that comes to mind is that the binding was somehow tied in to the Connolly bloodline. So when Archie died, the bonds got weak. Not enough to free the demon altogether, but enough so some energy could leak back and forth. Thus, the bad mojo."

"But Seamus was still alive!" Breda protested. "Didn't his bloodline count?"

I would have taken a bet it did, but not in the way Breda imagined. There'd been rumors of a ghost before, but as far as I knew he'd never appeared until a person of his bloodline took over the pub. It followed, then, that Archie Connolly had some reason to want his family well out of it and had sought me out as the person most likely to keep them and the demon well apart.

"I'm betting the binding happened before he was born. Some types of magic are person-specific. You have to be initiated into the circle before you're part of it. Seamus left when he was only eighteen. Archie might not have considered him old enough. Or, he might have wanted to protect his brother." Or keep him out of it for other reasons altogether; actually, thinking back on what Missy had told us that seemed more likely. And if Seamus had known about the demon and resented the exclusion, he might well have considered it reason enough to abandon his family after the war.

"But that means if my father thinks he'll have some kind of hold over the demon because of his bloodline…."

"He's really, really wrong."

That, in my opinion, would have been a suitably dramatic end to the conversation, but Breda had other ideas.

"What did you mean, about not wanting to mess around with a demon to whom you hadn't been properly introduced?" she asked, surprising me.

I hesitated a minute, thinking how best to put it. Then I said, "Most people practice one of two kinds of magic. Ceremonial Magic and Folk Magic. They're at opposite ends of a spectrum and everything in between mixes them up in varying amounts." My own abilities fell into a third category with very little relationship to that spectrum, but why complicate matters?

"If they're at two ends of a spectrum, they're closer to each other than they seem." She gave me a naughty grin.

"For the purposes of this discussion, let's not go there. Ceremonial Magic relies on the codification of symbolic actions. For example, once someone used a particular incantation to raise a demon and it worked, so now that's the incantation everyone uses when trying to raise that demon. You with me?"

Breda nodded. "Or once someone used rose petals in an effective love spell and so now rose petals represent love."

I raised my eyebrows. "Very good. I can see you have a natural bent for this."

"It must run in the family."

We both giggled. I'm sure it was the stress getting to us. At least, I knew it was getting to me.

"Ceremonial Magic also relies on the people—or entities—on both sides of the equation sharing a consensual reality."

"The demon responded to the incantation, so now it agrees that it has to respond every time."

"Right again. In the case of your love spell, or something where there's not another entity involved, the codification of the symbol boosts the faith of the practitioner to a point where, the-oretically, the energy she expends can make the world respond to her desire. That's why they say faith works miracles. It's also why so many books on magic include huge tables of correspond-ences."

"I sense you have a problem with this."

"You sense right."

"The problem being…?"

"The problem being that I'm not the kind of person who can believe rose petals represent love just because it says so in some book. I have a questioning mind. I want to know why. And maybe rose petals don't represent love to me. Maybe some creep dumped me by sending me roses. Maybe violets represent love instead. So if I use rose petals in my love spell, I'm not thinking of love at all; I'm thinking about rejection.

"That's where Folk Magic comes in. Folk Magic is about personal relationships to things. In Folk Magic you have to un-derstand that. And you must go out of your way to make sure your relationship to the unseen world is a good one."

"How do you do that?"

"You read many fairy tales?"

She seemed shocked by the question. "The usual ones, I guess. Why?"

"Because fairy tales tell you how. What makes a good rela-tionship in any world? Kindness. Respect. Generosity. Industry. Patience. The fairies always reward people who show those qual-ities. The cruel, the disrespectful, the lazy, the hasty—they get punished. They don't win the princess; they get turned into stone. It's all about manners."

"And this is relevant to the demon because…?"

"Because people who practice Ceremonial Magic exclu-sively tend to lose track of their manners. They have the formu-lae; why should they care? They're like telemarketers calling you up during dinner. You may feel obliged to answer the phone, but you're not going to like it when you find out who's on the other end. They act like you owe them your attention, simply because they have your number. It may be the only way you can get rid of them is to do what they want. You may hang up, though, or you may get wise and stop answering.

"It's the same with otherworldly entities. They might answer when they get the call, but they won't cooperate willingly, and they'll cause trouble if they can, just because they find the intrusion so annoying. That's why using Ceremonial Magic has a reputation for being dangerous. People like to say it's because the mage wasn't powerful enough or he got the formula wrong. But really, it's because Ceremonial Magicians don't understand that the way they go about things is just plain rude. They don't show the proper respect."

"I see."

"Now, imagine the same dinnertime call coming from someone you know. She hates to bother you, she says, but she's really in a bind and could use your help. You'd feel differently, wouldn't you? That's how Folk Magic approaches the unseen world—not with demands but with requests; not as a stranger, but as a friend, or at least an acquaintance. And that's why I'd rather nobody approaches this demon without a proper introduction."

"Do you think Archie can give you one?"

I didn't answer. My mind balked at looking past the present moment. Talking about magic was fine, but I had a feeling communicating with Archie was going to take more than talk.

"Caitlin," she said into the silence. "I'm really sorry I came here the other day. Without a proper introduction."

"Oh, Breda." I reached across the table and patted her hand. It had been a long time since I'd had a woman friend I could really talk to. I didn't know where the friendship would go or whether it would last once the situation at the Emerald Isle had been dealt with once and for all. But for the moment, I was sitting on the porch drinking tea with a woman I liked immensely. "I'm not."

Chapter Ten

Timber strolled in at six o'clock, bearing a large sack of carry-out from the Chinese place in Murtaw, where he had spent the last couple of hours drinking beer with Curtis Richards' concrete crew. He had the blueprints, too, rolled up under one arm, but he wouldn't let us look at them for fear of their being stained with hot mustard and duck sauce.

"Curtis poured the cement for the in-floor heating system." Timber delved into the sack, producing carton after carton, which he arrayed on the dining room table while I scrambled after plates, condiments and serving utensils. "Do you take chopsticks, Breda, or shall Caitlin bring you a fork?"

"Sticks, please," I heard her reply, and I searched through the kitchen drawers for an extra pair. I brought forks as well; they were always useful for cornering the last few grains of rice. By the time I got back to the dining room, Breda and Timber were already seated. I passed out the plates and joined them.

My husband bowed his head. "Thanks be to everything here that gave its life to feed us, and blessings on the Chinese people for preparing it. So mote it be," he intoned.

"Mote it be," I mumbled in hasty response, ignoring Breda's quizzical look at our unusual form of saying grace. "Well?"

"I got Mu-Shu Pork, Lemon Chicken and House Special Chili Pepper Beef. I hope that'll suit. Then I couldn't decide between eggrolls and pot stickers, so I got both."

"Timber!"

My husband piled rice onto his plate with an unrepentant grin. "Well, they had a bit of a go-round about the job, it seems. Curtis almost walked off when Brett—the general, you remember—handed him a schematic for the rebar."

I paused in the middle of ladling lemon sauce over my chicken. "A schematic for the rebar?"

"Curtis was rather put out about it." Timber nodded. "It was a complex pattern, and he hadn't allowed for the extra man-hours to follow it in his bid."

"But he did it?"

"Oh, aye. He drew up a change order and charged an extra couple of grand. Now he has a new favorite story about the strange whims driving wealthy property owners." Timber dipped an eggroll in hot mustard, bit, and chewed meditatively. "He said it was pretty, for all it was a pain in the arse to do. Lots of curves and spirals."

"That's interesting."

"So it is."

"Excuse me. What?"

I looked up; I had almost forgotten Breda's presence.

"Sorry. Didn't mean to leave you out of the loop. You know what rebar is?"

"Some kind of construction material, I gather." She studied her plate with an artist's eye. She had taken a little bit of everything and arranged it in sculpted mounds, with space around each item. As I watched, she added a miniscule dab of chili beef to an empty spot and squared the edges of her portion with her chopsticks.

"It's metal," Timber explained. "Or, metal rods, to be more specific. They're used to add structural integrity, especially when you're pouring a great deal of cement. Cement's hard, ken, but it's brittle. The more of it you have, the more likely it is to crack unless you put in something to reinforce it. So before you pour a floor, you lay rebar. Usually in a grid pattern."

"But my father wanted it in spirals and curves?"

"That's right."

"So what's the problem?"

"It's not a problem per se." I nibbled at my third pot sticker. "But it's interesting because spirals and curves are natural channels for magical energy, and because Jake, who designed the remodel, studied magical architecture. I've been wondering when we'd come back to that. I presume it was Jake's design?"

"Curtis didn't say."

"Magical energy in the floor," I mused. "That certainly supports the demon in the cellar theory. Is there a cellar?"

Timber shoved half a pancake loaded with Mu-Shu into his mouth and swallowed hastily. I was surprised he didn't choke. "I asked. Curtis said if there ever had been there wasn't one now."

So much for that bright idea. Oh well. As I'd told Breda, it was a long shot.

I filled Timber in on our excursion to the Historical Museum. He expressed a suitable level of interest at the news that we had confirmed Breda's relationship to Archie Connolly, but I didn't think he was the least bit surprised. He seemed much more concerned at the evidence that James and Archie might have bound some kind of demon to the site of their family business, and his reasons were much the same as mine.

"It's not really the way of it," he said, "to bind something when you can be rid of it, unless you get something from the binding. I wonder why they didn't lay the bastard?"

"Maybe they couldn't find a suit of clothes big enough," I submitted wryly. I couldn't help but notice that everyone now spoke as if the demon beneath the Emerald Isle were more than a mere supposition.

Timber laughed. "Aye, or maybe brewing in eggshells didn't impress it. Common folk methods for getting rid of something you don't want in your house," he added to Breda.

"That's a tangent I actually was able to follow." She had worked her way through all her little mounds of food; now she pushed her plate away. "I've read 'The Shoemaker and the Elves.' But the question isn't really why the Connollys didn't get rid of it. The question is, how are *you* going to?"

In answer, magic surged through me like a riptide threatening to drag me out to a stormy sea. I gasped at the sudden rush of power. A voice deep in my heart whispered, *Yes. Let go. This is how it should be.*

"What is it?" Breda's voice reverberated as though it came from under deep water, a great distance away.

The room pulsed around me. Senses heightened, I could see every detail. I marveled at the texture of the oak grain of our dining room table, at the intricacy of a fork's tines. Even the grains of rice on my plate seemed like living things to me. Timber's and Breda's faces glowed. In that moment, I had never seen anything so beautiful.

"Aye, love," Timber breathed, the words fraught with layer upon layer of meaning. "That's the way."

I wanted to sing or dance. I wanted to laugh and cry, both at the same time. I wanted to shout in ecstasy at this wonderful, wonderful gift.

I knew I could do anything I wanted, anything at all. No demon was a match for me. My hands crackled as I reached across the table for my husband, to gather him to me and tell him yes, this was life. To tell him he had been right. I saw his eyes gleaming with anticipation.

Then I saw it again: The hill with its shining, unfamiliar figure. The path to the fire, and the path to safety. The choice. *With divine power...* said the figure on the hill, and showed me the consequences.

My head spun with senseless images. I rocked with magic I could not control. My throat burned, screaming. And then:

Long, windowless, beige walls stretched away to a locked door in the far distance. I shuffled toward them on heavy feet, stolid and uncaring. Dim and dull-witted, moving because I had no will left to sit down and stop.

A small voice in my head said, *No*.

I began to struggle. It took all the strength of my will to push the magic away, but I did it, little by little. I pictured myself fighting against the tide that wanted to drown me, pulling towards shore. As it grew closer in my mind, the ecstasy receded. My sensed dimmed to their usual level. Part of me cried at leaving the wild ocean behind, but the rest felt only relief. I had beaten Fate, this time.

The world tilted. For a minute I thought it would shatter around me, but then all the pieces fell into place and I came to myself, sitting at the dining room table, my body all mucky with sweat and my face wet with tears.

Timber, who had been leaning towards me, jerked away as if I had slapped him. He threw his napkin on the table and stood up, all but knocking his chair over.

"If that's how ye want it, then," he said as he stalked out of the room. Soon I heard the back door slam shut behind him. I closed my eyes.

"What was that?" I heard Breda say. "What was that about?"

"Dinner's over," was my only reply.

Timber was singing in the downstairs shower. His clear baritone filled the house with the martial strains of "Donald MacGillavry," broken by the occasional swear word when he got soap in his eye. A comforting, normal sound—if you didn't know, as I did, that he only sang that song when distressed.

I popped into the upstairs shower to rinse off the sweat left over from my dinnertime struggle, wishing I could wash away the rest of my problems so easily. When I emerged, wrapped in a towel, I found Breda waiting for me in the hall. She had a hard time meeting my eyes. I knew right away that Timber's outburst had made her very uncomfortable. She didn't understand what had caused it or why I hadn't reacted differently, and I couldn't tell her without explaining things I didn't want to explain. Embarrassment poured off her, almost thick enough to touch. She needed distraction.

"Come on." Taking her by the arm, I steered her into the bedroom. "That's my closet on the right." I nodded towards it and sat down at the oak vanity I had salvaged from a dumpster in Boulder; it always astounded me what some college kids chose to throw away rather than move. I dropped my towel. "Pick me out something to wear, will you?"

She opened the bi-fold door and peered inside without much interest. Then her jaw dropped and her eyes lit up.

"Holy Cow!"

I grinned into the mirror. Most of what the band made went into expenses: travel, equipment and so on. But we split what was left, and I put almost all of my share into extravagant costumes to wear on stage. Hung side by side in the closet were a dozen such outfits, ranging from a green silk slip dress I had purchased in a moment of weakness though it showed rather more skin than I liked, to an Elizabethan fantasy of burgundy velvet and lace, complete with stomacher and train, that I donned once a year for the SCA Christmas banquet in Grand Junction.

Breda's fingers lingered on the slip dress.

"Not that."

"Why not? You have the figure for it."

Truly, I thought there was quite a bit more of my figure than a dress like that could cope with, but I didn't say so. "I may have to confront your father about the contract. I don't want him looking down my dress while I'm doing it."

She smirked. "It might be a useful distraction."

She had a point. "All right then." I yanked open the central vanity drawer, pulled out concealer, eyeliner and shadow and began putting on my makeup, Breda watching over my shoulder.

"You know, Caitlin," she said. "You're really quite attractive. I don't understand why you don't pay more attention to your appearance…"

"Instead of going about in skanky t-shirts and jeans and generally looking like a frowsy old farm-wife, you mean?" I glanced over my shoulder at the dress, chose blush in a pale shade of peach, and applied it to my cheeks with a gigantic brush. "Because, in case you haven't noticed, in my real life I spend most of my time grubbing in the garden plot and mucking around in the ditch. I suppose the tomato worms might actually appreciate a glimpse of my radiant beauty as their last sight on earth, but I don't often take their feelings into account."

"But you've got some great clothes here!"

"They don't exactly constitute daywear in Gordarosa. Do you know, I heard of a singer in Glenwood who wrote her entire stage wardrobe off on her taxes, because she couldn't use any of it except when she was working? The IRS sent someone to examine her closet, but he finally agreed with her."

Breda scowled at me. I puckered and put on peach lipstick.

"I used to put on makeup every morning," I went on after blotting. "Then I decided I'd rather sleep in the extra ten minutes."

"Don't you enjoy looking nice?"

"Sure I do. For about as long as it takes to get through a gig. Then I start feeling itchy. Inevitably, I rub my eyes and smear goop all over my face. Or my nice clothes get tight and scratchy and it's about all I can do not to rip them off and run down the street naked."

"Really. And what does Timber think of that impulse?"

"None of your business." I turned away so she couldn't see the color rising in my face. There had been one memorable occasion at a Beltane gathering in Boulder…but nearly everyone had been naked there, so I didn't stand out.

I got up, retrieved bra and a pair of cotton panties from my dresser drawer and put them on. "Right. Let's have it."

"You can't wear a bra with that."

I rolled my eyes, unfastened my bra and threw it on the bed.

The silk slid smooth and cool over my skin, which showed just as much as I remembered. I tugged at the front of the dress.

"Don't do that!" Breda scolded, and smoothed the plunging neckline back into place. "You look wonderful. Quite otherworldly."

"Just what I need," I muttered, wanting no more reminders of any other worlds to interfere with the rest of my evening.

"You need to do something with your hair, though."

"No one can do anything with my hair," I protested. But I let her sit me back down in front of the mirror and, at her instruction, produced a curling iron, brush, comb and hairspray from a bottom drawer. In less time than I would have thought possible Breda had the whole, waist-length auburn mass pinned in fetching curls up on the top of my head, leaving only a few coy strands trailing down the back of my neck.

"I look like a ho."

"You look fine. Jewelry."

I donned the amber and sterling set—choker, earrings, and bracelet—that Timber had given me for our last anniversary, and Breda declared me fit for consumption. And a good thing, too, for at that moment my husband started pounding on the bedroom door.

"Caitlin! It's a quarter to eight, and I'm naked!"

From the sound of his voice he was still mad at me. He seemed to forget it when he saw me, though. He nearly dropped the towel he had draped around his hips. That was kind of gratifying.

"I think I'd better go, now," Breda said.

"You're not coming to the gig?" Actually, I felt more relieved than disappointed. Breda and I had been in each other's company for almost twenty-four hours straight. I rarely even spent that much time with my husband, and I was beginning to feel the need for some space.

"I told you, I'm not into traditional music much. I think I'll go back to my hotel and catch a nap. But I could come by later to look at the blueprints."

The blueprints! I had forgotten all about them.

"Not tonight." Timber emerged from his closet, wearing his black leather trousers and the laced Jacobean shirt I'd embroidered for our wedding.

"But, Timber, we really need…."

"Not tonight," he repeated. "In the morning. Goodnight, Breda." He pushed her out through the bedroom door and shut it firmly in her face. She had the gall to giggle loudly before tripping away down the stairs.

"Timber, it is important that we look at the blueprints."

He stalked towards me. I backed up. He came closer. I tried to squirm away, but found his arms on either side of me, pinning me to the wall. My breath began to come short. I couldn't tell whether he was about to strangle me or kiss me. Just to be on the safe side, I decided on the former.

"Timber, please forgive me," I began. "I know it must be even harder for you than it is for me…"

He hushed me with a finger to my lips.

"There's nothing to forgive. Have I told you lately that you're beautiful?" he murmured into my neck. "The blueprints will still be there tomorrow. Everything will still be there tomorrow. Tonight, I want you to myself."

The words reassured me and I wound my arms about his strong body. Still, I couldn't help but wonder how long he'd continue to put up with my refusal to use magic—especially now that a demon seemed to be involved.

Unfortunately, we had a job to do before the happy interlude of Timber's desire could take place. Fifteen minutes later we were pulling up to the loading dock at the back entrance of the Emerald Isle. Once again, Frank and Lisa's green Subaru was already parked in the alley. Dared I hope punctuality was getting to be a habit with them? Maybe something good would come out of this situation after all.

I found Lisa in the usual back booth running through some scales—another wonder.

"Hey, Caitlin." The look she cast me over the bridge of her fiddle might have quick-frozen several circles of Hell. She was wearing a tight pink sheath and turquoise pumps; I hoped we wouldn't clash on stage. Her lip curled. "Nice dress."

I dropped my gig bag on the edge of the stage, wondering if I had time to go home and change.

"Wow, Caitlin!" Frank popped up from behind an amplifier. "You look stunning!"

The ice cube Lisa had force fed me melted in a flash flood of comprehension. Of course, Lisa was used to being the cute one. It probably irked her no end that tonight I looked better.

"Did you see Casey about the contract yet?"

"I'm on my way up there now." I pulled the document in question out of my bag, telling myself that I wasn't exactly lying. I was going to see Casey about the contract. I just had no intention of signing it. I still had no idea what excuse I'd give him, but, as Timber kept reminding me, I had a brilliant mind. Plus,

I had a keen gift for improvisation. I'd think of something. Either that, or I'd keep Casey looking down my dress until he drooled and passed out. That would buy me another day, anyway. And if Fate favored me, Timber would catch Casey ogling me and be forced to kill him, thus bypassing the whole issue.

I sighed. I should be so lucky.

When I went upstairs, however, Casey wasn't there. I forced myself to knock on his office door three times to be sure, but no one answered. I skipped downstairs feeling much lighter in my heart.

"Where's your boss?" I asked the bartender, more because I felt obliged to cover all my bases than because I really wanted to know.

He shrugged. "Haven't seen him tonight."

"Will he be in later?"

"Don't know. Maybe not. He doesn't always show up."

"Really?" You could have fooled me. Every time I'd been in the bar, Casey had been lurking around somewhere. I almost suspected he lived there.

"It's not like we need him. The place practically runs itself. You know, like magic. You want a pitcher of water back there, right?"

I ignored the reference to magic, told him we did want water, and made my way back to the rear room rejoicing over my reprieve. As I passed through the archway under the balcony, a deafening crash, as of several large metal objects and at least one body being tossed down a flight of stairs, resounded from the area of the stage. Over the dying echoes came the sound of my husband's voice, cursing aggressively in Gaelic. I ran up to find him sprawled on the floor behind the stage, buried in microphone stands. There was no blood, for which I was thankful. For a different reason altogether, I blessed the fact that Timber had not chosen to wear his kilt for the evening's performance.

"Bloody feckin' Hell, Frank!" he bellowed, picking himself up. His accent grew more pronounced with his irritation. "Why did ye string the power cords tae the back?"

I pulled my mind away from the interesting picture of Timber with his kilt up around his ears and looked at the site of my husband's misfortune. I had always found it a little bit odd that the stage was not flush with the rear wall, but stood out from it about three feet, making a kind of narrow corridor. Now I saw that, instead of being plugged into the outlets set into the rear of the stage as they usually were, the power cords for our PA and various amplifiers were strung across the gap and plugged into wall outlets. Apparently Timber had crossed behind the stage without looking and tripped over one of the cords.

Frank bustled over from the back booth, beer foam glistening on his upper lip.

"The stage outlets don't work," he explained, running a hand through his untidy black hair.

"Well why did ye no tape the cords down then? I could hae broken my neck, aye?"

Frank shrugged; either he hadn't thought of it or, more likely, the roll of duct tape that should be part of every working musician's gear had been commandeered for something at home and never found its way back to his gig bag.

"Wait a minute," I said as Timber rummaged in his own bag for his own roll of tape, still muttering. "What's wrong with the stage outlets? They worked yesterday, didn't they?"

My husband paused and flashed a lethal look in our bandmate's direction.

"Did ye no check the breaker box?"

"I don't know where it is."

Timber stalked to a metal panel set in the wall next to the back door. "It's right here," he growled, adding something under his breath that might have been, "you idjit." He opened the panel, studied the row of switches for a minute, and flipped one. "Try it now."

As Frank seemed incapacitated by the entire situation, I unplugged an amp cord from the back wall, plugged it into the stage, and turned on the power to the appropriate amp. Red lights glowed.

"Works."

Without another word, Timber returned to the stage area and set about re-stringing all the cords. Frank hesitated, then began to help; to his credit, he looked a little sheepish. I retreated to the back booth to assemble my flute and whistles. I wasn't sure how long the truce between the two male members of Red Branch would hold, and I didn't want to be near if and when it broke. Pretty soon, though, I heard the two of them laughing about something or other, the best of friends again. Guys. Sometimes you couldn't do anything but accept them. Still, I breathed a sigh of relief. *Please gods*, I prayed, *let there be no more crises tonight*.

For a while it seemed as though the gods had heard my prayer and, in a fit of perversity, decided to give me a break. The gig was another unusually good one, played to another packed house. No one threw bottles at us because we weren't playing rock 'n' roll, and no fights broke out—both of which had been known to happen even in venues without demons and ghosts. I was thankful, but I couldn't help wondering at the change in the place. Aside from hearing disembodied voices once or twice and seeing Archie Connolly walk through a wall, I had experienced nothing at the Emerald Isle that I would have expected from a site with such a peculiar reputation. It just didn't make sense. It especially didn't make sense if my theory about the presence of a demon, and Sean Casey's involvement with it, were correct. The disturbances should have been getting worse, not better. Yet to all outward appearances, the new Emerald Isle was just what Casey claimed: a pub in the old meaning of the word, a social center for the community, a place, in fact, where the whole family could enjoy an evening out without papa worrying that the kids would get robbed, stabbed, or propositioned. In short, not at all the sort of place convivial to a demon.

Our second set of the evening ended with one of my ballads, "The Unquiet Grave." I smiled wryly as I stepped up to the mic; there couldn't have been a song more appropriate to this particular venue.

"Cold blows the wind on my true love
and bitter falls the rain
I only had but one true love
in the Greenwood he lies slain…"

I began, enjoying the way the audience hushed as the plaintive tones of the lament soared out over the house.

"I'll do as much for my true love
as any young girl may,
I'll sit and mourn all on his grave
for twelve months and a day…"

The Emerald Isle might not be Archie Connolly's literal grave, but no one could deny its unquiet nature. Scratch that. At one time, no one would have denied it. Right now, however, an almost palpable stillness filled the place to the rafters, and it wasn't all a response to my singing. I had the sense of some great beast holding its breath: a whale in the moment before breaching, a mammoth in the tangled shade of some prehistoric jungle—waiting, waiting…

Waiting for what?

"When twelve months and a day was passed,
The Ghost did rise and speak…"

If only Archie *would* speak! He was probably the one person in town, aside from Sean Casey, who knew what was really going on. His spectral appearances and visits to my dreams might be an attempt to communicate, but he wasn't using any language I understood. And unlike the girl in the song, I didn't relish the notion of sitting here for twelve months and a day waiting for him to make sense.

I left the stage to thunderous applause and headed for the bathroom, still puzzling over the matter in my mind. At the sink, I ran cold water over my wrists to wash away the lingering heat from the stage. I would have splashed my face, but I didn't want to ruin my makeup. The wrist treatment wasn't as effective as I had hoped it would be, so I bent my head over the tap, searching for the pocket of cool that the water made.

When I straightened up, Archie's face hung in the mirror just behind my left shoulder. His mouth moved in little spasmodic jerks, like a dying fish.

My first, irrational thought was that he wasn't as old as I had thought him at first. If his disappearance had been due to his death, he would only have been forty-three at the time—not ten years older than my age now. Of course, in those days fifty was old. And some colors of hair did go grey early. And the smashed side of his head didn't make him look any younger.

Then I came to myself and realized that I was angry.

"Make sense, damn you!" I snapped. "What is it you want, you wee bastard? What are you trying to tell me?"

I whirled around to face him…and nearly collided with Lisa, who had just come through the door.

"Talking to yourself, I see," she commented, not without humor. "It happens to the best of us."

Archie floated behind her. His shattered mouth was still trying to shape words, and he was pointing at something. Pointing down. I opened my mouth to demand his meaning. But Lisa was standing there. I couldn't say anything in front of her, and besides, I already knew Archie couldn't answer.

"Caitlin?" I must have looked very odd, for Lisa's voice actually held a real note of concern. "Are you all right?"

Then I felt it, a thickening of the air like you feel during a storm just before the lightning strikes and after, when you hold your breath waiting for the thunder. The pressure built in my head and I squeezed my eyes tight shut to contain it.

It broke, all at once—not like a dam bursting, that starts with a trickle of water through a weak spot that gets wider and softer until the dam crumbles in a rush of mud and water, but like a gas main exploding when a match is struck in a perfectly quiet house, where there's been no hint of anything amiss. Or like a bird falling out the sky: one minute it's flying, the next it's there, dead at your feet. Or like…. I really can't say what it was like. I think I screamed, but I couldn't hear myself over the sudden clamor in my head. A horrible cry filled my senses, the psychic equivalent of a jet taking off next door, or of a Who concert.

And at the same time, the voice I had heard the first time I had stepped through the doors chimed in:

"… *HELP… PLEASE… PLEASE…HELP…NOW!*" Archie's mouth twisted into a rictus of pain and grief.

The first shock passed. Lisa was staring at me, her mouth wide. Had she felt it? She'd never given the slightest indication that she might be aware of anything beyond Mundane reality, but it had been so loud.

She clutched at my arm. "Caitlin…what…?"

She didn't have time for any more. At that moment a second wave more violent than the first rolled over the Emerald Isle. The voice in my head gave a great shout of wordless exultation. Archie sank out of sight as if pulled from beneath. My ears filled with the grinding sound of straining stone and twisting metal. Under my feet, the floor bucked and shook like a spooked horse.

And then I was falling.

Chapter Eleven

I grabbed at Lisa. Lisa grabbed at me. I heard the sound of cloth tearing and hoped it wasn't my dress. We hit the ground tangled in each other's arms and lay there while the floor continued its epileptic convulsions under us. I had some notion that during a seismic event one should run outside, or, if escape proved impossible, shelter in a doorway, but I couldn't make myself move. There's something surreal and terrible about having the ground shake under you. Under normal circumstances it's so stationary, so solid; your brain just can't wrap itself around the fact that what you're experiencing is real. As long as the shaking continues, you're in some other dimension outside time, where the rules you know no longer apply and anything can happen. Anything at all. All you can do is hold on and hope you're still alive when it's over.

That's what Lisa and I did. It seemed to go on forever. One of us was whimpering like a hurt puppy; I thought it was Lisa, but I couldn't swear to it. It may have been me, because just as I decided to slap her to make her shut up, the sound stopped.

All this time, the huge, hollow voice had been singing in my brain, a wordless, rhythmic chant on a rising note, like a prisoner on a chain gang straining against his bonds. Now the voice gave one last scream, filling me with an overwhelming sense of failure and futility, and died to nothing. Not much later, the shaking stopped, too. I held still for a minute, waiting for it to start again. It didn't.

"I think it's over," I said.

"Are you all right?" For just a second, Lisa sounded concerned. Then she seemed to realize she was lying on the floor, wrapped in the arms of another woman, and sat up with a jerk, like a marionette the puppeteer had just remembered. Her pink dress gaped open, torn down one seam. Thank gods, not my silk, I thought irrationally.

"Gawd, Caitlin, what's got into you?" she snapped.

"What?" I asked, mystified.

"You grab me and hurl me down to the floor, you roll around on the ground crying…I thought you were having some kind of fit!"

"You…you didn't feel it?"

"Feel what? Shit, my dress!" Lisa's slender fingers fluttered over the yawning seam. "I can't go back out there like this!"

"It's okay. I've got a sewing kit in my gig bag. Give it here; I'll fix it," I said, woodenly. It hadn't been an earthquake at all. It had all been in my head.

Lisa got to her feet and retreated to a stall. I heard the sound of a zipper, and the pink dress floated over the stall door, landing at my feet.

"I'll be right back." I glanced around the bathroom. For all appearances, nothing at all had happened there. I saw no cracked tiles, no doors hanging off their hinges, not even a fall of dust. I should have found that reassuring. I didn't.

Nothing seemed to have happened in the bar proper, either. All the patrons were laughing and chatting, and swilling beer just as usual. I saw Frank by the stage, signing a CD for a fan. Timber stood near him, tense and watchful. When he spotted me, he hurried to my side, and together we made our way towards our usual booth in the back.

"Caitlin! Thank all the gods," he whispered, laying a hand on my elbow. "Did ye feel that? Are ye all right?"

I nodded, glad to have some confirmation that I was not crazy. Not yet. "What was it for you?"

"A strike on the biggest drumhead in the world," he told me. "A cable snapping and lashing. A sound like thunder that went on forever."

"You're lucky. I got an earthquake. Did it affect anyone out here?"

He shook his head. "Not that I saw. But I nearly passed out, ken, so I wasna paying the closest attention."

"I grabbed Lisa. She thought I was having a seizure. Then she got mad at me."

"Typical. Where is she?"

"I left her in the bathroom." I brandished the dress and noticed that the hand holding it trembled. I might pretend calm, but the psychic storm had shaken me. "We've had a slight wardrobe malfunction. And that's not all."

As I made hasty repairs to Lisa's seam, I told him about Archie's appearance and the voice I had heard. After hearing me out, he was quiet for a time. Then he said,

"The demon speaks."

"I think so. I think we just felt it trying to break free." I bit off the thread and stowed my sewing kit back in my gig bag. "I wonder if it had help."

"Casey?"

"Who else? It would explain Archie, and he's not around. He hasn't been here all night."

With that grim pronouncement, I shook out the pink dress and went to roust Lisa out of the bathroom. All I wanted was to finish the set and go home.

The next morning I was jolted awake by something landing on my stomach. I knew at once that the something was not a cat; it was too small. Another something landed, and another. I opened my eyes. For a minute I couldn't make sense of what I saw. It seemed like a series of small stones flying through the open window. I watched as two more sailed across the bed and landed on Timber's chest. He woke with a grunt.

"What…? Shite, it's Breda, isn't it?"

"Oh…." I groaned, dragging myself upright. The room spun, and I put my head between my knees just in time to duck another shower of gravel. Regaining my equilibrium, I hauled myself over to the window and poked my head out.

"Knock it off!" I snarled. Breda paused in mid-throw. Her outfit today was rock-climbing chic: black tank top, khaki cargo shorts and light hikers, with her hair swept back into a perky ponytail. "What's with the movie tactics, anyway? Didn't your mother ever teach you to knock?"

"I tried knocking. I rang the bell, too. I called both your cell and your landline before I came over. Why didn't you answer? "

"Maybe because we were asleep." We'd unplugged the phone in the hall before falling into bed, and I'd left my cell downstairs to prevent just this kind of intrusion.

"You were?" She seemed truly mystified. "I've been up for hours."

You weren't playing a gig in a haunted pub until two in the morning, I thought. "What are you doing here?"

"Timber said to come back in the morning to look at the blueprints."

The blueprints. Right. We did, in fact, need to look at the blueprints. "Oh, all right. We'll be down in a second."

I withdrew my head from the window. Timber had managed to get out of bed and pull on a pair of sweats, but had apparently lost momentum soon after; he stood by the bedroom door, a vague expression on his face.

"Breda's here," I announced unnecessarily. "To look at the blueprints."

"Aye," he said, sliding to one side. Then he jerked upright. He had been asleep. "Aye," he repeated with a little more force. "I'll make coffee."

He set off down the stairs. I hoped he'd arrive in the kitchen without incident. A few vague minutes of my own later I pulled an old blue cotton sundress over my head—it seemed the easiest thing as it involved no zippers or buttons—wrestled my hair, still stiff with spray, into a braid and followed.

Breda was waiting at the front door.

"There's a dead rodent on your porch," she informed me when I opened it.

I peered past her to the disemboweled vole one of the cats had left on the doormat. On cue, McGuyver appeared and started batting at it.

"Lovely." I beckoned Breda inside.

"You look terrible," she commented helpfully as she bounced into the kitchen. Her eyes fell on Timber, who leaned on the counter, his eyes fixed on the coffee maker as though he could hurry it through its paces by force of will. "Both of you do. Rough night?"

"You could say so. You didn't happen to notice an earthquake at about eleven o'clock, did you?"

"An earthquake? No! Why?"

"I didn't think so." I told her about it. "No one in the bar experienced it but Timber and me. Or no one seemed to. But there may have been an effect all the same. They kept us playing until a quarter of two. They've never done that before, and I don't believe in coincidence." And Timber and I had been too tired afterward to indulge in any marital bliss. I growled to myself.

"What do you think caused it?"

"I think your father tried to loose his demon. I think he failed. Good thing for all of us."

A protracted silence fell.

"Coffee?" Timber offered with forced cheer.

"Yes, please."

Breda shook her head. "I've had some, thanks. Then it's even more important for us to locate Archie's cellar. Let's have the blueprints, Timber."

He retrieved the blueprints from the dining room hutch, where he had stashed them the evening before, and spread them on the kitchen table, weighting the edges with our coffee cups. For a long time we studied in silence. There was nothing. The curve of the bar, the curve of the stair, the kitchen, the stage—everything was just as Timber and I saw it each night Red Branch played. No mystical sigil indicated access to a demon. No red "X" showed where a door or secret passage was hidden. Not on the ground floor, not upstairs. Nothing, nothing, nothing. Even the design didn't look particularly mystical.

Or so it seemed to me. Breda had other ideas, though.

"Caitlin," she said, "you mentioned that Archie's ghost keeps walking through a wall?"

"Yeah. I've seen him do it twice. Three times, if you count a dream."

"Which wall?"

I pointed to a space on the blueprints, between the rear kitchen exit and the booth reserved for the band. "Right there. There used to be a door there; I saw it in one of the photos at the Historical Museum."

"What's on the other side?"

"Nothing." I shrugged. "A vacant lot. And a storm cellar, but that's been gone since the fifties or so. Besides, Missy told me the cellar was examined thoroughly, many times, and no one found anything strange about it."

Breda gave her head an impatient shake. "Not then. Now. What's there now, on the other side of that wall?"

"Western Realty." I glanced at my husband, baffled, but Timber didn't seem to be paying attention. As a matter of fact his eyes were closed and his mouth hung open, emitting soft snoring sounds.

"Then that must be it."

"That must be what?"

"The real estate office. Don't you see? The entrance to the cellar must have been in the empty lot. They built the real estate office right on top of it. That's what Archie's trying to show you by walking through that wall. To get to the cellar you have to start from next door!"

"Whoa there!" She looked so excited that I hated to burst her bubble, but I could see several problems with her theory. "In the first place there's a much simpler explanation for Archie walking through that wall. In his time, there was a door. He's used to walking through it. He has no reason to stop now there is no door, because he's dead and that kind of thing doesn't make a difference to ghosts."

Breda frowned.

"In the second place, even if the entrance was out in the lot at one time, why should it be there now? It might have been paved over. Or it might never have been found. The secret cellar is a local legend; if the people who built the real estate office had discovered it, it would be a huge deal. Everyone would know." And some enterprising Gordarosan would be giving conducted tours, and selling little cups of chicken blood to feed the demon, no doubt.

"They might not have told."

"Why not? Unless they knew about the demon in advance, there'd be no reason not to. And if they knew about the demon, or found out about it, the only reason to keep the secret would be that they wanted the demon to themselves. I don't always like real estate agents, but I can't quite bring myself to think Western Realty houses a whole nest of demon worshippers."

"They don't all have to be part of it. Maybe it's just a select few."

"Maybe," I conceded. Actually, when I thought about some of the people who worked there, the idea didn't seem so far-fetched. "But in the last place, even granting everything else, how would your father get access to the cellar in the dead of night when, supposedly, he conducts his demon-raising activity? Does he break in, or did someone give him a key?"

"Maybe he has some sort of understanding with the real estate people. It's kind of his demon, after all. It's on his property and his family discovered it. Maybe they even sent for him. I told you he has something of a reputation in arcane circles."

"I don't buy it." In my experience, ceremonial types were very possessive of their peculiar knowledge and rituals. Sharing wasn't likely.

"I don't know, Caitlin!" Her eyes blazed at me. "But it's an idea, and I think it's worth checking out. You're not the only one who can have ideas, you know."

Breda did have a point. It was an idea, and it was worth checking out, especially since for once I had come up blank in the idea department. Besides, what else was I going to do with my Saturday? Sleep?

"Okay. Let's go." I gulped the last of my coffee, got up and thrust my empty mug towards the sink. Another day on a single caffeine infusion loomed in my mind, and the picture didn't delight me. The evil thought flashed through my head that putting up with me in the state I would be in before much longer was no more than Breda deserved for getting me out of bed in the first place.

She seemed surprised at my sudden energy. "What, now? I thought we'd wait until night."

"And break in? Well, it may come to that, but I certainly don't want to do it without taking a look around first. That's much easier when the office is actually open."

"On Saturday?"

"This is Western Colorado. Real estate offices are always open." I nudged my sleeping husband, who roused and stared at me from red-rimmed eyes. "Timber. Go back to bed. I'll be back in a couple of hours."

He started to toddle off, but paused in the kitchen door. "Where are you going?"

I grimaced. Breda was already out the door, so she couldn't see my expression or hear the skepticism in my voice.

"I'm taking Breda to look for a house."

Western Realty was one of the older buildings in downtown Gordarosa, meaning that it had been standing for fifty years. Like most buildings downtown, Western Realty was snuggled in cheek by jowl with its neighbors, the Emerald Isle on one side and a lawyer's office where I had once worked for a few months on the other. Unlike most buildings downtown, it had never been used for any other purpose. It nearly went bankrupt during the mine closures of the eighties, but with typical western tenacity managed to hang on and now, with the Colorado housing boom in full swing, it employed half a dozen full time agents and as many secretaries, making it one of the biggest small businesses in town. Prosperity, as it often does, brought change; the building had undergone a facelift in recent years. The façade was newly stuccoed in a deep Santa Fe red, and a bright teal awning shaded the front window, where pictures of the properties Western Realty's agents had listed were displayed. In a side window, beneath the usual flyers for upcoming local events, a flat screen computer monitor flashed a never-ending digital slideshow of featured listings. Breda watched the show with interest.

"There certainly is a selection, isn't there?"

I read the price of one three-acre parcel and shuddered, remembering what I had paid for my five acres and farmhouse half a dozen years before. Some people would be pleased as punch to find their homes had risen so much in value. I couldn't help but feel that the constant increase was somehow immoral.

"It's the summer sport in these parts," I said. "People put their houses on the market, usually for outrageous prices, hoping some tourist will fall in love and make them rich." Some did. Most of them got bored with rural life after a year or two and moved on, but not before putting their recently purchased homes on the market for much more than they had paid for them. That encouraged locals to ask similar prices, and the cycle continued.

"The prices seem reasonable to me."

"You're from New York City," I pointed out. "Any real estate price under five million dollars would probably seem reasonable to you."

Inside, I stepped up to the reception desk while Breda examined the tiny lobby and picked up half a dozen free guides to Western Colorado real estate. She couldn't be serious, could she? As much as I liked her, I couldn't help feeling dismay at the thought. She was clearly a city girl. She might think herself ready for a change in her living situation, but Gordarosa would bore her to tears. Sure, life was exciting now, but….

"May I help you?" A motherly woman sporting grey pin curls and horn rimmed glasses popped up from behind the chest-high counter. "Oh, Ms. Ross! Good to see you!"

I had no idea of her name, but the fact that she knew me caused me no surprise. I had been given to understand that Timber and I stood out in a crowd.

"Is Debra in?"

"I'll check."

The receptionist spoke into a phone. "She'll be right up, Ms. Ross."

"Right up" in Gordarosa could mean anything from five minutes to half an hour, so I settled myself into a chair to wait. However, Debra appeared in a record time of thirty seconds, causing me to pop right back up again.

"Caitlin! How nice to see you!" She plunged around the edge of the reception desk and gave my hand a vigorous squeeze. Bouncy and blond, Debra Montaine was a woman of diminutive stature; the top of her head didn't quite come up to my chin. Like many small things, she was in a state of constant motion and her boundless energy put me in mind of a gerbil or a ferret. "How's your garden doing?"

It always discomfited me somewhat that, although I was ostensibly a professional musician, everyone in town completely ignored the fact in favor of asking about my garden. I had won a couple of ribbons at the county fair and I sometimes packaged up excess herbs and vegetables for sale at the local farmers' market, so maybe that explained it. But I couldn't help wondering if they declined to speak about my band because we were so bad.

"It's coming along. A little wilted; it's been so dry. And we don't have ditch shares, you know."

"Doesn't your place have a well?"

"It does, but with the drought it hasn't been putting out so much. I don't like to overtax it."

"We sure could use some rain. The weatherman from Junction says there's front moving in from Utah." The necessary summer subjects of water and weather thus dispensed with, Debra moved on to business. "So, what can I do for you?"

I shoved Breda forward. "This is my friend, Breda Ni Fhearraigh. She's new to the area and she's thinking about settling down." Again, I hoped she wasn't really. But the roles we were playing had to be convincing. "Breda, this is Debra Montaine. She sold me my house."

Debra's hazel eyes flashed over Breda. They must have seen something to indicate the presence of money, for Debra's mouth widened in an avaricious smile. Maybe it was the hiking boots. Those things don't come cheap.

"So very pleased to meet you, Breda," Debra gushed. "Won't you come back to my office?"

She led us down a narrow, white hallway with interior windows punctuating the walls at intervals on either side. Most of the windows were covered by mini blinds, but some were unobstructed and the inhabitants of the offices could be seen talking on phones, bending over desks and, in one case, nodding off in a big, leather chair. Breda seemed puzzled by the windows, but I knew from my stint in the lawyer's office that they were an absolute necessity. In a building admitting no outside light except at the front and back, a view of the hall gave the illusion of space and was often the only thing standing between the occupants and raving insanity.

"So, Breda." Debra closed the blinds on her own window and seated herself behind her paper-littered desk; Breda and I took two chairs facing her. "You're new to our little town? Where are you from?"

Breda looked at me. I poked her in the side. The small talk was part of the game, but it wasn't a part I intended to play for her. She cleared her throat.

"New York."

"New York! I spent my honeymoon in Saratoga Springs. It's pretty, isn't it?"

"Actually, I'm from the city. My family has a house on East Sixty-Fourth Street, near Hunter College."

Debra nodded wisely, but the location obviously didn't mean anything to her. It did to me. I had once been to a Bar-Mitzvah in that neighborhood. Pricey didn't begin to describe it.

"So what brings you west?"

"My father owns the Emerald Isle."

"Sean Casey's your father? What a dear man!"

She seemed sincere. I wondered if she'd sold him the Connolly Building. I wondered, too, if she really knew anything about him. Could Breda be right? I tried hard to picture Debra in a robe and hood, chanting incantations in a torch-lit cavern. I couldn't do it.

"And you came out here to be closer to him." Breda didn't deny it. "Well, we have plenty of properties that might suit a single woman—you are single?" Breda nodded. "Something in town? Or on one of the mesas?"

"I haven't seen much of the mesas. But I've spent my whole life in New York City. I think I'd like a little space. Something where I could get away from it all. Maybe a few acres," Breda said wistfully. She was serious, or she was doing a better job of acting than I thought she had in her.

"I suppose you want an existing house? Or are you thinking of building? We have several lovely building sites…." Debra reached in her desk for a folder, but Breda shook her head hastily.

"No! No, I don't want to build." She paled, and I knew she was thinking of Jake. "I just want to move in," she added with a nervous giggle.

Debra put the folder away, making a moue of frustration. I happened to know that some of those building sites had been listed for over a year.

"And have you thought about your price range?" Debra paused delicately.

"I have." Breda named a figure that wiped the moue from Debra's lips and made me catch my breath. I had known Breda had money, but I hadn't guessed how much.

"Well. There are quite a few options open to you. Let me just show you a few things…"

I shifted in my seat. Time for me to make my move.

"I need to use the restroom. Just go on without me, I don't mind."

"Yes, of course." Debra didn't look up as she waved at the door. "You know where it is, don't you?"

I left them in the office, bent over Debra's desk. Breda seemed thoroughly absorbed, but as I turned to shut the door behind me, she gave me a covert thumbs-up from behind the flyer she was examining.

I visited the restroom, both because I wanted my excuse to look as truthful as possible and because I had to. When I emerged, the hall was quiet and empty, with all the office doors closed. I drifted towards the back of the building, wondering where the cellar entrance, if it existed, might be concealed. If it were in one of the offices, I was sunk. I could explain lingering in the hall, if someone confronted me. But I had no excuse what-soever for rummaging through someone's office. I knew Breda would want me to check everything, though, so I tried a door-knob. It rattled but did not turn: locked. I had mixed feelings about that. Without making a full examination of every inch of the building, I couldn't disprove Breda's theory. And unless I disproved Breda's theory, she'd insist we come back after hours, something I really didn't want to do.

I found myself at the back door, which stood open to admit air; inside was pretty stuffy. Outside was a small employee park-ing lot with a lone car drawn up near the door; probably most people parked on the street. Several stacks of teal and white Western Realty lawn signs, each stack featuring a different agent's name and phone number, leaned against the wall. I took a few steps toward the alley, noticing that, though they shared an interior wall, the Emerald Isle was longer than Western Realty by a good fifteen feet, essentially enclosing the real estate agency's parking lot in a half-courtyard. I wondered if that meant anything. I tried to visualize the inside of the Emerald Isle as I made my way back. Here's the area just in from the loading dock where we stack our equipment. Here's the wall with the neon Killian's sign that should really be unplugged while we're play-ing. Here's the band booth.

I stepped over the Western Realty threshold. Here's the wall with Archie's door.

I turned to my right and blinked. A door stood right in front of me. I tried the knob; it turned. I went through, shutting the door behind me. Immediately, I was plunged into utter dark.

Something brushed my shoulder: a pull chain for an overhead light. I gave it a jerk, and a single hundred-watt bulb lit up, giving me a view of my surroundings. I was in a storage closet. A pretty big one, too—about seven feet square. Metal floor-to-ceiling shelving units stood along all four walls, leaving only enough vacant space for the door and one tiny window high on the back wall. All the shelves were crammed with office supplies: boxes of manila folders, boxes of printer and copier paper, shrink-wrapped rolls of adding-machine tape, stacks of legal pads, boxes of pens, pencils and business cards, all bearing the Western Realty howling coyote logo. It looked as though Lars Jensen, Western Realty's owner, was stocking up enough office supplies to carry his company through the next century. There was even an unused Xerox machine, standing in the center of the closet like an altar. A sweet, oddly familiar fragrance hung in the air, as if incense had recently been burned nearby.

My breath caught. Something protruded from beneath the Xerox machine. It couldn't be…could it?

I caught hold of one edge and shoved. The machine rolled grudgingly on its inadequate casters. The thing beneath it came into clear view. It was a padlock, and it was threaded through a hasp fastening a three foot by two foot trap door.

"It can't be that easy," I said aloud.

"What are you doing in here?" a male voice growled.

I whirled. The closet door was open and standing in it, silhouetted by the brighter light in the hall, was a very big man who did not look at all pleased to have found me there.

Chapter Twelve

"U h…" I stammered.

"No one's supposed to be back here." The man took a step forward, into the light of the hundred-watt bulb, and loomed over me in a threatening way. He was, as I mentioned, quite big: as tall as Timber, though not as broad, with craggy features blurred by dissipated living. He wore his hair in a spiky, gel-heavy style that would perhaps have been attractive on a younger man but did not suit his station or age; I took him to be in his late forties or so. The face triggered something in my brain. I didn't know him, but I thought I had probably seen him around somewhere.

"Debra sent me to get some file folders." I grabbed a box from the shelf at random, hoping it held the right kind.

He gave a thin-lipped frown.

"You don't work here."

"No. But my friend is with Debra now and I offered to run and get them. Seeing as I knew where they were kept." I flashed my best stage smile.

He took another step forward, shutting the door behind him. I held the box of office supplies in front of me like a shield. His eyes ran up and down my body, fixing at length on my face.

For a long moment he studied me. Then he gave a grunt of recognition.

"You're that musician. With that band."

His body relaxed and so did mine. I let out the breath I had been holding.

"Yes, I am." He might have been referring to any band at all, but under the circumstances I wasn't about to disagree with him.

He relaxed even more. "Yeah, I saw you the other night. You were pretty good. What you do isn't really my thing. I like rock 'n' roll. But you were still pretty good."

That's where I had seen him, of course. At the Emerald Isle.

"Thanks."

"Hey, you play the flute, right? You should play some Jethro Tull. That would rock."

"I'll take it under advisement," I said, irritated now my fright had worn off. Hearing pop jargon coming from the mouth of a person wearing a suit always set me on edge.

He ignored me, apparently having decided that, as a musician, I must be cool. I watched, mystified, as he walked farther into the closet, reached up and spun the crank to open the tiny rear window. Turning around, he leaned up against the nearest shelf and reached into his jacket, withdrawing a lighter and a telling twist of cigarette paper. The mystery of his presence abruptly became no mystery at all and I nearly choked, holding back the giggle bubbling up in my throat.

He loosened his tie, lit the joint and took a powerful drag, filling the closet with pungent fumes. That explained the odd smell I had noticed earlier. His eyes closed.

"You want some?" He thrust the joint in my general direction, still not looking at me.

"No. Thank you, though."

"This office is so stressful." He blew out a cloud of smoke. "A guy needs to unwind, you know?"

"Sure. Listen, it's been nice talking to you. I need to get back to Debra." I edged towards the door.

"Whatever."

I escaped into the hall and shut the door behind me, leaving my erstwhile adversary to unwind in solitude.

"Oh, brother," I sighed. My heart still beat too fast, so I leaned back against the wall for a minute, taking deep breaths to steady it. I wondered how long it would take me to disengage Breda from Debra's clutches so I could go home for a cup of tea and a nap.

When I returned to Debra's office, Breda was waiting for me in the hall.

"Through already?" I asked hopefully.

"Did you find anything?"

"Maybe." I told her about the trap door in the closet in as few words as possible, trying to make little of it. To my dismay, her eyes lit up.

"I knew it! I knew there was something fishy about this place the minute I walked through the door. It smells funny."

The semi-hysterical giggle I had been holding back since the closet incident erupted from my throat before I could stop it.

"What?" Breda frowned reproachfully at me, and noticed the box of file folders I still clutched against my chest. "What's that?"

"An alibi. Some guy walked in while I was in the closet. I had to think up a good reason to be there."

"You're kidding!" she gasped. "Did he threaten you?"

"He seemed pretty put out to find me there, but it turned out he was just looking for a private place to get high."

"No!" Breda goggled. "At work?"

I patted her on the shoulder. "You haven't seen much of the world, have you? Come on. I want to go home."

Breda squirmed. "Uh, Caitlin. You can't go home just yet."

"Why? I cased the joint and you're through with Debra, aren't you?" She didn't answer. "Breda. You are through with Debra. Please tell me you are."

"She's waiting for us out front. Oh, Caitlin!" Her face glowed and my stomach sank. "There's this darling little house! You have to come look at it with me."

One darling little house turned into two and two turned into a whole litter of the blasted things. I spent the next three hours going with Breda from property to property, trying hard not to pay any attention while she and Debra lobbed terms like "qualified borrower" and "motivated seller" over my head. I couldn't help but get involved from time to time, though. Breda seemed to know a great deal about the business end of things, but she'd never even considered buying a house before and, like any first-time buyer, she didn't know what questions to ask. She didn't know, either, about certain peculiarities of rural life, which I felt it my responsibility to point out to her. This house had a lovely view of the surrounding mountains, but it was on Smith Mesa, where there was no piped water. If she lived there, Breda would have to buy water from the public pump in town and lug it back to fill a cistern. That subdivision boasted ten-acre ranchettes—odious term—but its covenants allowed hunting access during rifle season, which meant residents stood a good chance of having to dodge bullets while hanging up the wash. I wasn't actively trying to scare Breda off; she needed to know these things. But I could tell that Debra took an increasingly dim view of my interference as Breda deemed property after property unsuitable.

After viewing all of Debra's listings and quite a few others, Breda narrowed it down to a choice between two houses, neither of which I could find anything overtly wrong with, and I was allowed to go home. I stumbled in the back door and through the kitchen, following the sound of humming to the downstairs bathroom, where I found Timber trimming his beard.

"So." He cocked his head and evened out a tuft on his right cheek. "Did she buy something, then?"

"Not yet." I sank onto the toilet. "But not for want of looking at everything within a five mile radius."

"You don't want her here? I thought you liked her."

"I do like her. I just don't want her to make a mistake. She has a lot going on; it's probably not the best time for her to make a life-changing decision."

"Isn't it?" He ran his fingers through the crisp, dark hair on his chin, causing a small shower of beard trimmings to fall into the sink. "I thought that's what the reading you did for her was all about. Breda changing her life."

Just what I needed, another person reminding me of what he thought I had said.

"I didn't think I had shared that with you," I said, nettled. He didn't seem perturbed.

"I know the cards, too, my love. Perhaps not so well as you but…." He laid the scissors down with a shrug and began rinsing hair down the drain. "Well enough to guess at what you didn't say."

"Hmph. Make sure you get those little pieces that always fall behind the faucet."

He splashed water where I indicated. "And did you find anything at the realty office?"

"Maybe…. Hey, I thought you slept through that!"

Timber chuckled. "I just didn't want to get involved. It's a crazy notion, as you pointed out."

"Maybe not so crazy." I told him about the trap door, and his eyes lit up just as Breda's had. I was beginning to suspect latent criminal minds surrounded me.

"We'll be burgling the place, then?" he asked with an eagerness confirming my suspicions—as if they had needed more confirmation where my husband was concerned.

"Tonight. After the bar closes." Little as I wanted to resort to burglary, there seemed to be no other choice and I thought it better to get it over with. Breda, of course, was thrilled with the prospect of breaking the law. "So I really need to get some sleep."

I got up and turned to go, but Timber caught my wrist and reeled me in. The next thing I knew, he had tossed me over his shoulder, which pressed into my stomach in a most uncomfortable way.

"What are you doing? You'll give yourself a hernia. Put me down!"

My demands went unheeded; he merely ducked through the bathroom door—narrowly avoiding whacking my head on the doorframe during the process—and started down the hall.

"Timber Alasdair MacDuff! You put me down this second!"

He paused in the living room, considering.

"No, I dinna think I will. I made a promise to you last night. I broke it then, but now I've a mind to keep it."

"Timber," I grunted as he carried me upstairs, his shoulder grinding further into my abdomen with every step, "I...really...need...to...sleep!"

"Hush up, Caitlin." He muscled his way into the bedroom, tossed me down on the bed and stood over me, leering, while I caught my breath. "You've nothing to complain of, ken. I'm just taking you to bed."

Timber was wise, in his way. Despite my protests, when I did sleep at last my rest came all the better for an interlude that did not involve burglary, demons, or any magic but the oldest kind. I woke in the evening feeling, if not optimistic, at least resigned to the coming larceny. And in the event that we got caught and sent to prison, I'd have the satisfaction of reminding Breda that I'd told her so.

Keeping in mind what I'd be up to after the gig, I chose to dress simply in a black camisole and black silk slacks fitting tight over the ankle but giving freedom of movement elsewhere—yoga pants, the catalogue from which I had ordered them called them. I wasn't stunning, as I had been in the green dress, but I had to admit there was a certain elegance to my appearance. Timber also dressed for villainy in black jeans and a black t-shirt several sizes too small that hugged the muscles of his chest in a way I found quite unsettling. He topped his outfit off with a black leather blazer I'd found at the discount store. Before we left, I caught him slipping something into one of the pockets. I knew exactly what it was, and I was thankful he understood his role in the night's work without my having to spell it out. Frankly, I wanted to pretend it wasn't going to happen at all.

The gig, for once, was unremarkable. It also ended much too early for my comfort, leaving us with a couple of spare hours before the bar closed for the night. Timber bought us a pair of beers and we hunched in the back booth, trying to be inconspicuous, a process which Frank and Lisa inadvertently helped along when they noticed we hadn't left and elected to join us. Frank downed two pints in quick succession and launched into a long retrospective of all the bands he had ever been in, with Lisa chiming in from time to time, pointing out how far those bands could have gone if they'd only taken Frank's advice. Then the both of them outlined their clever scheme to make Red Branch a headline act by the end of the year—a plan which involved sending out a great many gimmicky press kits but did not seem to include anything as banal as increased musical proficiency on either of their parts, although it did call for Timber and me to learn flash tricks with bodhrán and flute, respectively. I'd heard it all at least fifteen times in the years we'd been playing together, but I let them talk; it made good cover. To all intents and purposes, we were simply a band dreaming about the future over a couple of drinks after a week at a new gig. Besides, I was less disgusted than I might have been. Since we'd landed the Emerald Isle job, our performance had improved drastically—enough that I thought there might be something in the idea of becoming a headline act, after all.

At closing time, we loaded Frank and Lisa into their Subaru. I watched a little anxiously as they swerved off down First Street; any other time I would have made Timber drive them, but tonight I had other things on my mind and I figured as they only lived two blocks away and the streets were pretty much deserted, they'd probably make it all right. Timber and I got into our truck, drove a hundred feet down the alley, and parked in the shadows behind the theatre. We waited almost another hour before the crunch of gravel outside announced a new arrival. I glanced over my shoulder, half afraid and half hopeful of seeing the flashing lights of a police car.

It was Breda. She got out of her car, slammed the door much too loudly and walked over to the truck. Once again, she was dressed in her commando wear.

Timber rolled down his window.

"Keep it quiet!" he hissed. "We're no on a picnic!"

"No one's around," she replied. Timber must have glared at her, for she dropped her voice several decibels. "It's a ghost town down here."

I got out of the truck, closing the door as silently as possible behind me. "It might look that way, but in case you haven't noticed, there are houses on the other side of this alley. Houses where people live. Some of those people may be getting up before long, for the early shift in the mine. We have an hour."

I set off towards Western Realty, Timber and Breda following in my wake. The alley was eerily silent and dark, lit only by a few elderly street lamps that cast widely-spaced circles of flickering gold on the pitted gravel underfoot. Outside the lights, the shadows seemed much deeper than usual, a fact I noted with gratitude, although it seemed to give Breda pause.

"It certainly is dark here, isn't it?" she whispered. "I can't see a thing."

"You're in the country," I replied. "We don't have as much crime here as they do in the city, so there's not as much need to turn night into day. Most people don't even lock their doors. I doubt we'll find Western Realty so trusting, though."

She hadn't asked how we were going to get in. Maybe she had some notion of picking the lock with a hairpin. I wasn't going to give her the chance.

"Okay, Timber. You're up," I said as we stepped up to the door.

He grinned and handed me the tiny, high-powered flashlight that we kept in the glovebox of the truck. The door to the real estate office was situated exactly in the center of the dark space between two street lamps—something we'd checked on earlier, in a break between sets. At the same time, we'd taken the opportunity to remove the bulbs in the floodlights over the door, meant to guard against just the sort of thing we were attempting. Those bulbs now lay in my gig bag, wrapped in the flannel I kept for swabbing my flute. If we had time, we'd put them back.

"All right, then." Timber reached into his jacket pocket and withdrew the item I'd seen him place there earlier, a small roll of denim cloth tied up with an old shoelace. One-handed, Timber undid the complicated knot holding it all together and unrolled the denim, revealing a set of instruments that would not have been out of place on a dental hygienist's tray.

"What the heck are those?" Breda hissed.

Timber answered by crouching down, choosing two of the instruments and inserting them into the deadbolt on the door.

"Lockpicks? You have a set of lockpicks?"

"You were expecting plastique?" Timber growled He glanced at the roll of denim on his knee and chose a third implement.

"I wasn't expecting lockpicks."

"How in the world did you expect us to get in, then?" I snapped.

"I thought you could get your hands on a key!"

"Are you crazy? How was I supposed to do that?"

"You know everyone. I thought…."

Timber straightened up. "We're in."

He turned the knob and the door swung open without a sound. Timber and I got inside quickly; to my surprise, Breda hung back.

"What's wrong with you? Get in here!"

"What if there's an alarm?"

"This is Gordarosa. Not even the bank has an alarm. Besides, you should have thought of that before you insisted we burgle the place."

"But I thought you…!"

"Keep it down!" Timber reached through the door and dragged Breda inside by the collar of her sweatshirt; I closed the door behind them. "Ye didna think, aye? And *you*," he turned on me, "didna bother to get things clear. So quit your arguing. There's enough blame to go around. Now let's get done what we came to get done, and get out."

This seemed an eminently sensible suggestion, so I led the way to the closet door. It was still unlocked, and before another minute had passed we were all crammed inside.

"No light!" I said just as Breda reached for the cord. "There's a window; it might show."

I ran the flashlight beam over the floor.

"There."

The Xerox machine still sat half on top of the trap door. Timber rolled it out of the way and knelt by the padlock.

"Can you open it?" I asked.

"I could. But I dinna have to." He gave a yank, and the lock came off in his hand. "It's not latched, only turned."

"Was it that way when you were here before?" asked Breda.

"I don't know. I didn't have time for a close examination." A brief vision flashed through my mind in which a group of people, robed and anonymous, unlocked the trap door and disappeared through the floor. I shivered once before I realized it was silly; if there were anyone below the trap door wouldn't be latched at all. Someone had probably left it unlocked for easy access. What kind of access, there was no telling.

"Well, then." Timber undid the hasp and raised the trap door, which fell open with a thud that made Breda and me flinch. "I suppose I'd better have a look. Hand me the torch."

I passed him the flashlight. Timber took it and thrust it, and his entire upper body, through the hole the trap door had covered. The closet plunged into darkness.

"Be careful!" In my opinion, my husband was demonstrating much too little caution.

"Oh, aye, I'm careful." His voice echoed a little. He sounded, of all things, amused.

"What do you see?" Breda leaned over my shoulder, trying to get a glimpse down the hole.

"Pretty much what I expected." Timber pulled himself upright; there were cobwebs in his hair. "I'll just go down for a better look."

Before I could stop him, he jumped down into the gaping blackness. I gasped. Then I noticed that he had landed no more than four feet below where Breda and I stood. I got down on my hands and knees for a closer look. Timber crouched in what seemed to be a very small space, swinging the flashlight from side to side and humming to himself. When he had spent several minutes gazing in every possible direction, he popped back up through the hole and crossed his arms on its edge, which came up no farther than his chest.

"It's a crawlspace," he announced.

"What?" Breda joined me on her hands and knees and stuck her head down the hole. Timber grabbed her by the hair and hauled her out again.

"It's a crawlspace. Lots of insulation, wires, spiders." He shook a large one off his arm; it scuttled away to seek refuge under a shelf. "No sign of any outlet. The floor is all packed dirt. The stemwall isn't broken anywhere I can see. If there's a hidden cellar under the Emerald Isle, you don't get to it through here."

He pulled himself out of the hole and brushed himself off, filling the closet with clouds of old dust. I sneezed.

"You can't mean it!" Breda spluttered. "I was so sure…. It has to be here!"

Timber passed her the flashlight with a grin. "You're welcome to go down and see for yourself. I didn't see any Black Widows, but I might have missed them."

Breda shined the light down the hole and hesitated. I laid a hand on her arm.

"Come on, Breda. You saw how Timber came out of there. You can't really think a bunch of demon worshippers are going to put on their ceremonial robes, cram themselves into a closet and then crawl through the dust and the spiders to some other secret entrance under the building."

"It could be some kind of test," she said. But she handed me the flashlight.

"I doubt it." I motioned to Timber to shut the trap door and herded Breda out of the closet.

"Or maybe in one of the other offices…" she said as we waited for Timber to catch up with us.

"If there were access to any kind of cellar in one of the other offices, Timber would have spotted it," I assured her. "Face it, Breda. You had an idea. We checked it out. But it didn't come to anything."

She nodded forlornly and we stepped out into the alley. It was still dark, but the birds were stirring; I could hear a robin singing not far away. Just as Timber came out, a car started up in a driveway across the alley and pulled away down First Street. We'd finished just in time. Timber reset the deadbolt, we replaced the bulbs in the floodlights, and then we got into our respective vehicles and drove away into the growing dawn.

"You knew it would be a crawlspace," I accused my husband as we turned up Third Street, headed for home.

"I thought it might be something of the sort, aye. Rio Douglas did the Western Realty remodel, ken, and I remembered him mentioning it."

"Why didn't you say something then, you great lump?" If he hadn't been driving, I would have hit him. When he answered, I almost hit him anyway.

"I wanted to use the lockpicks. It's been years since I've had a decent challenge."

I groaned and leaned back against the headrest. I was glad the Western Realty adventure had ended without our discovering anything, but I couldn't help feeling a little bit disappointed that it had all been for nothing. Finding the cellar entrance in the real estate office closet would at least have answered a few questions. I had few enough answers and all too many questions, these days. I was beginning to wonder if the secret cellar, and the demon it contained, existed at all.

The first thought to cross my mind upon waking Sunday afternoon was that I had been involved with the Emerald Isle business for an entire week. I found the idea both reassuring and unsettling. It seemed like forever.

The second thought to cross my mind was that there was one particular piece of the Emerald Isle business I had managed to forget about for an entire twenty-four hours. Now I had remembered it, and I wished I hadn't.

"Casey," I groaned, sitting up.

Timber rolled my direction and opened one eye. "I'll no have ye calling out to other men in my bed, Caitlin."

"Perish the thought." I shuddered at the alarming picture that leapt unbidden into my mind. I threw my pillow at my husband to punish him for it; it was his fault. "I just remembered that Casey wants the contract dealt with before the weekend's over."

Timber made a rude suggestion concerning delicate parts of Sean Casey's anatomy. I grinned.

"I thought you didn't want me having anything to do with other men."

"Can we no have one day without that dismal place in it?"

"Would you rather take the chance that he'll track me down and inflict some ceremonial nastiness on me?"

I got out of bed and hunted for clothes as my husband considered the matter.

"Well, it might be interesting. I'd have to be invited, mind…Oww!" My hairbrush ricocheted off his shoulder. "Have you decided what you're going to tell him? To get out of signing?"

"I have. I'm going to tell him something that would make any businessman think twice about hiring a band."

"Aye? And what's that?" Timber got out of bed and began hauling on his own clothes—not the tight black t-shirt of the previous night, more's the pity, but an extra-large blue tank top and form-fitting jeans. Hmm. Well, the view was still fine, if different.

"Simple." I finished braiding my hair and smiled winningly into the vanity mirror. "I'm going to ask him for more money."

"More money? Are you daft?"

"Well, Mr. Casey, seeing as our band has brought more business into your establishment than you could have reasonably expected without our presence, I think the terms of the contract are in need of review," I recited with a smirk. "What do you think?"

"Not bad. Do you think you can pull it off?"

"Oh, I think I can." I walked over to Timber and stuck my hand in his back pocket, giving a squeeze. "Especially if a certain large Scotsman is there to back me up."

But an hour later, when I knocked at the door to Casey's office, no one answered.

"Damn. Now what?" Not that I felt any particular eagerness to see Casey, but now that I had a plan I wanted to get the contract matter dealt with.

"Try again," Timber advised from behind me. "There's someone in there. I heard them moving around."

I knocked again. Still no answer.

"Do you still hear anything?" I didn't, but Timber had preternaturally sensitive ears.

"Not now." I felt him shake his head. "They stopped moving when you knocked the first time. They don't want you to know they're in there."

"Mr. Casey? It's Caitlin Ross. Are you there? Maybe I should have checked with the bartender," I muttered, raising my hand to knock a third time. Before the blow could fall, the door jerked open.

"Oh!" Breda gasped, dropping something in surprise.

"Ack!" I exclaimed, as the thing she had dropped landed on my foot. It was a book. It appeared to be quite old, but before

I could get a closer look she snatched it up and thrust a loose piece of paper inside.

"I thought you were my father." She exited the office, closing the door behind her. "What are you doing here?"

"Looking for him. What are you doing in his office? And how did you get in there, anyway?"

She flushed the color of a tomato. "Ummm. I stole his keys the other night when he wasn't looking and ran down to the all-night Wal-Mart in Triangle to have them copied."

Timber raised an eyebrow at her. "And you didn't approve of my lockpicks? For shame, Breda."

"I wanted a chance to poke around when he was away. And I guess he is, because I haven't seen him in days."

Something in my brain went click. "Timber, did you happen to see Casey last night? I didn't, but I was pretty distracted."

"I didn't, no," Timber answered, retreating to a balcony table and taking a seat. "Why?"

I shook my head. "Nothing.... So what were you doing in there?" I asked Breda again.

"Looking for clues. For notes. For a way into the cellar. For anything." With a sigh, she joined Timber at his table.

"Did you...?" I began, but my husband interrupted me.

"I dinna think there is any cellar."

"What?" Breda sat up very straight, her eyes flashing danger. "What do you mean, no cellar?"

"Well there's no sign of one, is there? It's not in the plans..."

"You could hardly expect..."

"And Curtis didna know anything about one," Timber went right on over Breda's protests, his accent becoming more pronounced as his irritation increased. "We havena found any indication of an entrance."

I drifted over to the balcony railing and gazed down into the main dining room. Diners enjoying either an early dinner or a late lunch packed the place, and a line of customers waited outside. As I watched, the hostess called a name and a family came through the door. The hostess steered them around the edge of the staircase, past the pillared archway leading to the back room, and in to a small round table almost directly below me. It was a curious path, one that put me in mind of something having nothing to do with the restaurant business.

"If there's no cellar, where's the demon?"

"I'm not so sure there's a demon, either, when it comes to that. It was an idea Caitlin had, but we've seen no evidence…."

"What about the voices she's heard? What about the earthquake she felt?"

Both Breda and Timber's voices came from infinitely far away. And the magic gripped me again.

I fought, but this time I was a fish on a line and the hook was set. I felt it forcing me down, down into the dining room. My eyes slipped out of focus as the power enveloped me, and the room became nothing more than a pattern of shapes and energy. The curve of the stair flowed into the curve of the bar, which flowed into the curve of the big, round booth in the corner. The curve continued in a scattering of independent tables, drawing closer and closer together as they approached the center of the room. Glowing gold wreathed everything.

"Aye, well. I've no doubt your father is up to something. But we've no proof a demon has anything tae do wi' it. All Caitlin's seen is a ghost."

"A ghost that's trying to tell her something."

"For all we know he's trying tae tell her where he hid his last jar o' the pure."

The hostess called another name and another family walked the spiral path from the front door, around the stair and past the bar, shedding sparks as they went. The sparks danced into threads, which wove themselves into a cable. A distant, rational part of my mind considered and, I knew I'd seen that kind of thing before: life energy focused into an intense beam.

The hostess seated her charges at a central table. There were three of these, positioned seemingly at random with an empty space between. A strange sensation emanated from that empty space; touching it, I felt as though I were being sucked down a drain. I noticed that the gold light seemed to be sucked down as well.

Without a thought, I followed the trail of gold. I drifted down, ever down, to the floor and through it, through cement and dirt and solid rock to…

And then I remembered.

Glory wrapped the unfamiliar god, the god I had not sought. I stood before him, waiting to be burned. The burning did not come. Instead, he gestured down the hill behind him, where a smooth path led to a gate wreathed in fire.

The god spoke.

With divine power comes…

The fire flared up in the gate. I knew the ecstasy of magic, and the pain. Red fire battled white at my core, tearing me apart. I snatched at the white fire and tried to evade the red, but I could not grip one without gripping the other; I couldn't tell them apart.

I screamed, and could not stop screaming.

Long, windowless, beige walls stretched away to a locked door in the far distance. I shuffled toward it on leaden feet, unseeing, uncaring. Yet in my mind, something moved. I missed something. Something important, something cherished. I strove to find it and felt a fist of unease close about my throat.

Then a white figure came up beside me.

An abrupt shift brought me back to the present. Panicking, I struggled against the magic in earnest. My mind like thick honey, I labored up, away from the place that other will had taken me, thrusting power away with all the might I could. It was very difficult. Magic sang in my veins like a siren; putting it away was like bleeding to death. I was swimming against two currents, that of my own desire and that of the golden life force spilling

178 * KAtchеrіпe Lаmпe

down through the floor of the Emerald Isle. Both wanted me to give in, and part of me desperately wished I could. But I fought, and broke free, and finally found myself back on the balcony, leaning heavily on the rail, gasping for breath and staring into the dining room below.

And I saw something I had never seen before.

"What better place to hide your last drop than a secret cellar?"

"I'm telling ye, there is nae cellar. Nae cellar, and nae demon. If your father thinks there is, he's crazy!"

It was the floor. I had always known the Emerald Isle had a wood parquet floor. I might even have noticed that the wood was patterned in different shades of light and dark. If so, the fact had had no significance. Who looks at a floor? Even if I had looked, I would have been too close to see what I saw now. You had to be above it to get the full effect.

They had laid the parquet in the shape of an enormous spiral. Two spirals, one of dark wood and one of light. All the free-standing tables were arrayed on the light spiral. The dark was bare, as was the place where the two met, right in the center of the room. And surrounding it, as a guide, was a giant circle made up of the hostess station, the curved stair, the curved bar and the circular booths at the front of the room.

"You're wrong. Timber." My voice came out low and drugged-sounding. "There is a cellar. And there's something in it. Maybe not a demon, but something. And this whole place is built to channel energy down there."

I pointed, and they both looked over the rail. I heard Timber draw a long, shuddering breath as he took in what I had seen.

"Shite. It's a drill. It's a huge feckin' energy drill."

"What?" Breda peered closer at the floor, but she didn't see it.

"This building is a psychic drill," I told her. "It's drilling away at something underneath us. Something like a demon's prison."

I couldn't take my eyes from the customers coming in, walking the path, being seated and unwittingly feeding the process Sean Casey had set in motion, just by coming to spend an evening at his bar. I had fed it myself; every time Red Branch had played we'd stirred up energy to be filtered down through the floor and into whatever waited below. Now that I was aware what was happening, I could feel the whole building pulsing like a great engine.

"Oh, God," Breda said. "I knew it. Caitlin, you have to look at this."

She thrust two things into my hands, the book she had dropped on my foot and the paper she had crammed inside of it. I examined the paper first. I couldn't make head or tail of it. It seemed to be a diagram of some kind, a very old one; the paper was creased and yellow, the ink faded. I saw some rough shapes, both large and small, some of them connected by broken lines. A spidery hand had made miniscule notations by some of the shapes and lines: "50' from wall to wall," or "low ceiling," or a cryptic "too narrow to pass." The top right corner of the page bore a red ink stamp. "G.H.M." Gordarosa Historical Museum.

"This is what Jake took from the museum," I said, drawing my brows together. "But what it is, I have no idea."

Timber took the paper from me and gave it the once-over. "It's a map," he told me. "A map of a cave system, I think."

"What was it doing in the Connolly Building folder, I wonder?" I took the page back and scanned it again. This time, I noticed a set of initials at the bottom: "S.M.C." The mapmaker, I expected. Seamus Connolly?

"Where do you suppose they are?" asked Breda, eyes round.

I pointed down. "Under us. That would explain why Casey had Jake steal it. He didn't want anyone to remember they were there."

I turned to the book, a slim, leather bound volume. Its cover, cracked with age, bore neither name nor title. I opened it and saw that the pages were filled with cramped, spidery writing in faded ink, the same writing as on the map. A journal of some kind.

I read the first entry and my heart turned over.

"23rd May, 1917. Archie will not bring me into the secret, no matter how hard I beg. He says it is too dangerous and I do not understand. He says I am too young, although I will be eighteen next month. I have told him that unless he recognizes my claim I will run away to the war in Europe, but he only laughs as if at some childish whim. Perhaps making such a threat was childish, at that.

"So I'm through with begging and through with threats. I'm a Connolly and I have a right to my father's legacy, as I'm sure he would agree, were he alive. From tonight, I take matters into my own hands."

"I was coming to tell you," Breda said. "I found this and the map shoved to the back of Casey's bookshelf, covered up with some astrology books. I didn't know what the map was, but figured it must be important, since he took such care to hide it. As for the book, I only read enough to know what it is, but it might tell us a way to get in."

"What?" Timber looked from one to the other of us. "What is it?"

I closed the book and folded my hands on its cover.

"It's Seamus Óg's diary."

Chapter Thirteen

"*27th May, 1917. Last night I entered the cavern, but after our argument Archie must have suspected I'd do something of the kind, for he was waiting for me below and sent me right back up again. He was very angry. In vain I reminded him that our father used often to bring me to the chamber when I was but a child. He went as far as to say our father did a foolish thing, taking a boy where he had no business being and filling his head with ideas. He said our father was besotted with me because I had been born so late in his life and because I have my mother's face, who died giving birth to me. But I know our father meant for me to be part of the mystery. I remember his telling me, on my first glimpse of the circle, that when I came of age I also would be brother to the white flame, who is contained there….*"

"Does he say anything at all about how he got into the cellar?" Breda interrupted me for what seemed the hundredth time.

I sighed and rubbed my eyes. I'd just started the journal for the sixth time since bringing it home and they ached from deciphering Seamus Óg's cramped handwriting. Neither Breda nor Timber had even wanted to try. The prose was long-winded and flowery, peppered here and there with Gaelic. I wasn't fluent by any means, but I had some familiarity with the language from my singing repertoire and what I didn't know I was more than capable of looking up in the big dictionary that lay on the floor at my feet. So I had been delegated the official reader, a role of which I was heartily sick. Timber was no help. His childhood Gaelic had devolved into a large vocabulary of dirty words, and besides, he was Scots, not Irish.

"No. Not this time, and not the last five times I've been through it."

I glanced around the living room. A fire flickered in the grate, casting a cozy glow over the litter of soda cans, half-empty chips bags, the congealing dish of salsa and the large pizza carton lying open on the coffee table, empty but for a few grease stains and shreds of cheese. Timber was stretched out on the sofa, his eyes at half mast, a woolly afghan pulled up under his chin and Zathras curled up on his chest, asleep. My husband looked asleep too, but I thought otherwise. Breda occupied the tweed armchair by the window, her knees pulled up under her chin. Sometime during the course of the afternoon she'd kicked off her taupe pumps, which lay sticking out from under the otto-man, giving the odd impression of something that had crawled away to die. The purple nails on Breda's bare toes and her silver jewelry glinted softly in the firelight. Outside, the sky was the deep violet of late evening. Above the tops of the poplar trees separating our property from the road, a single star glimmered. It was a peaceful, reassuring scene, and in my chair by the hearth, with the book in my lap, I felt like some English nanny reading bedtime stories to her charges before tucking them in for the night. But the book I held was no volume of fairy tales. In fact, some of what it contained chilled me to the bone. That was the true reason for the fire; the summer night was quite warm.

Not everything in Seamus Óg's diary had to do with magic. He'd been a seventeen-year-old boy, after all, and although in the early days of the twentieth century a seventeen-year-old was counted a man, he still had many of the same concerns one would expect from any adolescent. He liked a girl, Nancy Sim-mons, whose father, the Presbyterian minister, deemed a tavern keeper's brother unsuitable. He chafed at having to do chores around the tavern when he had rather be hunting or fishing with his friends. He thought his older brother treated him like a child; he dreamed of a life beyond the tavern, of making a name for himself, of becoming a great man—though not, I noticed, of leaving the small town where he had been born. Archie scoffed at his youthful fancy and said his ambitions were no more than the myopic vagaries of an unschooled mind. He claimed to want better for his brother and urged him to explore a wider world than Gordarosa offered. Seamus Óg, of course, thought Archie's sole desire was to keep the family legacy to himself and refused to consider any options that would distance him from it.

The first few times through the journal I had paid close attention to everything, hoping to find useful information even in passages that seemed irrelevant. As the evening progressed, however, I began skimming large sections, skipping straight to the meat.

"*2nd June, 1917. Yesterday Archie received a large shipment of casks and barrels from his supplier back east and spent the entire afternoon shifting them to the cavern, where they would be safe from discovery....*"

"So he did hide his liquor in the secret cellar," Breda put in, unnecessarily.

"*I have told him before that I am more than willing to help him in this work and save him the weariness that accomplishing it alone surely must cause him, but he will have none of it. He will not have me enter the cavern for any purpose, even the most Mundane. This time I held my peace, knowing that after his labor my brother would retire early and sleep soundly, leaving me to look after the tavern in his absence. There being slight custom, I was able to lock up by eleven, and by midnight I had descended the hidden stair in pursuit of my desire.*"

"I can't get over the language," Breda said. "It's hard to believe he was raised in a frontier town and educated in a one-room schoolhouse."

"We are talking about the twentieth century. Gordarosa was pretty isolated back then, but it didn't quite constitute the back of beyond. They had cars and everything. Besides, I've seen some of the primers they used in those days," I replied. "Believe me, frontier kids, if they had any schooling at all, were better educated than most kids in public school today." I continued reading; I had come to one of the good bits.

"The chamber of the white flame was just as I remembered it. The feeble light of my lantern illuminated the great circle, etched into the floor by my father's magic, with its nine glyphs and encompassing star. Had my father lived I would understand these things. He would have taught me what they meant and how to use them to summon the white flame to my command. I am certain my brother knows, but he will share nothing with me. In his jealousy he keeps all to himself and uses the white flame for nothing more than to assure his pitiful success in his wretched business. He could be a great man in this town or in the wider world, if he but had the will. I lack not the will, only the knowledge, and this I will have to gain by stealth."

The next page was taken up with a crude drawing of what I assumed to be the circle in question. In a variation on a standard protective device, it consisted of two closely-spaced concentric circles, between which were inscribed, at what appeared to be equal intervals, a set of eight symbols or glyphs. Four of these—the ones set at the cross-quarters of the circle—I recognized as the alchemical symbols for the four elements: Earth, Air, Water and Fire. These were joined to each other by a set of lines describing a square. The two symbols at east and west looked familiar, though I didn't know them, and the two at north and south I had never seen anywhere at all. These four symbols were also linked in a square, and the two squares made an eight-pointed star within the circle. Nested within the eight-pointed star was a five-pointed star, a pentagram, oriented with its top point due north—or at the top of the page, anyway. In the center of the pentagram was a third circle, and this contained a ninth symbol, also unfamiliar to me. This last glyph was larger than the rest; it filled the central circle entirely and something about it put me in mind of a monogram.

"So Big James was some kind of magician," Breda said, not for the first time. "And he had something chained up down there."

"Aye, and he passed control of it over to Archie," Timber put in from the sofa. "We've been over this before. But we're no closer to knowing what it is, or how to get to this secret chamber, or what we're supposed to do if we find it, and I dinna think we will be if you read that manky book until Doomsday." He threw back the afghan, dumping Zathras unceremoniously to the floor, and stood up. Zathras glared at him for a minute before leaping back onto the sofa. "I'm going to bed. I've dry-wall to hang tomorrow."

He pecked me brusquely on the cheek and stalked off up the stairs.

"In a bit of a snit, isn't he?" Breda observed.

"I don't blame him. This…thing has taken over our lives." I sighed. "Maybe he's right. The diary's interesting and all, but I don't think it's giving us anything concrete to go on."

"Just go a little farther. Finish the story."

I opened the book again.

"*5th June 1917. Archie was invited to the McHenry place for supper this evening. I took advantage of his absence to search his rooms and I finally found it. I had always suspected he had not destroyed it when father demanded he do so. According to father, these things should never be written down, lest their power be diminished, but kept in the mind and the memory. But Archie's memory and aptitude for anything other than the running of his tavern are less than commendable.*"

"I don't think Seamus had room to talk," I muttered, for what followed was a list of Gaelic words he had obviously copied from some hidden document in his brother's possession, rather than memorize them. Next to each of the words he had drawn one of the symbols from the pattern on the floor.

Aer, Talamh, Uisge, Tine: Air, Earth, Water and Fire. Those I had expected. The next two, corresponding to the symbols that had looked familiar, I'd had to look up. *Fuil* meant blood. *Síol* meant semen ("Ugh!" Breda had said). Then came the two utterly unfamiliar symbols. The first, oddly enough, was simply identified as "Connolly." Some kind of family device, like the chop marks used by Japanese artists? I didn't know. Still more puzzling was the next: *Coimhthíoch*, which my dictionary defined as "foreigner." What did that mean?

Finally, set all by itself at the bottom of the page, was the ninth glyph, the one I thought resembled a monogram. This second rendering served to reinforce the notion; Seamus Óg had drawn it somewhat larger than the rest and I could see that it appeared to be a synthesis of the symbols representing "Connolly" and "*Coimhthíoch*." The Gaelic words beneath it were written large and underscored twice: *Tintri Fionn*. The White Flame.

"Curious," I said, and repeated the words aloud.

"Tintri Fionn?" Breda repeated, stumbling a little over the unfamiliar pronunciation. "What's that?"

Instead of answering right away I flipped back through the journal. Everywhere those words appeared they were in the Gaelic: "brother to Tintri Fionn," "the chamber of Tintri Fionn," "uses Tintri Fionn to assure his success…." After the first time, I had translated automatically. Now, however, I wondered if I had been right to do so.

"Well?" Breda prodded impatiently.

"It's what I've been translating as 'the white flame,'" I explained. "It's a very loose translation, actually. Tintri is fiery. Fionn is white or fair in the sense of fair-haired, blond. Two adjectives with no article and no noun that they're modifying…. I made the best sense of it I could. Maybe it would be more accurate to say something like 'the fiery blond one….'"

"That sounds like a person," said Breda.

I nodded slowly. "Yes, it does. A person. Or a name."

Breda snorted. "The Fiery Blond One? That doesn't sound like much of name to me."

"Not in English it doesn't, no. But maybe it was never meant to be put into English at all."

She stared at me. "So you're telling me Tintri Fionn is the name of…whatever it is that's down there?"

"I'm thinking it could be. And if it is, that changes everything."

"Why?"

"Haven't you heard the magical truism that names have power?"

She shrugged. "I took a cultural anthropology class once. The prof talked a lot about how members of some indigenous tribes keep their real names secret, to guard against their being used by witches. He seemed to think it was primitive superstition, though—like thinking having your picture taken will suck out your soul."

"It's truer than you might think. A name is a symbol of a thing. On a very basic level, knowing the name can give you access to the thing."

"You mean, we can just walk into the cellar…cavern…what have you, and yell for Tintri Fionn, and it will have to answer?"

"Umm…not exactly. For one thing, we haven't found the cellar." I managed a weak smile. "For another, name magic tends to function on more than the basic level. It's not enough to know the name. You have to understand it. You have to have a gut sense of why that name means that thing and no other thing, and when you use the name you have to be able to imbue it with that specific knowledge and power. Otherwise, who knows what you might get? At best, nothing will happen. At worst you could reach a nasty wrong number. It's a tricky thing. Kind of like ordering dinner in a foreign restaurant where the menus aren't in English."

"So why is this helpful?"

"Well, it's a place to start looking. You see, I was thinking of 'the white flame' as an abstract concept—'Brotherhood of the White Flame' sounds so nice and ceremonial, doesn't it? But if it's not, if Tintri Fionn is a name, we should have an easier time tracking it down. The sigil should be a help too."

"Sigil?"

I shoved the book across the ottoman at her and pointed to the monogram. "That's a sigil. It's another kind of symbol, one transcending language—like that squiggle the Artist Formerly Known as Prince came up with. Most of the major demons have them. Theoretically, if you know the sigil you have a better chance of reaching the demon because a graphic representation just by its nature accesses a deeper level of consciousness than words, which can get all tangled up in personal interpretation."

"And there are records of all these things?"

"Oh, sure. You've seen your father's library, haven't you? And there are whole Internet sites devoted to demonology. If Tintri Fionn is really this thing's name, we should be able to find him. It."

I dragged the journal back into my lap, hoping devoutly that Breda had not detected the note of false heartiness in my voice. As I had told her at our first meeting, I had never set much store by the modern so-called science of demonology; at best it struck me as dangerous rubbish. When I thought of perusing the vast number of Internet sites out there, with their detailed lists and descriptions of Hell's minions, I didn't know whether to laugh or cry. But facts really did seem to point to there being some kind of entity trapped underneath the Emerald Isle; it looked as though I were going to have to deal with it somehow, and I wasn't about to do so without knowing more about it. If that meant making a substantial change to my world view, well, I'd done that before.

Far from paying any attention to my vocal nuances, however, Breda was staring into space, a glazed expression in her eyes, like that of a recently deceased fish. I reminded myself that, despite her father and fiancé's hobby, she was still pretty new to all this. The best thing would be to finish out the journal one last time and send her back to her hotel to bed. I yawned. I needed bed, myself.

"*With what I have gleaned from my brother's careless notes,*" the entry after the list of correspondences went on, "*and what I remember of my father's teachings when I was a boy, I feel confident that I can induct myself into Tintri Fionn's circle and claim the place that should have been mine since reaching manhood. I wait only for a propitious night to conduct the ritual. Then Tintri Fionn's power will be mine, and Archie can make of it what he may.*"

I glanced at Breda. She was still staring into space, shaking her head slightly; she knew what was coming, as did I. Even knowing, I couldn't feel any sympathy for him. Seamus Óg sounded like a pompous, spoiled brat, and I thought he'd got off quite lightly, considering the headstrong way he'd messed around with things he didn't understand.

"*13th June, 1917. I have failed. I have failed and I do not know why. The moon and the hour being aligned, I made my way into the cavern. There I lit the fires and sprinkled the herbs as I remember my father doing. I called on the powers above and below and on the elements indicated. I spilled blood and seed.*" ("Ick," Breda grunted; I thought if we were going to be dealing with ceremonial magic she'd really better get used to references to sticky bodily fluids) "*and pronounced my name and that of his race, demanding by the power of all these things, by the sacred essences I shed, by his sigil and by his name that he come forth and do my will, and he did not answer. Again and again I called and again and again there was only silence, and the only fires burning were those I had lit. Then my brother found me and made me leave, and I had no choice but to obey. I had held out some hope that discovering what I was about would prove to him my determination to claim my rightful place and soften him towards my aims, but this was a childish fancy; he told me it served nothing but to show me unfit for an adult's responsibility, when I would so foolishly reach after that which those older and wiser than myself had determined I was not ready to understand. I know now he will never think me ready, and there is nothing for me here. If I am not to be part of this family in every way that matters, I will leave it forever. Tomorrow is my birthday. The war rages in*

Europe and thither will I go, called or not. Perhaps if I die in France there will be one who remembers me as a man of will, although to my brother I will never be anything but a child."

"And that's it," I said, riffling through the several blank pages left at the back of the book before closing it.

"Are you sure?" Breda asked predictably. She'd asked the same thing every time.

"Yes, I'm sure," I replied, a little waspishly. "There's no hidden map, nothing secreted behind the endpapers, nothing rolled up and concealed in the binding. There's nothing else in there."

To demonstrate, I held the book upside down by its covers and swung the pages back and forth. It was a shameful way to treat an old diary, which was why I hadn't done it before. The sole reason I did it now was that I was so tired and irritated.

To my utter amazement, a loose page detached itself and fluttered down to the floor.

"What the fu—?"

Breda alighted from her chair and snatched the page up, her eyes alight with eagerness. "It must have been stuck in those blank pages at the back."

I nodded, still stunned. I'd been through those blank pages—okay, not one by one, but I'd flipped through them several times, to make sure there was nothing else written there. I thought I'd have noticed something stuck between them, but obviously I'd been mistaken.

Breda got back in her chair, unfolded the page, scanned it, and blinked. "This is my father's handwriting."

"What? Let me see that."

As Breda made no move to pass me the paper, I got out of my chair by the fire and balanced myself on the wide, tweed arm of hers, where I could look over her shoulder. The page clutched between her fingers shook slightly and I noticed her hand was trembling. It didn't surprise me. Aside from the pattern on the

Emerald Isle floor, this page gave us our first solid evidence that Sean Casey knew what was going on and was involved in it.

There was no date, merely several paragraphs scrawled in peacock blue ink. But even if Breda hadn't recognized the hand, there was no question who had written it. He'd used his personal letterhead.

"Can you read that?" I asked, squinting. I could make out even the worst handwriting as a rule—Timber's was dreadful—but Casey's stumped me. It might as well have been Arabic, which it resembled.

"Yeah. I can." Breda's voice held a suspicious quaver. She cleared her throat and began:

"At first I assumed my grandfather's failure was due in most part to his lacking the demon's true name. Of course this is quite correct. There is no demon Tintri Fionn, which is clearly some uncouth Old World designation or descriptive term for one of the denizens of Hell whom the true sage will be able to identify with ease. The so-called sigil is also bogus. I am amazed that my great-grandfather survived his encounter with such a force as I now know this demon to be, much less succeeded in controlling it and binding it for such a period of time, given his appalling ignorance of what he was dealing with. But Grandfather Connolly always spoke of his father as a man of forceful personality and extremely strong will, and sometimes those are enough to see the unenlightened safely on a path where a wiser man would hardly dare to tread."

"Yikes!" I said. And I had thought Seamus Óg pompous! "He doesn't think much of himself, does he?"

"That's my father, all right," Breda agreed through tight lips. She worked her jaw a few times and continued,

"Having determined the demon's true name, I thought back on the many conversations I had with my grandfather before he died, and I am convinced now that another element contributed to his lack of success in making the beast respond to his will. Time and time again the old man repeated that his father was to have introduced him to the demon, that his brother refused to introduce him… One of the last things he said to me was that 'the key was in the blood, the father's blood.' I must admit I was

initially tempted to put this down to the dementia he seemed to suffer at the end. Then I began to wonder if the 'father' he mentioned was not his literal father but the person who stood in his father's place—the head of the family—and if access to the demon were somehow attainable only through direct intervention by this person."

Breda looked up. Are you getting this?"

"Maybe." I nudged her with my knee. "Keep reading."

"Were this so, the demon would be shielded from any attempting to interfere with it until and unless the head of the family deigned to introduce him. Unfortunately this means my own access is cut off. My grandfather's story seems to indicate that Archie Connolly was the last keeper of the ritual; as far as I have been able to determine he had no descendants and did not initiate any other. Because of this fact, it no longer matters who is the head of the family; the demon cannot recognize him. Therefore, my first task must be to break through the shield. Jake has helped me come up with a plan to do this."

Breda's fingers opened convulsively and the paper floated to the floor.

"So that explains the drill," I said. "Whatever has bound the demon is also keeping your father from it, and he's trying to break through by force. About as subtle as using a hammer on an eggshell, if you ask me." And a million times more dangerous. If Casey succeeded, a moment would come when the demon was free and not under anyone's control. A lot could go wrong in such a moment.

I picked up Casey's page and smoothed it across my knee. "Pity there's not more of this. I wonder why he put this one page in Seamus Óg's diary?"

Breda shrugged. Seeing Jake's name in print had shaken her.

I glanced down at the paper in my lap. There was one last thing written on it. The words ran across the bottom of the page in big, block letters that even I could read:

TINTRI FIONN = FLAXON

I must have made some sound, for Breda looked up, startled at last from her reverie. "What is it?"

I showed her. "Unless I'm very much mistaken, it's your father's best guess as to what we're dealing with."

"Do you think he's right?"

I thought about it. Fionn, Flaxon…they were both words for fair-haired, weren't they? Was there a demon known as the fair-haired one? I was too tired, I couldn't think.

"I don't know…. Listen, we've done enough for tonight. Tomorrow we'll…"

A soft snore met my words. Abruptly as a child, Breda had fallen asleep, taking refuge from too much information and too much shock in a place that was dark, warm and quiet. I thought about waking her, but ended up merely covering her with the afghan from the sofa and leaving her to her dreams. She'd probably have a crick in her neck from sleeping in the chair when she woke in the morning. But I thought she'd prefer it to waking in a cold hotel room, all alone.

Chapter Fourteen

I was awakened Monday morning by the fleeting scent of spearmint toothpaste and a whiskery but pleasant kiss.

"Mumphle," I said, leaning into it.

"I wish you'd informed me we had company," Timber murmured, giving my ear a loving nibble. "I went downstairs in my altogether, strode boldly through the living room, and ran headlong into Breda as she was coming out of the shower. The shock of it took ten years off my life." His voice quavered like an old man's.

So of course he'd chosen to punish me by getting me up at the inhuman hour of seven-fifteen. "How'd Breda take it?"

"Heathen wench! D'ye care nothing for your husband's health?" The voice deepened to match tones with a furious Puritan minister's. Then it lowered to a glum mumble. "The wee bitch laughed at me. And me in my manly splendor."

Manly splendor, indeed! I opened my eyes hoping for a glimpse of it, but he had already put on his work clothes, cheap jeans, a cheaper t-shirt and a worn flannel over all. A flowered bandana covered his dark mane, giving him a piratical air. I licked my lips, then sighed. He did, after all, have to be to work by eight.

"Is she still up?"

"Drinking coffee in the kitchen."

"Did she seem…all right?"

"Well, the best look I got of her she was a bit red in the face and gasping for air, but that was from the laughing, ken. Why?"

I gave him a brief account of what we had deduced from Seamus Óg's journal and the paper of Casey's that we had found stuck in the back. "The mention of Jake seemed to unnerve her a little."

Timber emitted a soft curse and settled himself on the edge of the bed. "I expect it would. D'ye ken, with everything else, I had all but forgotten that looking for him was what brought her to you in the first place."

"I hadn't. And neither has she. Do you know she keeps a picture of him on the dash of her car?"

He shook his head slowly. Of course he hadn't known.

"Caitlin…." he hesitated. Beneath the edge of the bandana his blue eyes went suddenly dark and serious. "D'ye think there's a chance of finding him?"

"I don't know," I said too quickly. "Probably not."

"Caitlin." He didn't address me by name so much as a rule; most often he used endearments like "darling," or "sweetheart," or "my love." I remembered telling Breda about the power of names and shivered a little. "I'm not asking just anyone. I'm asking you."

"Timber, I…."

If I thought to get some use out of the power of names myself, he thwarted me handily.

"That's right. It is me asking and no other."

All at once the room went very still, as if the words had had some ritual significance, and I wondered if he had done it on purpose.

"You know I've been trying to keep things on a Mundane level."

"Aye, I ken it." His voice dropped to almost a whisper. I could see his struggle to keep calm, but his accent got more pronounced, indicating his emotion. "I've kent it for five years. I've seen how ye fight it, too. Ye canna keep it up."

"You just want me to take back the magic so you won't feel guilty when you do yours." Even as I made the accusation, I knew it wasn't true. It was my fear speaking. But the words poured from my mouth before I could stop them, and once they were out, I couldn't recall them.

He jerked as if I'd shot him, and his eyes went black with bitterness and hurt. Very deliberately, he got up from the bed and walked to the front window. When he reached it, he turned to face me.

"You're blind," he said roughly. "If ye could but see yourself…" He jerked his head in my direction with an expression close to contempt. "I've tried, Caitlin. I married ye in spite of everything. But ye've never told me what's behind this…obstinacy. Love is all very well, but there must be trust."

I blanched. "Timber, I…"

He held up a hand. "And now ye know what's at stake and ye still…" He heaved a great sigh and his expression turned to heartbreak. "Caitlin. I love ye with all my heart and I always will. We both have our secrets, and that's as it should be. But I canna stay with a woman who wilna step up. I hate to say it, but there it is. And ye can have no idea what it means to me, to tell ye that."

My heart lurched sideways. An invisible fist clenched around my throat. To lose Timber… Since he'd come into my life, he'd been my mainstay. To be without him would be worse than death.

But would it be worse than Fate? a traitor voice whispered in my head. I knew what was in store for me if I took up my powers again. In my head, the unfamiliar god waited with his choice.

I swallowed and closed my eyes. I had no choice. Between my fear and Timber, I'd choose Timber every time. "What can I do?"

He regarded me narrowly, not quite convinced. "There's the drill. It should be disabled."

"I could do it if I could find the nexus point of the spell. That would mean going to the bar… I'd have to do it under Casey's nose." Telling myself I wasn't making excuses, I went on in a rush, "No. No, it's not good enough. Timber, I need something else. Something now. I need…I need to know you'll be home tonight."

"Look for Jake," he said at once.

I gave a sigh of relief. I could do that. Using the Sight did not even take magic. I might yet escape Fate.

I slid out from under the sheet to perch on the edge of the bed, bare feet flat on the floor, arms limp at my sides and hands resting light as feathers on my thighs. The old oak floorboards were hot under my toes where the sun had warmed them. I took a deep breath, smelling hay, flowers and ripening fruit mingling in the breeze from the open window. The birdsong was very loud. I opened myself, and it got very quiet.

In the next moment, the room did not seem warm at all; in fact it grew quite cold. Goose pimples rose on my arms, and I wanted to hug myself against the chill, but I did not. I could not. I had become very heavy and could not lift a finger; my body felt as though it were bound to the bed with lead straps. I felt an intense pressure in my temples and behind my eyes, another in my stomach, as if I had swallowed an egg that was about to hatch. The two pressures met somewhere in my throat and I found myself swallowing convulsively.

When I heard the words, I knew they were coming from my mouth but I could not for the life of me think how they had got there or how they were getting out.

"Jake Carruthers lies beyond the Dark and beyond expectation, and the sight of him is not to be hoped for."

Bile rose in my throat, filling the empty space where the words had been, and I fell across the bed retching and shuddering uncontrollably. Timber grabbed my fleecy purple bathrobe from its hook on the back of the door and wrapped me up in it. He sat beside me and for a long time patted my back, humming reassuring nonsense under his breath, everything but compassion swallowed in my need.

"Gods, Caitlin." He smoothed my hair away from my face. "I had forgotten how it can take ye. I'm sorry. So sorry."

"I'm fine." I sat up, clutching the bathrobe around me. I was not fine. My voice sounded thin and stretched and my whole body felt as though it had been beaten with sticks. With a groan I fell back onto the bed.

"Remind me after this not to prophesy anything before I've had my coffee."

I smiled wanly up at him. He smiled back, just as wanly. We weren't altogether all right again, but that would come, now. For a minute there was a welcome silence.

"Well," said Timber at last. "At least we know."

I nodded. Prophecy is often a convoluted affair, but the one I'd just uttered didn't seem to leave much room for interpretation.

"Do we tell Breda?"

I opened my mouth to say, "Yes, of course!" and shut it again slowly.

"Not yet," I said, sitting up once more.

"I think she needs to know."

"Eventually she does. I'd prefer it to come some other way, though." My husband raised an eyebrow. "Oh, come on. What am I supposed to tell her? 'Breda, I just happened to peek behind the veil this morning and guess what?' I had no business looking, Timber, and you had no business asking, and we both should have known that. I wouldn't have done it at all if you hadn't…" I stopped myself before I could say "blackmailed me." I didn't want to argue again.

"Aye, you're right." He gave his head a slow shake. "She probably would have asked if she'd known what you could do. She did come to you for help in locating him, after all."

"Well she didn't ask, and I didn't offer, and I feel like a terrible snoop. I may have to tell her, but it will be in my own time and in my own way."

"All right," he agreed grudgingly. "I suppose you know best." He glanced at the clock on his nightstand. "I have to go."

"Go, then." I clutched the bathrobe tighter.

He didn't move. I chanced a glimpse at his face. He didn't appear at all like a man who had just won a battle that had been going on for five years. He looked tired, and for the first time since I had known him I could see the old man he would become.

"I'll be back tonight," he promised me. He leaned over and planted a kiss on my cheek. It was not his usual kind of kiss. This one felt dry and hesitant.

I nodded. Only then did he stand up and leave the room, and in a little while I heard the truck pulling down the driveway.

Even though I knew Breda was waiting for me, I took a very long, hot shower. I did not think about my fight with Timber, or the implicit promise I had made him, to take up my powers again. I tried not to think about Jake. That part was not as difficult as I expected it to be. The mind has a tendency to turn away from things it does not want to know, and although my path lay straight through the middle of it all, the addition of a ritual murder—or what seemed very likely to be one—to the confirmed presence of some kind of demon, black magic, and general bad mojo fell firmly into the category of things I did not want to know. Not yet.

My efforts to pull myself together must have been at least halfway successful, for when at length I made my way down to the kitchen, Breda did not take one look at my face, turn pale, and shriek, "My God, what happened to you?" She merely grunted and waved at the coffee maker, with barely a glance up from the tattered novel in her hands. It was an historical piece of a thousand pages or so and Breda had already read a good third of it. I had kept her waiting for some time.

I poured myself a cup of coffee and took a good, long swallow, reminding myself all the while not to think about Jake. When I turned around, my expression was as cheerful as I could make it. The coffee helped; Breda had brewed it extra strong.

"Right. Ready to hunt some demons?"

That got her attention. She closed the novel without even marking her place.

"You're kidding, right?"

"Only a little."

"Do I need to be armed?"

"Not really. We'll be using modern methods. Come on."

I led the way back to my office, a tiny room off the back hall that had once been a pantry of some sort. Timber had knocked a couple of windows in the walls and installed some corner shelves, and I had painted the whole room bright purple. At six feet by eight, the space was cramped; with the desk I had bought at the Salvation Army shoved up against the far wall, a file cabinet in one corner and two chairs, it was positively claustrophobic. I loved it beyond reason. One window looked out onto the kitchen garden; the other, onto an ancient apple tree, the last survivor of an orchard planted when the house was built. I spent hours in all seasons sitting at my desk and staring out, watching the sky change color from summer blue to winter grey, while birds went about their business among the branches. I also conducted most of the band's business from this room: sending out mailings, running off contracts and updating material on the several free music websites to which Red Branch subscribed.

I sat at my desk, woke up my computer and called up my internet browser while Breda pulled up the empty chair. A click of the mouse took me to Google.

"So what are we looking for, exactly?" Breda asked.

"Exactly? I don't know." I shrugged. "More about this Flaxon character, I suppose. Your father seemed to know of him; at least he had reason to equate him with the mysterious Tintri Fionn. I'd like to know why."

"If my father thinks Tintri Fionn and Flaxon are one and the same, I'd be inclined to believe him," Breda said with some heat; after everything, she couldn't help defending the old man. I wondered what she'd say if she knew what I did about Jake, and restrained myself from commenting. "After all, demonology is his life's work."

"Especially the search for this particular demon," I agreed. "All the same, I want to know for myself. Maybe I spent too long in the academic world and maybe I'm just cynical by nature, but I have a hard time taking anything anyone says for granted. I need to check my facts." At least, I needed to check them as much as one could when dealing with occult maters, where so much was left to speculation and inference.

First thing first. I typed "Tintri Fionn" into the search engine and clicked "Google Search." I got a list of horse racing statistics, all in Gaelic. No help there. I added quotes to the name. That search turned up nothing at all.

I tried "*coimhthíoch*" next. That turned up 152,000 results. After the first seventeen pages all proved to be references to the same Clannad album, I decided to pass. I couldn't waste the day trying to hunt down the demon that way, and I had no idea how to narrow the search parameters to give me a more manageable list.

Okay. I cracked my knuckles over the keyboard and typed in "Flaxon." The results came back almost immediately.

"Now showing results one through twenty of…one hundred and thirty-six thousand!" Breda read over my shoulder.

"We'll never get through all that. Would we like to refine our search?"

"Yes, I think we would," I said. To "Flaxon," I added "demonology." That brought the results down to a mere one hundred and eighty-two; not bad. Trying to narrow the options further, I added "sigil." The number of results jumped back up to six hundred and three. I sighed and returned to the previous search.

The very first link led to an on-line copy of *The Book of the Sacred Magic of Abramelin the Mage* by S.L. MacGregor Mathers, 1898.

"My father has that book," Breda said. "I saw it in his office. He keeps it locked up."

"Let's hope that's a good sign," I replied, and clicked.

Compared to a lot of websites, the page that came up was stark, with plain black Roman text on a white background. There was no detailed information in sight, merely a list of names beginning with Chief Spirits and Sub-Princes and continuing with their servants, rather like the employment records of a large corporation. The Chief Spirits were pretty much the ones I had expected: Lucifer, Satan, Belial and the rest. The servants were a different matter altogether; I'd never heard of any of them. The entries didn't provide much information—just the relevant demon's name and its possible derivation. But halfway down the list of the servants of Ariton, I found it.

"Flaxon. Greek: About to rend, or be rent asunder."

And that was all.

"Well, that was helpful," I muttered, and returned to my original search.

But none of the links turned up much more. The "Index of Angel names, magical words and the names of God," listed Flaxon's name, but nothing about his nature. Same with the *Demonic Bible*. Trying to access the full text of the *Sholl S Humanitome* led only to a page requesting I become a member of some public library in a place I had never heard of. And then the search results suddenly thinned themselves from nearly two hundred to a mere seventeen, and the bottom of the page told me,

"In order to show you the most relevant results, we have omitted some entries very similar to the 17 already displayed."

"What do you think?" Breda asked. "Should we 'repeat the search with the omitted results included?'"

"I don't know." I didn't really think that would get us anywhere. Still, I wasn't eager to go back to the original "Flaxon" search with its hundred and thirty-six thousand results. I clicked one, last link.

"Hey, this looks promising!" I said.

The page began with a long history of Goetic magic, including sections on organization, philosophy and initiation. The specifics of conjuring and working with various demons were addressed in some detail. I felt hopeful until I came to the list of useful spells and noticed that many of them included the dice score necessary for the spell to succeed.

"Summoning Flaxon requires a roll of seven or higher… Arrgh!" I said. "It's a gaming site! Why didn't he say so in the first place? There ought to be a law."

With a grimace I returned to the "Flaxon" search. Right away, I saw that most of the sites mentioned were more gaming sites. There was a Flaxon Technologies, which I did not supposed to be a nest of demon worshippers, although the webmaster did describe himself as evil. Then I noticed that a surprising number of the sites seemed to use mistake "Flaxon" the demon for "flaxen" meaning fair-haired. My hand froze on the mouse and I swore.

"What?" Breda asked in a timid voice.

"Well, I was hoping to get some clue as to why your father is so sure this is the demon we're dealing with. But if Abramelin is his source, there's nothing in the name about whiteness, or fire, or any of that."

"My father said Seamus Mór was wrong about that."

"He did, but Seamus Mór actually dealt with the demon and your father didn't. He bound the dratted thing in his cellar; he must have known something about it. He must have known its name." I tapped my fingers on the desk.

"It could have been luck."

"I don't believe in that kind of luck. Hand me the dictionary, would you?" I pointed to a tattered, red New American Heritage edition on the nearest shelf.

Mystified, Breda did. I flipped pages, muttering to myself.

"Faithful…fictile…Flag Day…here we go, flax. 'Any of several plants of the genus Linum…' No, I don't need that. 'Flaxen: made of or resembling flax; having the color of flax fiber, pale yellow.' But that's 'flaxen' with an 'e' of course, I knew that; how could I be so stupid?"

"Caitlin! What are you on about?"

"It's not spelled the same."

"So what?"

"So, flaxen, the English equivalent of the Gaelic word, fionn, isn't the same as Flaxon, the name of the rending demon."

"And?"

I slammed the dictionary shut.

"Your father went into this believing he knew more about it than the Connollys, even though they dealt with this entity for years and all Sean Casey knew of it was a rumor. He decided right from the start that there was no demon named Tintri Fionn. It was just some old country nonsense."

"My father…"

"Has a very specialized knowledge. But Breda, how could he possibly know every demon that ever existed? How could he know for sure that Tintri Fionn isn't the thing's true name?"

Breda's white skin went a shade whiter as the implications of what I was saying sank in. She swallowed. Then she gave a hollow laugh.

"He does get pig-headed when he's convinced he's right."

Like father, like daughter, I thought, but had the sense not to say so.

"So how did he come up with this Flaxon being?"

"My guess? He'd already decided the demon must be one mentioned in one of his precious texts. If he's like other Ceremonial Magicians of my acquaintance, he probably thinks the path he follows is the one straight road to power and all the others are so much malarkey."

"That sounds about right."

"He thought the name, Tintri Fionn, referred to some attribute. So he probably did what I did: translated it to find out what those attributes were. And probably the source he used defined *fionn* as fair-haired or flaxen. At that point, Sean Casey made a huge leap in logic. He equated the English definition of the word with the name of a demon he'd seen before, even though they're spelled differently and likely have completely different origins."

I flipped to the back of the dictionary. "See here: 'flax' comes from the Germanic root 'plek,' meaning 'to plait.' But there's another word, 'plēk,' meaning 'to flay.' Casey got his roots mixed up. Flaxon being a Renderer and the Connolly building having the violent history it does probably reinforced his opinion, but the fact is he found that demon because that was the demon he wanted to find. That's my guess, anyway."

"So he doesn't know what he's dealing with at all." Breda's blue eyes narrowed, making her look disconcertingly like the man under discussion.

"Doesn't look like it."

"And that's bad."

I wanted to tell her, not necessarily. Sometimes ignorance was actually safer, if you couldn't access what you didn't understand. Seamus Óg hadn't been able to break through the barrier, after all. Then I thought of the psychic storm, and the drill, and I thought that a child didn't have to understand fire in order to be burned. I shook my head.

"It's really bad."

She blew out a breath from between compressed lips. "What are we dealing with?"

"I wish I knew." I thought hard about the name, about the Connollys and about Seamus Óg's diary. Then I turned back to the computer and typed in "Irish demons." Another huge list. I added "sigil" and that reduced the list, but not by much. I added "*coimhthíoch*" and struck pay dirt. Six entries. Six. That was definitely a number we could work with.

"God, Caitlin, how long do we have to keep doing this?" Breda complained. "It's got to be time for lunch."

"Just a little longer," I assured her. I stared blankly at the list. The Clannad album was mentioned again. So was what seemed to be an Irish Heavy Metal band offering free MP3 downloads. There were a couple of links to Irish language dictionaries. And there, at the bottom of the page, one last link.

Na seanfhaclan agus béaloideas.

Proverbs and Folklore.

"Come on, Caitlin, I'll take you out to that Mexican place," Breda pleaded.

"Okay," I said. "Just let me check this one thing."

I didn't have much hope. After all, what did proverbs and folklore really have to do with demons, Irish or otherwise? Still, I clicked, and the kind of luck I didn't believe in must have guided my hand.

There it was.

Chapter Fifteen

Despite the name, the site was in English—and thank all the gods for that, as the limited Gaelic I had learned in the course of my career with a Celtic band definitely did not measure up to the task of translating an entire website. A large green and gold banner at the top of the page proclaimed the site name, along with the standard *Cead Mile Failte*, a hundred thousand welcomes, but that was all.

The wallpaper caught my eye more than anything else, though. The beige background bore an exact copy of one of the symbols from Seamus Óg's book: the symbol associated with the Gaelic word for foreigner, *coimhthíoch*. The giant image floated like a dead fish just beneath the print, filling my awareness to the point that I was hard put to take in any of the actual information the site offered until Breda jabbed me hard in the ribs.

"I'm still hungry," she reminded me.

"Okay, okay." I blinked and started scanning the page.

"Would you mind telling me what we're looking at and why it's important enough to delay my enchiladas?"

I swiveled my chair to stare at her, astounded she couldn't see it. I kept forgetting that, despite her ancestry and despite the company she'd been keeping, Breda was still new to all this. To her, the sigil on the wallpaper was just another interesting clip-art motif, if she noticed it at all.

"Do you have Seamus Óg's journal there?"

She held it up by way of answer.

"Turn to the entry with all the symbols."

She did so and I tapped the page. "Take a good look at that one, the one he calls *coimhthíoch*. Then look at this website again."

Breda studied the book for several minutes before raising her eyes to the monitor. This time, she gasped softly. "It's the same as the wallpaper."

"A-plus."

"What does that mean?"

"It's the first confirmation we've had of this symbol's existence outside of Seamus Óg's journal. Other than that, I don't know. Not yet."

Proverbs and Folklore was an oddball site. In addition to a section on demonology, the table of contents on the home page served up a mishmash of every conceivable subject that could possibly be covered by the name: fairy lore and legends, history both real and mythic, a map for a walking tour of ancient sacred sites, instructions for brewing pocheen, recipes, and the wit and wisdom of somebody's Grandmother Oonagh, to name just a few. Looking at it, I couldn't help but wonder at the choice and variety of material. It made me think of stories where the hero has to sort through all the dross in some old hag's storehouse, searching for the one item of value concealed there. I glanced again at the wallpaper with its prominently displayed symbol. Maybe I already knew what that item of value was.

Even though my search had called up the link, the one word that should be there, *coimhthíoch*, didn't appear anywhere. But towards the middle of the list—nothing was in any kind of order, alphabetical or otherwise—I saw something that made me pause.

"Alien Encounters," I read.

Breda shifted impatiently in her chair. "Caitlin, we're looking for a demon, not for little green men."

Aliens. The word *coimhthíoch* meant "foreigner," not "alien," true. But on the other hand, aliens were about as foreign as you could get. I crossed my fingers and clicked.

At first it seemed my intuition had led me astray. The page appeared to be no more than a survey of supposed extraterrestrial activity in Ireland, as rambling and incoherent as most of what I'd read on the topic, complete with abduction accounts and vague hints at government cover-ups. The expected parallels were drawn between modern alien activity and ancient supernatural occurrences attributed to fairies and the like. Nothing new, nothing helpful, but I scanned the entire page just to be sure. To my puzzlement, the page continued past the place where the text ended. I scrolled through a long expanse of blank screen, expecting at any moment to hit the links generally found at the bottom of any web page, the ones taking you home, or back to the top, or to the site map. They never appeared.

What did appear, after a minute of scrolling that seemed like an eternity, was the symbol. It sat as if trapped in a narrow little box, all by itself at the center of the screen, the black lines of it standing out like a nasty bruise. And when I passed my mouse cursor over it, the cursor changed from an arrow into a hand. The kind of hand that, in Internet language, means: click here and you will be taken somewhere else.

I clicked.

Without delay or warning, the black lines of the symbol went scarlet, as if they had been comprised of some extremely flammable substance to which I had just touched a hot match. This, it seemed, was not far from the truth, for the now-scarlet lines turned into flames, which flickered realistically enough to cause shadows to dance across the office walls and spread to engulf the whole screen. As the flames spread, they also increased in brightness, until I had to turn my face away from the monitor; it actually seemed that if I continued to look, I might be blinded.

"That's some good animation," Breda said.

Animation? I wasn't so sure. It seemed much, much too real. So real, in fact, that I was afraid if the intensity of the light got any stronger, it might do serious damage to my system. I glanced down at my equipment tower, half-expecting to see smoke pouring out of it. There wasn't any, but the tower was alarmingly hot to the touch. My hand hovered over the reboot button.

And then the screen went blank.

"Shit." I said.

"Maybe you needed a password." Breda's voice quavered, not entirely with laughter.

I leaned over and laid my hand on the tower. It was cooling rapidly, and I could feel the vibration within that told me something was still functioning. Straightening, I looked at the screen. It stared back, as dull and grey as a dead eye.

"Shit, shit, shit!" I chanted. I wanted to pound on something, but everything within reach was breakable and I knew I'd regret it later. "Now what?"

"Reboot and try again?" Breda suggested.

"I don't know…." On impulse, I glanced up at my DSL and router boxes and saw all the lights flashing a normal green. "We're still on-line. I wonder…."

At that moment, the screen gave a shiver, almost a convulsion, and a single word appeared, blinking, stark white against the grey.

Loading...

"Loading? Loading what?"

"A new page, I'd guess." All at once I felt hopeful again. "That was obviously some kind of blind, or maybe a test."

"Test? Of what?" Breda sounded skeptical.

"Patience, maybe. Whoever constructed it needed to know we were serious about finding out…"

I had been going to explain all the myriad precedents for tests of intention where quests for mystical knowledge were involved, but my words trailed off as the new screen appeared. It was not like anything I had imagined it would be.

We were looking down into a one-room cottage, as if from a window set high up in the wall. The cottage so exactly resembled the sort of thing you'd expect to see if you somehow stumbled into a fairy tale that it gave the impression of a Hollywood set dressed for a remake of Hansel and Gretel. The walls were irregular grey stone; the floor was packed earth and what I could see of the ceiling, just apparent at the top of the screen, was reed thatch over smoke-blackened beams as big around as my thigh. From our vantage point we had a good view of a worm-eaten plank table surrounded by slat-backed chairs, a dry sink and counter built in along the right hand wall, and the open front door, through which sunlight streamed. The table bore a bowl of fruit: apples and pears. The curtains at the one window I could see were checked red and white, and seemed to be woven of the same coarse cloth as the towels folded neatly on the counter. Some sort of wreath hung on the front door.

The one thing missing was a hearth, and from that I deduced our position.

"We're over the fireplace. Maybe in a picture, or a mirror…."

"What?" Breda's voice had the flat, impatient tone of someone too worn out to marvel. "Caitlin, what is this? Animation? A movie? Real time video?"

"Hush." I had just noticed the room's single occupant. A bent-willow rocking chair was drawn up into the patch of sun leaking in through the door, and in this an old woman sat knitting; I could hear the click of the needles. She wore a nubby grey shawl over her bony shoulders, and the head bent over her work was completely white, with the hair pulled back into a tight knot. The bare toes peeking out from beneath her long, shapeless skirt were horny and nearly black with dirt.

"Who's that?" Breda asked, seeing the old woman at the same time I did.

"I don't know. Grandmother Oonagh, maybe?"

As if my saying the name had caught her attention—and for all I knew it had—the old woman looked up. She squinted in the direction of what I took to be the mantelpiece. Then her eyes widened and she chuckled.

"Well. It seems I have visitors." Her voice had a rusty quality, like a mill wheel that had not been turned in a very long time. It also did not emanate from the speakers attached to my computer system. Rather, it seemed to come from all around us, filling my little office until I felt there was scarcely room to draw a breath. Breda must have felt the same, for she shrank towards me, clutching at my arm.

"It's been a goodly while since anyone has got past my wards, I can tell you," the old woman said.

"Wards?" I asked. I don't know what prompted me to speak aloud; my computer wasn't equipped with a microphone. But she heard me, and I wasn't surprised.

"Oh yes. Not just anyone can find this place. I can't be bothered answering questions for every fool who thinks he has something important to say. It takes a special combination of elements to bring someone here, the Will, the Sight, and the touch of the Other."

"The touch of the…"

"Now I can tell by looking that you have Will and Sight in plenty, though you aren't much of a one for using either, are you? But the touch of the Other, that's a rare thing, make no mistake. How did you come to have dealing with one of that race?"

"What's she talking about?" Breda hissed.

"Shut up, will you?" I returned my attention to the old woman, who had laid her knitting aside and stepped closer to whatever mystical device was allowing us to see each other and converse.

"Don't be too hard on the young one," the old woman said with another eerie, though not unkind, chuckle. "Her journey is just beginning. Can't you remember your own first steps?"

"I can't say as I do."

She gave me a long, considering look, then shrugged. "Well, perhaps not. There's Old Blood in you. Some are born on the path."

I grimaced. The last thing I wanted to discuss with this old woman was my path. "So you know something about...about the *coimhthíoch*?"

I wasn't sure I should use the word, but it didn't seem to faze her. "An old race, to be sure, and not one native to this shore or any other of this world."

"Evil?"

She shrugged again. "I would not say so. But very, very dangerous."

"This one...the one we suspect is here...seems to incite violence."

"They manipulate strong feeling, and when it is strong enough, they feed. Violence is easy to provoke. Some say they prefer the taste of love, but true love is harder to come by."

Great. Just what I wanted: a philosophy lesson.

"All true magic is a matter of philosophy, child. Never forget that," said the old woman with a smile.

"I'll keep it in mind. So is that the only reason they're dangerous? Because they provoke strong feelings?"

"Oh, no." She shook her head. "That's the least of the danger. You see, they're strangers. Aliens." She said it as if it should have profound significance.

"And?"

"They have no true connection to this world. They come and they go, but do not make a home. The rules of this world cannot bind them. The magic of this world is to them as the wind through the leaves; they feel it, and it means nothing. They are without form, without center. They have no names."

"This one has a name," Breda put in from behind my shoulder. "Tintri Fionn."

The old woman waved one gnarled hand in a dismissing gesture. "For a name to have power there must be…it must be able to attach itself somewhere, you understand? A *coimhthíoch* has nothing like that. No place for a name to root, no place for a hook to catch. They do not answer when we call, save as it pleases them."

Well, that went hand in hand with my personal philosophy about demons, at any rate. Hearing her say it was strangely gratifying, though not helpful.

"We may invent things to distinguish them, but to them our distinctions are meaningless. The word we call them is just a word; in other places, there are other words. Even the sign by which you found this place is merely for the benefit of those who know, a way of signifying that which cannot be signified. To the coimhthíoch themselves, it is nothing."

"This one has a special symbol," Breda persisted.

"Again, it is nothing. Someone recognized this particular stranger and created a sign for it. It is like putting a label on a jar of preserves, but the preserves know it not. The label does nothing to keep them in the jar."

"What do you suggest we do, then?"

She gazed at me with something like pity in her eyes. "What any creature must do when faced with forces too great to be contained. Wait for them to subside and go away. The coimhthíoch rarely stay long in one place. Perhaps this one will not do too much damage before leaving."

"You're not very helpful." Breda stirred; I could feel her getting angry. "Why go to the trouble of all that misdirection if you have so little to say?"

"I say what I know."

"Well it sure isn't much! What are you hiding?"

Hiding from, *more like*, I thought. Unless I missed my guess those wards were designed to do more than frustrate random inquiry. But why the interesting key? There couldn't be many people out there who had both the Sight and the Will to find the place. Add in actual contact—however tenuous in my case—with the entity called *coimhthíoch* and the numbers would diminish still more. I couldn't imagine there were a lot of those strangers walking around; if there had been, information about them wouldn't be so hard to come by. There would be more myth, more legend. At the very least someone would have used the term as a basis for a nasty creature in some role-playing game. But there was none of that at all.

So what did Grandmother Oonagh want? Breda was right; the old lady wasn't giving out any useful information. So the *coimhthíoch* were really not of this world and really not subject to its laws—so what? We could have guessed as much. Or could we?

I tapped my fingers on my desk. Breda and the old woman were still facing off across the void of cyberspace, not saying anything, just glaring at each other. For the merest second, though, I thought I saw the old woman's eyes slide in my direction, and in that brief contact I noticed something I had not noticed before. Behind the daunting fierceness of her expression lay a shadow of fear, and lurking behind that, almost imperceptible, lay another shadow still. A shadow of hope. When I saw that, I knew.

She had said it herself. What does any creature do when faced with forces too great to be contained? Hide and wait for them to pass. And maybe while you're hiding, someone else will figure out a way to deal with it.

Grandmother Oonagh wasn't there to give out information at all. She was hoping information would come to her.

"Tintri Fionn is bound," I said.

For the first time, the old woman looked flustered. Flustered, and at the same time, eager. I knew from that my guess had been spot on. She was hiding from a *coimhthíoch* herself.

"Bound? To a place and time? But such a thing cannot be…. The *coimhthíoch* do not…. No one has ever…"

"Someone has." I grabbed Seamus Óg's journal from Breda and waved it before the monitor. "We found references to a ritual, and a diagram of a circle."

"Show me." She stepped very close, so that her wrinkled face filled the screen.

Feeling more than a little foolish, I opened the journal to the page with the diagram and the symbols and held it up to the monitor. The old woman studied it for a long time, then took a step back, looking shaken.

"Blood and seed and the family name," she muttered, wiping her hands on her skirt. "Yes, that might be possible, if one could contain the stranger long enough. A net spell might do it, but the person casting it would have to be very powerful and strong of will."

"By all accounts Seamus Mór was that."

"But what, then, is your problem?" The old woman made a visible effort to pull herself together, smiling a smile that looked painted on. I felt more than a little miffed. After all, I'd just handed her the answer to her own, personal puzzle; she could have thanked me. Instead, she seemed in a hurry to get rid of us. Oh well. I could hardly blame her. Who knew how long she'd been stuck in that cottage, wherever it was. "If it is contained, surely the stranger can be no trouble to you."

"The problem is, someone is trying to loose it."

"My father," Breda added, unnecessarily.

"Ah. That is grave. And has he broken through?"

"He's having difficulty. But I think he's succeeding." I told her about the psychic storm and the drill, and she nodded.

"He thinks it's some normal demon. One he knows," said Breda. "One he can control."

"That is unfortunate. Once the stranger is free, it will not be compelled and attempts at control will only anger it further. You must stay your father from this unwise course." She spoke with the certainty that comes from experience, and I thought I knew why she was hiding.

"I'm not sure we can." Hell, I wasn't even sure we could find Casey, let alone force him to do anything he didn't want to do. For all I knew he was holed up in the cellar with the demon right at that moment, working his mystical way with it. And we couldn't even find the entrance.

A wave of dizziness hit me as the magic pulsed and the Sight rose unbidden. I saw Sean Casey, long robes trailing behind him, making the circuit of Tintri Fionn's prison. I clutched at the arms of my chair and pulled myself back to the present.

"Then my only advice to you is, gather all that is dear to you and flee. Protect yourselves in any way you can. For when the stranger is released, he will be very, very angry. And very hungry. Now I must go. I have matters to attend to."

And with that, the old woman reached into the pocket hanging from the knotted cord serving her for a belt and withdrew a handful of what looked like dryer lint. She threw it down, into what I supposed was the fire; anyway, a great cloud of black smoke billowed up, obscuring the screen. Breda and I both flinched away, instinctively covering our noses and mouths with our hands.

When the smoke cleared, a very familiar message met my eyes.

Error 404: Page not found. If you think you have reached this message in error, click your browser's back button or try again later.

Somehow I didn't think we'd get through Grandmother Oonagh's wards a second time—if she would even still be there, now that she knew what to do. Hands shaking, I turned off the monitor. After a moment's thought, I shut down my computer altogether.

"Wow," said Breda. "That was weird."

"Yes. Yes it was."

"Do you still want lunch?"

"Sure."

As she had promised, she took me to the Mexican place downtown. I don't remember what we talked about—Mundane things, probably. She ordered tomatillo enchiladas and I had the relleno plate. We both claimed to be extremely hungry after the morning's exertions, and we both made appreciative noises when the food arrived. But I couldn't help noticing that despite that, neither of us ate very much.

Chapter Sixteen

"**S**o was that old woman a witch, or what?" Breda asked me.

We were making a circuit of downtown after our so-called lunch, both burdened with carry-out boxes. I already knew I carried mine for form's sake only. I'd take it home, put it in the fridge and forget about it, and two or three weeks later, when its contents were unrecognizable as food, throw it away. Or Timber might delve into it during one of his midnight forays after sustenance; anyway, I would never taste those chile rellenos again. I had no idea what Breda would do with hers. Her bed and breakfast might have kitchen facilities and it might not. She might not care. For all her nice clothes and attention to her appearance, she might be one of those people who would eat leftover chicken that had been sitting in a hot car.

"Caitlin?"

"What? Oh." I still did not want to discuss Grandmother Oonagh, but didn't see how I could avoid it; I had already learned that trying to change the subject when Breda had her mind set on something was like trying to change the course of an oncoming train by standing in the middle of the track and waving your arms. "Depends on what you mean by the term. I doubt she's a neo-Pagan religious feminist who uses the word as a means of achieving personal empowerment, for example."

"I don't think that's what I meant." We passed a trash container painted with childish suns and daisies, a public works project of the Gordarosa grammar school. Breda glanced at the carry-out box in her hand and tossed it in, thus affirming my estimation of her character; she was not a skanky chicken-eater. After a minute, I tossed mine in after it. The guilt I felt at wasting food lasted a second or two before being replaced by the sense of wicked freedom that comes from doing something one's parents would frown on. I wiped my hands on my jeans with a rueful smile. "What's a neo-Pagan?"

Breda's question recalled me to the present and I raised an eyebrow. "How long did you spend in Boulder? Neo-Pagan is a term pertaining to any number of small, non-standard religions with origins in the Spiritualist movement of the late nineteenth century, which incorporate as doctrine practices their adherents believe reflect much earlier, indigenous ritual systems."

"In layman's terms, New Age stuff."

"If you want laymen's terms, you should ask for them. I wrote a thesis on this."

"No shit?" She looked at me with a new kind of respect and I realized that, for all the time we'd spent together, she'd been thinking of me, not as a specialist in a field, but merely as a person with some wacky ideas that happened to make some kind of sense at this point in her life. It was typical Seeker mentality, grasping at anything, not in any expectation of finding real answers, but in the hope of stumbling upon some justification for staying exactly the same and doing nothing while feeling good about it. It would have annoyed me but for two things. I sympathized with her, and I'd given her little reason other than a few conversations to think of me in any other way.

"No shit. So do you want to hear more or not?"

"I'm fascinated. But try to use smaller words."

"I'll see what I can do." We paused outside a gift shop, where I pretended to admire a display of Black Hills gold while gathering my thoughts. "New Age is a catchall for any non-standard thought system—or maybe I should say, non-Western-standard, because New Age stuff, as you call it, can include Eastern practices like meditation and yoga. Neo-Paganism is a specifically Western-oriented subgroup: Wicca, modern Druidism, sects based on supposed ancient Egyptian practices or Aboriginal or Amerindian beliefs. Although," I added thoughtfully, "some of them get quite messy with their gods—invoking Kwan Yin and Coyote in the same breath, for example."

"And this is a problem because?"

She said it with a smirk and I could tell she was humoring me, but I couldn't help but answer. She'd asked, after all. "Well, aside from its being disrespectful to co-opt deity from any source you please just because you think it's cool, and inconsistent to invoke an Eastern Goddess into a Western ritual, it's just sloppy. I mean, a Chinese Bodhisattva and a Navajo trickster? Will they work together? They might not even know each other. Best to pick a pantheon and stick to it, I say."

We passed the drugstore at the end of the block. Outside, a young mother struggled with a boy of three or four, who had apparently snatched up some small toy on the way out the door and refused to relinquish it. He was howling and red-faced; she was screaming, equally red. As we watched, she raised a hand and slapped him, hard, across the face. He dropped the contested toy—a Star Wars Lego—with a whimper; his mother retrieved it and, looking dazed, led him back inside the store.

"I hate seeing stuff like that," Breda said, glancing over her shoulder as we crossed the street.

"So do I. It's funny, though…."

"What?"

I shook my head. I knew the mother slightly. Dee-Dee Scranton had two older children besides the toddler. They were all remarkably well-behaved and she was more patient than most young parents with the expected slip-ups. I'd never known her to raise her voice; until today, the thought of her slapping one of her brood would have been unimaginable.

"What about Satanism?" Breda asked, examining the petunias in the planter outside the bank.

"Don't get me started about that."

"Why not?"

"Why are you asking all these questions?" I countered.

"Because it's interesting. Because my father is an evil magician who's trying to raise a demon and I want to know if I'm destined to follow in his footsteps. Because, as the old woman said, I'm on some kind of path and I gather you've been down it. So lead on, MacDuff."

"The exact quote is, 'Lay on, MacDuff,' and it has nothing to do with following anything."

"Whatever. So, what about Satanism? Is it neo-Pagan? Or is Satanism only a myth?"

I sighed and gave a reflexive glance over my shoulder. My theories on the subject were not best made public in a conservative rural town. "Oh, it goes way back. There were people practicing a form of Satanism in seventeenth century France; it was all the rage at court. But it's not neo-Pagan, no. Satanism is a Christian sect."

"What?" Breda exclaimed so loudly that heads turned among a group of old ladies gathered outside the library, on the other side of the street.

"Shh! Satan is a Judeo-Christian deity, the dark half of the Father God. It's a standard duality. See, wherever you have a religion that extols a particular set of ideals to the exclusion of all others, there inevitably develops at least one sect that does the exact opposite. So where the accepted doctrine is love, light and forgiveness, the reactionary sect will practice hatred, darkness and revenge, for example."

"Okay, I get that. But how does it make Satanism a Christian sect, if it's a perversion of what Christianity stands for?"

"Because it's a perversion of what Christianity stands for." Seeing Breda's perplexed look, I went on. "Socially speaking, rebellion is defined by the dominant paradigm. The rebel isn't outside society; he's part of it. There's no crime without law and no behavior is immoral unless there's an established moral code. On the other hand, without crime or immoral behavior, there's no need for a system of law or morals to regulate things. One feeds the other and both make the whole. Classical Satanists get up to all manner of intensely disturbing stuff, no doubt about that. But most of it—perverting the Mass, reversing the cross, reciting the Lord's Prayer backwards, orgies in the temple—is designed to spit in the face of the Christian God. A truly independent Pagan religion wouldn't give two shakes what the Christian God thought; He's not relevant. All that immoderate display meant to show just how free a practicing Satanist is from the strictures of the Christian church does nothing but show that the religion is completely defined by them. So Satanism is a Christian sect."

Breda shook her head. "You are bound to be burnt at the stake."

"Don't think I haven't thought about that."

We crossed the street to the Post Office, which was crowded and noisy. At the counter, an old man in irrigation boots was arguing loudly with the clerk about the cost of sending a parcel to his son stationed overseas. A line was piling up behind him and none of the customers seemed in a very good mood. I checked my box in a hurry, decided it contained nothing I needed to bring home, and retreated.

"Man, it's weird down here today," I remarked when we regained the relative calm of the sidewalk.

Breda shrugged; she hadn't noticed. I opened my mouth to explain, then thought the better of it. She was from New York; no doubt she walked through worse every day just going from her front door to the corner to hail a cab. Like as not we could have what passed for a riot in Gordarosa and she wouldn't flinch.

"So was she a witch? Outside of the religious sense."

"Hard to say. Outside of the religious sense, we modern Westerners don't have a very good definition of what a witch is," I hedged.

"What's your definition, then?"

"Look, Breda, I really don't know that I'm comfortable discussing this in the middle of the street."

"Why not?" She hauled up short outside the deli on the corner and gave me a very pointed look.

"All right, then. There are a couple of kinds of witches. First you have your classic medieval witch: the ugly old hag who gets her powers from associating with the forces of darkness, who wreaks havoc around the village by making the crops fail and the milk sour. You might go to her for spells to smite your enemy, if you're desperate, but she's nobody's friend and you don't want to cross her. This, by the way, meshes with lots of indigenous witch concepts."

I sat down on the bench outside the deli and motioned for Breda to join me; this might take a while.

"Then you have your wise woman. She's similar to the first, except there's no connection to the forces of darkness. She's often a healer or midwife, and she has some knowledge of the way the unseen world works."

"Like you."

"Ha, ha," I laughed mirthlessly. That was as close as I wanted to go to my personal space. "According to some feminist theories, wise women suffered the most from witch hysteria, because any woman who preferred to live alone and demonstrated power and independence threatened the natural order of things as defined by the Catholic Church. So when natural disasters occurred, they got blamed.

"Then there are fairy tale witches. Most of the ones you hear about are the bad sort. They're kind of female ogres—eat little children, turn knights into stone and what not."

"Like in Hansel and Gretel."

"Right. But there's another kind, more analogous to the wise woman type: the witch-challenger. She operates according to a complex set of rules that she isn't allowed to break. Generally she's difficult to find; you have to pass a test or series of tests just to come to where she is. Then she sets you a task, and if you complete it to her satisfaction she rewards you with something that will aid you in your quest."

"What if you don't complete the task?"

"She eats you." Breda gulped and I couldn't help but grin. "I said this type wasn't necessarily evil; I didn't say they weren't dangerous. But I think we passed."

"So you're saying Grandmother Oonagh was a challenging witch?"

"She could have been just a wise woman, I guess. But I think not. Those wards…and the way she just took over my computer…. There was more to that than herbs and scented candles. She had some real power."

"Then if we passed her challenge, what's our reward?"

"I've been thinking about that." I realized suddenly that both my hands were clenched into fists in my lap; with an effort, I relaxed them. "We have more information about Tintri Fionn than we did before."

Breda snorted. "Not much. All that stuff about strangers are not of this world—we could have done as well by guessing."

"Maybe. But we learned at least one thing we didn't know to begin with. Seamus Mór contrived a way to bind an entity whose nature makes it immune to binding. And if it's been done once, it can be done again."

"What, you mean invent a spell or something?"

I wiped my palms on my jeans, but said nothing.

"I thought spells came from old, mouldy books."

"They came from somewhere before they were written down. Someone made them up."

"And you think you can? What gives you that idea?"

That was something I wasn't ready to answer. If things kept on the way they were going, someday I'd probably have to tell Breda everything about my powers. But not today.

"That's crazy, Caitlin. What if it goes wrong? Look at how my father's mucked things up. This *coimhthíoch* thing is dangerous. I'm not even sure we should get involved at all."

"I'm already involved." I swallowed back the nausea that rose at admitting it out loud. "This is my home, Breda. I'm not going to let some pissed off demon destroy it because your father was an idiot."

Breda slumped on the bench, her chin in her hands. "I don't see what you're going to do about it. Something tells me Internet searches and repeated visits to the Historical society aren't going to make a lasting impression where Tintri Fionn is concerned."

I shook my head. "No. I'm going to have to…come up with something else."

I swallowed. Coming up with something else was the very thing I'd been trying to avoid, all along. But my agreement that morning with Timber made any more avoidance impossible.

"So we're back to the spell thing." She sighed, then brightened. "Hey, I know. You're in contact with Archie Connolly's ghost, right? Why don't you just ask him what Seamus Mór did?"

"I've thought of that. The problem is, he never says anything coherent. It's like there's something blocking him from telling me anything important and I can't figure out how to get through."

"Maybe what's blocking him is the simple fact that he's dead. I don't suppose your thesis covered rituals for communicating with spirits?" She gave a nervous giggle.

"There was no practical examination, no."

"Man. Too bad you're not a witch."

"Yeah. Too bad about that." I didn't quite manage to keep the irony from my voice, but Breda didn't notice it.

"I want to go back to my hotel and change. Walk me there?"

I nodded. We got up, crossed the street and headed back the way we had come.

"Maybe things aren't as bad as they seem," Breda offered hopefully as we passed the theatre. "It's been quiet since your psychic storm, after all."

The words had hardly escaped her mouth when a huge crash rocked the street. Two doors down, the plate glass front window of the Western Realty offices exploded outward, spraying glass everywhere. Shocked passersby ducked and covered their heads; one screamed and staggered into the street, bleeding.

A minute later, a body came hurtling through the broken window and landed face down on the sidewalk.

"What the…?" Breda and I both ran to see what was going on, as did everyone else who happened to be downtown. We pushed our way to the front of the crowd just in time to see a briefcase follow the body through the window, and I ducked in reflex. The briefcase burst open, scattering files and papers before clocking the prone, suit-clad figure on the sidewalk square on the temple. He had just been in the process of picking himself up, but went down again with a grunt when the briefcase hit him. Still, in the moment that he was upright I got a look at his face and beneath the bruises I recognized him. It was the guy who had been smoking pot in the storeroom. Needless to say, he'd been fighting. From the look of his clothing, his opponent had used him to break the window before tossing him through.

"And don't let me catch you back here again!" a voice bellowed from within. Hard after it, another suited man came through the demolished window, this one under his own power. Lars Jensen, the owner-broker. He strode over to the cringing form on the sidewalk and aimed a kick at its midsection. "I don't run this office for scum like you to stink it up with dope!"

"God, overreact much?" Breda murmured.

The kick didn't land. Its intended target grabbed Lars's leg and jerked, pulling Lars to the ground beside him. I cringed as I heard the distinctive crack of a skull striking pavement. Then my pot-smoking acquaintance leapt astride his boss—former boss—and began pummeling him in the face, his craggy, dissolute features a mask of unholy glee.

"It's a shitty job anyway!" he screamed, grabbing the briefcase and smashing it over Lars's head.

A couple of cops ran up—the police station was right across the street—and tried to separate the pair, but only succeeded in being drawn into the fray. I grabbed Breda by the arm.

"Come on. Let's get out of here before this spreads." I dragged her back to the porch of the Mexican restaurant, where we stood, panting. And just in time, too; several other bystanders had been drawn into the fight and were now duking it out in front of the real estate office. I hoped no one would think to pick up pieces of the shattered window as weapons.

Somewhere in the distance, a siren sounded. In my head, the earth gave a slight shake, like a horse twitching flies from its skin.

"Okay, you're right, "said Breda. "It's weird down here today. Or does this sort of thing happen often?"

In reply I pointed across the street, at the shiny front door of the Emerald Isle. Grandmother Oonagh's parting words rang in my head,

When the stranger is released, he will be very, very angry. And very hungry.

Unless I missed my bet, Tintri Fionn was, at that moment, enjoying a snack.

"There's nothing else we can do up here. We have to get down there," I said.

Timber didn't look up from wetting down his bodhrán, a task that, though unnecessary in more humid parts of the world, was vital in Gordarosa's desert climate. Reaching for a tipper, he gave the drum an experimental roll and, finding it produced the requisite dull thud, laid the spray bottle aside.

"Aye. So you've said. Again and again."

He sounded aggrieved and I couldn't blame him. I'd had precious little else to say since coming home Monday afternoon. It was now Tuesday evening and I'd spent the intervening hours poring over the Emerald Isle blueprints, Seamus Óg's journal, the cave map, photocopies of Historical Museum documents and anything else I hoped might hold the slightest clue to the location of the cellar entrance. I'd even gone looking for Grandmother Oonagh again, but, as I'd suspected might be the case, she was no longer accessible. In fact, the entire Proverbs and Folklore website had disappeared. If I'd eaten or slept, I couldn't remember it. I certainly hadn't spent any kind of quality time with my husband.

"Timber, this is really important. You weren't there; you can't possibly imagine what it was like, seeing downtown erupt in violence the way it did. It's a miracle no one was seriously injured; next time might not be so lucky. We have to put a stop to whatever it is Casey's doing and to do that…"

"We could work on the drill," he pointed out. "Putting it out of commission would buy us time, at least."

I sighed. I actually had gone to the Emerald Isle Monday afternoon when things had calmed down. I'd stood on the balcony and stared at the thing working away beneath me. And I'd seen no way to disable it. Timber knew that. I'd told him so several times.

"I think it must be tied into the cellar as well," I said yet again. "I need to get down there."

"You're beating your head against a wall. You're not going to get anywhere going over the same things again and again."

"It's here somewhere, I know it is."

"Perhaps it is. But you're trying too hard to see it. You need to relax and think of something else and let the pieces fall together. That's all I'm saying. Now come on and get your flute out. Frank and Lisa will be here any minute."

"Be still, my heart," I grumbled, but I thrust the Emerald Isle papers into a pile on the coffee table and reached for my gig bag. A Red Branch rehearsal ranked low on my list of ways to relax, but it would without a doubt get my mind off ghosts and demons—of one sort, anyway.

Twenty minutes later—which was to say, fifteen minutes late—the doorbell rang, announcing the rest of the band's arrival. Lisa looked frumpy in an oversized sweater and tattered black jeans; she stalked over to a corner by the fireplace, plunked her fiddle case down and pulled a magazine out of the basket on the hearth without saying a word. I wondered if she and Frank had been fighting again, but if so, her partner didn't show any sign of it. Frank bounded into the living room like an excited puppy, waving a slim pamphlet that I recognized as a Carvin equipment catalogue. I rolled my eyes, having seen this manifestation of mania before. Now, instead of getting straight to work, we'd have to spend half an hour listening to Frank extol the virtues of the latest gadget he'd found that would make the band great without his having to practice.

"Come on, people," I said. "We're supposed to start at seven. Get your instruments out, get tuned up and let's get to it. I'd like to start with those original reels."

Lisa gave a pained sigh, laid her magazine aside and pulled out her fiddle, which she began plinking at in a put-upon way. Frank acted as if I hadn't spoken.

"Caitlin, I've just got to show you this one thing. This sound system—it's perfect for us." He thrust the catalogue into my face.

"We have a sound system." I pushed the catalogue away.

"Yeah, but now that we have a steady gig we need something better."

"What needs to be better is our playing, Frank. Get your guitar out."

"Just listen to this!" He sidestepped me and shoved the catalogue at Timber, who, to my extreme annoyance, actually examined it with interest.

"A twenty-four channel mixer with built-in effects and a two-band EQ, two dual fifteen-inch six-hundred watt three-way speakers and a DCM2000 amp," Frank recited. "Doesn't that sound great?"

"A twenty-four channel mixer! Frank, Red Branch is a four-piece band! Do you expect us to play six instruments at a time?"

"And if we add in mics, cords and cables we can get it all for just $2699!" he went on, undaunted.

I did the math automatically. Even under the terms of Casey's new contract twenty-seven hundred dollars added up to a lot of gigs, with none of us drawing pay.

"We don't need that much power." I glanced over my shoulder at Lisa in the vain hope she'd support me. She'd put down her fiddle and picked up the magazine again. "We're playing in a bar, not a stadium."

"It's never too early to plan for the future. Red Branch is going places, Caitlin. I can feel it."

"The next place we're going is the Carbondale Mountain Fair. They provide their own sound, but they aren't going to play the set for us. So we need to rehearse," I said through clenched teeth.

Lisa glanced up from her magazine. "God, Caitlin, relax! You always get so uptight before a gig. No wonder you never have any fun. Anyway, we're doing fine at the Emerald Isle, so what's the worry?"

I counted to ten and reached for my flute. "I'm going to start playing in thirty seconds. I'd appreciate it if you'd join me."

"It's really unprofessional to start rehearsing without tuning up," Frank said with a professorial glance over the tops of his glasses.

"Then I guess we'd better tune up, hadn't we?"

I gazed at Frank expectantly until he subsided onto the ottoman and took out his guitar. Another stare induced Lisa to trade her magazine for her fiddle once again, and for a few minutes the living room rang with the sound of strings being twanged and adjusted. When the guitar and fiddle were in as good tune as their players could make them, Frank struck a D chord so I could bring my flute into the mix.

"You're sharp," Lisa snapped, as if I had done it on purpose.

I pulled out the head joint to compensate and tried again. This time the tone was spot on.

"All right, then. The new reels." I nodded at Timber, who gave the beat, and after a count of eight we were away.

Or, I was away. Lisa stumbled through the first phrase, missed half the notes in the second, and dropped out. Frank did somewhat better; at least, he hit the appropriate chords on the downbeats. The rest he neglected to play at all.

Halfway through the first tune I stopped.

"What was that?"

Lisa looked away. Frank shrugged.

"Maybe we should take it at half tempo."

"We spent the better part of our last rehearsal playing this set at half tempo. We agreed to come back ready to play up to speed. Did you guys even practice? Where are your charts?"

Frank fumbled around in his guitar case. "I think I have them here somewhere…"

"Well get them out! I didn't spend hours copying them for you to leave them in your guitar case." I whirled on Lisa, who at least had the charts spread out on the floor in front of her. "What's your excuse?"

She gave me a pathetic, wide-eyed stare. "It's been so hectic at work this week. I just didn't have time to practice. You know how it is. And I don't learn things as quickly as you do, anyway."

I closed my eyes and counted another ten, breathing deeply. It didn't help.

"Go home," I said, my eyes still closed.

"What?" I heard Frank's guitar hit the ground with a soft vibration of strings.

"You heard me." I opened my eyes to see every member of the band staring at me aghast, my husband included. "Go home. I'm tired of wasting my time like this."

"But Caitlin!" Lisa's eyes got even wider. "The Mountain Fair! It's big deal; we have to be ready!"

"We're doing fine at the Emerald Isle, so what's the worry?" I mocked savagely. "If you guys don't want to learn anything new it's no skin off my back. Now get out of here."

I set my flute down carefully, got up from the sofa and stalked down the hall to the kitchen, where I stood, shaking, until I heard the front door close behind them.

"It's all right," Timber called. "They're gone."

I couldn't move, I was so angry. I bent my head over the kitchen counter and watched little drops of water roll off the tip of my nose and splash onto the Formica without realizing I was crying. After a while, I felt my husband's arms around me. I turned, buried my face in his chest, and bawled.

"Shh," he whispered, stroking my hair. "They had it coming."

"I guess." I wiped my nose on the back of my hand and allowed him to lead me back into the living room. "It's just…I'm so tired of it all."

"I know."

We sat on the sofa. Something crackled under me and I pulled the Carvin catalogue out from under my leg. I threw it at the wall.

"Gods! What will it be next! A new…bloody…sound system!"

"It's a nice one," Timber said, amiably. The sole reason I didn't punch him was that I knew he was trying to distract me and I was perfectly willing to be distracted.

"Yeah, for a metal band. What in the world is Frank thinking? No, don't answer that, I already know. But really! What could a primarily acoustic Irish band want with so much juice? We probably couldn't even run it. We'd blow a circuit or something."

"Actually, the stage wiring is heavy duty." Timber wound a lock of my hair through his fingers. "You could run a metal band through it without any problem at all. There's three fifty amp fuses on that circuit."

"That's a lot?" The numbers meant nothing to me.

"It's a lot."

"But we already blew it once, remember?"

"We didn't blow it. Someone had turned it off. See, when a fuse blows, the switch flips back only part of the way. When I checked the breaker box that time, the switch was flipped back all the way. So someone turned it off intentionally."

"Why would anyone do that?" I closed my eyes. The emotional storm was passing and I felt warm, and safe, and dreadfully sleepy.

"Dinna ken." I felt Timber shrug. "Maybe Casey was having some work done on the stage."

And then, all at once, I did not feel sleepy at all. The disturbing, familiar sensation of puzzle pieces falling into place in my head jolted me wide awake, and I sat up with a start.

"On the stage…Timber, I need you to make a phone call."

"You've thought of something."

"I have. I need you to call Curtis Richards and ask him a question."

He raised an eyebrow at me when I told him the question, but he dutifully trotted upstairs to the bedroom to retrieve his cell phone. When he didn't come back for a long time, I followed.

Timber was sitting on the bed, a dazed expression on his face, his cell phone in one lax hand.

"How did you know?"

I shook my head and plucked my own phone from my nightstand.

"What now?"

"I have to call Breda." I was already punching in the cell number she had given me. She picked up on the first ring. "Hey, it's Caitlin. Do you still have the keys to the bar?...You do?...Great. Meet us there at three."

"Three in the morning!" Timber groaned. "Woman, I'm supposed to be working on the roof tomorrow!"

I flipped my phone closed. Despite the ongoing sleep deprivation and despite the disastrous rehearsal, I felt better than I had in days. I had finally discovered where the secret cellar entrance lay hidden. In a few hours, we'd be standing in the circle of Tintri Fionn.

"Pray for rain," I said.

Chapter Seventeen

"When is a stage not a stage?"

My question echoed through the deserted bar, an eerie melody played over the syncopated click of our footsteps on the parquet floor. Was it my imagination, or could I feel those seven words being drawn down through the ground to add their small energy to the drill grinding away at Tintri Fionn's prison, bit by bit? I shivered.

"Oh, wait; I know!" Breda's voice came from so close behind my ear that I jumped. "When it's a jar, right?"

I'd wanted to leave her behind. Timber and I meant to descend into the cavern, but we had no idea what we'd find there. It was stupid and dangerous and we had no other option, not if we wanted to get a clear picture of what we were dealing with. All Breda had had to do was unlock the bar for us and leave. Of course, she would have none of it.

"That's a door," growled Timber from the rear, still disgruntled at the necessity of another pre-dawn foray. We'd tried to catch a few hours' rest before setting out on this latest venture; we'd even been successful. But waking to an alarm at two in the morning is never a happy event. And prayers for rain and subsequent cancellation of the next day's work had gone un-heeded. Outside the sky was bright and full of stars, without a cloud in sight.

"When it's a blind," I said.

I wove a twisted path between the tables in the front room, trying not to touch anything. I didn't like being there and didn't want to leave more trace of my presence than I could help. I'd have hated for something stupid like dandruff to form the basis for a nasty bit of retaliation, if Casey ever got wind of this. If he wasn't there already.

"I don't get it," said Breda after a minute.

"It's not a pun. Watch yourself here; they left the chairs down at this table." Everywhere else the chairs had been turned upside down on the table tops at closing, but at the two-top nearest the entrance to the back room both were down and sat slightly removed, as if they had been vacated moments before. I wondered if that meant anything and hoped not. I told myself the closing staff had just been lazy.

"I don't see why we can't have a light. I'm here with a key, after all."

"Aye, an hour after closing and dressed for mayhem." All of us were black-clad again, though Timber had left his leather jacket and lockpicks at home. "Perhaps you'll want to explain that to the nice policeman when he comes knocking on the door to see if everything's all right."

"I could tell him I came in late to do the books."

"With two friends."

"There's plenty of light from outside," I said, forestalling further argument. There was; a street lamp on the corner shone right in the Emerald Isle's front window. It made for a lot of disturbing shadows, but we could see easily enough if we paid attention. "We can turn on one of the table lamps in back, maybe."

I edged into the narrow aisle between the bistro tables and headed for the stage, Breda and Timber following.

"So how is a stage a blind?"

"It's a form of misdirection, like in a Vegas magician's act. Put a band on it, and no one questions it or wonders why it's there. Nights when the band's not playing, well, it's still a stage. Because everyone knows a band has been there. But take away the band and what do you have? A big platform that conceals a substantial portion of the floor."

"Oh," said Breda. Then, with more significance, "Oh!"

I nodded. "That's why Casey needed to hire a band, even a half-assed band like Red Branch. He probably could have managed without it. You see a platform in a bar and you just assume it's a stage, whether a band's playing on it or not. There's always the possibility of a band. But never having a band might lead to awkward questions. I'm sure that's something your father would have wanted to avoid. Okay, I think we can risk some light."

Timber flicked on the lamp on the table nearest the stage. It seemed terribly bright, and it took a minute for my eyes to adjust. When they did, I found myself staring up at our sound system, all set up as if Red Branch would be beginning a set at any minute. It reminded me of my recent dream, and I shivered.

"Strangely enough, I have Frank to thank for putting me onto this," I said. "If he hadn't brought up the issue of a newer, more powerful sound system, I would never have found out that this stage carries way more juice than it should. And Timber would never have told me that the power had been turned off before our gig last Thursday night."

Breda sat on the edge of the stage. "I don't see what power has to do with it."

"The stage circuit carries three fifty amp fuses," Timber explained. "About three times the juice Casey would need to supply any band he'd be likely to hire. So what's the rest of it for? Our guess is that shutting off the power to the stage reroutes it somewhere else."

"Somewhere else, like the cellar."

"Aye. So when you threw the switch in the breaker box upstairs, you'd be powering up the cellar."

"That's a lot of could-be's."

"I know. But I'm pretty sure I'm right because of Curtis Richards' answer to a very important question," I said.

"Curtis Richards? He's the cement guy, right? What did you ask him?"

"Was the stage in place when he poured the floor? Curtis said yes. Which means, he had no idea what was under it." I gave my husband a withering look. "Really, I'm surprised it didn't come up during your conversation. I thought you asked him if he noticed anything unusual about the job."

"I did. He didn't mention anything but the rebar. Perhaps the stage thing didn't strike him as odd. A lot of these old buildings have unusual features you have to work around. You get used to it after a while." He shrugged.

"So when you figured out the switch had been turned off…."

"Well, I wondered why someone would do such a thing, of course. And that made me think hard about the stage. And the pieces just fell into place."

"And now?"

"Now we check it out."

Hoping I showed more confidence than I felt, I made my way to the breaker box, opened it, and threw the switch over. Almost at once the room seemed to grow quieter, as if a distant humming sound just below the normal range of hearing had been suddenly silenced. I almost had convinced myself the silence was in my imagination when Breda spoke up.

"Anyone else notice that?"

"Aye." Timber came around the stage to join me, flexing his arms as if preparing for battle. "What do you think, love? Do we move some of this equipment?"

I eyed the stage with dismay. My brainstorm had panned out so far, but I wasn't sure how to proceed.

"I don't know. Let's have a look."

The three of us walked around to the back of the stage and stood staring, perplexed, at the tangle of power cords running from our amplifiers to the outlets.

"Okay. Unplug these," I directed. "And shove the amps to the sides, I guess."

Timber immediately moved to do as I had directed. Breda hesitated.

"What are you going to do?"

I sat down on the floor. "Meditate and hope something comes to me."

Breda snorted, but reached for the nearest amp cord and began arranging it into a neat coil. I stared at the flat, plywood back of the stage in front of me. To my eyes, it appeared unremarkable; I couldn't see any latches or hinges. No button marked "push here for secret cellar access." Nothing like that.

"Come on," I muttered. "Where are you?"

The stage declined to answer.

No avoiding it: time to make use of my something extra. If the entrance were here and Casey accessed it regularly, he'd have left a residual energy trace. With a little effort, I should be able to find it. I drew in a deep breath and tried to relax, remembering how looking for Jake had affected me.

I closed my eyes and reached out with my mind. Almost at once my fingers began to tingle. I felt my hands lift of their own accord; my arms stretched out to the stage back. Something was there; I knew it. The thought filled me with a sudden exhilaration, which I quashed with difficulty; now I needed to feel and pay attention, not get distracted by random ideas and impulses. My hands floated to the top of the stage, wandered over it for a second, and drifted down. They found a lip where the top of the stage overhung the back by nearly an inch. The underside of the lip was very smooth to the touch.

"What's she doing?" I heard Breda ask above me.

"Hush," came Timber's distant reply.

My fingers walked the lip of the stage, spiderlike. At a distance of a foot apart, they found nothing. Eighteen inches, two feet, nothing. But just at the point where my arms extended as far as they could go, the tips of my fingers felt metal and I experienced a sudden jolt like an electric shock. Further exploration identified two sliding catches, like the ones on expensive luggage, and two buttons. I depressed the buttons and slid the catches in sequence, but nothing happened. I reversed the sequence, and nothing happened again. But when I held the buttons down with my thumbs and manipulated the catches with my fingers, I felt something lift. I pushed, and a three foot square section of the stage slid back on well-oiled guides, exposing a very deep, very dark hole.

"Wow," said Breda.

I got to my feet, blinking. Looking into the hole, I saw a metal ladder leading down into the darkness. Still feeling as though I was not quite operating under my own power, I set my foot on the topmost rung.

"Wait a minute." Timber grabbed me by the arm and pulled me back. "I'm going first, aye? Better for me to meet any surprises than you."

I swept my eyes over the big, construction worker's muscles in his arms and nodded.

He didn't go down right away. Instead, he picked up the nine-volt flashlight he had brought, switched it on, and shined the beam down the hole. I could see motes of dust floating a long way down, but no bottom.

"Deep," he said. "Thirty, maybe forty feet. Well, here goes."

Flashlight in one hand, he swung into the hole and started down the ladder. Breda and I crowded over the entrance, watching the light quiver and bob with his progress. From time to time, the light paused and swept from side to side as Timber examined his surroundings. After what seemed an eternity, the light stopped one last time and described a circle.

"All right." Timber's soft call echoed from the depths. "It looks clear so far. Come down."

I don't like ladders at the best of times. Climbing down a dark hole into a magician's secret stronghold, even with a loving husband waiting for me at the bottom, is not high on my list of experiences I'd like to repeat. My heart beat a painful rhythm in my chest, and I fancied I could hear Breda's doing the same as she came down after me. The rungs of the ladder were cold and sharp, making me wish I'd had the foresight to wear gloves. I couldn't see a thing, so the whole descent had to be done by feel. More than once my foot slipped and I barely caught myself before falling. The only positive aspect of the entire affair was that it was not damp.

I thought about Casey. I thought about the demon. I wondered what I would do if either of them was really there, and shivered. I'd promised Timber I'd take back my powers, but even if I did, I wasn't sure what use they'd be. My powers ran to the defensive. Shielding myself, hiding myself. I could unweave others' workings; that was the power I hoped to use to undo the drill spell if I could. But, if Casey were down there, it would be up to Timber to subdue him. Our only advantage lay in the fact that he would not be expecting us. He was a Ceremonial Magician, not a true mage. Ceremonial Magic took time to prepare.

And the demon? What about it? I told myself Tintri Fionn was still bound, and swallowed my fear, and kept going.

The end came without warning. Reaching for the next rung, my sneakered foot hit an unexpected patch of rough ground; my ankle turned sharply and I bit back a cry. In a stupid reflex, my fingers released the rung they were holding and for an instant I fell backward. Then Timber's steady arms closed around me and I heard his reassuring whisper close to my ear.

"Got you."

He swept me out of the way just in time for Breda to alight, as gracefully as if she descended thirty-foot ladders into scary pits every day.

"Oof. Chilly down here, isn't it?" She tugged the zipper of her hooded sweatshirt up as far as it would go. I rubbed my bare arms, feeling goose pimples, and wished I had worn something more sensible than a camisole.

We were crowded into a black bubble perhaps six feet in diameter. Not a perfectly spherical bubble, like the kind kids blow from soapsuds, but a one squashed a little flat, as if someone had stepped on it. The floor was rough and stony. Overhead, the ladder led back up through a fissure in the ceiling.

"Caves," I said. This whole area had been chock full of volcanoes back in the day. Gordarosa, on a rise sloping down to the flood plain of the Gordarosa river, could well be riddled with them.

"Aye." Timber shined his light back up the ladder. "That rock chimney goes up a good long way. Casey didn't have to excavate far to reach it, only about ten feet. I wonder how he knew that would be?"

"Seamus Óg." I asserted. "The diary said his father used to bring him down here when he was young. I'm almost certain he made that map."

"Must have been." Timber turned away from the ladder and swept his light over the wall opposite it, where a narrower fissure gaped. "I believe that's our path."

I eyed the fissure askance. I didn't like the idea of plunging into a dark, cramped corridor without having a good idea of what lay ahead.

Breda seemed to share my reluctance.

"I thought you said there would be power down here," she said.

Timber took a step into the fissure and ran his light over the walls and up to the ceiling. The walls nearly touched his shoulders.

"It's wired." He pointed with the flashlight and we could all see the bare bulb screwed into a socket in the rock overhead.

Electrical wire ran from the socket, presumably to another bulb further along.

"Great. Then all we need is to find the switch."

Breda made as if to seize Timber's flashlight and begin an examination of the cave where we stood. I stopped her.

"I'm not sure that would be wise."

"You think it's a good idea to stumble around in the dark?"

"No, but I also don't think it's a good idea to go flicking switches without thinking. We might not be alone down here. Turning on the lights could alert…someone…to our presence."

"You think there's someone waiting at the end of the tunnel?" Breda sounded skeptical. "In the dark? Please, Caitlin. The trapdoor was shut. How would he have got in?"

"If someone is there, he's heard us by now," Timber put in. "Sound carries underground, and we havena exactly been keeping our voices down. Let's be a little quieter, aye?"

"Granted, it seems unlikely," I whispered, chastened. "But I just don't know. This business scares me, and we'd best be careful. That's all I'm saying."

"Do you want to go back up?"

Breda's voice held a nasty, taunting note and I glanced sharply at her set face, pale as a moon in the shadows. She was just as scared as I, maybe more so.

"No. I've come this far. I want to see what's down here."

I jerked my head at Timber, who squeezed himself into the fissure and started down it, his light bobbing before him. With a last glance over my shoulder at Breda, I followed.

The floor sloped upward at a steep grade, with dips and rocks making the footing tricky. Concentrating on making my way forward, I did not hear Breda come up behind me. She touched my elbow, and I flinched, suppressing a little scream.

"How did he do it? My father?" She seemed desperate to know.

"It's no such a big job." Timber shrugged, full of a construction worker's confidence. "A crew of five could do it in two, three weeks, including building the stage."

"But the electricity…the excavation…How did he keep it a secret?" Breda stuttered, and I knew what was bothering her. History was full of tyrants who murdered the workmen who built their castles, to keep their secrets safe.

Again, Timber answered her. "It wouldna have been too difficult. Put out word that you'd pay well for a crew who would keep their mouths shut. Keep them in a hotel out of town and work at night. Then when it's done, tell them to get lost." The flashlight beam passed over the walls. "Aye, this has been widened a bit. You can see the marks of the power chisel here, and here."

"There'd be the electrical inspection to pass," I couldn't help but put in. I wanted reassuring as much as Breda. "He couldn't hide that funny breaker box."

"Aye, he'd have to keep the electrician around for a bit. Perhaps even have him do the legitimate work; I never asked about that. But Red only inspects the work he knows is there, ken. You'd get everything ready to go, have the inspection. Then when you got your certificate, the electrician could come back and connect the secret wiring to the box."

"Oh," Breda said in a weak voice, not sounding comforted.

"It happens all the time," Timber said in a matter of fact way that made me wonder what kind of job sites he'd been working on.

The fissure went on at a slight curve for a dozen or so more paces. Then I sensed the walls receding on either side, and the air felt less heavy than it had. We had reached the big cavern on the map, I thought. If I was right, this would be Archie's cellar, where Tintri Fionn was bound. I took a hesitant breath, half expecting my lungs to contract against the ozone tingle of deep magic. When nothing happened I breathed more deeply. The heady rush of oxygen told me I had not done so in far too long.

"Right. Stay close," Timber said. He veered off left, keeping along the wall.

Breda and I needed no encouragement. We entered the chamber right on his heels. So when Timber stumbled over something on the floor near the wall, we all went down in a heap together.

"Hell!" Timber flailed out with both hands to catch himself, losing the flashlight, which rolled a little distance towards the center of the cavern. There was a sickening crunch. I had just time to mouth a brief prayer that the crunch had nothing to do with any portion of my husband's anatomy before I caught my foot on his outstretched leg and fell too, jamming my knee painfully on something sharp that was not a stone. Breda collided with my back, sending me the rest of the way to the ground and coming to rest on top of me.

For a brief moment we all lay where we had fallen, stunned. The silence was total but for Breda's heavy breathing in my ear; I couldn't hear Timber at all. Panicked, I reached out a hand and found what I thought was his thigh. I clenched my fingers around it and gave it a shake.

"Timber! Are you all right."

"Reach a little higher and I'll be just fine." He sounded breathless but not in pain. I released my hold and jerked my hand away. "Stay here while I get the light."

I heard him crawl off towards the place where it had landed. A sudden lessening of the weight on my back told me that Breda had rolled off me, so I sat up.

"You okay?" I groped for her hand in the darkness.

"I think so." Her fingers found mine and gave a quick squeeze. "What about you? Your hand is sticky."

"I think I cut it on something. It's not bad."

"Serves you right for making us wander around in the dark…. Oh, God."

Timber had returned with the flashlight and we could all see, now, exactly what we had tripped over.

It was a pile of human bones. I tried very hard not to remember any stories of warriors being sacrificed and buried in the foundations of old buildings, so their ghosts would watch over the places for all eternity.

"Pay a crew to keep their mouths shut?" Breda sounded ready to throw up.

Timber crouched down and picked up a femur. "Och, these are old. Look how clean and dry they are. Besides, if you sacrificed a person to act as your watchman, you'd lay him out with some dignity, wouldn't you? Provide him with weapons, too." He tossed the femur aside and rooted through the pile. "This poor fellow's all in a heap. I'm guessing he was already here. Casey probably just found him and stuck him somewhere out of the way."

"Why do you know these things?" Breda glanced at the pile of bones, shuddered, and looked accusingly at me. "Why does he know these things?"

I shrugged. I didn't think it quite the time to explain my husband's outré interests.

"Ah. Here we are." Timber lifted up a skull and held it in the light. No mystery as to what had killed this guy. The whole right side of the cranium was caved in. With a little more rooting, Timber came up with several bone fragments that fitted into the spot. "Archie Connolly, I presume."

I squeezed my eyes shut, but that didn't block out the sudden memory of my first encounter with the ghost, gazing apologetically at me as his brains dripped down the side of his face. My stomach heaved.

"Poor guy." Breda reached a tentative finger towards a section of ribcage, but drew it back without touching. "So this must be the place. And he did die down here. Murdered, you think?"

"I don't know." I shook my head, swallowing back bile. "At first I thought so. Now that we've found him, though, I'm not so sure. No one knew about this place, except the Connolly family. The only person who could have murdered him here was Seamus Óg, and we know he never came back."

"The demon, maybe?"

"It's bound, remember? I don't see how…." The pile of bones blurred before my eyes. They had something to tell me if only I would listen. I felt an almost overwhelming compulsion to reach out and take the skull from Timber's hands into my own and hold it up to my ear. Resolutely I turned away, telling myself this was not the time. I blinked, and the bones came back into focus.

"Let's look for a light, aye? I'm fairly certain we're alone down here, and I dinna fancy tripping over anything else. Unless you feel something."

Timber waved his flashlight at me. I dashed away the cold sweat that had broken out on my face, nodded and reached out into the dark with my mind.

"Nothing," I said after a moment. "Just cold."

From his pocket Timber produced a mini Maglite, which he passed to me. "You two keep to the wall. The beam of this doesn't go very far; it'll be safer. I'm going across."

Nodding, I got to my feet and twisted the Maglite on. Timber started boldly, if slowly, into the center of the cavern, his light bobbing before him. For a cowardly second I wished I were by his side, not left here on my own with Breda to look after in the bargain. With a sigh I skirted the pile of Archie's bones and headed left along the wall. Breda followed close as a shadow.

We hadn't gone far when my flashlight beam gleamed on metal.

I stopped, unable at once to assimilate what I was seeing. Stacked against the wall were half a dozen hav-a-heart traps, the kind of metal cages people use to catch raccoons and rabbits and the like and transport them off their property, in lieu of setting out poison or lying in wait with a shotgun. Leaned up against them was a big bag of generic pet food, half empty.

"What the heck?" Breda asked.

All the traps stood vacant, but several showed signs of recent occupation, and I remembered Frank's casual mention that there had been a lot of ads for missing pets in the last week's Mountain Market. I shivered. This was getting worse and worse.

"My guess? Someone's been conducting animal sacrifices."

"Animal...?" Breda shuddered.

"Blood's a powerful tool in magic. And Seamus Óg's journal did mention it."

"Caitlin."

Timber's voice drifted out of the gloom behind me, soft yet insistent, and I turned to meet it. I could see the beam of his flashlight somewhere in the center of the room, pointing at the ground.

"Come here to me. No, Breda, you stay," he added as she began to follow. He must have heard something that occasioned the comment; he couldn't possibly have seen her. "Caitlin, give her your flashlight."

I handed the Maglite over and started off, hoping there was nothing in the way; it was utterly dark but for the pinpoint of light to tell me where my husband stood. The cavern got colder as I approached its midpoint, until at one spot, near what I supposed to be the center of the ritual circle, I passed through an area cold as ice. I shook off a shudder and kept going without thinking about what it might mean.

When I reached my husband, I found him crouched over something on the floor. I laid a hand on his shoulder and he jerked upright, whirling to face me. I had a brief impression of a grim, set expression on his face and then his flashlight beam pointed straight into my eyes, blinding me. I had no doubt he had done this on purpose and there was something behind him he did not want me to see.

"What is it?" I shielded my eyes with my arm, but it didn't help much. I glanced at the ground but I could only make out the shape of Timber's legs, set wide in a fighting stance.

"I want you to take Breda and get her out of here. I'll be along soon. No questions. Do it now."

"You found something."

"I said no questions!" he barked in a tone I only heard from him in situations of extreme danger. The shock of it startled me into obedience and I began to turn around. But by that time it was too late. Breda had found the light switch.

All around the cavern walls bulbs behind pearlized shades popped on. The light was still dim—some part of my mind that insists on keeping track of such things recognized the bulbs as no more than twenty-five watt ones—but after the long dark, the effect was that of a sudden sunrise. I stood blinking at what the light now revealed as a vast, volcanic cave, roughly circular, with walls nearly fifty feet apart at their widest. The ground was packed dirt, and standing out darkly from the dirt at the center-most part of the cave were the lines and patterns of Tintri Fionn's prison. I was standing in the southern portion of the circle, near the glyph for "Connolly."

That was all I had time to notice before Breda screamed.

She had worked her way around the wall and now stood almost directly behind Timber; I could see her clearly over his shoulder. Her position also gave her a perfect view of the thing Timber had not meant for either of us to see, and though she was a good fifteen feet away there was no doubt that she recognized it for what it was. Being much closer, I recognized it, too. It was a body.

Blood magic, indeed.

Breda screamed again and dashed forward, a move which found me totally unprepared; in her place most people would likely have fainted or at least headed for the exit. Timber leaped over the body and caught her before she could throw herself down on it. She struggled and pummeled him, but he had a foot and a hundred pounds on her and had no trouble holding her fast. After a brief contest she subsided against him, heaving. Over his shoulder, wild eyes fixed on the still form on the floor.

"Oh God. Oh God," she chanted. "Who is it? Oh God— is it Jake?"

I shook my head. It was not Jake. "Timber, let her see."

My husband released her and moved aside. Breda took one step forward and then another. Then she hurled herself onto the corpse with a strangled wail.

It was Sean Casey. He was dressed in dark robes, just as I had seen him in my last flash of vision. And his throat had been cut from ear to ear.

Chapter Eighteen

"He's been dead a while," Timber said.

"How long?" I turned my face away. Now that the initial shock had worn off I recalled my marked distaste for looking at dead things. I could imagine all too easily the quickness with which life could be snuffed out: one minute there, the next minute gone.

"A few days. Maybe more." He took a closer look at the edge of the wound in Casey's throat, gaping like a second, grotesque smile. "It's hard to tell. The cold down here has kept him pretty well preserved."

Breda made a strangled sound. It had taken us several minutes and a lot of fighting to pry her off the corpse; now she huddled on the ground beside me, her head in my lap. Absently, I stroked her hair. She shuddered once and grew still.

"'Who would have thought the old man to have had so much blood in him,'" I quoted in a whisper. It was everywhere. A huge, dark splotch of it showed where it had been poured on the Connolly glyph. Some had splattered the floor six feet away. Casey's ritual robes were clotted with it.

"'What need we fear who knows it, when none can call our power to accompt?'" Timber murmured in reply. "It looks like someone did call his power to accompt."

I sighed. "Well, now we know why he hasn't turned up at the bar in so long." As far as we knew, no one had seen Casey since the previous Thursday. That same night, we had discovered the stage power had been switched off. And then both Timber and I had felt that terrible psychic force. Maybe this horrible murder had been taking place right under our feet. Maybe it had been meant to release Tintri Fionn. "And what Archie was getting at Thursday."

"Aye."

"We have to call the police," Breda said from my lap.

Timber's eyes met mine over the body. He shook his head. I cleared my throat.

"I don't think we can do that, Breda."

"What?" She sat up, swiping tears and snot from her face with the back of her hand. Her eyes were red and swollen and she looked almost inhuman in her grief. "Why not? My father's been murdered, Caitlin. This isn't a game anymore."

"I never thought it was. But Breda, if we call the police this whole cave will become a crime scene. It'll be guarded. We won't be able to get down here again, and we'll lose any chance we have of preventing Tintri Fionn from breaking free."

"Do you think I care?" For a single second, Breda's eyes blazed like twin blue fires. Then they dimmed as a fresh wash of tears put the fires out. "Anyway, my father's dead. Whatever plans he had are over."

"It's not so simple. The drill he built is still functioning. The binding is already cracked. You saw what happened downtown. Unless we repair the damage, things will get worse and worse. We have to have access."

Breda sniffled, but nodded. I thought I had never seen anything so brave as the way she pulled herself together then. "I guess you're right. I wouldn't want his legacy to be mass insanity in Gordarosa. Maybe if we put things right it will redeem him somehow."

Timber patted her on the shoulder. "Aye. Perhaps it will." He stood and glanced around the cavern. "I think perhaps it would be best if we left now. Unless you wanted to look around more…?"

I got to my feet as well. "I suppose I should see if I can find where the drill is connected," I said without any eagerness. I'd had my fill of the cave, and my friend needed me. I prepared to open myself to the magic.

"Wait a minute," Breda said, forestalling me.

I turned back around to see her standing close by her father's body, swaying a little on her feet. She had a very strange expression on her face, part confusion, part desperation.

"We're not just going to leave him here, are we? I thought…. I thought we could bury him. Not officially, I understand that…but somewhere."

Already touching my Sight, I saw it in her mind: a grave scooped out of the alkaline soil somewhere in the adobe flats between Gordarosa and Murtaw, a brief prayer, a candle burning. I looked away, heart torn in pieces by the wasteland of her face.

Timber spoke before I could.

"No, Breda love, we canna do that either."

"But why? I understand about the police, really I do…"

"Breda." I moved forward and touched her gently on the arm; she started like a half-trained colt. "You said it yourself, your father was murdered. Not by a demon, but by a person. Someone was in this with him, someone we don't know about. With luck, that person doesn't know about us, either."

I had a very strong suspicion of that person's identity. Only two people knew about Tintri Fionn, other than us. One of them had been Casey, but Casey was dead. Dead for days, according to Timber, yet the psychic drill still functioned as strongly as ever. If Casey had constructed it, as I had thought, the magic would have begun to break down with his death. So it must be the other. The one who had a much better motive for wanting to control a demon.

"But…"

Breda's eyes were glazing over—belated shock, I thought. It put me in mind of something small and frail frozen in a pool of ice. The notion of some final ritual had been the sole source of her strength and courage, and I was taking it away.

"Whoever did this left your father here. He'll expect to find the…body…when he comes back. Removing it would tell him someone has been here and knows what happened. We can't afford that. At best, he'd panic, throw a lot of power into some last ditch effort to break through the binding before we could stop him. He might even succeed."

"Then maybe we *should* go to the police. If they put the cavern under surveillance, whoever did this couldn't get in either. We'd have time for more research, and when the investigation ended we'd be ready."

The idea tempted me more than I wanted it to. But I shook my head. "And in the meantime, your father's confederate would come looking for us. He's killed once already. I doubt he'd balk at doing so again, if he thought we stood in his way. I'm sorry, Breda. It's safest just to leave things as we found them."

She looked at the ground. Under my hand, her arm was as tense as a plucked harp string; I could feel it vibrating with each breath she took.

"I see," she said, after a long time. The harp string quivered a final time and stilled.

The flatness of her voice should have warned me, but I wanted too much to believe she understood, and didn't hear it. I gave her arm a squeeze, feeling her pain, promising in my heart to make it up to her somehow.

She lifted her eyes and the hatred in them hit me like a slap.

"I wish I'd never met either of you."

She pushed past me and stalked away through the cavern and up the tunnel without looking back. Stunned, I took a step after her, but Timber caught my arm.

"Let her go."

"But Timber…."

"She's been through a lot. Ye canna make it right for her. Give her time; she'll come around."

Or she won't. The words he didn't say hung in the air.

I stared down at Sean Casey's body, wishing I could cover his face with his robes or fold his hands on his breast, knowing I could do neither. All I could do was hope that in some distant place beyond the world we knew, he had found some kind of peace.

I had forgotten all about the drill.

Timber found the light switch and flicked it off, plunging the cave back into darkness. His flashlight bobbed towards me; he took my hand and led me out through the tunnel and up the ladder. While he slid the trap door closed, shoved our equipment back into place and switched the power in the breaker box back over, I stood mute by the stage, unable to think, unable even to feel. I couldn't comprehend what was wrong with me. It wasn't my father whose body we'd found and been forced to leave there, alone in the dark.

Outside, false dawn painted the street an eerie yellow-grey. A finger of sun poked over the horizon to point at the empty space where Breda's car had stood moments before. I let Timber load me into the truck, drive me home and tuck me into bed. He disappeared for a moment and I heard his soft voice on the phone in the hall, telling the contractor at his job that something had come up and he wouldn't be in to work today. Then he crawled into bed beside me, and before long I heard his soft snoring.

I lay looking up at the ceiling for a long time.

The next few days went by in a blur. When I woke late Wednesday afternoon, the strange, hollow feeling in my gut had abated somewhat, but I was still disoriented and unable to concentrate. I puttered around at household tasks, leaving them half-finished when my mind fell on something else that needed doing and I wandered away. I waited for my brain to kick into gear, but it never did. I tried calling Breda, but she didn't answer and after leaving several incoherent messages I gave up. Timber was right. She'd come around. Or she wouldn't.

I couldn't believe how much I missed her.

Downtown, the mood remained tense. No fights broke out as I sleepwalked through my daily round of errands, but I heard more than one squabble threaten to escalate before a glimpse of the police car cruising back and forth on Main Street called the participants to their senses. In the shops, the clerks were harried and angry, the customers impatient and snide. I recognized the demon's touch and knew I should do something. I knew that if Tintri Fionn were freed, no number of police cars would keep Gordarosa from tearing itself apart. Yet I couldn't make myself care enough.

One time Timber said to me, "I ken you're grieving, love. But there's work to be done."

I stared at him and didn't answer, and soon I heard the sound of his frustrated drum wafting from upstairs, ineffectual as I felt.

Thursday night came, and with it our next gig. I considered blowing it off. I didn't want to set foot in the Emerald Isle again. I didn't want Red Branch to supply any power to the arcane drill boring into Tintri Fionn's prison, cracking it ever wider open. But Frank and Lisa didn't know that about that; I certainly wasn't going to tell them, and I didn't feel up to inventing a plausible excuse to cancel on short notice. So when eight o'clock arrived I put on my makeup, chose something pretty from the closet and went.

The bar was a madhouse, and not in a good way. The atmosphere hit me almost as hard as it had the very first time I'd walked through the door. In a way it was worse, because the bar had been empty then; now people crammed every corner and I could feel their roiling emotions like a nest of snakes in my belly. The jovial atmosphere had been twisted into something ugly, no doubt due to the demon's increasing influence; I sensed fear, and anger, and a kind of insatiable hunger. I had played to similar audiences before and it never turned out well.

Frank and Lisa were nowhere to be seen. I wondered if my tantrum of Tuesday night had scared them off for good and almost hoped it had. I would have welcomed a good excuse to turn tail and run.

"This is not good." I plunked my gig bag down on the stage and set off for the bar.

"It's a nasty crowd." The young bartender flashed frightened eyes over my shoulder as I approached and poured me a whisky without being asked.

"Thanks." I bolted the drink.

"I thought you might need it. I know I do. This has been the week from Hell. I wish Mr. Casey would get back. He had some kind of knack for keeping people happy. Almost like magic." He grinned to show he was joking; I thought he'd probably hit close to the truth. "Since he left…."

"You haven't heard from him?" I tried hard to keep my voice casual.

"His daughter came in earlier. Said he had been called away of a sudden on some kind of business trip."

Silently I commended Breda for her quick thinking.

"She left something for you, though."

He slid an envelope across the bar to me. I opened it with a mixture of curiosity and fear, half expecting a letter telling me where to go. What I found, however, was a cheque: two weeks' payment by the terms of the contract I had never signed. There was no note at all.

A beefy, unshaven man in a muscle shirt appeared at the other end of the bar, bellowing for a round of boilermakers and cursing the waitress, who had disappeared—if she had any sense, she'd taken refuge in the kitchen. The bartender left to deal with him and I slipped away, deciding not to bring myself to anyone's attention by insisting on the free drinks due Red Branch by contract.

Frank and Lisa had arrived by the time I made it back to the stage. Neither of them said a word about the aborted rehearsal, which suited me fine. I just wanted to get the night over with and escape.

The gig was an unmitigated disaster. We had barely limped into the first set before I realized just how spoiled I had been by playing at the Emerald Isle and just how complacent it had made me. I had never questioned the way our performance had improved on Casey's stage or the enthusiasm with which the audience received everything we did. Nor had I questioned how uncommonly well the bar had succeeded in its first few weeks of operation. As I muddled my way through a set of reels I had been playing for years and should have been able to pull off asleep, drunk, or dead, I considered the bartender's words in a new light. The psychic drill would be no good at all without the energy to power it. There must be something else at work, something to draw people in, give them a pleasant experience and make them remember it, so they'd keep coming back. What better way to accomplish that, than to ensure the house band gave a good show?

I glanced at the stage; it pulsed and glowed in the light of my gift. So did the walls. So did the bar and the door. The whole place crawled with charms: charms of attraction, of enjoyment, of success, fulfillment and good fellowship, to name the ones I could identify. I felt a moment's admiration; I hadn't thought

Casey had it in him. But with the magician's death, the work had begun to fall apart. Gaps and odd blurs marred the patterns, rendering them ineffective. In the normal course of events that might not have mattered. All charms faded with time; the fact didn't necessarily spell disaster. In this case, however, other forces were at work. Blood—Connolly blood—had been spilled, cracking Tintri Fionn's prison enough that the demon's influence could leak out.

They relish strong feeling, Grandmother Oonagh had said. *Violence is easy to provoke.*

And still the drill ground away, prying the crack ever wider. It took its power from energy; it didn't care what kind. I should have done something about it.

I glanced around the stage. Lisa stood beside me in a daze, scowling down the length of the fiddle tucked under her chin as if she didn't know what it was or how it had come there. Every now and again she'd lift her bow to the strings, saw ineffectually for a few notes, and drop it again. Frank's left hand seemed frozen to the neck of his guitar; his right jerked spasmodically as he played the same chord over and over again in no particular rhythm. I quashed a familiar surge of irritation. This time, at least, no amount preparation could have improved any aspect of our performance. Frank and Lisa were not to blame, and giving in to anger would only feed the beast below.

Of all of us, Timber alone seemed able to rise above the demon's influence, pounding out the beat on his bodhrán as if he could keep us all in line through sheer force of will. His red face dripped sweat, betraying his intense concentration. He edged towards me, still pounding, and stuck his whiskered lips in my ear.

"We canna keep this up. It's only making things worse."

About that time, the first bottle hit the stage, exploding in a spray of shattered glass and expensive beer. The audience didn't want any more music. They wanted blood.

I dove at Lisa, knocking her aside before a second bottle could smash her in the face. A mass of sweaty humanity surged forward, making an inarticulate noise like a stormy sea and I dragged her, unresisting, toward the back of the stage. Timber was already there, unplugging instrument pick-ups from the soundboard. He turned towards Frank, standing between the two main speakers, staring without comprehension at the impending riot, and gave him an ungentle nudge.

"Move!"

Frank woke with a start and leapt off the stage, cradling his guitar in his arms. The rest of us followed, trailing the cords from our pick-ups like thin tails. Timber got the rear door open; we swarmed onto the loading dock and he slammed it shut behind us, breath coming in harsh gasps. I found a push broom someone had left outside by the dumpster and slid it through the door handles as a makeshift bar. It wouldn't hold back a determined effort for long, though, and I held myself tense, waiting for the inevitable moment when our pursuers would break through.

It didn't come. Instead, I heard from within, muffled by the walls and the thick steel doors, the unmistakable sound of our equipment being smashed to bits.

I thought about the rack of expensive whistles I had left behind in our flight and closed my eyes. Lisa crumpled to her knees. She had another fiddle in there, one for which she had paid quite a lot.

"Well!"

I opened my eyes to see Frank gazing at the door. To my amazement, he was grinning.

"I guess we'll be needing a new sound system after all." The grin turned into a smirk as he glanced in my direction. "You still have that Carvin catalogue, right?"

I had never wanted so badly to punch anyone in my life.

Very late that night—or very early the next morning, depending on how one chose to look at it—I unlocked a door down the hall from the bedroom where Timber lay sleeping and entered a room in which I had not set foot for five years.

I had expected it to be stuffy, as closed rooms often are, especially at the height of summer, but the oak boards under my bare feet were cool and a chill ran over my arms, raising goose bumps. I remembered Tintri Fionn's cavern and shivered harder still. Like the cavern, the room before me lay in utter darkness. Outside, the moon was waxing towards full, but heavy shades covered the room's two windows, blocking any view of the sky. Only the dim pink glow of the cat-shaped nightlight in the hall lit my way, and when I shut the door behind me that, too, vanished. I stepped forward, prodding the path ahead with one bare toe, not knowing whether there might be some unexpected obstacle in my path. I'd not been in the room in five years, but Timber used it and he wasn't always great at picking up after himself. But nothing impeded my progress, and I reached my goal, a long bureau shoved up against the north wall, without incident. I yanked open the center of the bureau's three drawers and felt around inside, locating by touch a thin taper and a box of kitchen matches. It took me several tries to get the taper lit, holding it and the matchbox awkwardly in my left hand while striking a match with my right. But finally my nervous fingers accomplished the task, and I used the taper to light the two fat, pillar candles standing on either end of the bureau. Then I shook out the taper, returned it to the drawer and gazed around me.

The room looked very much like any little-used room, one where a family might store odds and ends when moving into a new house, until they could be sorted through and transferred to their appropriate settings or relegated to attic or garage. Boxes lined the walls, some half opened to give shadowy glimpses of mysterious, newspaper-wrapped objects, others still neatly sealed with tape. Aside from the bureau, the sole furniture was a trio of bookcases near the door. Two stood empty. One was half full of hand bound journals: Timber's. A round drum, similar in size and shape to a bodhrán, leaned against one of the bookcases, hide-wrapped beater thrust into the sinew holding the drum head to the frame: Timber's ritual drum, which provided the driving force for his shamanic journeys. On top of the bookcase stood a deep, pine box. Before the box sat a mahogany incense burner lightly dusted with ash, a bronze candle holder in the shape of a voluptuous woman, a bundle of sage tied with red thread, one end of which was charred, and a fan made of a magpie's wing. The scents of sweetgrass and copal hung in the air, faint as the memory of a dream; my husband had made use of the space recently. That very night, perhaps, while I'd been in the bath, trying to soak away the lingering disquiet of the events at the bar.

I'd never meant to come here.

That wasn't strictly true. When we'd bought the house as a retreat, six months before I'd left Boulder, I'd assumed I would be spending a great deal of time in this room—at some point, if not immediately. It had been my special charge, weekends when we'd come up to work on the place. I'd rolled on the paint. I'd stained the trim; I'd chosen the symbols for the walls. I'd even begun stenciling a border of moon phases up near the ceiling. It ran two-thirds of the way around the room before ending abruptly as a world dying.

I'd assumed I would be spending a lot of time here. But the fear that had sent me fleeing from Boulder, and the life I knew there, had changed everything. Since coming to live in Gorda-rosa I hadn't set foot in the room once. I thought I never would again. Everything here—the boxes and their contents, the candlelit altar (for it was an altar, not just a bureau; I had to be honest with myself now), even the paint on the walls and the shades over the windows—was part of an existence I had renounced.

A lot of mystics say no one can walk the path knowing. It's too dark and too dangerous—not because of monsters hiding in the shadows, though there are some—but because the farther you go the more you're forced to admit that the world in which you've believed all your life is not solid, but changes with every footstep. Your most dearly held beliefs are revealed as nothing more than the ambiguous symbols from a dream. Even your notions of self—especially your notions of self—dissolve and blow away like fine sand, leaving you with nothing: no shield to hold between your assumptions and the truths you cannot bear to know. This is why, those mystics say, every true Seeker must trick himself into finding wisdom. If you tell yourself you are on the straight path, you have already turned aside. Only by turning around and going in the opposite direction, as Alice did in the Looking Glass Land, can you hope to reach your destination. Only by allowing yourself to become involved in something completely beside the point can you come to the place where the unexpected truth hides, waiting to snatch you by the throat when it's too late to run.

This is why so much magic involves long, seemingly pointless, ritual.

I had always laughed at this idea. During the course of my life I had faced more than my share of unbearable truths; what was one more to me? I knew the voices of my personal demons intimately and, though their words still stung, they had no power over me. There was no belief, no world view, I couldn't relinquish at a moment's notice. I could make my own choices. I had no need to trick myself into going wherever I wanted.

How we lie to ourselves. How we cling to fear. Even telling Timber I would embrace my magic again, I had clung, hoping against hope that I could avert my Fate. Now it was time to let go and accept the consequences.

I closed my eyes and again relived the vision of the bright, unfamiliar god on his hill. *With divine power comes divine…* Struggling with the two fires. Screaming until my throat grew raw with it.

And the long, beige walls closed around me.

I shuffled between them on dead feet, suffused with an unbearable weariness. Something rolled in my mind and tried to surface, a whale coming up for air, not yet breaching. I grabbed at the rare thought. For only an instant, mingled grief and rage warred in my mind. I felt tears on my face and a shout in my throat.

A white figure came up beside me. There was a pressure on my arm. Then darkness, silence, and a sense of devastating loss fading into nothing.

Maybe getting over my fear had been the point all along. For all I knew, the Universe had constructed this whole situation—bringing Sean Casey here, even bringing the *coimhthíoch* here—for the sole purpose of making me claim my power.

The thought made me want to throw up.

I searched along the wall for a particular box, one I remembered packing in haste on one of my rare trips back to Boulder after my flight, without giving much care to the contents. After Timber had agreed to join me. In fact, I had begged Timber to take the whole of its contents to the dump or throw it on the fire. He'd refused, telling me it was my business, which of course it was. But I'd found I couldn't dispose of those things either. So they had all gone, higgledy-piggledy, into the box and the box had come here, to be stored with the rest of the magical paraphernalia in the room I swore I would never use. From time to time I told myself I'd destroy or scatter the contents, but I never had.

I read somewhere once that when you renounce something in fear, you're only putting off the inevitable.

The box had once held Captain Morgan's Spiced Rum, and I found it right on the top of a pile in the corner nearest the altar,

almost as if it had been waiting for me. The black marker label-
ing it Caitlin's Things was so shaky I hardly recognized it as my
writing. Maybe it wasn't. Maybe Timber had done that much. I
honestly didn't remember.

I lifted the packing tape with a fingernail and tore it off.
The lid flaps opened, releasing a heady rush of sage scent and
dust. I bent the flaps back, braced myself, and thrust my hand
inside.

A thick layer of coarse salt covered the contents. I remembered doing that. Under the salt lay an assortment of variously-
shaped lumps, hastily wrapped in newspaper. I flinched as I
touched them, yet there was comfort, too, like putting on a
worn, old sweater you remember your mother wearing while
baking cookies on a rainy afternoon. Deliberately shutting that
image out of my mind, I pawed through the box. I was looking
for something specific, and now that I had made up my mind to
act I didn't want to waste any time on relics and nostalgia. The
long, thin, shape, though—that was my wand. Timber had
carved it for me out of a rowan branch, and the dark stain at its
tip was my own blood. That weird bundle contained my chalice,
a cheap piece of pottery with a bright blue glaze, which I had
found at the top of a trash bin outside a Sorority house on Uni-
versity Hill at the end of a semester. And that….

"Stop it," I told myself sternly, and laid the objects aside,
unwrapped.

What I sought lay at the very bottom of the box. I knew it
at once, both because of its size and shape and because of its
feel—I hadn't wrapped it in anything at all. That was really stupid, and gave a clear indication of my state of mind at the time
I had packed the object away. I drew it out slowly: a big, squat
candle, one of those pillar candles as big around as a child's
thigh, blood red, with three wicks. I had bought it for a specific
purpose and had spent hours in a trance state, carving symbols
and patterns into the wax. Despite its being unprotected, the

carvings were unmarred. I breathed a sigh that might have been relief and might have been despair.

I had lit it but once. The wicks bore scant evidence of charring; I had extinguished the candle in great haste after a conversation so frightening that even the memory of it made me want to…. No, don't go there. I carried the candle over to the altar and positioned it precisely at the center, aligning the wicks in a triangle whose apex pointed north. Then I hesitated. Timber and I had meant to consecrate the space with a ritual that would situate the workroom beyond time and space, at the borders of everywhere yet actually located nowhere. This would have had the double effect of making any magic performed there more effective and providing protection from potentially harmful elements. But we had never done it, and I doubted the wisdom of calling on the powers I intended to call without it. A temporary circle would achieve the same thing, but casting a good one required tools and time—more of each than I wanted to deal with.

I sighed. I was about to throw a pound into the pot and here I was balking at an extra penny.

"Circle," I said, low, and one sprang up around me. It was small, just enough to contain me, the altar and a little piece of floor.

The rest of it was so simple, it almost seems silly to mention it at all. I found the taper in the drawer and lit it from one of the pillar candles—the one in the east, the direction of choice. With the taper, I lit the three wicks on the big candle, starting with the one in the north. There was no invocation, or anything like that. The symbols I had carved years ago took care of all that for me.

When the big candle was burning well and in no danger of going out without warning, I shook out the taper, stepped back and sat on the floor.

"All right," I said. "You win."

Chapter Nineteen

The first indication I had that my unorthodox prayer had been received was that I suddenly found myself, not in the dark Workroom at the top of my house, but seated at a table at the Emerald Isle. To this day I don't know whether I had been somehow transported there in body, or whether I was experiencing a particularly vivid vision or dream state. My eyes flickered around the room and fell on Sean Casey, slit throat and all, seated at a piano in the corner. Did the Emerald Isle boast a piano? I didn't think so. Probably a vision, then. Still, I couldn't quite tell.

Casey was all dressed up like a saloon piano player from some musical set in the 1890s, in shabby black pants, a bow tie, and a white shirt with the sleeves rolled up above the elbow and secured by ruffled garters. His fingers caressed the ivories, playing something slow and bluesy in the style of Pinetop Perkins. Later I realized the tune had been that old standard, "Blind Girl," and was glad I hadn't recognized it at the time.

Archie Connolly sat across the table from me, wearing the same old-fashioned tweed suit and derby hat. He mopped at the blood trickling down the side of his face with a much-soiled handkerchief. Then he consulted his watch.

"Not long now," he said. He shook his head sadly. "The whole thing's coming down."

As if in answer, the earth gave a slight tremor.

"Archie." I took his hand, surprised at its warmth. "You have to tell me how to stop it."

"Can't stop it. Not once it's begun. It's a matter of the way you go on, you see."

"What?" I cursed in my heart. I should have been more specific in my request to my newly reclaimed patron gods; the help they were giving me was no help at all.

"There's but one to keep the pact. And I wish her safe."

"Pact? You made a pact with Tintri Fionn?"

"The blood can help but so much. Help or harm."

At that moment the piano music stopped in mid-note and Sean Casey swiveled around on his stool.

"Caitlin Ross," he said. "It's been so long. About time, too. You've nearly left it too late."

I bristled. "Excuse me. I'm trying to have a conversation here."

"Archie can't help you." Casey shrugged. "Not in this place. In fact, he's not really here at all."

"Oh?"

"He's a shadow. A projection, if you like. He's the form your thoughts take. That's why he can only tell you what you already know."

Casey waved his hand and Archie was replaced by another Caitlin, clad in the same grey sweatpants and camisole I had donned after my bath. She had a vacant look in her eyes, and I glanced down, embarrassed. Then I noticed my own clothes for the first time: a loose, midnight blue velvet gown heavily embroidered with Celtic knotwork. I knew for a fact that gown was still packed away in a box in the Workroom. My throat convulsed in something between a swallow and a gag.

Casey saw it. "Oh, come on. You made the dedication; you may as well look the part. Unless you didn't mean it."

"I meant it."

"Good." He turned back to the piano.

"And who are you? Another projection?"

He smiled at me over his shoulder. The way he craned his neck around made his head seem about to fall off.

"I'm the owner of the bar."

That took a minute to sink in. "Oh," I said, even as my mind gabbled, *Which one?* My true patron? Or that bright other? I didn't want to consider the matter, so I shoved it aside.

"So what is it you want, exactly?" He tinkled off a string of notes. "I have time for one request; make it a good one."

I thought hard. My original idea had been to ask for a way of rebinding the *coimhthíoch*, but if the piano player was to be believed—and if I didn't believe him there was no point in my being here—I already knew that was impossible. Likewise, I already knew the method of releasing the binding was extremely important, that it involved some sort of pact and that the pact had to be passed from the one who held it to another of his choosing. All of that led me straight back to one place. Archie Connolly was the last person to have held the pact. His death hadn't negated that. So, dead or not, Archie had to pass it on.

"I need to be able to speak to Archie Connolly. The true one, not just a shadow. I need to know what he knows."

"And finish what he started." The piano player in the shape of Sean Casey nodded enigmatically. "You didn't specify that, but I'll throw it in for free. That's a complex tune. You sure you're up to it? You're out of practice."

"I make a fast comeback."

"All right, then." He cracked his knuckles over the keys and began to play a haunting, almost dirge-like melody, which the musician's portion of my mind identified as a minor mode, probably Mixolydian.

"There once was a knight from the Low Country," he sang in a surprisingly light tenor,

"A secret he took to his grave

A red-haired witch came out of the north
His secret for to have, to have
His secret for to have.

She called to the East and she called to the West
She called to the North and the South
She called to the place where the dead knight slept
With the cold clay in his mouth, his mouth
The cold clay in his mouth.

Nine times she walked 'round the place where he lay
Nine times she named him aloud
Nine times she burned the nine sacred herbs
All on the dead knight's shroud, his shroud
All on the dead knight's shroud.

She sang to the North and she sang to the West
She sang to the South and the East
She sang to the place where the dead knight lay
And his ghost did rise and speak, and speak
And his ghost did rise and speak."

"There you have it." The piano player ended his song abruptly, closing the keyboard cover with a bang. "Now you'd better be off. There's work for you, and not much time to do it in. Oh wait. There is one more thing."

He reached into a shirt pocket I hadn't seen before and drew out an enormous bronze key. The thing was so big it could not have fit in the pocket at all. He dusted it off on his sleeve and tossed it across the bar to me; it spun glittering toward my hand. When my fingers closed around it, it felt warm, almost hot.

"What's this?" I asked.

"What does it look like?"

I examined the key. It appeared heavy, yet it didn't weight as much as a feather in my hand. "What does it do?"

The piano player grimaced at my stupidity. "What do keys do?"

I stared at him. Finally he said grudgingly, "It unlocks a door, of course."

"A door to?"

"You can be very irritating at times." He heaved a put-upon sigh. "Very well. It leads to a place to keep things you can neither dispose of nor use. An attic, as it were. Now really, you'd best be off."

Without any more warning or ceremony, I found myself in the workroom, flat on my back before the altar. The candles had all gone out, smothered by their own wax, and a faint scent of smoke hung in the air. And there was something around my neck that hadn't been there before. My fingers groped toward it and found a tiny key on a chain. I clutched my hand about it, wondering what it meant.

"Open," I croaked, and felt my hasty circle dissolve.

I picked myself up, groaning. I had no idea how much time had gone by. I wasn't too stiff, though, and when I lifted a shade to peek out the window I saw it was still quite dark. Maybe only a few minutes, then.

I started for the door, paused, and turned towards the altar.

"Thanks," I said with a nod.

I wasn't sure if I meant it.

At that point I wanted nothing more than to crawl into bed and sleep for a hundred years, hopefully to be awakened by a kiss from a handsome prince in the form of a certain shaggy Scotsman of intimate acquaintance. But I knew visions, like dreams, had the annoying habit of making marvelous sense while they were happening and dissolving into an incoherent mess the minute they were over. The significant details of my experience were already fading, and there was one thing in particular that I couldn't afford to lose.

I left the workroom and tiptoed downstairs, not without a longing glance at the bedroom door. In the living room I paused to fish a whistle from the collection in the wide-mouthed glass vase on top of one of the bookshelves—these were the cheap whistles I took camping or hiking when I felt the need for some music maker in my back pocket, not the custom-made ones I had left behind in my flight from the riot at the bar, which I thought of with a pang. On the shelf where I kept my music books, I found a notebook of staff paper with some space in the back and a pen stuck in the spiral binding. All this I carried out to the front porch, where I sat in one of our cheap, green plastic lawn chairs and proceeded to write out the song Casey had given me, words and music both. The music might not turn out to be important. Clearly the lyrics were instructions for a spell, and the spell did speak of singing, but there was no indication that the air to which the spell had been set had anything to do with it. Still, better to be thorough. I played it through on my whistle several times, hoping I'd gotten the key right; these things can make a difference.

E Mixolydian. I smiled to myself as I scribed a single sharp beside a treble clef, feeling more than a little proud that I'd recognized the mode back in the vision bar. It's funny how little things like that can boost one's confidence.

Despite my good intentions, I must have fallen asleep over the work. The next thing I knew, someone was shaking me, softly yet insistently, by the shoulder. I opened my eyes to daylight and immediately praised the gods that our house faced west, the porch roof creating a refuge of shade. From the look of the yard, it was already gearing up to be a typical late-July day for Western Colorado, bright and scorching hot, without a cloud in the sky.

"What time is it?" I asked the tattered, brown sweatpants hovering near my left knee.

"Six-thirty." Timber shoved a warm mug into my hand: coffee. I took a healthy swig. "You must have been tired, to fall asleep out here. Why didn't you come to bed?"

"Shit." I sat up with a jerk, narrowly avoiding sloshing coffee all over my lap. Timber relieved me of the mug before I could do any real damage and I glanced around for the whistle and notebook, finally locating them on the glass-topped wicker table that shared the porch with the two plastic chairs. I snatched up the notebook and sighed with relief.

"I got it. I got it all down."

"Got what?"

In answer, I passed him the notebook and he took a seat to study it. His chest was bare, and a large hole in a vulnerable area of the sweatpants gaped alarmingly. Noticing my stare, he crossed his legs primly.

"You were struck by a sudden inspiration and you came out here in the middle of the night to write a song?" He lifted an eyebrow in my general direction. From the tone of his voice it was clear he thought I had slipped a gear, maybe two.

"It's not just a song. It's a spell. And it was given to me."

"Given to you…?"

I watched his face change as he digested the information, wondering what his reaction would be. But he only glanced back down at the notebook.

"I see. What does it do?"

"It lets me communicate with Archie Connolly. And hopefully he'll be able to tell me how to get rid of this demon, once and for all." I *see?* Was that it? I'd done this huge thing and that's all the comment he had? After all his poking and prodding and telling me I only had half a soul? After threatening to leave me? I opened my mouth to tell him what an insensitive prick he was, but he laid a big hand on my knee, forestalling me.

"What did ye want me to say, Caitlin? Ye said ye'd do it. Was I wrong to believe ye?"

"No," I whispered.

"Well, then. There's no more to say about it. I'm a bit surprised ye left it so long, mind."

I did tell him what I thought of him, then. He only raised an eyebrow at me.

"Och, love. Now ye want to pick a fight with me because you're scared and I'm safe, but that wilna change anything. Ye canna go back. Eventually we'll both have to face what it means, the good and the bad. And I'm not fool enough to believe there'll be no bad. But right now we have to take what ye were given and find a way to use it, or else ye did what ye did for nothing."

"Okay," I grunted, still miffed.

"D'ye ken how to work it? The spell?" Abruptly he was all business. To my surprise, the shift in his manner took the edge off my pique.

"It's fairly explicit. The knight from the Low Country would be Archie."

"Gordarosa isn't exactly low. As a matter of fact, it's pretty high up."

"I know, but 'Low Country' is trad-speak for someone with magic powers in a lot of songs. Whenever a maiden meets some mysterious person on the road, he's always from the Low Country."

"And he usually turns out to be the Devil in disguise."

"Well, I don't think Archie's apt to show me a cloven hoof. I hope not, anyway."

Timber grunted. "And the red-haired witch would be you, I take it."

"That's my take. I did come from the north—originally, anyway. Then the rest: Circle, invocation, symbolic action. It's pretty obvious. The only thing it doesn't spell out is what are the nine sacred herbs I'm supposed to burn."

"Those would be herbs promoting spirit communication, I expect. I can come up with those. Since the spell isn't specific, there's probably room to tailor it to what's available. When are you planning on doing this?"

"As soon as possible. I want this over, and we have the Mountain Fair next weekend."

"Sunday night? The bar closes early on Sundays, and it will give us time to prepare."

"I wish we could do it sooner," I grumbled. "I've wasted too much time, and Sunday night is three days from now. Anything could happen. Anything could already have happened."

"I dinna think it has," Timber mused. "Surely we'd ken it if the demon had been freed. And, love, these things canna be rushed. Ye ken that."

I nodded, conceding the point. "I'll call Breda. We'll need her to let us in." I shuddered at the thought that she might not respond. Then I shook myself, this time voluntarily. I couldn't waste time worrying about Breda. We'd do what was necessary.

For the moment, it was necessary to deal with the Mundane aspects of life. Some people might have found this anticlimactic, and it was, but it was also a relief. After Timber left for work, I puttered about the house for several hours, catching up on neglected chores. At eleven, when the Emerald Isle opened for lunch, I phoned the bar to confirm that we were not expected to play our usual Friday set in light of the previous night's events. Then I called Frank and Lisa to inform them of the cancellation.

I hoped to get their machine. Instead, I got Frank.

"Cancelled?" he wailed, predictably. "What do you mean, cancelled?"

"We have no sound," I reminded him.

"That's not a problem. I can call Cassie and borrow her PA. I don't think she has a gig tonight." Cassiopeia Jones was a fiftyish accountant-turned-singer-songwriter, who played a mostly solo act at various coffeehouses. We'd borrowed her sound system several times before purchasing our own.

"If she's heard about last night, I doubt she'll want to lend it to us."

"Then we can play without…"

"Frank!" I cut him off. "It's not a question of sound or no sound. They don't want us to come."

There was a moment of silence. Then, "Are we fired?" he asked, sounding on the verge of tears.

"No, we're not fired." The bar owner has been ritually murdered, there's a demon under the stage and some unknown person is preparing to unleash it on the whole town, but the band has not been fired. "They just have a lot of cleanup to do after the incident last night and they'd prefer us to take the rest of the week off." Or at least that was how I'd chosen to interpret the incipient hysteria of the dining room hostess, who by default was the one left to deal with the mess and felt mighty resentful of the fact.

"But what about the Mountain Fair? We'll never be ready if we don't play…"

"Frank, calm down. We'll meet tomorrow since we don't have the gig. We'll have our regular Tuesday rehearsal. We can meet Wednesday and Thursday if we need to. We'll be fine." If I wasn't dead by Monday morning, that was.

I got rid of Frank with a few more rote reassurances that made me wonder who'd come up with the myth that a bandleader's job was glamorous, as in my experience it consisted mainly of managing time and money and nursemaiding insecure personnel—hardly the stuff of which rock 'n' roll legends are made. To my horror I noticed I was pondering the question with a kind of nostalgia for the days, not many weeks past, when frustrations about the band were the worst thing I had to worry about. I was actually looking forward to tomorrow night's rehearsal as a reprieve.

It was, of a sort. At least, it gave me a chance to turn off my brain and run on autopilot for a while, which I hadn't done in twenty-four hours. From the time Timber came home Friday evening until the time Frank and Lisa arrived, we were busy with our spell preparations, taking as little time as possible away from them to eat and sleep. A simple charm wouldn't have required so much work, of course, but this was a big one; I was, as the piano player in the shape of Sean Casey had pointed out, out of practice, and I wanted to get it right.

I shouldn't have worried so much. It came back surprisingly quickly, like the proverbial riding a bicycle. As we worked, I felt myself suffused with an eerie confidence that came from doing work I knew well—work I was born to do. It was like suddenly stumbling upon a straight road after being lost in the woods. Discussing the spell with Timber, I heard myself speak in tones of command I had thought lost to me in all my ineffectual struggles with the band, and a small, cynical part of my mind wondered how long I'd go on kidding myself that I could find happiness as a musician. This was rightness. I was a witch and that was all there was to it.

Finding the herbs presented the only real difficulty. It didn't take Timber long to come up with a list of things that might work, but narrowing it down to nine that were readily available, had the desired effects and wouldn't poison me was something else again. Hemlock, for example, was quite potent in rituals raising spirits and it grew wild all over Gordarosa, but nothing in this world or any other could induce me to burn hemlock, even in the high-ceilinged vault of Tintri Fionn's cavern. I wanted to talk to a ghost, not become one. Salts of Osiris, on the other hand, were perfectly safe, equally potent, and only available if we managed somehow to time travel back a couple of millennia to a certain marketplace in Ancient Egypt. For a while I seriously considered despair. But Timber kept at it, and by late Saturday afternoon we had our nine herbs, all nicely wrapped in separate waxed paper packets.

The spell song had only mentioned the herbs as necessary ingredients, but there were other things I'd need as well: charcoal and matches, candles, a ritual knife. Stuff like that. Stuff any witch or magician knows to bring to a ritual without thinking about it. You can do a spell without any of that junk, of course—well, not without the charcoal, not if burning herbs is an integral part of it—and I had, but for this particular event I wanted more about me than just my wits and my will. Too, I was counting on being able to deal with the demon immediately once Archie told me how. That might require supplies. I didn't know what supplies exactly, so I spent Sunday morning unpacking boxes in the Workroom, making piles of things that seemed likely and trying to figure it out. This activity only resulted in my getting very dirty and creating a lot of piles, so I finally gave it up and decided on the old stand-bys: knife, sage, salt. It would be enough, or it wouldn't. As I packed them away in my leather Renfaire scrip with the herbs and charcoal, I reflected I'd rather have fewer things and a gift for improvisation than a lot of useless crap weighing me down.

At noon I called Breda. She didn't answer.

"Breda, it's Caitlin," I told her voice mail. "I think I can stop…this thing, but I have to get into the bar after hours tonight. Meet me there at one. Please," I added before hanging up.

I turned around to find my husband looming behind me, looking grim.

"You've left it late."

I shrugged. "I didn't want to spend three days wondering if she'd call back and jumping every time the phone rang."

"It would have given you time to come up with an alternate plan."

"I have an alternate plan. Bring your lockpicks."

"If that's it, you needn't have called Breda at all."

I didn't have an answer to that. Or maybe the answer was obvious. Anyway, I didn't say anything.

We slept. We did other things. We made love a couple times without mentioning that we needed the comfort of each other's bodies to shelter us from the knowledge of the night's work. It's funny how normal everything seemed. I tried several times to remind myself that I was preparing to do something entirely beyond the pale of most people's daily experience—something that would be incredibly dangerous if things went wrong. All the usual cautions against strong magic unwound in my head, a ceaseless litany bent on convincing me that the coming night's work was definitely foolish and possibly crazy: Magic isn't real; it's just some form of mass hypnosis, an addiction to the alpha rhythms of the brain. Demons and ghosts don't exist. They do exist but can't be trusted. You aren't powerful; you're deluded. You'll be swallowed. There's nothing to swallow you. Not to mention the one fact I hadn't quite managed to forget: there was another player in this game, a player willing to kill, and he might not take kindly to interference. None of it had any impact. I'd experienced worse nerves before a big gig.

That, too, I filed away to look at later.

Night fell and it was time to get ready. Timber shut himself in the Workroom; from within I could hear the slow, sonorous tones of his drum, interspersed now and again with the high-pitched chatter of a gourd rattle. I took a long bath in a darkened room with candles and rose petals floating in the tub, then rubbed lotion all over my body before getting dressed, a thing I didn't often take the time to do. I felt myself falling into the light trance state that precedes any ritual, the one where every sense becomes preternaturally, paradoxically heightened—less a shutting out of the material world than an opening to include the world unseen, as well as the world seen, one heightening the experience of the other. People try to reach that state by using drugs, unaware of, or perhaps just ignoring, the fact that drugs diminish real-world perceptions, without which the visions they seek become so much garbage, strings of nonsense syllables without context. I'd done those drugs and recognized the so-called insight they brought as what it was: the ramblings of a half-wit, open to any kind of interpretation. Free of their influence, I knew better than to lose myself in the way the candle flames seemed to expand into miniature suns or the feel of the blue velvet dress as it slid over my skin. I steeled myself against finding undue significance in the pattern of the bathroom tile, grey with sparkles of gold that I had not noticed before. These things were beautiful, but the beauty contained no message, other than that it was. And that, also, was without meaning, although I was glad for it. Glad beauty existed in the world.

I finished dressing, grimacing a little as I slid my battered rafting sandals over thick Connemara wool socks in a shade of heather that clashed horribly with my dress. Breda's fault that I noticed it at all. Associating with her had woken a vain streak. Well, I was going to work magic, not have my picture taken. The cavern was cold, the floor uneven and sensible footwear was in order. I still didn't like it. But if dowdy footwear was all I had to worry about tonight, I'd count myself lucky.

I was ready. I blew out the candles and went down the hall to knock on the Workroom door. The drumming trailed off into silence.

"Time," I said. And despite my best intentions, the word held more significance than any other word in the world.

Chapter Twenty

Breda was waiting for us, a hunched dark shape in a sleek dark car parked in front of the drugstore, across the street and several businesses down from the Emerald Isle, in a pool of shadow where the light of two street lamps did not quite meet. *She's learned caution, at least,* I thought as Timber pulled our truck into a space several car-widths down. This late Sunday night (or Monday morning), the streets were deserted but for our two vehicles: no good at all to cause undue suspicion by parking too close together. If anyone were watching. If it weren't suspicious enough that we were there at all.

She jumped out of her car almost as soon as she saw us, the sharp slam of the door echoing through the still night like a shot. Timber and I exchanged a glance and followed suit more slowly, without as much noise. The three of us met in the middle of the deserted street. Breda nodded at my husband before turning stiffly to face me. Tension rolled off of her in waves, her body so brittle with it I thought a breath would shatter her. Her blue eyes looked through me. Her lip twisted.

"Nice dress." I'd last heard those exact words, in that exact tone, from Lisa the night of the earthquake—it seemed like a hundred years ago. I remembered Breda fussing over my hair and giggling at Timber's reaction to the green silk slip dress, and the irony in her voice now hit me like a punch to the gut. I'd known she had a mean streak, but I had never thought it might be turned on me. Useless to tell myself there was nothing personal in it. It was personal. She meant to hurt. She meant to hurt *me*. And I couldn't let it matter.

I swallowed, tasting blood, feeling cold pain like a razor, all the way down.

"I didn't know if you'd come," I said. My voice came out eerily calm, admitting no vulnerability. I stated a fact, no more.

"I came for my father." The words were awash in bitterness and hostility. In my sensitized state, it was all I could do to keep my knees from buckling under the weight of it. In case I hadn't gotten the point, she added, "Not for you."

She turned and stalked off towards the bar. Clear through the still night, I heard the musical jingle of her keys as she fetched them from her pocket, the snap of the lock turning. My eyes caught a flicker of movement as she put the keys away, another as she abruptly faced me once again. Our eyes met over the wide expanse of the asphalt street.

Then she turned and walked away, disappearing around the corner.

I felt Timber's hand, warm and strong, on my elbow.

"Come on, then. Let's get this done."

He steered me across the street and through the doors. Inside, the pub looked almost too clean, too orderly, as if it had been disinfected. I wished I could believe that it had, because then I could just go home and forget all about what had brought me there.

There seemed to be several fewer chairs upended on the tables than I remembered, and I wondered if they had been smashed in Thursday's brawl. I wondered, too, if business had been calmer since then, without Red Branch's music to raise the energy.

We made our way to the back room and Timber snapped on one of the green-shaded lamps. Here, too, everything was orderly, the bistro tables arranged with almost military precision in straight rows. Something about the sight made my stomach turn over. Someone had piled what remained of Red Branch's equipment in the booth we had used; I restrained the urge to paw through it to see if any of my whistles had come through intact. There would be time enough for that later, if there was a later. I supposed anything beyond salvaging had found its way to the dumpster out back. At some point I should probably go through that, too.

The stage was utterly bare.

Timber went to the breaker box and switched over the power. I released the catches unlocking the trap door—it was easier now that I knew how. Together, we pushed back the panel to reveal the hidden ladder. But when Timber would have started down, I stopped him.

"I need you to stay here."

He stared at me. "Ye canna be serious."

"Utterly serious."

His face contracted in a belligerent frown; the green light from the table lamp made him look ghastly, like something seeking vengeance from beyond the grave. Not a comforting thought, considering. I reached for his hands and squeezed them between my own.

"Someone else is involved in this business, Timber. For all we know, that person might have decided this is the perfect night to finish what he started. I count us lucky that it hasn't happened already."

"He might be down there already."

"I doubt it very much. The power hadn't been switched over," I pointed out. "I'm going to be very vulnerable, you know that. This is the only way in. I need you up here, standing guard."

"I could stand guard down there much better," he sulked, his heart not in it. He knew I was right.

"And if the worst happens and you have to fight someone off? I don't want that going on anywhere near the demon or anywhere near the spell. It will be hard enough without that kind of distraction."

Timber gave in with a sigh. "What d'ye want me to do?"

My eyes ran over his big, muscled frame, his large, strong hands. They took in the twenty-inch dirk he wore at his hip. Most people thought it a stage prop, but he kept it razor sharp and knew how to use it.

"Whatever you have to," I said, and my husband gave a grim nod. We'd talk morals later.

"At least let me come down and help ye get set up." Timber patted the canvas shopping bag, loaded with various supplies I hadn't been able to fit in my scrip, slung over his shoulder. "Come on, love. Surely ye dinna want to lug all this down the ladder yourself, in the dark."

"I don't," I admitted. "All right, then. But you leave before I start."

He nodded and lowered himself through the hole. I followed close behind. It was, as he had pointed out, very dark, the shadows heavy and tangible, like a blanket. I seemed to draw them in with every breath and knew a momentary panic, feeling I might smother. I stopped to gaze up the shaft at the dim green light coming in at the trap door above. It seemed very far away.

"Are ye all right?" I heard Timber call.

"Yeah. Fine." I gave my head a brisk shake and started down again.

By the time I reached the bottom of the ladder, Timber had fired up the lights. We had argued about that part. Despite the inherent difficulties in setting up a complex ritual space with only a flashlight for guidance, I felt very strongly that using the cavern's electric light, even for the sole purpose of setting up, would be inappropriate. With all the candles I planned to use, there'd be light soon enough. Timber's good sense won out, though, and in the end I was glad.

When we reached the cavern, we saw that sometime since we had last been there, Sean Casey's body had been removed. I was more than a little relieved that I would have neither to drag it outside the circle nor work around it; more than a little disturbed by this forcible reminder that a sinister third player was in the habit of coming and going. As if I could have forgotten that. Still, I was glad Timber would be above, watching my back.

I returned to the work at hand. Eight virgin white pillar candles went around the outside of the circle, positioned precisely at the quarters and cross-quarters, just beyond the eight symbols etched into the floor. At the center of the circle, on top of the ninth symbol, I placed an ornate brass censer full of sand, on which I laid several quick-lighting charcoal bricks. My other tools went around the censer. There were the nine packets of herbs, of course. Beside them I set a lighter, a plain white taper in an unglazed clay holder, a sage and sweetgrass smudge stick wrapped up prettily in red thread, a small dish of sea salt, and my black-handled ritual knife. I followed no particular pattern in laying the things out except what felt right to me. I finished too soon.

"I'm ready," I said to the room at large. I hoped I wasn't lying.

"Light the taper and I'll go." My husband's voice came from somewhere outside the circle of candles. I did as he directed without looking up. There was a pause.

"Be safe, Caitlin," Timber said at last. He started for the cavern entrance.

"Timber."

I felt him turn. "Aye?"

"You know who to watch for."

"Aye," he said. "I do."

Another pause, and then I heard him start the trudge down the corridor. The electric lights went out, and I knew Timber had flicked them off before starting up the ladder. My single taper suddenly seemed very small.

"I'm ready," I repeated under my breath, not feeling it.

I knelt before my taper for what seemed a long while, not wanting to start anything until I was sure Timber had reached the top of the ladder. Even after I knew he must be in the bar above me, I waited. I should begin centering myself, paying close attention to my breathing and drawing up power from the earth beneath me to prepare myself for the task ahead, but I couldn't make myself focus. I had done the exercise so many times it should have come without any effort at all, but every time I tried to imagine the standard pillar of white light leading up from the earth to connect with my spine, I found my mind somewhere else. Or I'd suddenly hit upon some ludicrous image of my tailbone as a giant, three-pronged plug searching for an outlet in the earth's core, and be overcome with a sense of absurdity. Or the whole visualization would shred in my mind, leaving only tattered flickers at the edge of my sight, like the ones that herald a migraine. The second time that happened I had the disturbing thought that I might actually bring a migraine on by trying so hard, and I decided to give up. Blinding physical pain wouldn't help me at all. I was as grounded as I was going to get.

First things first. I closed my eyes and reached out with my mind, seeking the psychic drill. I hadn't told Timber I planned to disable it; in fact, I hadn't known myself. It almost seemed ludicrous, a waste of energy. But if I failed, if something happened to me, I wanted it dealt with. At least disabling it would thwart the person wanting to free Tintri Fionn. And its absence might buy Timber, or whoever came after me, some time.

I found the threads of the spell without any problem at all, a thick knot of them directly over the center of the circle. I touched them with a tentative tendril of thought and felt the knot give almost at once. Interesting. The spell was not nearly as strong as I had feared. That fact gave me confidence. The magician who had cast it was no match for me at full strength. I began to believe I would get through the night. In fact, I hoped I would meet that other magician, so I could deal with him once and for all. With that hope fierce in me, I punched a hard fist of power right through the center of the knot. It exploded, firing tendrils of magic in all directions, where they flared briefly before dissipating. I felt the drill grind to a halt.

So easy. I should have done it before.

On to the main event. I got up off my knees, stumbling a little. Well, maybe disabling the drill had affected me more than I had thought. For a moment, I rested with my head down, getting my balance. Then I picked up my taper and walked to the easternmost of the eight pillar candles. When I reached it, I just stood there, wondering if I remembered what to do. A prayer seemed in order.

"Goddess, let this work," I murmured and lit the candle.

I repeated this unconventional invocation all the way around the circle, as I lit each of the candles in turn. As I touched my taper to the wick of the eighth, a sudden silence descended; I felt a sharp change of pressure in my ears. Working my jaw to release it, I went back to the circle's center and replaced the taper in its holder. Something was happening, at any rate. Not a full circle casting, but a beginning.

Next, I lit the sage stick, fanned it until I was sure it wasn't going to go out on me, and walked the circle again, the sweet herbal scent trailing in my wake. By this time, lack of focus no longer troubled me. All my senses were preternaturally sharp, yet not in a way that allowed for distraction. Rather, anything on which I turned them leaped out at me and filled my reality, leaving no room for anything else. I saw the sage stick in my hand, the edge of a wall beyond the candlelight, my left foot as I extended it to take a step. I felt I journeyed through a series of still shots, or from frame to frame in an animated sequence slowed almost beyond the perception of progress. Yet I must have progressed, for soon I arrived back at my starting point, feeling another shift of pressure in my ears as the silence deepened.

Back at the center of the circle, I extinguished the smudge stick and took up my ritual knife. I'd thought about this next bit a lot. According to the song:

She called to the East and she called to the West,
She called to the North and the South.

In an ordinary circle casting, one moves always clockwise from east, through south and west, to north, as I had done twice now. I had elected to cast a formal circle, which meant going through the pattern three times: once with the candles, to establish the space, once with the sage, to purify it and now, once with the knife to cut this piece of time out of the fabric of consensus reality. But I didn't know whether the song described the circle casting or took it for granted. If the former, it seemed to indicate I should invoke the directions out of order. I didn't feel quite comfortable with that. I wanted to believe that, in naming the directions out of order the song had merely taken literary license to make the rhyme work. But I didn't know.

On the spur of the moment I decided to go through the knife portion of the program in the usual manner and pray that it did nothing to jeopardize the spell. At each quarter, in order, I used the knife to draw a pentagram in the air above the appropriate candle. As I drew it, each pentagram flared blue, then vanished. Once that had happened, I called on the guardian of the direction—Eagle in the East, Lion in the South, Whale in the West and Bull in the North—to lend me strength and watch over me in my work. I used whatever words popped into my head. Some people used long, complex invocations read from a book, but that had never seemed natural to me; anyway, what I did worked and that was what mattered. As always, conversing in picturesque language with entities who didn't always allow themselves to be seen made me feel extremely silly. I imagined some Mundane stranger watching me from somewhere beyond the circle, wondering what the heck that lunatic thought she was doing. For some reason, in this particular instance the feeling of being watched hit me with especial strength. I was glad when a knee-shaking rush of energy and another blue flare told me the circle was complete and I could move on to the meat of the matter.

Back in turn to East, West, North and South, where I announced I had come to call on Archie Connolly, if he would be so kind to appear. I was getting into the rhythm of the thing now, humming the eerie little tune I had been given under my breath as I danced from place to place. The cold cavern grew increasingly warm and I felt sweat trickling down my face. In the ring of candles, everything shone gold, awash with light; outside the circle shadows crowded in, so pitch black there might not have been any outside at all. For all I knew, there wasn't.

She called to the place where the dead knight lay...

I had wondered about this bit, too—Archie's bones were well outside the circle, at least now. But I understood all at once that this, at least, was poetic license. There was no cold clay in Archie's mouth, nor did he have a shroud on which I could sprinkle the nine sacred herbs. It was the pattern of the thing that mattered. I danced to the center of the circle and raised my arms over my head.

"Archie Connolly, come forth!"

I heard the words roll out of my mouth, low and strange. The cavern echoed with them like a struck bell.

Nine times she walked 'round the place where he lay...

I started the first of my nine circuits of the circle, swaying with a peculiar little grapevine step that took me on a path that spiraled inward from the north edge to north again at the center. I sang the spell song as I went—not so much sang, actually, as chanted, tunelessly rhythmic, in time with my pattering feet. I had lost my sandals and socks somewhere, somehow; I didn't know, nor did I care. The earth rolled under my bare feet, partnering me in my dance.

I knew a moment of hesitation when I reached the center of the circle and realized I had forgotten to light the charcoal. Only a moment—hardly enough for it to register before I picked up the half-consumed taper and touched its flame to the censer. A great gout of purple fire leapt up with a whoosh, nearly singeing my eyebrows off my face and giving me all the proof I needed that the magic was working. I'd rarely seen charcoal do that before.

I reached for my packets of herbs and opened the first, patchouli flower to represent the power of Earth, over the glowing charcoal. It was from an old stock of incense herbs that had lain in a box in the Workroom back home for years and far from fresh, but the characteristic scent still leaped upwards, along with a great cloud of purple smoke. Pretty.

"Archie Connolly, come forth!" I sang out again, and danced away before the echoes died.

Seven more times I whirled around the circle, lightfoot on the increasingly unsteady ground. Seven more herbs I cast in the fire: peppermint from the garden for the element of Air; cardamom from the kitchen cupboard for Water and tobacco for Fire. Then came the herbs we had chosen to do the real work of the spell, each one representing a quality I wished to contact. Myrrh, the ancient funeral gum, made it clear that I was attempting to communicate with someone long dead. Allspice gave me the power to do it. Lavender to reinforce the communication and cloves for divination to pierce the veil. Each time as the smoke went up, I raised my arms and called Archie's name. The air in the circle grew heavy with a scent that called to mind an Indian restaurant with a bath oil shop in the foyer.

By the ninth circuit it seemed I had spent eternity down here, dancing around the circle and throwing herbs on the fire. I had reached that state where exhaustion gives you more energy, but things around you look increasingly surreal. I felt I could go on indefinitely, yet knew I was about ready to fall on my face. I reached the center of the circle for the last time with a vague sense of relief, mingled with anticipation.

The last of my nine sacred herbs waited for me, looking lonely in its twist of waxed paper. Timber and I had argued about this choice long into the night, but I had my way in the end. I tore open the packet and withdrew a single blossom from the Angel's Trumpet vine in the front yard. It was still moist and soft.

Datura, for opening doors.

Timber had thought it too dangerous. He had wanted to use bay leaf—after all, he reasoned, the Oracle at Delphi had burned bay to cause visions. And he was right about that…but it hadn't seemed right to me. I wasn't trying to prophesy, but contact the dead. Datura had been used time out of mind by shamans attempting just that sort of thing. Besides, it was just one blossom. More of a symbolic gesture than an effective drug.

I threw it on the fire. I had meant to stay well back from the upward rush of smoke, but somehow it caught me right in the face. It smelled terrible, like mildewed leaves burning. I staggered back, then recovered.

"Archie Connolly," I called for the ninth time, "Come—!"

It's a funny thing about ritual circles in real life. If you believe Hollywood convention, you'd assume they act as a kind of barrier, so things can't just wander in and out of your magic space at will. And to a degree, they do. But they're more to guard against psychic interference than physical. Oh, quite often people experience an aversion to breaking into the circle. Sometimes it almost confers a kind of invisibility. That's why you can hold a ritual in the middle of a public park and after the circle is cast people will jog right by without paying you any attention at all. They forget you're there and if they remember they don't find what you're doing at all interesting or unusual. Except for animals and small children, of course. They're immune to the effect.

The point is, a circle, for the most part, happens in the mind. A disciplined, aware mind can get around a circle very handily just by refusing to participate. And that's why when someone decided to walk straight into my circle, sneak up behind me and clock me on the head, well, there was nothing to stop him.

I went down to my knees all at once, exactly as if all the bones in both my legs had been abruptly removed; they just folded up. I blinked. I didn't yet understand what had happened; part of me thought it was the datura. The edges of my vision went all fuzzy, like they get sometimes when you stand up too fast. The name for that phenomenon flitted through my brain: postural hypotension. I was proud of myself for knowing that. Except I hadn't stood up. I'd gone down.

My head felt really, really heavy. With an immense effort, I managed to lift it and found myself staring into a pair of eyes. Whether they were near or far I couldn't tell, but I knew I'd seen them before, and not long ago. After a minute it came to me. I'd seen those eyes over asphalt in front of the bar that very night.

Breda's.

Then something hit me again and I went down into darkness.

I came to face down in the dirt of the cavern floor with no idea how much time had passed. My mouth was full of bitter dust and I lifted my head, spitting and choking. I acted without thinking, only afterward remembering to flinch as pain shot through my skull. I was well into the flinch when it hit me that, in actuality, my head didn't hurt. Not at all. Cautiously I raised my hand to feel for the lump I knew must be there; whoever had struck me hadn't pulled the punch. But there was no lump anywhere I felt. Curious.

I rolled onto my side and raised myself up on one elbow, blinking dirt out of my eyes. When they cleared, I noticed another curious thing. I was still at the center of the circle. But my ring of candles had vanished. That should have meant darkness, except it wasn't dark at all. In fact, the cavern was quite light.

The light had a rosy quality I associated with early morning. My first thought was that whoever hit me must have turned on the power. I thought I remembered the shades over the wall fixtures as bluish green rather than pink, but I could have been mistaken. Then I happened to glance up at the nearest wall and I discovered a third curious thing. The wall fixtures weren't there.

I sat up suddenly and scuttled backwards like a bug trying to escape a small boy with a jar. I didn't get far before bumping into something behind me.

"Come, then. Get up. We don't have much time," said a voice over my head.

"Give her a moment," drawled another. This second voice came from directly behind me. I couldn't quite get up the nerve to turn around and see who was speaking, however. Instead, I groped behind me in the dust. My hand found something quite close by; in fact, I was half sitting on it. When I looked down, I saw it was a shoe. A shoe with a foot inside it.

"Ack!" I squawked, and butt-hopped to the side.

"A moment may be more than we have," said the first voice. I didn't know it, but it had a familiar cadence. A trace of an accent, maybe. I thought hard, but was too disoriented to identify it.

"More than you have, maybe," replied the second voice. "It doesn't matter to me which way things go."

"Does it not? You worked hard enough to influence the matter."

A hand entered my field of vision, a brown, gnarled hand with short nails. The nails were somewhat grubby. The edge of a slightly frayed tweed sleeve hung over the wrist.

"Come, then," the first voice repeated.

After a second's hesitation, I grasped the hand and allowed it to pull me to my feet. My head swam a little. Another hand on my shoulder steadied me.

"Can you stand all right?"

I nodded and both hands released me. I felt their owner take a step back.

He was, I saw when I finally managed to look up, a middle-aged man in a brown tweed suit that had seen better days. The suit jacket was open, revealing a yellowish-white shirt of some coarsely-woven fabric—muslin, probably—and scarred leather suspenders. The suspenders attached the old-fashioned way to buttons sewn into the waistband of the tweed trousers, which sported no belt loops. The man himself had a pleasant, round face made rounder by grizzled side whiskers. The hair on his head was equally grizzled and extremely wiry, and receded from his brow in a widow's peak. His eyes were a good-natured blue, but the expression in them was more than a little worried.

It took me a minute to place him, but I did it at last.

"Archie Connolly. I didn't recognize you with your head in one piece."

He gave a stiff little bow. "At your service, Miss…?"

His hesitation surprised me. After all the history we had, I had expected him to know my name.

"Learning anything new is extremely difficult for a ghost," said Archie with a wry smile. "Being, as it is, that a ghost is a kind of message itself. A message sent into time."

Well, that made a kind of sense. "Ross. Caitlin Ross."

"A pleasure to meet you, finally."

"So the spell worked."

"In a manner of speaking. Or would have done in another moment. The final word was all it lacked. I was getting all ready to come to you. But it seems you came to me instead. Perhaps it's for the best."

I swallowed, hard. "Am I dead?" I'd known there'd be a price to my using magic, of course. There always is. But I'd thought it would be something entirely different. And I hadn't expected to have to pay it so soon.

To my relief, Archie chuckled. "Oh, heavens no! Just visiting. But that means we don't have too much time, you see. Only until you wake up. Less, if…." He didn't finish that thought. "And there's quite a lot I need to show you, so we'd better get started."

So, I was unconscious. That explained a lot—the missing lump on my head, for one thing. The altered state of the cavern, for another. I wondered what was going on back in the world where my physical body lay, and experienced a peculiar reluctance to find out.

"First," Archie went on, "there's someone else here you need to meet."

Of course. The second voice. Having identified Archie, I had a pretty good notion to whom it must belong. My suspicions didn't make it any easier to face him. I hung my head, stomach churning. Archie made a clucking noise under his breath, laid both hands on my shoulders and turned me around, as if I were a youngster he was forcing to greet an unloved relative.

"You've come this far," he said, prodding me forward.

I looked up to a very strange sight. The center of the circle was taken up almost entirely by a large, brown leather chair. Beside the chair stood a marble-topped occasional table bearing a shaded hurricane lamp resting on a lace doily. The lamp burned with a dull flame, not enough to account for the rosy light all around. And in the chair…

…in the chair sat a young man in a tweed suit very much like the one Archie wore, except where Archie's jacket was open, the young man's was buttoned up as far as it would go. His shirt was also buttoned all the way up to its stiff, starched collar, and he wore an equally stiff-looking black necktie with the knot shoved up under his chin. Despite all this Victorian stiffness, the suit was rumpled looking, as though the young man had been wearing it for a hundred years without changing. A hundred years would be about right, at that.

It was evident at a glance that this young man was not human and never had been. His skin was not just pale, but white: white like paper is white, or snow, or white sugar—skin devised by a person who has been told that some human beings have white skin, but who has never actually seen such a person. It seemed oddly thin, and there were lights burning underneath it, giving him more than a passing resemblance to a man-shaped paper lantern. The lights were pinkish-gold; in fact, they were the exact same color as the light in the cavern. I understood, now, where that came from. Above the starched collar and tie, the young man's head was triangular, with a wide brow and pointed chin. It put me in mind of a praying mantis, an impression strengthened by his habit of holding his head cocked to one side. The features of his face seemed deliberately chosen. The delicate bow of the bloodless lips, aristocratic nose, high, sharp cheekbones and huge colorless eyes seemed beautiful at first glance; at second they resolved into a frightening parody of beauty. His carefully arched eyebrows were the same color as the fine, straight hair on his head: dead white.

"Tintri Fionn," I said.

He shot a little smile at me, showing the barest hint of teeth.

"Forgive me if I don't get up," he replied, not sounding at all as if he cared whether I did or not.

That's when I noticed he was tied to the chair. I didn't see how I could have missed it; the rope winding around and around him was heavy as a hawser. His thin wrists were secured to chair's armrests with manacles that seemed to sprout directly from the leather, and a thick chain ran between his ankles.

I blinked and both rope and chain flickered and vanished. Okay.

"So you're the cause of all this," I said with some asperity. I was remembering that I had recently been knocked unconscious and was not feeling gracious about it.

"All this?" Tintri Fionn raised a white eyebrow. "Hardly." His eyes wandered over my shoulder and I heard Archie shuffle his feet in an embarrassed way. "The actions of men brought the world to this present."

Archie cleared his throat and Tintri Fionn's superior, almost bored expression transformed into the petulant grimace of a small child caught out in a lie.

"Well your father started it," he whined. "You can't blame me for wanting to get out of it any way I can!"

"Hush. There's no time to bicker." I felt Archie at my elbow. "You came here for information, Miss Ross, and you shall have it, but only if you attend to me now. And only if you agree to do exactly as I say."

"And this information will help me…restrain Tintri Fionn?" I thought about the ropes and chains, which I gathered were this plane's symbolic representation of the spells binding the *coimhthíoch*. They seemed secure; certainly they didn't allow Tintri Fionn much movement in this place. But I knew what I knew.

There was a long silence. Tintri Fionn and Archie exchanged a glance over my shoulder. I could feel something passing between them; I didn't know what, but I was fairly sure I wouldn't like it if I did.

Archie sighed. "As to that…. There's a great deal you do not know. Perhaps when you do, you'll understand."

"So, tell me."

"Better to show you."

"Show me, then."

"That I will."

With no more warning than that, Archie turned to face me. I had a brief impression of his craggy face so close to mine that our noses almost touched. His eyes—the same ice blue as Sean Casey's and as Breda's—filled my vision, merged and became one. Then he laid a hand on my forehead, and everything went black.

Chapter Twenty-One

The blackness cleared with infinite slowness, as of lights coming up for the first act of a play. First I saw the hints of shapes where the darkness lay thick only moments before. The shapes grew gradually more distinct, becoming the shapes of things, but what the things were I still couldn't determine. Then full brightness, centered on a scene directly in front of me. It was a kind of courtyard between buildings; on three sides, I could see walls stretching up into nothingness. The ground was packed, yellowish grey dirt. To the right someone had stacked a bunch of barrels; to the left, I could make out a cellar door set almost flush with the ground. What looked like a plow stood in the rear corner. The scene was uninhabited, increasing its resemblance to a stage set waiting for the first actors to enter.

My perspective troubled me. It was too high; I looked down on the scene as if from a balcony. I glanced down and got a shock. I had no body. I was a pinpoint of awareness floating about fifteen feet off the ground, in what seemed to be the far downstage left corner of the courtyard—the right side of the scene, from my point of view. I tried shifting my focus. I couldn't get any lower, but after a little experimentation, during which the scene spun wildly around me, making me wonder whether, body or no, I was going to be sick, I found I could "turn around" and get a glimpse of what lay "behind" me. That turned out to be a street of some kind. I could see a row of buildings—most of them wooden façades, with a few of brick—on the opposite side of the street. People walked up and down, and on occasion a wagon rumbled past. Both people and wagons remained indistinct, mere stage settings, not players.

I focused on the courtyard again. By this time I knew it for the yard beside the Connolly building, home of Western Realty in the present day. About the time I established this fact, a door slammed and the play began.

"Two jars!" a gruff voice called from off stage. "The big dills, mind. And be quick about it."

"Aye, Da." The boy who had just come through the door at the side of the building was a red-haired, freckled lad of nine or ten, but his face showed signs of the man he would become. Archie Connolly stood scowling to himself for a moment, hands thrust deep in the pockets of his too-short trousers, his bare toes working in the dirt. Plainly he would rather be doing anything than the errand on which he had been sent. I knew, as one knows things in a dream, that he hated and feared going into the cellar and at times like these, which came all too often, he hated his father for sending him there.

After a minute, the boy gave a sigh and approached the cellar door. Taking his hands from his pockets, he heaved at it; it was obviously heavy, almost too heavy for him to open. At last he succeeded, though, and the door fell to one side with a muted crash. The boy started down the cellar stairs.

Now what? I wondered, but almost before the thought had formed I found myself heading down into the cellar myself, floating just behind and above the boy's right shoulder. I was getting used to my odd circumstances by this time, and again I thought of being in a dream. As in dreams, I was there and not there, able to watch but not act, and I had the same helpless feeling of knowing I witnessed something with far-reaching consequences I could not affect at all. I hated the sensation. But I knew it was important for me to pay attention, and so I did.

The cellar was very dark, the only light the thin strip of day from the open door. However, it seemed Archie didn't need any more light, for at the bottom of the steep stairs he veered automatically left, towards what seemed to be a shelf of canned goods in the far corner. He was sorting through them by feel—looking for the big dill pickles, I remembered—when the earth gave a little shake. A shower of dust fell from the ceiling. Archie paused, shrugged and went back to his work, intent on getting through his task and back above ground as quickly as possible.

Then the earth gave a great big shake, and Archie—and I with him—fell through the floor. He landed with a jolt that knocked the wind out of him. Just as he seemed about to recover, the earth gave another little shake, and he tumbled down a slope into pitch blackness. At least, I imagine the nine-year-old Archie found it pitch black. For me, it was more like what passed for pitch blackness in a movie. The background was indistinct and full of odd, distorted shadows, but I had little problem seeing the action.

Archie sat up, spitting dirt, seemingly unharmed.

"Da?" His voice quavered. He got up, brushed himself off, and looked around, squinting. I could tell he couldn't see a thing. He stumbled into the sloping wall down which he had just rolled. With a supreme effort, he clambered up on top, stretching his arms above his head. The hole in the cellar floor was directly above him, and ten feet out of reach.

"Da!" he screamed. "DA!"

Light flared like a sudden sunrise. It did not come from above. Archie whirled around, blinking. I saw what he saw: a huge cavern filled with white-hot fire that roiled and swirled like something alive. Like a bag of ferrets in a furnace, I thought.

"Well." Tintri Fionn's voice was very soft, the merest murmur, yet it seemed to fill the whole cavern. Though without source, it seemed to come from everywhere at once. "What have we here?"

Archie didn't answer. Someone else did.

"There you are," said the deep, gruff voice I had heard sending Archie on his errand. It was just as sourceless as Tintri Fionn's. However, before I had time to ponder the fact, it barked a command in Gaelic, and the swirling white fire collapsed on itself with a noise somewhere between a hiss and a cry of rage.

"Got you," said the deep voice.

Blackout.

"He sent me down there on purpose," Archie's voice whispered in my ear. "Over and over again, hoping something of the sort would happen. He knew it came there, you see, but he couldn't do anything until it revealed itself. He made me the bait." Ghost that he was, he could not keep a hint of bitterness from his voice.

"A child's fear…" Tintri Fionn put in. I felt him give a little helpless shrug. "It's hard to resist."

"The net he caught it in was only temporary." Archie went on. "He had to keep renewing it—no, reinventing it, because as soon as the *coimhthíoch* learned the way of it, it would no longer hold him."

"But he did make it permanent eventually," I said.

"That took years," Archie replied, and the lights came back up.

I would have known years had passed even had Archie not told me, just from the change in the cavern. A lot of work had been done there, and from the sullen expression on the face of the red-haired youth who stood near my vantage point I could guess who'd done most of it—under duress. The walls had been smoothed somewhat, and torches burned at intervals along them. The hole from the initial cave-in had gone, but near where it had been a steep passage led up into darkness. I still didn't know where access to the cavern had originally been—probably in the old cellar, if the position of the passage gave any indication—and wondered if I'd ever find out. But the most conspicuous change was the pattern chiseled into the floor. I knew it in its present, worn state; here it was sharp-edged and new, the symbols almost leaping out at me. They had been darkened with some inky substance—tar, maybe—that put me in mind of a ritual scar. I wondered if Archie had had to do that, too. One element was missing: the ninth symbol, the monogram at the circle's center, the one I didn't understand.

The *coimhthíoch* was confined near the circle's north edge, not quite on top of the glyph symbolizing it, but so close as to make no difference. It had no shape as yet, being merely a dense, white spot almost too bright to look upon. Its sickening, unrestrained writhing had been stilled somewhat, but it still flickered and pulsed, on occasion flaring like a sun as it sent a tongue of its substance lashing out to test the bonds holding it. Once or twice the invisible container seemed to give a little, causing Archie to flinch, but it always held.

I couldn't tell Archie's age at this point—fifteen? Seventeen? Old enough to shave—a razor cut stood out livid on his pale cheek—but not quite a man. He'd grown some from the boy who had fallen through the cellar floor, but I knew already he'd be stocky rather than tall. He wore what I thought of as school clothes, although at his age he had probably long since left school: better than work clothes but not quite Sunday best. The pressed trousers and shirt spoke of a woman's touch, and I remembered that at this point his mother would still be alive, Seamus Óg not yet born. His boots shone with polish. I wondered if his mother knew where he was and what he was doing. Probably not.

Archie stood in the extreme south of the circle, directly over the glyph for "Connolly." He was staring fixedly at the *coimhthíoch* opposite him, and my attention followed his. So it wasn't until a movement by Archie's right elbow caused him to look up that I realized the cavern held a third person. I had never laid eyes on Seamus Mór before that moment, but I knew him at once. Not that he resembled his son; he didn't in the least. He was, indeed, a big man, massive and broad where Archie was wiry and compact, with hands that looked capable of crushing rocks. His sleeves were rolled up to expose heavily muscled forearms and his collar gaped around a throat as big around as a bull's. He didn't get that build by keeping a general store, I thought, and wondered what he had done before. Sweat skimmed his handsome, lined face, as if he had recently been engaged in heavy physical labor. Grey touched his black hair only at the temples, crawling down into bushy sideburns that were almost white, the lone indication that he neared sixty. The sole feature he shared with Archie was his ice blue gaze. When I saw it, I realized with a start that he did resemble someone I knew. He looked like Sean Casey would have, had he lived to be so old.

The aura of power surrounding him was unmistakable. I thought of Casey's pretensions towards magic and would have laughed, if I could have. Casey had not possessed even a shadow of his great-grandfather's presence. He had been a dilettante with delusions of grandeur. Seamus Mór was the real thing.

The air in the cavern was tense and expectant, heavy with the echoes of words recently spoken. A fresh cut on Seamus Mór's forearm still streamed blood in a thin trickle. I had arrived in the middle of something.

"So, then," Seamus Mór said in his deep, gruff voice. The liquid syllables were Irish Gaelic; I shouldn't have been able to understand him, but I did. "It's one more chance I'll be giving you."

The white light at the edge of the circle pulsed and flickered. "And my answer will be the same." The demon's reply might have been Gaelic, or it might not. It sounded directly in my mind—probably in Seamus and Archie's minds as well, and I knew that whoever received the message would understand it, no matter what his native tongue.

"Still, it's I who'll be asking. Will you go from this place and leave me and mine alone?"

The whiteness rippled with unmistakable sardonic laughter. "Why should I?"

As if in answer, a lopsided diamond of blue fire flared upwards within the circle's confines. At a gesture from Seamus Mór, it contracted towards the whiteness until the coimhthíoch had to condense itself to avoid it. I had the impression of a person being backed up against a wall.

"The four powers bind you," Seamus Mór remarked in conversational tones, and I saw then that the blue fire connected the glyphs representing Earth, Air, Water and Fire. "You can neither feed, nor flee, nor fight me while this is so. I'm offering you your freedom in exchange for one promise. It's no little thing."

"Your four powers cannot hold me forever. They're of this world as I am not, anchored to the rules and symbols of this world as I am not. Even now they weaken." To demonstrate the truth of what it said, the whiteness flexed and stretched; the blue diamond shivered. Seamus Mór grimaced and the diamond held, but it seemed larger than it had been, allowing the demon to expand as if drawing breath. It flowed outward past the *coimhthí-och* glyph. "Soon I will break these bonds and you will not be able to prevent me."

"Very well, then." Seamus took a deep breath; I felt it fuel the words he was about to speak. The air in the cavern thickened.

Archie Connolly chose that moment to interrupt.

"It's a cruelness you're doing, Da," he said. "Trapping and tormenting a starving thing."

His words were very soft, but his father whirled on him as if he had shouted.

"Have you learned nothing all these years? And what would your pitiful starving thing feed on? Pain and grief and violence, the terrors of your family and your home. It would have had you long ago, had I not been waiting for it."

"It was you that sent me to it." No emotion colored Archie's voice, none at all. All the same, I saw plain the damage his father had done him.

"And I'd do so again, to bring the beast into the open," Seamus replied more calmly. "Only so could I trap it and prepare for what comes next. For your safety, and this town's."

Archie withered visibly. And I saw then what I hadn't before. Over the years he'd come to identify with the demon trapped in the circle. In his own way, he also was bound by his father's spells, with a binding that would outlast his father's death and his own. He would never leave Gordarosa, as he dreamed of doing, for to do so would mean binding some other creature to the guardianship of the cavern. And such a thing he would never do. His prison was too bitter for him to inflict it on anyone else—even someone who claimed to want it. For that and nothing else he had alienated his brother, to prod Seamus Óg into a life Archie had never been able to live.

I saw it all then, though the main part of the spell remained uncast, the brother as yet unborn and the ultimate end to the story a mere hint of tragedy in the future, my future. Then Seamus Mór raised his arms and began to speak, and I forgot it all.

"Formless you were, but formless no longer!"

The old man's voice tolled like a great bell. The air in the cavern shimmered as with heat, and the black lines of the circle and the symbols at its edge turned red.

"Void you were but void no longer. I bind you to this realm by Earth; I bind you to this realm by Air; I bind you to this realm by Fire; I bind you to this realm by Water: here to be embodied and here to remain."

The diamond of blue fire blazed white and leaped up to the ceiling, thrusting the *coimhthíoch* away from the circle's edge and towards the center. The brighter white flame of the demon stuttered, somehow giving the impression of a man staggering under a heavy blow and falling to his knees. The cavern held its breath. After a minute, however, the demon recovered; its lurching steadied and it flared into brilliance again. But it seemed smoother than it had been, more condensed: a ball of light, rather than barely tamed tongues of flame.

"In this place I claim you: Blood of my blood, seed of my seed, by blood and seed I sign you! Nameless you were, but Nameless no longer!"

I didn't understand what Seamus Mór was getting at. The demon, apparently, did. At the mention of naming it went mad, or as mad as it could, as spellbound as it was. It pulsed frantically, straining against its bonds like a lunatic against a straightjacket. The cavern rocked with its efforts. A shower of dirt and small stones fell from the ceiling, only to be swept away by a whirlwind that sprang up from nowhere. The floor heaved and Archie stumbled; his father grasped him by the elbow and held him firmly in place.

"Tintri Fionn I Name you, White Flame of the Connollys," Seamus Mór bellowed into the chaos. "Let this name be upon you! Let it make you one with me and mine and all who come after! One in the blood and one in the seed and one in the Name, bound from this moment by all that binds the Name to the World, in time and through time for all time hereafter, and bound through the Name to this Place until one of the Name shall release you! By the power I call, by the power in me, So Let It Be!"

The white flame of the demon contracted almost to the vanishing point. Then, in a burst of brilliance so dazzling it almost blinded me even in my disembodied state, it exploded up towards the ceiling, a Roman candle igniting. For a moment I thought it had broken free. But a similar flame, this one green, shot up from the glyph where the young Archie stood, engulfing the young man until all I could be see of him was a vaguely human shape outlined in fire. The two flames, the green and the white, met over the exact center of the circle, impacted, and detonated, sending a sheet of pure energy straight down into the cavern floor. The flash when it hit was blinding. Everything went black and I thought, though I knew better, though I knew what I saw to be only an echo of events that had taken place a hundred years ago or more, that the spell had backfired and the cavern and everything in it had been consumed in that blast of magical power.

Then my vision cleared. I saw Archie crumble gracelessly into a heap at his father's feet. Only my knowledge of future events told me he had not been struck dead, so pale and still he lay. I expected his father to show some concern, but Seamus Mór did nothing of the kind. His attention was fixed elsewhere, on the circle's center. After a minute, I looked there too.

The ninth glyph had appeared there, fresh and new, burnt right into the stone. From the first I had thought it resembled a monogram, and that was exactly what it was. A monogram was essentially a written symbol of how families—and individual family members—were linked through blood and name ties. I gazed long and hard at the intertwined symbols for Connolly and *coimhthíoch*, and I understood what Seamus Mór had done.

The problem of a *coimhthíoch* was that it did not belong to this world. It didn't obey the world's laws because it didn't acknowledge them and nothing could make it do so. To bind it permanently, Seamus Mór had had to make the *coimhthíoch* part of the world and subject to its laws. He'd done so by magically and ritually making the demon part of the family: wrapping its essence up with his son's so tightly that that there was no longer any telling where one left off and the other began. It was brilliant. Brilliant and sad.

I looked up. The air at the center of the cavern still shimmered in the glow coming off the new-made glyph. As I watched, the glow darkened, thickened and took on substance and form.

A young man, unnaturally white-skinned and long-limbed, but still discernibly human-shaped, appeared on top of the glyph. Heavy chains bound him, naked and shivering, into a position that looked extremely uncomfortable. Even knowing what he was and what he was capable of, my heart went out to him.

He opened one colorless eye and fixed Seamus Mór with a baleful stare. The bloodless lips parted to emit a single, bitter word of greeting.

"Father."

Lips and eye both closed. The embodied demon turned its face away, and I floated in darkness once again.

"You understand what he did?" Archie's voice sounded close to what would have been my right ear, if I'd had ears. I tried to nod, remembered I had no head, and replied in a word instead.

"Yes."

"He bound me with blood." The demon's voice still held a note of bitterness and, I was surprised to note, chagrin. "He made me one of his blood and thus, part of his world. I didn't think it could be done. I still don't know quite how he managed it."

"He was an unusual man. Powerful and creative," Archie replied with grudging admiration.

"A dangerous combination," Tintri Fionn agreed. A weighty silence followed, during which I felt a peculiar, crawling sensation all over, a sensation I associated with being subjected to intense scrutiny. I shivered, and spoke to distract myself from the feeling.

"But what happened? As I understand it, Seamus Mór meant to prevent you from ever having influence in this world. Yet you managed it, enough to give this place a reputation for violence. Did the binding weaken with time?"

There came a long, pregnant silence. Once again, I got the impression of Archie and the demon exchanging a look over my head. Whatever the answer to my question turned out to be, I really, really was not going to like it.

"Show her," Tintri Fionn commanded tersely.

"Ummm…" Archie seemed very uncomfortable. If he could sense my irritation, I didn't blame him.

"You knew it would come to this. Are you going to back out now?"

"No." Archie sighed helplessly. "That I'm not."

"Then you must show her. Things are moving in the world. We haven't much time."

"I thought you didn't care about time," I said. Or thought I said. Or tried to say. But before I could get the words out, the lights came up for the last act.

It started in the bar. Or perhaps I should say, it started in Connolly's Tavern, for it was a much different place from the Emerald Isle I had come to know so well. The furnishings were not so rich and there were fewer of them, a handful of farmhouse tables and rough-hewn chairs was all. Each of the tables was large enough to seat a family of eight, but they seemed small in the cavernous front room. After a minute I saw that this was because the room actually was bigger, encompassing half of what would be the back room in my time. The rest of that section was walled off, with the bar in front of it, close to where the stage now was situated. A swinging door behind the bar led to what was probably the kitchen. To the left of the bar, where the restrooms were now, a rickety staircase led up to the second floor living quarters.

It was clear at a glance that the tavern had fallen on hard times. Everything I could see had a dusty, disused quality, from the tables and chairs to the row of glasses behind the bar. It didn't take me long to figure out why. No liquor was in evidence anywhere. The shelves that should have held gleaming bottles of bourbon, rum and fine whisky were empty. There wasn't even a beer keg to be seen. Prohibition had hit the nation, and in Archie Connolly's case it had hit hard.

My thoughts seemed to have summoned him. The kitchen door swung and Archie stepped through, a much older Archie than I had last seen, the Archie that I knew. Like his tavern, he had seen better days. His hair was unkempt and he hadn't had a shave in a while. His once fine suit was worn at the collar and cuffs, as was the muslin shirt underneath it. His boots, which had probably been fine when new, were run down at the heel and scuffed at the toe. It wasn't simply the wear of hard work. The suit wasn't one kept in reserve and donned when its owner was required to do manual labor. It was all he had. He was a man fallen from prosperity to poverty, trying to keep some semblance of dignity on the way down.

Just how far down he had yet to go he couldn't know, but I could. The suit was the same one I had always seen him in. Archie wasn't just at the end of his resources. He was at the end of his life.

He hummed softly to himself as he examined his appearance in the mirror hung behind the bar, straightening his collar, dusting his sleeve. He produced a comb from a pocket and ran it through his hair, but did not quite persuade it to lie flat. He felt his chin, frowned at finding it stubbled, then shrugged. His appearance as crisp as he could make it, he turned and gazed for a long time out over the empty room. Then he gave himself a little shake, came out from behind the bar and exited through the side door.

I followed.

Once outside Archie headed, to my surprise, for the cellar. I kept following—I hadn't any choice in the matter—but I couldn't help but wonder if I was wrong in thinking I knew what was coming. I had supposed Archie was headed for the cavern; according to everything I'd heard, the cellar did not conceal the entrance. Missy Phillips had said so. The way she told it, everyone had said so.

I was about to learn, however, that everyone was wrong.

The cellar didn't look much different from my first sight of it in the vision that had taken place close to forty years before. That is, it was dark. The thin strip of light coming in from outside showed me a claustrophobic space of dirt floors and cobwebby brick and board shelves cluttered with a wide variety of stuff: canned goods, old tools, broken bits and pieces of unidentifiable objects and the like. It looked a lot like my cellar at home. Archie rummaged around on one of the shelves and produced a candle lantern. He lit this with a match from a box on one of the other shelves and set it down on the floor. Then he took a long pole with a hook at one end from a dark corner and started back up the stairs. About halfway up he stopped. He thrust the pole up, caught the edge of the cellar door on the hook and pulled, grunting with the effort. The door slammed closed. For a second the cellar was plunged into darkness. Then the candle lantern flared, or seemed to flare; anyway, there was a sudden transition from pitch blackness to a homely, golden glow by which I could see Archie picking his way back down the stairs. At the foot of the stairs he stopped, turned back around and reached up with both hands towards a contraption I had never noticed before: some kind of rope and pulley arrangement; I couldn't make it out clearly. Archie grasped the rope with both hands and tugged. The mechanism was well-oiled and moved smoothly, without a sound. The cellar stairs lifted up, revealing a deep, dark hole with a ladder leading down.

After everything I'd seen and everything I'd been through, finding out the answer to the penultimate riddle was the most demoralizing anti-climax I'd ever experienced. I didn't have time to dwell on it, though. Archie was already on his way down the ladder, lantern bobbing in one hand.

At the foot of the ladder, he set the lantern on the ground. The circle of gold spilling out of it, which had seemed so bright in the cellar above, shone pitiful and fitful in the looming dark. Archie glanced down once with an odd, almost fond look on his face before leaving the lantern's inadequate comfort and facing the gloom.

"Tintri Fionn!" he called. "It's Archie. Will you have a word with me?"

I was struck by his tone: not commanding, but requesting, respectful and, yes, even cordial, like a visitor calling without warning, who is well aware he might be turned away. He saw himself, not as a powerful man with a demon at his beck and call, but as someone who shared a fence line with an eccentric and rather unpredictable neighbor. And as the rosy light blossomed and Tintri Fionn answered, I realized that the demon felt the same way.

"Hello, old man." Since his binding and subsequent transformation, the demon's voice no longer seemed to come from everywhere at once. It no longer seemed as powerful, either. Tintri Fionn had been bound for twenty years, and he was starving. He couldn't die, perhaps. But it was obvious he was weaker than he had been. Weaker than he was now, in my time.

When I'd last seen him, he'd been naked but for the chains shackling him to the floor. Somehow in the intervening years, Tintri Fionn had acquired the suit I had seen him in. I wondered if the clothes were from some working of Archie's and decided they probably were; I couldn't imagine Big James showing so much mercy, even in the name of modesty. The chair of my time hadn't come into being yet. Instead, Tintri Fionn was chained in a horrible, hunched position to a kind of pillory. He looked very thin and frail, which made the chains seem especially heavy and large. The suit did not so much resemble a straitjacket as a burlap sack, so loose did it hang. All in all, the sight of him put me in mind of a young scholar sentenced to the stocks for printing libels.

"What will you with me? As usual, I am totally at your service." Tintri Fionn made as if to shrug. The chains rattled.

"Whist. You should know me better by now. I said I'd like a word and that's all I want." Archie dragged a boot toe through the dust on the cavern floor, back and forth, back and forth. "It's sad times, Tintri Fionn. Sad times."

"Spare me your maudlin reminiscences. You're walking free out there."

"So I am," Archie returned acerbically. "And so would you be, if you'd not been so high-and-mighty that you turned up your nose at what was offered you."

"It's bad manners, Archie Connolly, to taunt someone who can't get away from you."

"And it's worse manners, Tintri Fionn Connolly, to dwell on your own troubles when another is in need."

They like each other! I realized. For twenty years, they had been bound together, and they shared something neither could ever share with anyone else. Was it so strange that enforced proximity should grow into friendship? I'd seen old men at the post office twit each other in exactly the same way, drawn close, even against their will, by the simple fact that they had survived.

"What do you want?" asked Tintri Fionn, the grudging affection so clear now I had seen it.

"As it happens, I want to do something for you. If you'll let me."

"You can't do anything for me, unless it were to set me free."

There was a long, long silence, and from it I knew exactly what Archie intended. Tintri Fionn got it in the same moment; the light of him flared painfully bright, as with hope.

"It's sad times," Archie said again. "I can't keep the tavern going, the way things are. I'm not too old to start over, but with Da gone, and young Seamus, there's nothing to keep me here." There was longing in his voice as he spoke of leaving. "It's California for me, and that as soon as I'm able. But I can't leave you trapped here, you poor, starving bastard."

Tintri Fionn's light flickered with suspicion. "And what do you want in return?"

"I want you to go. Gordarosa's like to dry up and blow away in any case. But even if it doesn't, I won't have you taking revenge here for what my father did. Leave. Go back to wherever it was you came from."

The demon shook his head sadly. "I'm bound to this plane, now. That path is no longer open to me. Unless...?"

"I'm truly sorry to hear that." Archie frowned. "For un-Naming you is something I cannot do. You're a Connolly until you die."

"I can't die."

"Until the end of time, then. But I can release you from this cavern, and that I will do, if you'll leave Gordarosa and promise to take no vengeance on me and mine."

Tintri Fionn seemed to consider. "It's not much of a choice."

"It's the only one I'm offering you."

The demon hesitated, but it was just posturing and I could tell Archie knew it.

"Very well. Release me and I'll do as you ask. I'll leave Gordarosa and take no revenge on any you name."

Archie nodded, once. Then he cleared his throat, and with no more preparation than that, began the ritual that would release Tintri Fionn Connolly into the world.

It was as different from his father's ritual as it was possible to imagine, and I remembered, as if it had been a hundred years ago, explaining to Breda the difference between Ceremonial and Folk magic. Archie used no tools. No ceremonial sword, no incense, not even a candle. He sketched no new sigils on the floor. He made no offering of blood, or any other bodily fluid. He didn't stride or boom or make expansive, meaningful gestures. He simply walked—no, strolled—around the cavern, speaking in a quiet voice that reminded me more than anything of a farmer coaxing a skittish cow through a gate,

"Hello, you powers of Earth. You remember old Archie, then? I'd be asking a favor of you, if you'd oblige me by listening…"

It seemed they did listen. Listened, and responded better than I'd ever known them to. As Archie passed each glyph and cajoled the element it represented, the glyph flared blue and stretched out tendrils to its neighbor until the whole circle glowed with a sapphire radiance almost too bright to look upon.

You old codger, I thought in voiceless admiration. *You're the best magician I've ever seen.*

"Now, show me what you're doing to my friend Tintri Fionn, here," Archie requested.

The elements were happy to oblige. Blue spokes shot out from the edges of the circle to the center. There, they became one with the chains holding the demon in the pillory—one with the pillory itself—and I could see how each reinforced the rest,

and the whole tied itself into the floor, making it impossible for
Tintri Fionn to break free.

"Ah, you've been holding that for a powerful long time,"
clucked Archie in sympathy. "And it's grateful I am for your
hard work. But now's the time you can set your task aside."

The links of the chain twitched. Tintri Fionn, sensing freedom at hand, also twitched. And the cavern, bound to Tintri
Fionn at its center, twitched too.

A shower of small stones fell from the ceiling.

"You be quiet now," Archie told the demon in the same
calm tone. "I don't need you fighting me."

"I'm not fighting. I'm helping."

"I don't need your help, either." Archie continued to stroll
widdershins around the circle, halting at last in the southwest,
near the Connolly glyph. Something about his position caused a
shiver of apprehension to roll through me. But I couldn't think
of why that would be, so I ignored it.

"Come now, you powers of Earth, leave off your long task
and let my friend go. You powers of Water, of Fire and of Air,
set Tintri Fionn Connolly free. My father bound you to this
work, and it's I who tell you the work is over."

The links of the chain thinned imperceptibly, dimmed imperceptibly…and held. Tintri Fionn, who must understandably
have found this frustrating, made a noise something between a
roar and a growl and strained against his bonds again.

More stones fell from the ceiling. Bigger ones.

"Tintri Fionn Connolly," warned Archie. "Be still." He
gazed at the chains for a moment, considering. "Once more, I
think. All at once."

For the first time, he raised his voice. It was less cajoling,
more demanding, yet nonetheless loving: a mother telling her
child to stop this nonsense and come to bed this instant.

"Come now, you powers of Earth, powers of Water, powers of Fire, powers of Air. Give up your hold and release Tintri
Fionn Connolly from bondage. I, Archie Connolly, tell you your

work is done. Lay aside the task and go on to your own places. So mote—!"

And then it happened. Despite Archie's warnings, all this time Tintri Fionn had been testing the chains, intending to rip himself free the moment they became loose enough. With each heave, the chains gave a little, which only encouraged the demon. But also, with each heave, the floor shook a little harder; the ceiling shed a few more stones. Just as Archie was about to tag the ritual, the demon's struggles dislodged a great big rock from directly over Archie's head. It crushed him as a boot would crush a beetle. And the two words that would have released Tintri Fionn entirely were never spoken.

Chapter Twenty-Two

I t was dark. So very dark. I lay on my stomach with my cheek
pressed into a hard, dusty surface; my mouth was bone dry
and my lips seemed gummed together. I tried to swallow
and gagged; my mouth wouldn't open and I feared choking on
the bile that burned my throat. My head hurt. My arms hurt, too.
For some reason they were twisted back behind me; my shoulders ached with the strain of it. I tried to bring my arms forward
into a more comfortable position and couldn't.

Far away, a voice chanted in the dark. Nearer, another
voice whispered in my ear in a lilting, familiar tone,

"Caitlin. You must wake, now. You must wake up."

I tried to turn my head to see who spoke. It was so dark.

"You must do the task I set for you," the voice continued.
"And you must protect her."

Task? Protect? I thought, but I couldn't speak and the voice
went on, insistent, unheeding.

"You have the power. It's what I chose you for. Come now,
girl, wake up."

I tried hard to understand. My head hurt so badly. There
was an answer in that, if I could only see it. I couldn't see anything, though.

A third voice spoke, quite loud, nearer to me than the chanting but not quite so close as the whisper.

"Are you ready for me yet?"

The chanting broke off in mid-syllable. "Not yet." My ears, which seemed to be the only portion of my anatomy functioning as expected, identified the speaker as a male, irritated. "I told you not to interrupt. Now I have to start over. You'll know when it's time."

"It's taking too long." I thought I knew that voice, but its petulant tone confused me.

"It will go quicker if you keep silent and do as you're told."

"I want what you promised me." The sound grated at me, almost a whine. The male voice sighed, impatient, but the words it spoke next were conciliatory.

"And you shall have it, but only if you do as I say. Now why don't you check on our guest? I think she's waking up."

Footsteps approached, a muffled sound like rain hitting a dusty street. Something—the toe of a boot?—poked me in the ribs.

"She's not going anywhere."

"Keep an eye on her, all the same. I don't want any more interruptions."

The chanting started up again.

Paying attention to that snatch of conversation had helped my mind to clear somewhat. My head still hurt abominably, but I understood that this was because someone had hit me—presumably, one of the two people I had just overheard. One of those two people, or maybe both of them, had also tied me up. That was why my arms were in such an awkward position. I couldn't feel my legs at all. I chose to believe they had also been tied, and rather too tightly. The alternative, that the blow to the head had permanently damaged me, I could not even consider.

I had no memory of being tied up, nor could I recall when or how the chanting had started. This pointed to my having been unconscious for some time. Fifteen minutes popped at random into my head. I had the distinct impression that something important had happened while I lay unconscious, but that seemed absurd. If I hadn't been aware of being tied up, how could I have been aware of anything else, important or not? Still, the feeling wouldn't leave me. I cast my mind back, trying to remember.

It didn't come. What came instead was a vision of the last thing I had seen before falling senseless to the ground. Breda's blue eyes.

Hers was the voice I had recognized, of course. I mulled that over for a minute or so, trying not to flinch at the implications. Sometime in the last few days, she'd fallen in with a magician. *The* magician. Jake Carruthers. I had suspected it ever since we'd found Casey's body. Someone else might know of the cavern. No one else knew of the demon. But my grief at Breda's abandonment had crippled me, and my preoccupation with the spell had blinded me. Most of all, words of my own speaking had lulled me into thinking I had more time.

Jake Carruthers lies beyond the Dark and beyond expectation, and the sight of him is not to be hoped for. At first I'd thought it meant he must be dead. Knowing that Oracles always speak in riddles, I'd wondered, especially after finding Casey. Still, I'd hoped to control the outcome somehow—by always expecting him, by not hoping to see him at all. But when I'd disabled the drill so easily, I'd stopped expecting any problem. I had begun to hope that I would face him. Now the terms of the prophecy were fulfilled. Now he was here.

I wondered how he'd swayed her to his side. What could he possibly have offered her? He must have offered her something. Because if not, the only explanation was that Breda had been playing me all along, and I just didn't want to believe I'd made such a horrible mistake.

"I know you're awake. I didn't hit you that hard. You might as well open your eyes," Breda said from somewhere above me.

At any other time I would have felt like a royal idiot at being made to understand that the only reason I'd been suffering in the dark all this while was that my eyes were squeezed tight shut. However, at this particular moment in time, I could not possibly feel any stupider. I blinked, opened my eyes, and looked around as well as I could, considering I lay prone on the floor of a cavern lit only by candles. The angle of my head gave me a good view of Breda's boots: maroon leather and snakeskin in a faux cowboy style. I had never seen them before. Presently, she slipped the toe of one under my ribs and flipped me up onto my side.

"Jake's going to make me a star," she announced casually, squatting down by my face. "After he's dealt with the man who ruined his family. And anyone else who gets in his way."

I frowned. After saying she was tired of the bustle of the city and she wanted to get away from it all, she wanted to be a star? It didn't make sense.

Breda peered into my eyes as if willing me to understand something. I tried to feel her thoughts, but my head still ached too fiercely and I couldn't catch them. All I understood was that I had been very wrong about her. The Breda I thought I knew would never have wanted celebrity. She had played me. Played me like a pro.

I started to reply, but only managed a kind of strangled gargle. My mouth had been covered by several strips of duct tape, a very effective silencer.

"We couldn't have you mucking things up," Breda explained. "We heard your little song. Jake says there's power in your voice. Best to keep it quiet."

Power in my voice. They knew about that part, but they didn't know about my other, purely mental abilities, the ones my Old Blood gave me. Jake was a Ceremonial Magician; for him, everything depended on ritual and incantation. He might not even believe in pure magic. I wondered if I could turn his ignorance to my advantage.

Then another thought turned my heart to ice. If Breda and Jake were here, they'd come through the trap door in the stage. The trap door I had left Timber guarding. He wouldn't have let them past without a fight. At the very least, he'd have found some way of warning me…

…if he'd been able.

I tried very hard, then, not to think of Sean Casey's bloodless body, tried very hard not to imagine my husband in the same position. I couldn't manage it. My throat constricted until I thought I'd pass out again for want of air, and my vision blurred with tears. I blinked them away, furiously. There was no time for them, now. No time for grief.

Just then, the chanting stopped.

"Breda, I'm ready for you," Jake began, then paused. I couldn't see him yet, but I felt his eyes turn my way. The sensation of them on me was both sharp and slimy, like being cut with a pus-covered blade. I shuddered.

I felt, rather than heard, him come towards me. "So, she's awake. Get her up."

Breda grabbed my shoulder and hauled me into a sitting position. For the first time in a while I was able to see my surroundings, and I took a good look around. It gave me a shock to see that so little had changed. I sat almost at the center of the circle. All around me, at the quarters and cross-quarters, my white pillar candles still burned. Close by lay the censer in which I had burned the herbs. It had been tipped on one side and spilled a small pile of ash from which a lingering scent of spices still rose. The grey-black smear of it was vivid as a new bruise against the tan background of the dusty floor. All in all, the only remarkable additions were the two people looming over me. Breda was conspicuously Mundane in her cowboy boots, designer jeans and button down shirt, but Jake made up for that in a long, blood-red robe printed with what I assumed were cabbalistic symbols in stark black. A black hood was thrown back to reveal his handsome, dark face. I examined that face closely for signs of the evil I knew it hid, but there was nothing. No lines of dissipation, no hint of unnatural red in the eyes, no scattering of scales across the bridge of the nose. His teeth, when he smiled down at me, were not pointed. It was the same face I had seen in the photo of Breda's dash. Just a face.

"You should have let me kill her," he said.

He held a knife in his hand, a wide, curved blade that narrowed towards an almost ridiculously stubby hilt cross-wrapped in leather. I remembered watching a horror movie with Timber. "Why is it that whenever they want a strange looking knife in a movie, they always use a kukri?" he'd complained. "Because they look cool," I'd replied. Apparently Ceremonial Magicians thought the same.

Oh, Timber...

"You were the one who said her blood might contaminate the ritual space," Breda reminded him. "Besides," she swayed close to him and ran her hands seductively down the front of his robe. I thought I was going to be sick. "I want her to watch. Then we can let the demon have her."

I stiffened. The demon! Crap! All at once everything I had learned from Archie and Tintri Fionn came rushing back so forcefully that my sight went black. When it cleared, everything in the cavern had changed. My candles were still there, as were Breda and Jake—more's the pity. But I could also see the lines of shimmering blue fire joining the quarter points of the circle and the radiant tendrils reaching out to the center where Tintri Fionn Connolly sat chained. I could see him, too, leather armchair and all. I was practically sitting in his lap. His colorless eyes met mine and he smiled down, as if from a throne.

"You know what to do," he said. "If you can." From his leer, I knew he thought the possibility of my accomplishing the task before me was a slight one.

I glanced up, wondering if the others had heard him. It didn't seem that they had.

I did know what to do. Or, I knew what I was supposed to do, which wasn't quite the same thing. I was supposed to finish the ritual Archie had started to set Tintri Fionn free. I still wasn't sure I thought it such a good idea. But releasing the demon was bound to cause a powerful diversion and that might be my best chance to get out of this mess. However, to finish the ritual I had to be able to speak. And my mouth was sealed with duct tape. I couldn't make a sound, much less utter a coherent word.

Jake preened under Breda's touch. His hand—not the one with the knife—reached up to caress her hair. He drew her mouth towards his. They kissed wetly. Disgusting.

"You're right," he murmured. "We'll let the demon have her."

"And then I'll be a star. I'll have the world at my feet."

He looked at her for a long time, smiling a mysterious, scary smile. "Of course you will."

He took her by the elbow and guided her off toward another part of the cavern.

I thought furiously. I'd disabled the drill, but not as soon as I should have. The bonds holding Tintri Fionn were weak, weak enough that Jake thought he could break through them somehow. I knew he wasn't magician enough to do it with a simple command. What was it planned?

Then I saw where Jake had led Breda and I knew.

She was standing right on top of the Connolly glyph. I remembered Sean Casey's body lying in that exact spot. I remembered the psychic blast I had perceived as an earthquake. Jake had used blood before, Connolly blood. He just didn't think he'd used it at the right time, or used enough. And the last remaining scion of the Connolly line was standing right in front of him.

Protect her.

Despite my certainty of Breda's defection, a scream of warning bubbled up in my throat; I couldn't let her die that way. The scream couldn't get past my sealed mouth. I squirmed against my bonds, but they held tight, as tight as those bound the demon who seemed, beyond all sense, my only ally.

Jake started speaking again, long, sonorous syllables in some language I didn't know; even so, I found it compelling.

Anything that heard his words and understood them would be bound to obey.

Still chanting, he raised the knife in both hands, offering it to the sky. Breda followed his every movement with glowing, trusting eyes. He had killed her father in just this way, and still she believed he would do her no harm. Gently, slowly, Jake put his hands on her shoulders and turned her around. He held her against his chest in the circle of his arms for a long moment. Then one hand reached up in a sickening parody of his earlier caress and grabbed her by the hair. Every movement was as slow and deliberate as a dance performed under water.

I glanced at Tintri Fionn, who was watching the ritual in a disinterested sort of way. Desperate to get his attention, I flung my head wildly in the general direction of his tweed-clad legs, fully expecting to meet nothing but air and go rolling onto my side. Instead, I contacted something with a meaty thunk that made my head swim. Tintri Fionn glanced down at me with a frown, like a woman whose child's tantrum has distracted her from her afternoon soaps.

Aren't you concerned about this? I thought as hard as I could in the demon's direction. *Isn't there anything you can do?*

He smirked at me. "You don't understand, do you? She's the last of the Connolly line. When her blood is spilled it will free me just as surely as Archie's spell would have—maybe better. All I care for is to be free. I don't much care how that is accomplished, so long as it is."

His words his me like a sudden slap in the face and all at once I understood what I hadn't before.

You set this up.

"From afar? Hardly. But once Sean Casey and Jake had come, it did not pose much of a problem to influence their minds in the direction I wanted them to go. The bonds were already loose, you see. Jake's mind was particularly fertile ground." He went on, a little petulant, almost as if he felt the need to justify his actions. "I couldn't know that you'd come nosing around. I couldn't know that Archie intended you to complete what he had finished. And as I said, it's all one to me, either way."

I looked back at Breda and Jake. Time seemed to have stopped in that strange way it does in moments of crisis; they stood just as they had. Could he be having second thoughts? If so, I couldn't count on them lasting long.

Jake began to raise the knife.

I struggled against my bonds, trying to feel my own power, my mind desperately seizing and discarding one option after another. Sight? Useless. Shield spell? No; I had small skill at shielding others, only myself. Illusion? That had possibilities, but I rejected it too. The balls of light I had played with as a child might distract Jake for an instant. I couldn't count on them doing more.

Seamus Mór's net spell. I didn't know how to do it, but it might work. I cast my thoughts to the *coimhthíoch* again.

Show me what Seamus Mór did to you, I begged. *Show me how you were caught in the first place.*

Tintri Fionn turned his face away and didn't answer.

At last, I hit upon one, final possibility. I had punched through Jake's drill with a fist of power. Could I do the same to a human being? I knew I could make a shock, but I had to be in contact. Could I use pure energy?. It might do nothing. It might kill him. Still, I had no other choice and time was running out.

I pulled up as much power as I could and hurled it straight at Jake's head.

He staggered backward as if he'd been hit in the face with a two-by-four, releasing Breda and dropping the knife. And to my astonishment, Breda whirled on him, kicked the knife aside, and went at him with her fists.

At that same instant, a bellow of rage echoed through the cavern. I whipped my head toward the source of the sound and saw Timber plunging out of the cavern's entrance, heading not for Jake, but straight toward me.

I didn't have time for more than a moment of joy at seeing him. For just then all the energy Jake had been channeling, with no guide now that his concentration was broken, erupted.

Jake screamed, stiffening, and Breda leapt back as a pillar of black fire sprang up from the magician's body, wreathing him in smoke and flame. The fire shot straight to the ceiling, impacted, and split into writhing tendrils that whipped back down to the cavern floor, which bucked and heaved like an unbroken bronco at a rodeo, no mere psychic storm this time, but a real earthquake, real as the one which had killed Archie Connolly. The walls began to buckle, dislodging great rocks from above. Ruin rained down.

Tintri Fionn, frustrated that his plan had gone awry, pulled hard at the chains of light that bound him and let out a roar loud enough to split my already aching head. I fell over onto my side, and felt a trickle of blood as I cut my cheek on something sharp.

Timber raced to my side, leaping over cracks and rifts that had opened underfoot. Kneeling beside me, he started sawing at my bonds with his dirk, the sharp blade parting the ropes with scarcely an effort. I shook my head, hoping he could read the urgent message in my eyes.

He did. His free hand came up and ripped the duct tape from my lips. I opened my mouth to gasp in a deep breath and began to speak. Then I hesitated. I considered Tintri Fionn. And I knew that whatever Archie wanted, I could not loose this thing on the world.

Timber finished sawing. The ropes that held me parted and I staggered to my feet, wincing as blood rushed back into my legs. I glanced back over my shoulder. Jake had recovered, and now he and Breda were locked together in what looked like mortal combat. Jake was screaming threats and imprecations in words I couldn't make out; Breda held her own in grim silence. But Jake was taller and stronger, fueled by rage at the wreck of his plans, and as I watched, Breda's knees began to crumple.

"Help Breda," I gasped to my husband.

He hesitated, clearly not wanting to leave me until I had regained more strength.

"Help her!" I insisted. "I'm fine. I have something to do."

At that, Timber gave a curt nod and dashed off through the shaking cavern. I spared only a second to watch him thrust his body between Jake and Breda, shoving her aside. Then I faced the *coimhthíoch*. Slowly, as if I had all the time in the world, I walked forward until my blue dress brushed Tintri Fionn's knees. I stared into his colorless eyes.

"I need a binding promise from you. The same one you made Archie. If I free you, you'll leave here. You'll take no revenge. You may feed on the emotion you can find, but you'll provoke no more violence. A big city ought to provide all you need. I suggest you find one."

Tintri Fionn glared at me, but did not speak.

"Promise," I said, "or you can stay here and starve."

If anything, the *coimhthíoch's* expression increased in malevolence. Still he made no answer.

I glanced back at the battle going on behind me. Timber and Jake stood a little apart from one another, Jake breathing heavily, Timber hardly seeming to breathe at all. It seemed my husband had broken Jake's nose, for blood streamed down the magician's face. As I watched, Jake threw himself at Timber, trying to bear him to the ground by main strength. Timber didn't even stumble, but stood under the onslaught like an oak tree. Then he thrust Jake away with one big hand. The other came up in a straight punch to Jake's jaw. The magician's eyes rolled up in his head and he fell like a sack of rocks. Timber took a second to dust himself off, then straddled Jake's supine body, pressing the dirk to his throat. Timber wasn't even sweating.

Another tremor rocked the walls, but I felt no pressing need to move. I thought there was a little less force behind it; Jake's spell must be petering out. Still, I had no desire to be in the cavern if the whole building decided to come crashing down.

"Very well," I told Tintri Fionn, and turned to go. *I'm sorry, Archie,* I thought. *I'm sorry I couldn't do what you wanted.*

Just then I felt a hand on my shoulder, holding me back.

"Wait," Archie Connolly said.

I could see him now, too. He looked as he always had, tired and worn, his head caved in at the side. It didn't bother me anymore.

"Tintri Fionn Connolly," he said. "Don't be a stupid arse. She's trying to help you. She's trying to help us both. Now be a good lad and make the promise."

Fionn gazed at Archie for a long, long minute. Then he bent his head in the barest nod. His voice came soft and sullen, but it came.

"Very well, Archie. I'll be good."

Still, I wavered, unsure I could trust his promise. He and Archie both stared at me, and I could see no hope at all in either of their faces. If I refused to free Tintri Fionn, I doomed both of them to an eternity down here. An eternity of haunting, an eternity of starving. But what promise could the *coimhthíoch* give me that I would believe?

Then I thought of the original binding, and it gave me the answer.

"Swear by your name," I demanded. "Your full name."

Tintri Fionn didn't falter. "I, Tintri Fionn Connolly, promise to be good."

I saw the power of the oath settle on him in a flash of gold. It contracted around him, smaller and smaller. When it vanished at last, I saw a heavy, gold ring on the third finger of his left hand. I nodded, satisfied.

I raised my arms in invocation and drew up a great breath from the center of the Earth. As my lungs filled, I felt myself charged with living power. The blue fire of the circle contracted about me, expectant, listening.

"Earth, Water, Fire, Air!" I bellowed. "Your long work is finished! Let Tintri Fionn go! In my own name, Caitlin Ross, and in the name of Archie Connolly, who chose me to end what he started! So Mote It Be!"

For a minute, nothing happened. Then the room got very still. Something unbelievably large rose up before me. Something large, and white, and made of fire.

It passed right over me and everything was flame. It passed over Breda and she shone like the living heart of a diamond. It stooped on Timber like a hawk diving, bathing him with its light until he blazed like a man made new. Even Jake, now conscious with his mouth hanging open in astonishment, appeared beautiful in its glow, and I knew for the first time what Breda had seen in him.

It uttered one word, a huge booming sound that threatened to split my skull.

"FREE!"

The fire circled the cavern, once twice. Then it rushed up through the ceiling and was gone.

I glanced at Archie. He smiled, and gave me a nod.

"Good work," he said, and melted away as if he had never been.

I sagged. One thing taken care of. But I had not finished yet.

My mouth set in a grim line, I approached the place where Timber held guard over Jake. The floor still trembled, but I had been right; it was quieting. The danger had passed and it was time to deal with the ending.

"Well, love," Timber said as I drew nearer. "What d'ye want to do with this one?"

I considered. Little power remained to Jake Carruthers now. In fact, he had never had much, beyond what hatred and lust for revenge had given him. Had I not been so reluctant to embrace my own magic and with it my Fate, I could have dismantled his plan practically before it started. I regretted that more than I could ever tell.

He watched me from dark, apprehensive eyes. An attractive man, covered in dust, face bloodied, he lay still under the knee Timber pressed into his chest, cowering as much as he was able away from the dirk lightly held at his throat. His failure had broken him, and I almost felt pity. Almost. But I couldn't forget that he had done murder.

"What did you do with Sean Casey's body?" I asked, hearing my voice stern and remote, like that of a judge. Which, I supposed, I was.

Defiance flared, just for an instant. "Disposed of it. What's it to you?"

Behind me, Breda gave a dry sob. She surged forward and booted Jake in the ribs, once, hard. Then she walked away without another word.

"Well?" Timber repeated. He lowered his voice, out of consideration for Breda, I thought, because it didn't keep Jake from hearing. "We canna let him go."

"I know. Stand aside, Timber."

He jerked his head up, alarmed. "Ye canna…"

"Stand aside," I ordered again, and this time he did.

"Get up, Jake," I commanded, but he didn't move. He just lay there, staring at me as if he had no idea what I had said. I glanced at Timber. "Get him up."

My husband hauled Jake to his feet, then took a step back. Jake staggered a little, his ritual robes swaying about him. He raised his eyes to mine and I saw terror in them.

"What are you going to do to me?"

I smiled a little. "I'm going to give you a choice."

The terror receded, just a bit. "What choice?"

"We know you murdered Sean Casey. You admitted as much. But no Mundane court would ever convict you without evidence, which we don't have."

He managed to laugh in my face. "No Mundane court would believe you, even if you had the evidence."

"Very likely. So what to do? I don't want executing you on my conscience. It wouldn't go down well with my patron." Actually, I thought my patron wouldn't mind, her being a pragmatic sort. As for my other, unofficial patron…I didn't know. I still didn't want to have to do it. "But I can't let you go."

Breda came up behind me. "Give him to me. I'll kill him myself," she said, just as Timber chimed,

"I'll take care of the bastard."

I had to steel myself not to start; I hadn't expected that. Breda had every reason to want revenge, and Timber took a very dim view of black magic. But to kill a man in cold blood? I didn't think either of them could.

Jake did, though. His eyes wavered from Breda's set face to Timber's, and he paled under his dark skin.

"What's your choice?"

"I can send you elsewhere. Somewhere you can do no harm. I'll be honest with you; I don't know exactly what it's like there." *A place to send things you can neither dispose of nor use*, the Sean Casey in the vision bar had said. An attic. I saw Jake sitting among dusty boxes, broken furniture, old photographs. "For all I know, you may even be able to get back. In time. If you prove useful."

Again he looked from Breda to Timber. Then his gaze fixed on me. "Not much of a choice."

"It's the only one I've got to offer you."

Jake thought for a long while, and I held my breath, watching him weigh the options. Finally, he said, "I'll go."

I nodded and raised my hand to the key on the fine chain about my throat.

I pointed at Jake and spoke. The word, no word I had ever heard before, rolled off my tongue, nearly charring it to a cinder with power. Brightness blossomed behind Jake, as if a door had opened, showing the way into a brilliantly lit room. The brightness increased in intensity until it became nearly blinding. I felt Timber flinch. Breda shielded her eyes, but I steeled myself not to look away. I saw the light grow to engulf Jake, dwindle abruptly, and die.

And when it had gone out, Jake had vanished.

"Gods," Timber breathed. "Caitlin, what did you do?"

I hardly heard him. The magic drained away like blood from a cut vein. At the same time, my perceptions swelled. My aches and pains vanished, leaving me with a sense of well-being that made me giddy, it came as such a relief. I felt the velvet of my dress, so soft against my skin. Under my bare feet, the cavern floor seemed to roll and shift, delicious in its rough caress. I giggled.

Where Jake had stood, the brightness of the doorway still shone. It appeared so solid, I wondered what it would be like to touch it, run my hands over the unyielding luster of it. But even as I gazed at it, fascinated, it fractured into splinters. Each fragment flared into colored diamonds, fuchsia, green and gold. The colors came together in patterns that seared me with a sense of infinite significance, not that they had importance beyond themselves, but only that they were. If only I could grasp that significance, I could understand...everything.

That struck me as so delightful and strange that I began to laugh, a high-pitched, piercing sound that echoed through the cavern like the chime of insane bells. I laughed so hard I doubled over, clutching my stomach, tears streaming down my face.

"Caitlin!" I heard my name spoken from very far away. The sound reverberated in my ears and it had no meaning.

The patterns circled all around me now, enticing, inviting. I reached for them with my mind...and they broke apart, revealing the shadows that lay beneath.

My laugh turned into a scream.

"Caitlin!" someone said again, and I felt myself taken by the arms and hauled upright. A hard blow landed on my cheek, and another. Still shrieking in terror, my only thought to fight off this new threat, I hurled power at my attacker as I had at

Jake. But nothing happened except that another pitiless slap came out of the darkness, making my ears ring with its force.

Then, all at once, I returned to myself. The shadows shredded into wisps and dissolved. And I was standing in the cavern, at the edge of Tintri Fionn's now-deserted circle, Timber holding me up with one hand while the other was raised to strike me again. He must have seen sense return to me, for, very slowly, he lowered his hand and let me go.

I stared at him, lifting my own hand to my stinging cheek.

"You hit me," I said in wonder, and collapsed to the ground.

I came to in my own bed, in my own room, with no notion how I had got there and Timber holding my hand. My head ached a little and my face stung, but other than that I felt very well. I sat up. My husband was seated on the edge of the bed. He gave a start to see me move. Then he wrapped me in his arms.

"What time is it?" I asked against his chest. "What day is it?"

Timber held me at arms' length, examining me for damage. "Aye, you seem all right," he said after a minute. The words were careless, but his face told another tale. "You're tougher than you look. It's Monday morning. About ten o'clock. You've been out nearly five hours. It took Breda and me both to get you out of that place. Hauling you up the ladder was no joke, ken."

I only caught one word in all of that. "Breda?"

"I'm here," said her voice from nearby.

I disengaged myself from Timber and found her sitting in a chair drawn up beside the bed. Without a second thought, I reached over and slapped her.

"You bitch!" I shrieked. "How could you do that to me?"

Her hand flew to the red mark I had left on her cheek. For a second I thought she would fly at me. Then she gritted her teeth.

"I deserved that," she sighed. "But when Jake showed up at my hotel, I didn't know what else to do but string him along until you were ready for him. As soon as I saw him, I knew he'd killed my father. And I knew if I didn't convince him he'd fooled me, I'd be dead meat."

"You almost were anyway. How did you plan to get away, with me trussed up like a Yule goose?"

She rolled her eyes. "Caitlin, I've lived in the city all my life. I started taking self-defense lessons when I was twelve. I could have gotten away from Jake any time I wanted."

"You could have fooled me," I muttered, unwilling to let go of my anger. "And what was all that about wanting to be a star? I thought I'd be sick."

"It was a code," Breda explained with great patience. When I just stared at her, she went on, "I thought you'd know I'd never want anything like that. So you'd know I was really on your side."

"Your confidence in me appalls me," I growled at her, and I meant it. "At the least, you could have called me. How could you know that I'd ever be ready to face Jake at all? I never told you about that side of me."

She laughed. "Do you really think I'm that stupid? I've known you were a witch for ages."

I slumped back on my pillows. "You are definitely that stupid. You could have got us both killed, and Timber too. How did you get past him?"

Timber coughed behind his hand. "It seems we were stupid as well. We never examined that cavern as thoroughly as we ought."

"What do you mean?" I asked suspiciously.

"There's a back door," Breda replied. "It comes out behind some sagebrush in a ditch near the railroad tracks. Jake showed it to me and I convinced him to use it. It wasn't hard. He didn't want to go through Timber. But don't feel too bad about not finding it. It's hard to see from the inside, even when you know it's there."

I closed my eyes, trying not to imagine how everything could have gone totally, fatally wrong.

"I need a whisky," I said to the dark. "A large one."

"I'll get it," Breda offered, and I heard her close the door as she left the room.

The bed jiggled as Timber moved closer to me. I felt him lay a hand on my arm.

"Hush now," he crooned. "It's over. It's done."

Only then did I realize I was shaking. I let him pet me for a minute or two before I heaved a deep breath, willed my body to stop shuddering and opened my eyes.

"How did you know to come?"

"I heard you. Plain as plain, I heard you say my name, and I knew you needed me." His hands tightened. "As long as I live, I'll always come when you need me."

I leaned into his body and lost myself in tears. Only a minute, it was, though it seemed much longer. Then Timber took me by the shoulders and held me away from him. He peered into my face.

"Caitlin," he said hesitantly. "What happened back there? After you sent Jake…wherever you sent him?"

Breda's step on the stairs saved me from having to answer. Soon the door opened and the woman herself appeared. I thought how much different she looked from when I had first laid eyes on her. It wasn't just that her clothes were rumpled and stained and covered with dust, though that Breda would have taken the time to shower and change. No. She looked older and a little wiser. She had seen things she never expected and had come through it. That changes a person.

I remembered the Tarot reading I had done for her, it seemed so long ago. In my mind's eye, I saw the Lightning Struck Tower falling to pieces and releasing a bolt of pure energy to pierce the sky.

Yes. That reading was over, and Breda had come through just fine.

She set a tray bearing three large glasses of amber liquid on my nightstand. One of the glasses she passed to me, another to Timber. The third, she kept for herself. Before drinking, she raised it in a toast.

"Here's to magic," she said, sliding her eyes at me. "The good kind."

"*Slàinte,*" Timber and I chorused.

We clicked our glasses together.

epilogue

On a Saturday evening almost a month later, I found myself downtown, my fingers wound through the gaps in the nine-foot chain link fence surrounding an empty lot on the corner of First Street and Main.

Nothing remained of the Emerald Isle. The building had sustained substantial structural damage in the strangely localized earthquake at the end of July, and the city had condemned the place and torn it down. The Historical Society had made some outcry about that, the Connolly Building having been a prominent historical site. A tour through the wobbly pub had convinced even Missy Phillips that there was no hope, though. The full moon rising over the drugstore across the street showed only a shadowed, flat expanse of gravel and dirt, with the occasional jagged end of a charred beam poking up like a broken dinosaur bone. Even I had to strain my imagination to believe a building had ever stood there; still harder to believe in the cavern where Tintri Fionn had been trapped for almost a hundred years.

Breda owned the property now. Actually, her father still owned it in name. Sean Casey's body had never been found, and years would pass before Breda could declare him legally dead. However Timber, using one of his more dubious skills and a contact whose name I didn't want to know, had provided her with a convenient power of attorney, so she could do with the place whatever she wished. She had told me that Debra Montaine was after her to sell the corner lot as a building site. We both shuddered to think of that possibility. True, Tintri Fionn was gone. But who could tell what kind of bad mojo might have accumulated in the spot, or what might be called up, should another business take hold there? Neither of us wanted to find out.

"What do you think you'll do with it?" I asked her. "I don't think the town will smile upon its staying an empty lot forever."

Breda jiggled the thermostat on the living room wall of the turn of the century farmhouse she had recently purchased on Geary Mesa.

"I can't get this to work."

"Breda, it's the middle of August. Why do you want to turn the heat on?"

"I was cold last night." She shrugged. "It must be the dry; I'm used to summers with ninety-degree heat and one hundred percent humidity."

I straightened up from the box I was unpacking, one of the mere half-dozen Breda had shipped back from her last visit to New York. All of them contained mementoes of her mother. Sean Casey's collection of books and magic paraphernalia had been turned over to Smith's Bookstore for auction.

"Is your coal stoker working?"

Breda looked blank. "Coal?"

"This house has a coal furnace; a lot of the old ones do. Please tell me you knew that."

The blank look turned to one of horrified chagrin. "Well, I…"

"Breda! Did you even have the place inspected?"

"I loved it at first sight!" Her face was bright red now. With her hair, it gave her a close resemblance to a tomato peeping out from beneath a frost-blackened vine. "I walked in the door, took one look and told Debra I'd take it. Geez, Caitlin, haven't you ever made an impulse purchase?"

I had, but my acquisitions were generally limited to shoes and jewelry. I sighed.

"I'll send Timber around to give it the once over." With luck, there wouldn't be anything major wrong. "Now, what about the lot downtown?"

"I thought maybe a public park. Just a little place with flowers and a few trees, where people could go sit." There was a catch in her voice and she looked away, but not before I saw the tears welling in her blue eyes. "My father wasn't really a bad man. It would be a nice memorial to him."

I remembered her words as I gazed through the fence, imagining green grass and flagstone pathways, whispering trees and flowerbeds in a riot of color. It *would* be nice. For myself, I wasn't sure Sean Casey deserved such a memorial. But I could think of someone who did. A man of great heart and compassion so limitless it could even encompass the sufferings of a demon. A man who, all unrecognized, had sacrificed dreams for duty. It hadn't been necessary, really, that Archie Connolly remain in Gordarosa. He could have left any time; once set, Seamus Mór's spell would not have required his son's presence. Only an overriding sense of responsibility had kept him: responsibility to a brother who despised him, responsibility to a town that took his presence for granted, responsibility to the thing that his blood had trapped in a world not its own.

He was free now. At least, I hoped so. I was the one who was bound. Not to a place, or to a person, but to a path. A glimpse of that path's ending had caused me to renounce magic five years before. Helping Archie had set me back on the path again, and this time, I thought, there would be no turning aside.

I didn't blame him. *I should never have got you involved. But you looked so pretty up there, singing that song,* he'd said, and I believed him. I'd made my own choices. Like Archie, I could have walked away. That I hadn't was no one's fault but my own.

Still, I felt the need to let him know that. If the vanished dead could look down and see the consequences their actions have brought to the living, I wanted him to have no cause for regret. So I'd come downtown on the night of the full moon, to grant Archie Connolly absolution the only way I knew how. Standing there on the street corner, I sang for him one last time.

"Slan abhaile, Slan go foill
Beidh mo chroi seo briste gan thu a stor.
No go gcasfad aris orainn
· *Eist is bi ag smaoineamh*
Ar an gceol 'ta ag teacht
O mo chroi seo amach."

Good luck to you; go safely home.
My heart is broken now I'm left alone.
Until we should meet, think on me and hear
The music so deep from my heart, oh my dear.

"He's not there, you know," a voice said from behind me just as the last notes of the song died away.

"I know." I turned. When I had last seen Tintri Fionn, he had been a pillar of raging white flame. Now, he was just…a guy. A weird guy, with colorless eyes, stark white skin and white hair curling to his shoulders. A seriously thin guy, whose tight white jeans clung to legs like sticks and whose white t-shirt clearly outlined every rib. But a guy, all the same.

"Why do you sing to him if you know he's not there?"

"Sometimes when a person you know has…gone on, if you go to a place that was important to him, it's as if you can still feel him there. So you can talk to him and tell him things you think he might like to know."

Tintri Fionn gazed at me with a face as blank as Breda's had been at the mention of a coal stoker. I tried again.

"Some people think that there's a kind of portal between the last place a person was in life, or the place where he's buried, and wherever he goes when he dies. So if you visit the portal, you can contact him."

Tintri Fionn blinked, once.

"It's a thing mortals do, okay? It makes us feel better."

At that he nodded. "Like Breda visiting Jake's grave."

Now I blinked. "Jake has a grave?"

No one but the three of us who had been there—and Tintri Fionn, it seemed—remembered Jake Carruthers at all. He had been a name on a set of blueprints, an Outsider who never appeared, not important to anyone. Still, sometimes I wondered if there were more to it than that. My hand crept to the tiny key I always wore about my neck, now. For all I knew, it had erased him altogether from this dimension when it sent him to that bright other.

Not much of a choice, he'd said, and he'd been right. But I'd had no other. I hoped that, in time, I would learn to live with it.

"She made a place in the hills. She takes him flowers and tells him she's sorry." Tintri Fionn frowned slightly. "She should not be sorry. She didn't kill Jake. No one killed Jake."

He paused for a moment, regarding me with puzzled eyes.

"You sent him away. Are you sorry? I would have killed him," he added as an afterthought. "I don't understand why you didn't."

I wondered whether Tintri Fionn was capable of understanding the complexities of human responsibility, human guilt. It was not something I felt up to explaining to him.

"What are you still doing here? You promised you'd leave Gordarosa." I glanced at his left hand and saw the gold ring of his oath still there.

He smiled and the moon glinted off his pointed, white teeth. "I promised to be good. I have been good." Seeing where my gaze lay, he clenched his fist. The ring stood out against his pale skin, bright as the full moon. "It chafes," he complained.

My blood turned to ice and I backed away a step. It was as far as I could go; I felt the cold chain link pressing into my shoulder blades. I wondered what "good" meant to a demon.

"I freed you," I whispered in growing horror.

By appearance, he was just a guy. So easy to forget what he really was. So easy to forget the rules for human behavior didn't apply.

"You did," Fionn agreed. He stretched a long, thin finger out towards my cheek. His nails were as sharp as his teeth; it was like being caressed by a cold razor blade.

"I do not feel gratitude." He pulled his finger back and licked its tip, his tongue startlingly pink against the white of his skin. His eyes closed in pleasure.

"It's good," he murmured. "The taste of unexpected fear. So good. Like nothing else."

His eyes popped open.

"However. I do understand debt. The one I owe you is substantial. You mortals seem to value your emotions almost as much as you value your lives. I give you both. You and yours are safe from me."

I closed my eyes in relief, but did not step away from the fence. My knees had turned to jelly and the fence was the only thing holding me up.

"You'll be leaving, then?" I asked, looking at him again.

A strange look of pain passed over Tintri Fionn's face and he spread his hands, an oddly helpless gesture for such a powerful being.

"Where would I go?" he asked softly.

In that moment I understood Archie Connolly better than ever before, for I pitied Tintri Fionn. Not quite a man, he was no longer quite a demon. He was still powerful—I had seen that for myself—but the one power denied him was the one he most wanted, the power to go home. He was bound to this plane, a stranger in a strange land, and Gordarosa was the only place he knew.

That didn't mean I wanted him there, however.

"You'll get pretty hungry, if anyone I claim is safe from you."

"My dear Ms. Ross." He gave an avuncular chuckle. You can't possibly expect to claim the whole town. When I said 'you and yours,' I meant those to whom you have a sincere emotional attachment. You. Your husband. Possibly even those other noisemakers you hang about with, though I don't know about them. I can sense your deepest feelings, remember, and your feelings about your…bandmates…are unclear at best."

I opened my mouth to argue that point, but snapped it shut as I realized I couldn't. In fact, shameful as I found the feeling, there was something deeply satisfying about the thought of Frank and Lisa having to fend for themselves.

"What about Breda?"

"Breda." Tintri Fionn repeated thoughtfully. "She's a special case. We're related, after all. And I find the notion of feeding off my relations strangely unsettling."

I sighed, wondering how Breda would feel about counting an ex-demon as part of her family. Of course, some people might say that weird family was better than no family at all. I didn't know if Breda would be one of them.

Tintri Fionn turned to go, his boots loud on the silent street. Before stepping off the curb, he stopped.

"Don't worry about Gordarosa," he called over his shoulder. "I don't have to kill to feed, you know. I don't even have to interfere too much. Mortals emote a great deal, even without my stirring the pot."

"That doesn't mean you won't."

"No. It doesn't." His white form receded until it was no more than a blur in the night. Then it seemed to turn to one side, and it vanished.

I sagged back against the fence, which responded with a hollow chime.

"What have you got me into, Archie?" I murmured.

There was no answer. But then, I hadn't expected one.

It was several days before I got up the nerve to tell my husband a secret I'd been keeping for five years.

We were sitting in the living room after dinner, as we did most every night. A cup of peppermint tea sat on the low table in front of me, steam curling up from it like incense smoke. Beside me on the couch, Timber was attempting to drink Earl Grey while McGuyver walked back and forth on his chest. The front window was open wide, and the last vagrant summer breeze smelled of the rain that had fallen earlier in the day. All in all, it was a peaceful domestic scene and I wanted more than anything to let it remain so.

But I had to tell him.

"Timber," I began. "About magic…"

My throat closed. I couldn't go on. I had never told anyone why I had stopped using my powers and run to hide in the country like a fox going to earth. I could barely form the words in my own mind, much less get them out.

"Aye?"

"I never told you exactly why I gave it up."

He set down his teacup with a grunt and gazed at me over McGuyver's back. "Ye dinna have to."

I drew in a sharp breath. My heart thumped wildly; I was excused. I didn't have to say anything. I could hide the secret deep in my heart and forget the events of the month past. Everything could be as it was before.

I raised my eyes to my husband's face and saw it full of compassion. Even now, he would let me do this. But I thought about trust, and about the promise I had made him, and I knew I couldn't. Everything had changed, and I could not turn back.

"Yes, I do. I freed Tintri Fionn. I shouldn't have done it. He's a powerful, dangerous being, a master of manipulation, and I should have expected he'd twist his words. But I did it, and that makes me responsible."

Timber nodded. His hands moved absently over McGuyver's fur, calm and gentle. I wanted those hands on me.

"There's more. As long as we've been here, we've thought nothing magical ever happens in Gordarosa. We were wrong. I found out about the Emerald Isle because I stumbled into it. What if I hadn't? There could be other dangers, dangers I've been ignoring. I can't do that anymore."

"I've dealt with a few…problems," he admitted. "I didna want to throw it in your face. But you're right. Gordarosa is no dead zone."

I lowered my eyes and took the deep breath of a swimmer about to plunge into freezing water. "So I need magic. But there are complications. I'm going to need your help."

"Ye ken I'll always help you."

I wondered. I wondered if he would, when he knew everything.

"Do you remember the last…situation in Boulder?" I didn't think he could have forgotten. It had been a huge mess, and in my fear and my haste to leave everything magical behind, I'd abandoned him to deal with it by himself. The real magic was that he had ever come back to me.

"The Ring of Omicron? I mind them, aye."

Something in his voice distracted me and I glanced up at him again. His face held an odd wariness, and he didn't meet my eyes.

"I never asked you how you managed that," I said.

Timber's expression went absolutely blank. I felt his thoughts, guarded, small and still, like a mouse crouching in the shadow of a hawk. Curious.

"Aye, well." He scrubbed a hand through his hair. "I do have some talents of my own. But we were talking about you."

"We were," I sighed. "There were so many of them, working such…evil. I didn't think we could manage them with the power we had." I pondered again how he might have done it and decided I'd have the story out of him one day, if it took the rest of my life.

"So you went looking for more."

"I did. Maybe I shouldn't have done it without letting you know, but it seemed a private thing between me and my goddess. She'd grant my request or she wouldn't. If the latter, you'd never have to know and we'd be no worse off. At least, that's what I thought at the time."

"And what did she say?"

"She didn't say anything. I couldn't find her."

"So then?"

"I found someone else."

I had been so careful. I had always been careful. I despised sloppy magic, which I saw all too often in other people's rituals. When I tried to contact the gods, I made no invocations to some vague Feminine Principle, some Male Counterpart more amorphous still. I knew these powers were real and one must be very specific to reach exactly the entity one intended to reach, to aid one in achieving a particular goal. When I called on the gods, I called them by name.

My special patron was the goddess Cerridwen, a goddess of change and transformation, death and rebirth. It was her symbols I carved into the candle that would be my focus. I carved the cauldron that brewed the potion of wisdom and brought the dead to life; the hen that ate the grain that would be born as the Bard, Taliesin; the three drops of inspiration; the greyhound that ran down the hare. All the while, I thought on Cerridwen and on her story, charging my candle to bring me to the one with whom I desired speech. Her and only her.

What had gone wrong?

"When I lit the candle, I at once found myself walking down a lonely road across a lonely moor," I told my husband. "I wasn't bothered. I thought if I kept walking, I'd find her sooner or later. I could see up ahead the road went over a hill, and there was a figure standing on the hill's crest. But it wasn't Cerridwen. It wasn't her at all."

I didn't know who it was. It seemed to be male, but it wasn't any of the gods with whom I was acquainted.

"What did he look like?" Timber asked.

I closed my eyes, the better to remember. "It wasn't clear. Young. Dark-haired, wearing purple trousers and some kind of fur cloak. I remember thinking he looked Greek, and that puzzled me because the Greek gods and I have never had much to say to each other."

He stood before me on the path, blocking my way. Behind him, down the other side of the hill, the path was bathed in two kinds of fire, white and red.

"I knew if I went on I would be burned, but I wasn't afraid. I wasn't afraid until he spoke. 'Your path is the path of power,' he said. 'But power does not come free. There is always a price, and yours is the choice to pay it or not.'

"Well, of course I thought he was going to tell me that if I took the path of power I'd risk doing great evil, or die young, or any of the usual things. That didn't bother me. I thought I was capable of keeping my evil impulses in check. And, well, dying young didn't seem so bad if I could accomplish something in the meantime."

Timber gave me a black look, which I took to mean that he wouldn't at all approve of my dying young. But he didn't say anything and I went on.

"I asked him what the price was, or wasn't I allowed to know? Because it does happen that way, though it hardly seems fair. But what he said was, 'With divine power comes divine madness.'

"He showed me what he meant. I can't describe what I saw. It was glorious and frightening, all at once. The ecstasy of magic. The dread of darkness. All of it too much to bear. I screamed until my throat was raw. And at the end of it… Shuffling feet. The prick of a needle. Walls closing in on me. Closing me in forever.

"The god—I suppose it was a god—stood aside when it was finished. And I turned, and walked away from the fire, back into the Workroom of our old place in Boulder. I put out the candle as quickly as I could. And the next day I started packing."

Timber blinked. "That's it? Divine madness?"

I nodded.

"Well, that could be anything, couldn't it? It could just mean that you'll get so involved in some higher purpose that you'll lose track of the now from time to time." He patted my knee reassuringly. "Dinna worry about it. I'll make sure you eat."

"I don't think it's that simple," I snapped. How dare he make light of something that scared me so badly? The occasional missed meal hardly seems a fitting price for divine power. Besides. It's already begun. You've seen it."

Comprehension dawned on his face. "When you dealt with Jake."

"Yes. I used magic I had never before used, and suffered the consequences. I don't know if it will happen every time, or only when I exercise what might be called 'divine power.' But I'm afraid. Timber…" My voice trailed off and I swallowed. "I know how it ends. With the walls and the shuffling feet. I know what that means. My mother…" I took a deep breath. "My mother had me put in an institution when I was fifteen because she wanted to shock the magic out of me. I was there for a year."

"Gods, Caitlin." His voice shook. "I'm sorry. I didna realize."

"There's no way you could have. It's all right." I forced a little laugh. "Needless to say, it didn't work, though they tried. But Timber...I don't want to go back, ever. I don't want those walls to close in." My voice fell to a strangled whisper. "I don't want to go mad."

"I won't let you go, love. I'll never let you go."

He reached out to pull me close to him. For just a minute I rested against his chest, feeling the solid warmth of his body. He was my anchor. As long as he was in this world, I could always find my way back.

The doorbell rang. We sprang apart and Timber glanced out the window with a curse.

"Well, if you dinna want to go mad, I wouldn't answer the door," my husband said. "Because unless I'm very much mistaken, that's Madness and his wife right now."

I had forgotten the day. It was Tuesday night, band night, and for once Frank and Lisa were right on time.

I glared at the door. Then, suddenly, I laughed. Not a forced laugh, this time, or a mad laugh, but a peal of pure mirth. Timber was right. The gods spoke in riddles all the time. Despite what had happened, for all I knew, my fears were groundless.

Besides, going mad couldn't be any worse than what I went through every time Red Branch played a gig. It might even be better.

"We'll talk more about this later," I said.

"Aye. I expect we will," Timber replied and got up to open the door.

Frank bounded in, waving yet another Carvin catalog. Lisa stalked in behind him, threw herself into the big chair and buried her nose in a book that she pulled out of her gig bag. I sighed. Some things never changed.

"Come on, people. Let's tune up and get to work."

Timber reached for his bodhrán, narrowly avoiding being smacked with the catalog Frank was thrusting under his nose.

"…and it's got four 50-amp speakers and a 32 channel mixer, with mics and cables all for just $3999…!"

"I don't see what the hurry is." Lisa looked daggers at me over her book. "We just got here. And it's not like we have anything important lined up since we lost the gig at the Emerald Isle."

She said it as if it were my fault.

I guess it was.

The End

Special Preview
She Moved through the Fair
Second in the Caitlin Ross series

WEDNESDAY

"Please explain to me again why I am doing this."

My husband, Timber MacDuff, jerked the steering wheel of our Chevy truck around to avoid colliding with a compact car hastily backing out of a handicapped space in front of Gordarosa's Main Street Theater.

"Feckin' idiots." Accident prevented, at least for the moment, he relaxed back into his bucket seat, left hand resting on the wheel in a manner I could almost call negligent. His right hand reached out and squeezed my thigh.

"Because you told Bill you would months ago, aye?" he said in the soft Scottish lilt that nearly thirty years in America hadn't managed to erase. "Come now. It won't be so bad."

"I suppose." I glanced across the cab at him, but his eyes were on the street, scanning it for a parking place. He wouldn't find one. At seven-thirty on this last Wednesday evening in September, cars packed the three-block strip of downtown, all carrying people to the opening event of the First Annual Gordarosa Harvest Festival.

"I didn't mind when it was just Bill," I went on, as if we hadn't had this conversation a dozen times or more in the last month. "I liked the idea of a performers' showcase."

"But...?" Timber turned the truck up Church Street, hoping to find a space off the main drag.

"It's been blown out of proportion. An arts festival at this time of year...I'm not sure the town can support it." Gordarosa's population of fifteen hundred did include more than its fair share of musicians, poets, potters and other artists, as well as a great many alternative-minded people. But the bulk of the citizens were ranchers and coal miners, farmers and small business owners. I couldn't convince myself they'd be all that interested, especially not when half the events took place on weeknights.

It had started innocently enough. Bill Jamison, the bandleader for local rock group Right as Rain, also owned and acted as chief engineer for the Gordarosa Valley Recording Studio, which he ran out of the basement of the house he shared with his partner, Eva Destruction, Right as Rain's bassist. Most of the local musicians went to Bill's studio to record their CDs. So Bill had come up with the idea of putting together a sampler CD featuring all those local artists and staging a concert where folks could see them all in one place at one time. I'd agreed to participate because my Celtic band, Red Branch, had been one of the groups to record a CD at GVRS, and it had seemed like good exposure. I hadn't reckoned with it becoming a huge deal.

"Breda thinks it can." Timber's black leather pants squeaked as he shifted his weight and spun the wheel again, taking the truck up to Orchard, still in search of a parking space.

"Breda's lived here two months. She has no idea what this town can support." My best friend, Breda Ni Fhearraigh, late of New York City, had recently been hired as the manager of the Gordarosa Arts Center. Approached for her business acumen, she'd taken Bill's original idea and run with it, transforming a one-night performers' showcase into a four-day festival complete with a poetry reading, artists' studio tours, a pub crawl and a fair in River Trail Park on the north side of town.

My husband grunted in satisfaction at finally finding a place to park as he pulled the truck into the Methodist Church lot, a quarter of a mile from downtown and almost empty. Lucky for us the Methodists didn't hold Wednesday night services, as some denominations did. "We're here. Grab your gig bag, love. We've a bit of a walk, and we're on in less than an hour."

"We should have walked from home." I got out of the truck, twisting my ankle in the process, and cursed under my breath. "I had no idea it would be so crowded down here."

"Thus proving your fears about the viability of a festival groundless."

I glared at him. Timber leaned on the hood of the truck and grinned back in his lazy way, a stray lock of his wavy, dark hair falling into one twilight blue eye. Six-foot-four and built to match, the sight of him, as always, sent a thrill through me. I had much better things to do with my Wednesday night than play a twenty-minute gig for which I was not being paid.

"At least we've got a forty-minute set on Saturday night," I grumbled, grabbing the satchel containing my flute and whistles out of the back of the truck. We weren't being paid for Saturday night, either, but the gig would keep the rest of the band happy. As I reached for my gig bag, my waist-length hair fell over my shoulders, getting in my way. I pushed the offending locks back with an impatient growl, caught my gig bag on the edge of the truck bed as I tried to haul it out, and dropped it on my toe.

"Do you need help?" Timber had already claimed his own gig bag and slung the case containing his bodhrán over his shoulder, and started out of the parking lot.

"No. I need to cut off my hair." Auburn and as straight as if it had been ironed, I couldn't do anything with it but let it hang or braid it back. I'd chosen the former for tonight, and it was annoying me.

"Och, don't do that. Maybe Breda will fix it for you if there's time."

I sniffed. Breda often dealt with my hair before gigs; she alone could make the mass of it perform to any standard. But Breda had already been downtown at the theater setting up for tonight's show when the time came for me to get ready. Besides, I was so irked with her over the whole festival thing that we were barely speaking.

"Come on. Let's go." I caught up with my husband in a few steps, but my ankle twisted again on the rough pavement and I stumbled. My brown, high-heeled boots had not been made for walking.

"You should have worn different shoes." Timber caught me about the waist with his free hand, steadying me. He kissed me on the neck, his beard scratchy on my skin, and his fingers trailed over the bodice of my green lace dress. I slapped his hand away.

"None of that. I would have worn different shoes if I'd known half Colorado would be here and we'd have to walk a mile to the venue. What's Steve going to do with them all? The theater only seats a couple hundred."

Timber merely shrugged and let me go. Clearly he did not consider the theater owner's tribulations any of his concern.

"Why so cranky?" he asked as we started toward Main Street in the gathering twilight. "Is it just the gig?"

I paced beside him for half a block in silence before answering with a sigh.

"I don't like festivals. There's always too much crazy energy, with the crowds and the noise. It gets to me. And Frank and Lisa are always on their worst behavior." Frank Delacourt and Lisa Bristol comprised the other half of Red Branch, as guitarist and fiddle player, respectively. "I hate having to ride herd on them and make sure they get the job done instead of swanning about lapping up adulation they haven't earned. Honestly, Timber, these days I don't know why I ever thought I liked being a musician in the first place."

"You love being a musician. You hate being a bandleader."

"Wise man. I should listen to you more often."

"Aye, you should."

We joined a herd of bodies all hastening down First Street to Main and the concert. I stumbled and almost fell again as someone jostled me; Timber took my arm and steered me aside.

"Looks as if the press release did its work," he commented.

Breda had advertised the Gordarosa Harvest Festival in every paper from Aspen to Moab, hoping to draw a more moneyed crowd than our little town could provide. What's more, she had enlisted Vic Houston, a bluegrass artist on the Honey Ridge label, who had retired to Gordarosa a year ago, to contact his friends in the music industry on the festival's behalf. He promised promoters and label reps, both at the performers' showcase to which we were headed and at the big concert Saturday. This had gone a long way to mollifying tempers of musicians who were going to a lot of effort without being paid. Canny, my friend Breda. Pity she hadn't been able to do anything to solve my problems.

Reaching the alley leading to the theater's back entrance, Timber and I peeled off the crowd and started down the rutted gravel. I spared a glance for the empty lot on the corner or First and Main, surrounded by chain link fence, where the Emerald Isle pub had stood until the past July. The rubble of the bar had been cleared from the site not more than a month ago. Most of it had been used to fill the gaping hole that had once been a demon's prison—once been, because I had freed the demon myself last summer to prevent its being controlled by a magician with an evil agenda. The street lights cast a harsh, bluish-green glow over ground not entirely smooth. Breda, who owned the lot because her late father had owned the pub, was always saying she intended to turn the lot into a memorial park and garden, but she hadn't got around to it yet.

Breda and Timber were the two of the three people in town who knew I was a witch, Breda because that magician last summer had tried to sacrifice her to gain the demon's allegiance, which I had prevented by slapping him in the face with magic; Timber because he was my husband and a shaman as well. I trusted both of them with my secret. I wasn't sure I trusted the third person in the know, the demon himself. When I had released him I'd thought he'd leave the area. Instead, he'd taken up residence. Consequently, since last July, I'd been keeping my inner eye peeled for any untoward magical activity in Gordarosa, either from the demon or anything else. So far, I'd spotted nothing requiring my intervention.

Midway down the block, the back door to the aptly-named Main Street Theater stood open to the mild September night, spilling soft gold into the alley. Timber and I hastened through it into the dressing room, a cavernous space of cinder block walls that had once enclosed a tractor garage. Musicians and their gear crammed the room from wall to wall; the performers' showcase featured a dozen bands. Not all the members of all the groups were present, but enough were to fill the air with a heavy musk of Patchouli oil and perspiration. The atmosphere hummed with anticipation.

I forced my way between two members of the bluegrass band, Mama's Choice, who were sharing a suspicious pipe on the back step, and plunged deeper in, looking for a place to stow my gig bag until our turn came. Spotting what seemed to be a free area in a corner, I made for it, only to find it occupied by a small, porcelain saucer and a matching bowl. The bowl sported a rim of white inside, indicating the recent presence of milk or cream. I frowned at it.

"Steve's keeping a cat?" I asked Timber as he came up behind me.

He gave his eloquent shrug again. "If he is, it's hiding now, aye? Over here."

He guided me through the crowd to the other side of the room, where a familiar guitar case stood propped against a wall. In its shadow lay an equally familiar fiddle case. Sighing, I plunked my gig bag down with the things belonging to Red Branch's other, less talented half. Timber set his own gig bag, crammed with a dumbek and various other percussive noise-makers, next to mine and laid his bodhrán case on top. Then we both straightened up and glanced around for the rest of our band.

I found them soon enough, more by sound than sight. Frank's nasal voice rose above the others of those clustered by the refreshments table where, beer in hand, Frank held forth on the merits of various types of guitar strings to a dark haired young woman in a white dress—Sylvie, a high school senior with a stunning voice. Her eyes glazed as she looked at him; I thought she was searching for an opportunity to get away. Lisa's braying laugh erupted from the group gathered around a TV in one corner. The TV displayed a closed-circuit video of the action on stage—a necessity, since no one in the dressing room could have the least idea how the show was proceeding without it.

A sigh of relief left my lips at seeing both band members present and accounted for; they had been known to wander off at inconvenient times. Both were attired appropriately, as well: Lisa in a sleeveless blue velvet mini dress and Frank in black slacks and a tuxedo shirt. Good. Presenting a professional appearance at a gig seemed so obvious to me that I rarely gave it a second thought. With Frank and Lisa, I could never be sure. Most of the time they got it right. But I had never forgotten the time Lisa had showed up to play a wedding wearing tattered old jeans and a sweater covered in dog hair, and I'd had to send her home to change.

Sylvie disengaged herself from Frank and disappeared into the crowd. Frank grabbed another beer from the refreshments table and headed for the back door. At a jerk of my head, Timber took off to keep track of him. I gave a mental hike to my skirts and went to join Lisa.

"Who's up?" I asked as I squeezed into the gang watching the show on the TV

"Andrew Rose," Julian, the drummer from Right as Rain, informed me. "He's singing about his sagebrush."

"Gawd, he's *awful!*" Lisa bellowed.

A frosty silence fell. Glancing around, I noticed the expressions on the faces around me had become rather fixed. I grimaced. Lisa had it right; Andrew Rose, a singer-songwriter with pretensions of spirituality, *was* awful. But in the close-knit musician's community of Gordarosa, that kind of thing went better unsaid.

My eyes strayed to the clock over the back exit and then to the order of performance posted on the stage door.

"Right." I touched Lisa; she jerked away from me as if burned. "Mama's Choice is next and then it's us. I'm going up front, but I should be back in fifteen minutes or so."

She nodded, her eyes glued to the screen. I did not tell her to stay put. She would only have uttered some scathing comment designed to keep me in my place. Besides, she didn't look likely to go anywhere.

I returned to my gig bag, collected a stack of CDs and left through the back door, giving a cursory nod to Timber and Frank as I passed. I didn't hear what they were talking about, but I noticed that now Timber's eyes looked glazed. Rounding the corner of the theater, I took the shortcut through the narrow park between it and the Oddfellows' building. The park, usually empty at night except for the odd group of bored teenagers, was full of people taking a break from the entertainment, having a smoke, getting a breath of air, or standing around in groups, chatting.

When at last I broke through into Main Street, I found it even more crowded than the park. In the block in front of the theater, people milled around like cattle. Half of them didn't have a hope of getting inside and didn't seem to care. Some seemed to be coming, others to be going. Some just stood around hoping to see and be seen. A number had small children in tow, not all of them well-behaved. I saw Rain and Sky Montoya dragging their six-year-old son, Tobias, away from a friendly black Lab with a bandana around its neck. His screams for a puppy of his own cut through the general rumble, as did his mother's increasingly shrill protestations that this was impossible.

Performers circulated, signing CDs. A Mariachi band had set up in front of the Mexican restaurant on the corner. At the other end of the street, a Folk duo played Kingston Trio covers in front of the bank. My head began to pound from all the unrestrained energy beating at me like a hammer. I'd been loath to put up a shield before; a performer needs to feel the mood of the audience, after all. But I'd be no good to anyone if I didn't get some relief. I drew up some earth energy and threw it around me, and felt better at once.

The shield helped me as I shouldered my way through the crowd, my stack of CDs cradled in front of me like a child. People sprang away from me by instinct, leaving my path clear. Gaining the front door of the theater, I burst into an area of relative calm and let my shield drop. My headache returned, but it wasn't as intense and I could ignore it. I wiped sweat from my forehead and wondered if there were any way I could make it back to the dressing room in the less than fifteen minutes I had left. A burst of applause from the house told me Andrew Rose had finished his set. Allowing for a five minute changeover and a twenty minute set for Mama's Choice, I decided I had plenty of time.

Spotting the long table to one side of the lobby where CDs by the various bands playing in the showcase were displayed for sale, I slipped along the concession stand to dump my wares before folks taking advantage of the set change to stretch their legs could cut me off. A couple of people were already there, scanning Bill's compilation CD. I waited to one side, wanting a word with the person running the counter. Then the couple moved along and the beautiful, raven-haired woman behind the table raised her ice blue eyes to mine.

"Caitlin!" Breda Ni Fhearraigh's voice was tart as a bowl of lemons. "How wonderful to see you. I always loved that dress. Your hair sucks, though."

I plopped my stack of CDs onto the table beside a fishbowl bearing the legend, "Donate to KGOR, YOUR volunteer-run radio station!" in bright blue crayon on orange construction paper.

"Hello, Breda," I replied, pretending to straighten my CDs. "Look, can we call a truce?"

Her eyes flashed. "I'm not the one who decided to pitch a fit about this festival. I can't believe it, Caitlin! Sometimes I wonder if Frank and Lisa aren't right about you. No fear like fear of fame."

That stung. "Frank and Lisa can…" I hissed.

All at once Breda relented. "Let's forget it. No good you getting upset before your gig."

I regarded her from narrow eyes. I missed Breda quite a lot and wanted her friendship back, but I couldn't help but suspect there would be a high price on her renewed goodwill.

She returned my gaze, the picture of innocence in her black silk jacket and plum camisole. The silver on her fingers gleamed in the low lobby lights as she brushed her bobbed hair back behind one ring-bedecked ear.

"All right. And…I'm sorry," I mumbled.

"Well, you can make it up to me. In fact," her face glowed as she sprung her trap, "you can make it up to me tomorrow. Come to the poetry reading with me tomorrow night and all will be forgiven."

"The poetry reading?" I groaned. "Oh, Breda, please. Not that."

"I need you to come."

"Why? You know how I hate poetry readings. All that angst. It gets under my skin." I gave her a meaningful glance, to be sure she got it.

"I do know." She returned my gaze; she got it, all right. Other than Timber, only she knew of my powers. "I also know you're not exactly helpless."

"But…."

"I need you to come because everyone knows how much you hate readings." I must have looked as mystified as I felt, because she went on, "I'm worried about this, Caitlin. The Writers' Guild wanted Friday night, but I couldn't give them Friday night because of the pub crawl. I promised them we'd have a great turnout even on a Thursday. Everyone knows how much you hate readings, so if I can leak that you're going, everyone will think there must be something pretty terrific in store to attract you, and they'll come too. It's simple."

I stared at her. "You have an evil mind."

"So you'll do it? I'll fix your hair," she wheedled.

I sighed. "Oh, all right. But I'll have to take a rain check on the hair. We're on in…" I glanced up, noticing that the lobby had become very still. Only a few people loitered, some getting popcorn or beer, some chatting in the alcove in front of the restrooms, and a couple pointedly waiting for me to be done with Breda so they could have a chance at the CDs. The high, lonesome sound of Mama's Choice drifted through the heavy velvet curtains separating the lobby from the theater proper. The clock over the concession counter read eight-twenty. "Crap. We're on in ten minutes. Gotta run."

Spinning around, I suited actions to words, but only made it as far as the door before colliding with a couple just coming in. For a few seconds the three of us did a stupid little dance, trying to get out of each other's way. Then the man grabbed me by the elbows, picked me up and set me aside, grinning.

"Caitlin!" he exclaimed. "How's it going?"

Vic Houston's official bio described him, in not very original terms, as "a long, tall drink of water." It did not mention that his wiry frame was all muscle; I am not a small woman and not many could have manhandled me as casually as he did. His craggy good looks had something of the wolf about them, with shaggy blond hair gone almost all the way grey, a sharp nose and chin, and melting brown eyes. I saw something of the wolf in his grin, too. He looked as though he couldn't decide whether to romp with me or eat me. Maybe both.

If I had been the one on Vic's arm, I would have objected most strenuously to his turning such a grin on another woman. Cassiopeia Jones, however, was one of those rare people who looked for the good in everyone around her and found it more often than not. A warm smile in her grey eyes, she held out her blue silk-clad arms to me. I hugged her, taking care not to snag my dress on any of her expensive turquoise jewelry. She had quite a lot of it on, from matching necklace and earrings set in silver to a rope of rough stones looped around her left boot. She didn't usually go around flaunting her wealth, but she would be playing later tonight and had dressed the part.

I knew Vic would be joining her for a song or two, but he hadn't taken any trouble over his appearance. In fact, he looked almost drab in his faded blue jeans and Guatemalan shirt. Around his neck he sported a macramé hemp and bead choker of the sort I had seen on a lot of the alternative crowd in recent days. Vic's was remarkable in its ugliness. The beads were a nasty bluish-purple color, with streaks of green like an old bruise, and the cord was grimy, as if he had been wearing it for a while without bothering to wash. A single blue crystal teardrop lay in the hollow of Vic's throat, the sole thing of beauty about the piece.

"Have you been on yet?" Cassie asked as she released me.

I shook my head. "We're on next." I listened for a minute to the faint sound of a mandolin solo coming from the theater. "In fact, I need to get backstage. It sounds like Mama's Choice is finishing up."

"Oh, I wanted to hear them!" Disappointment rang clear in Cassie's voice. I kept my face blank. Mama's Choice was the new act in town and everyone wanted to hear them. It had been a couple years since a Red Branch gig held that kind of appeal.

"You'll get a chance on Saturday," Vic soothed her.

I heard the mandolin solo end in a flourish, then a number of cheers and a crescendo of applause. Out of the corner of my eye I saw people begin to shove their way through the lobby curtains.

"I've really got to…" I began, attempting to shove my way between Vic and Cassie. Vic grabbed my arm.

"You'll never get around; the street is jammed. Anyway, I wanted to ask you something about Saturday."

"What about it?" I began walking backward through the lobby, dragging him along. Cassie trailed in our wake. My gaze met hers over Vic's head; she rolled her eyes at me.

"Well, Bill and I were wondering if Red Branch would consider switching spots with Mama's Choice."

I froze. I knew the order of performance. Mama's Choice had an afternoon spot at four-thirty, when people would be tired from spending the day in the park and thinking about going home for dinner. Red Branch had a prime evening spot at seven, when all those folks would be rested up and returning ready to party.

"No." I said.

"But your music is more restful, Caitlin," Vic pleaded. "Better for winding down the afternoon. Mama's Choice is…"

"I don't care what Mama's Choice is." Restful? I'd give him restful! Let him try dancing a few jigs and reels and then tell me if he thought Celtic music was restful. Anyway, I knew it was bullshit. Bill and Vic wanted to put us out of the way because we didn't fit in. Celtic music didn't have the same draw Bluegrass did. Besides—I had to admit it—we weren't very good. After almost three years of playing together, Red Branch couldn't match the polish Mama's Choice showed even in their infancy.

"We fixed the schedule a month ago, Vic," I told him. "Next festival you can do whatever you want. Not this one. Now I have to go."

As if on cue, I heard Timber's voice roar from the theater.

"Caitlin! Get in here!"

I tore my arm out of Vic's grasp. His grin had vanished, replaced by a flat, cold look of disapproval. I remembered he had a reputation as a bad man to cross.

Ever the peacemaker, Cassie came up between us. "Are we going to have coffee soon?"

What an inane question, I thought, but I said, "Sure. Call me."

"Caitlin!" Timber bellowed again. I heard laughter from the audience and my face burned.

I turned and ran, across the lobby and through the curtains, and down the center aisle to the stage where my band awaited me, Timber concerned, Frank smiling into his guitar, and Lisa looking thunderous, as usual. *They had better play well tonight,* I thought as I grasped Timber's outstretched hand and he hauled me up beside him. *It's only four songs; surely we can manage that much.*

Timber thrust my flute at me. I took it in my left hand, grabbed my mic stand with my right and flashed my best stage smile out over the house.

"Good Evening!" I sang out. "We're Red Branch and we're going to be playing some songs and tunes to lighten your heart and your feet, so kick off your shoes and clear the aisles! We're going to start off with a set of jigs; this is 'The Kesh,' 'The Lilting Banshee,' and 'The Connaughtman's Rambles.'"

I gave the beat and raised my flute to my lips, smiling all the while. But I couldn't help noticing, with a sinking sensation deep in the pit of my stomach, that half the audience had vanished.

About the Author

Although some claim she is a mythological construct, **Katherine Lampe** does, in fact, inhabit a small town in Western Colorado. She can be seen when the rays of the full moon in Pisces shine on the north face of Jumbo Mountain. At other times, you might locate her by turning over various large rocks. Or, you can like her Facebook page, found at www.Facebook.com/KELampe, read her blog: theshadowsanctuary.wordpress.com, or follow @KeleGrrl on Twitter. Follow the rest of Caitlin Ross's adventures! Books, social media, and more: www.independentauthornetwork.com/katherine-lampe

A Final Note

Independent authors do not have huge advertising budgets, as a rule. We rely on word of mouth. If you enjoyed this book, please consider recommending it to a friend and/or posting a review on Smashwords, Amazon, Goodreads, or your favorite book-oriented site. Good reviews boost a book in a site's internal search engine, allowing more readers to find it and helping authors continue to do the work they love. Thank you.

Printed in Great Britain
by Amazon